naughty bits

AN ANTHOLOGY *of* SHORT EROTIC FICTION

2

naughty bits

AN ANTHOLOGY *of* SHORT EROTIC FICTION

2

Jenesi Ash

Portia Da Costa

Charlotte Featherstone

Lillian Feisty

Cathryn Fox

Megan Hart

Lisa Renee Jones

Elliot Mabeuse

Alison Paige

Saskia Walker

Spice

NAUGHTY BITS 2

ISBN-13: 978-0-373-60541-5

Copyright © 2010 by Spice Books.

The publisher acknowledges the copyright holders of the individual works as follows:

CHANCE OF A LIFETIME
Copyright © 2008 by Portia da Costa

THE PRIESTESS
Copyright © 2008 by Gregg Robinson

TAKEN
Copyright © 2008 by Michelle Scheibe

FAVOR ME
Copyright © 2008 by Jasmine Communications, LLC.

MEDUSA'S FOLLY
Copyright © 2008 by Paige Cuccaro

PRIMAL INSTINCTS
Copyright © 2008 by Cathryn Fox and Lisa Renee Jones

THIS IS WHAT I WANT
Copyright © 2007 by Megan Hart

IMPROPER PLEASURE
Copyright © 2008 by Charlotte Featherstone

CAUGHT IN THE ACT
Copyright © 2008 by Saskia Walker

For questions and comments about the quality of this book please contact us at Customer_eCare@Harlequin.ca.

Spice and Colophon are trademarks used under license and registered in Australia, New Zealand, Philippines, United States Patent and Trademark Office and in other countries.

www.Spice-Books.com

Printed in U.S.A.

CONTENTS

CHANCE OF A LIFETIME

Portia Da Costa

RAIN. PERPETUAL RAIN. I'M CERTAINLY NOT going to miss the British weather. I'll miss a lot of other things, but not this.

I stare out of the window, down the gravel drive and out across the park of Blaystock Manor. I'm here filling in with some temp work, while I wait to take up my dream job, my chance of a lifetime working in the Caribbean at a luxury resort as a junior manager. This gig is just cleaning and helping with renovations, donkey work really, but it's all extra money to pay for my new tropical wardrobe.

Actually, it's a free day today. The marquess is pretty good about that. We get plenty of time off, plenty of breaks and other perks, and despite the fact he's strapped for cash and putting everything into this project, we're pretty well paid for our labors. Everyone else has gone off in a minibus to visit a local monastery where they brew apple brandy and make luxury biscuits and stuff, but me, I've got my own diversions here.

I'm alone in the house. Even the marquess drove off a short while ago in his decrepit gray Jag. And I'm free to indulge my wicked secret vice.

I discovered this little sitting room a couple days ago, when I was a bit lost and searching for the Blue Salon, where I was supposed to be polishing the floor. I stumbled in here and found a room that was homely and pretty lived-in, and sort of cozy. And, being irredeemably nosy, when I saw an old VCR and a bunch of tapes, I had to investigate.

Boy, oh, boy, oh, boy! What a shock I got.

And now, while the house is empty, I slip another tape into the machine and settle down in a battered old leather armchair to watch it.

It's a home movie. Filmed, I think, in this very room. And it stars my latest crush, the marquess himself, and a woman who must have been his girlfriend at the time. Obviously it was taped many years ago, because His Lordship had short hair then, and now it's long, down to his shoulders.

Here he is, possibly sitting in this very chair. His knees are set wide apart and his girlfriend is facedown across them.

He's spanking her.

He's really laying it on with his long, powerful hand, and she's squirming and patently loving it!

And I'm loving it, too, and I don't really know why. Okay, I knew people played spanking games for sexual kicks, and I'd sort of hinted to various boyfriends that I'd like to try it. But it's never happened and I've never really worried about that.

But now. Now I've seen it. I bloody well want it!

I'm so turned on now I can barely see straight. And I certainly can't stay still in my chair. I'm sweating and my skin feels like it's already been spanked, all over. And between my legs, I'm drenched, my panties sopping with intense, almost inexplicable arousal. My sex is aching, tight and hungry, as if I want to be fucked right now, but at the same time have my bottom thrashed, just like the woman in the video.

The marquess really seems to be enjoying her pleasure, even though his cool, handsome face is exquisitely impassive. It's an old, well-worn tape, but I can still see the mask of stern, beautiful composure that he affects…and the wicked dark twinkle in his eyes.

It's no good, I've got to play with myself. I can't help it and I can't bear it if I don't. My sex is so heavy and so tense, I've just got to do it.

As the woman on the screen writhes and wriggles and shrieks as His Lordship's hand comes down, I unzip my jeans and shuffle them down to my knees, dragging my soggy panties with them. There's something wickedly lewd about sitting here with my clothes at half-mast like this, and the forbidden exposure only excites me more and makes my need to touch my body ever more urgent.

"Oh, God…" I murmur vaguely as I slip my fingers between my legs and find my clit. It's swollen and ready for my touch like a throbbing button. I flick it lightly and my vagina flutters dangerously. On the screen, the spanked girl tries to touch her own sex, wriggling her hand beneath her belly as she squirms and cries, but the marquess pauses midspank and gently remonstrates with her.

"Come, come, Sylvia, you know you mustn't do that. No pleasure until you've been a good girl and taken your punishment."

His voice is soft, even, but shot through with sweet steel and authority. It pushes me closer to coming just as powerfully as the spanking show does. I suddenly wish I could get to know him better, and make this all real.

"Oh, my lord…" I whisper this time, closing my eyes and turning on an inner video. This time it's me across those strong thighs. Me who's writhing and moaning, with my bottom flaming.

Oh, the picture is so clear. And it's the marquess of today who's doing the business, not the one in the video.

He's wearing his usual outfit of black jeans and black shirt, and his beautiful hair is loose on his shoulders like sheets of silk. There's a sly, slight smile on his pale, chiseled face, and his long, cultured hand comes down with metronomic regularity.

I'm rubbing myself hard now, beating at my clit, but not stroking the very apex of it. I daren't; I'm so excited and I don't want to come yet. In my fantasy, he allows me to touch myself while he's smacking me.

I writhe and wriggle, both fighting the pleasure and savoring its gathering at the same time. I throw my thighs wide, rubbing my bottom against the seat of the creaky old armchair. The sensation of the smooth surface against my skin is even more pervy. I press down harder, squashing my anus against the leather. I imagine him spanking me there, and even though I've no idea what it would really feel like, I groan, wanting it more and more and more.

"Oh, my lord…do it…do it…" I burble, eyes tightly closed and half out of my mind with desire and longing.

"Actually, my dear, I think you're 'doing it' quite well enough on your own. Do continue."

What?

It's like I'm falling, dropping through reality into a parallel universe. I know what's happened, but somehow I can't stop rubbing myself.

My eyes fly open though, and there he is.

The marquess.

Somehow he's walked into the room without me realizing it, moving softly on the rubber soles of his black running shoes.

In a few split seconds, I take in his glorious appearance.

So tall, so male, so mysterious. Long, dark hair, pale smiling face, long fit body. Dressed in his customary black shirt and jeans, his elegant hands flexing as if preparing to copy the actions of his image on the screen.

I snatch my hand from my crotch and make as if to struggle

back into my jeans. My face is scarlet, puce, flaming…. I'm almost peeing myself.

"No, please…continue."

His voice is low and quiet, almost humming with amusement and intense interest. It's impossible to disobey him. Despite the fact that I think the aristocracy is an outdated nonsense, he's nobility to his fingertips and I'm just a pleb, bound to obey.

Unable to tear my eyes away from him, I watch as he settles his long frame down into the other chair, across from mine. He gives me a little nod, making his black hair sway, and then turns his attention to the images on the screen.

So do I, but with reluctance.

But I do as he wishes and begin to stroke my clit again.

Oh, God, the woman on the screen is really protesting now. Oh, God, in my mind, that woman is me, and I'm laid across the marquess's magnificent thighs with my bottom all pink and sizzling and my crotch wetting his jeans with seeping arousal.

I imagine the blows I've never experienced, and just the dream of them makes my clit flutter wildly and my vagina clench and pulse. I seem to see the carpet as I writhe and wiggle and moan, and at the same time his beautiful face, rather grave, but secretly smiling.

As his eyes twinkle in my imagination, I come.

It's a hard, wrenching orgasm. Shocking and intense. I've never come like that before in my life. It goes on and on, so extreme it's almost pain, and afterward I feel tears fill my eyes.

Talk about *le petit mort* and postcoital tristesse. I've got tristesse by the bucketful, but without any coitus.

My face as crimson as the buttocks of the spanked woman in the video, I drag my panties and jeans back into place and lie gasping in the chair. I scrabble for a tissue. I'm going to cry properly now, not just a few teardrops, and I know I should just run from the room, but somehow I just can't seem to move.

Something soft and folded is put gently into my hand, and as I steal a glance at it, I discover it's the marquess's immaculately laundered handkerchief. Still gulping and sniffing, I rub my face with it, breathing in the faint, mouthwatering fragrance of his cologne.

Shit, I fancy this man something rotten, and I've been fantasizing about him fancying me back, and falling for me, and now this has happened. I'm so embarrassed, I wish I could burrow into the leather upholstery and disappear out of sight.

A strong arm settles around my shoulders, and the great chair creaks as he sits down on the arm beside me.

"Hey, there's no harm done," the marquess says softly. "Now we both know each other's dirty little secrets." He squeezes my shoulders. "I get off spanking girls' bottoms and having them wriggling on my lap. And you get off watching videos of it and playing with yourself." He pauses, and I sense him smiling that slow, wicked smile again. "And quite beautifully, I must admit. Quite exquisitely…"

I beg your pardon?

Hell, I must have looked awful. Crude. Ungainly. Like a complete slapper.

I try to wriggle free, but he holds me. He even puts up a hand to gently stroke my hair. I still can't look at him, even though part of me really wants to.

"I'm so embarrassed. I'm so sorry. I had no business coming in here and prying into your private things."

One long finger strokes down the side of my face, slips under my chin and gently lifts it. Nervously, I open my eyes and look into his. They're large and dark and brown and merry, and I feel as if I'm drowning, but suddenly that's a good thing.

All the embarrassment and mortification disappears, just as if it were the rain puddles outside evaporating in the sun. Indeed, beyond the window, the sky outside is brightening.

Suddenly I see mischief and sex and a sense of adventure in those fabulous eyes, and I feel turned on again, and somehow scared, but not in a way that has anything to do with an awkward situation with my employer. It's a new feeling, and it's erotic, but so much more.

"Indeed you didn't. That was rather naughty of you." His face is perfectly impassive, almost stern, but those eyes, oh, those eyes—they're mad with dangerous fun. "Do you think we should do something about that?"

I feel as if I'm about to cross a line. Jump off a cliff. Ford some peculiar kind of Rubicon. This is the chance of a lifetime, and I'm a perfect novice in the world portrayed in his video, but I understand him completely without any further hint or education.

"Um…yes, my lord."

Should I stand? Then kneel? Or curtsy or something? He's still sitting on the arm of the chair, a huge masculine presence because he's tall and broad-shouldered. Everything a man and a master should be.

I'm just about to stand, and I feel him just about to reach for me, when suddenly and shockingly his mobile rings, and he lets out a lurid curse.

"Ack, I must take this. Money stuff," he growls, and nods to me to mute the television as he flips open his phone.

I make as if to leave, but he catches me by the arm and makes me stand in front of him. With almost serpentine grace, he slides into the armchair and pulls me across his lap. Then, as he has a terse conversation that I don't think he's enjoying much, he explores the shape of my bottom through my jeans.

He doesn't slap or smack or hit. He just cruises his fingertips over the denim-clad surface, assessing my contours and the resilience of my flesh.

Slowly, slowly, as he gets slightly cross with someone on the other end of the line, he examines my cheeks, my thighs and then, without warning, squeezes my crotch. I let out a little yelp, and that's when he *does* hit.

It's just the softest warning tap…but it's electrifying. I almost come on the spot and I have to bite down on my lip to stifle my groans.

I start to wriggle and he cups my sex harder, from behind, pressing with his fingers. Pleasure flares again as my jeans's seam rubs my aching clit.

I'm biting the upholstery, squirming and kicking my legs and grabbing at his legs and his muscular thighs through his jeans. He rides my unruliness, his hand firm between my legs as he owns my sex like the lord and master he truly is.

Eventually his call is over, and I'm a wrung-out rag. He flings aside his phone and turns me over, then kisses me.

I expect domineering hunger and passion, but it's soft, light and sweet, almost a zephyr.

He wants me. He's hard, I can feel it beneath my bottom. But as if his own erection means nothing to him, he sets me on my feet then stands up beside me.

"Much as it pains me to leave so much undone and unsaid at this moment, Rose, I have to go." His eyes are dark. Is it lust? Regret? Something more complex? "I need to go to London, and I'm going to have to get a bloody taxi because I've just left my car at the garage." He pauses, then leans down to kiss me on the lips again, a little harder this time. "But when I get back, we'll reconvene. If that's agreeable?" He tilts his head to one side as he looks down on me, and his exquisite hair slides sideways like silk.

I nod and mutter something incomprehensible that doesn't make sense even to me, and then he pats me on the bottom again and strides away across the room.

At the door, he gives me a wink, his dark eyes twinkling with mischief.

"Enjoy the rest of the video," he says, then suddenly he's gone.

* * *

But I don't watch it. After he's gone, I just shoot off to my room, tucked up in the aerie of the old servants' quarters, feeling strange and weird and disoriented, as if I've been in a really vivid dream, and I've just woken up. Then I sort of snivel a bit, not sure of my emotions.

The marquess is our boss, and up until now, he's been a sort of admire/adore-from-afar-type man. I'm not into all this hero worship or celebs and aristos for the sake of it, but he's got genuine charisma and blue-blood charm. He's also got some weird history. Apparently, he was in the army at some time, then a dropout, and was now getting his act together and sorting out the manor on behalf of his father, the duke. The whole family is strapped for cash, but Blaystock Manor is just the right size for a deluxe, high-end hotel or conference center, and the marquess has thrown just about every penny he possesses, and some he doesn't, into restoring it and bringing it up to standard.

And somewhere along the line in this convoluted story of his, he was married, but she died and now he's alone. No doubt his dad is pressuring him for progeny, to continue the family line, but so far it seems he's resisted, and there's no marchioness.

Some very silly thoughts drift into my mind as I get ready for bed and I push them smartly back out again. I've got my dream job waiting for me in the Caribbean. I won't be here all that long.

Although I would love to see what the manor looks like when it's finished.

I suppose all this pondering is to avoid thinking about the fact that the marquess has seen me masturbate, and almost, but not quite, spanked me.

Do I really want to be spanked, though?

In the video, he was doing it for real, and that woman— whoever she was, surely not his wife—was squealing and crying out. So obviously it hurt like hell. Lying in bed later, I tug down my pajama bottom and give myself a slap on the thigh. It's a pretty halfhearted effort, but it makes me squawk and rub the place to take the sting away.

Immediately though, I'm drifting into fantasy.

In my mind I'm back in the little sitting room, and this time the phone stays silent. And the marquess bares my bottom and starts to caress, caress, caress it, then lands a blow.

I slap myself again, trying to recreate the feeling. It bloody hurts, but I do it again, moaning, "My lord…"

I slap and slap and moan and moan, and suddenly I just have to play with my clitoris. I'm so turned on imagining him spanking me that my wet sex aches.

Within a few seconds I come, softly crying his name, seeing his face.

The next day, I worry. What's going to happen? Is anything going to happen? Or has the marquess quite sensibly decided to dismiss our stolen interlude as an aberration. Something of no consequence. It must be bred in his blue English blood to dally with underlings for his pleasure without a second thought.

I certainly don't see him for the next couple of days, and the cleaning, dusting and polishing goes on without incident. I work cheerfully with the rest of the team, as if nothing has happened.

But then, after a long day, when the others are all off to the pub, I slip back to my room to change, and find a little note upon my mat.

I'm sorry we were so rudely interrupted, it says in a fine, almost copperplate handwriting. *Would you care to join me in the small sitting room at seven o'clock this evening? I feel that there's much we could explore there in the furtherance of your education and the pursuit of mutual pleasure.*

It's finished off with a single word.

Christian.

Christian? Who's Christian?

Then it dawns on me. Duh! The marquess is just a normal person in that, at least.

He has a first name.

I wonder if he'll want me to call him Christian? Somehow it doesn't seem right or respectful. Especially in view of what we're almost certain to be doing. It'll definitely be "My lord" or "Your Lordship," or just sobs and moans of pain and pleasure in equal amounts.

At seven o'clock, I'm staring at the door to the little sitting room. It was half in my mind not to turn up, to try to pretend that what happened beyond that slab of oak never happened. But doing that would be to miss…well…the chance of a lifetime. I might never meet a man again who's into the things that the marquess is, and I might go through life having perfectly ordinary, perfectly satisfactory sex, but still wondering what it would have been like to try the extraordinary kind with spanking and strange mind games.

I knock as firmly as I can on the door, and immediately that deep, clear voice calls out, "Enter!" from within. Crikey, he already sounds like a stern schoolmaster summoning his tardy pupil.

I tremble.

But there's nothing fearsome or intimidating when I step into the room and close the door behind me. It's cozy and welcoming, with a nice little fire burning in the grate to ward off the unseasonal damp chill. The thick curtains are drawn, and soft lamps emit a friendly golden glow that flatters the fine old furniture and makes it gleam.

It flatters the marquess, too, not that he needs it. He looks stunning.

He's all in black again, as ever. Tight black jeans embrace his long legs and the splendid lean musculature of his thighs and his backside. As he rises to his feet from the depths of one of the armchairs, I imagine, for a fleeting second, spanking him.

Blood fills my cheeks in a raging blush, and I falter and hang back. A huge waft of guilt rushes through me at even thinking that. I open my mouth, but I can't speak, and he smiles at me.

"Come on in, Rose. Would you like a drink?" I notice that he has a glass with something clear and icy set on a little table beside his chair. Vodka? Water? Gin? Who knows…?

"Um…er…yes." I flick my glance to the sideboard and a few bottles, but I can't seem to compute what's there so I just say, "Whatever you're having…please."

"Good choice…and do sit down." He gestures like a Renaissance courtier toward a free chair by the fire and watches me as I make my way there; I'm terrified I'll trip or something, despite the fact my heels aren't high or spindly.

I take my seat and watch him mix my drink, swiftly combining clear spirit, ice, mixer and a sliver of lemon. He prepares the concoction perfectly, despite the fact that he's studying me intently almost all the time.

I've dressed carefully.

Jeans are awkward to wriggle out of, especially if you've got a curvy bottom like mine, so I've chosen a soft, full summer skirt that almost sweeps the floor. A miniskirt would be too obvious, not ladylike, and as I'm here with an aristocrat, I'm compelled to make an effort to be worthy of him.

On my top half I've got a little buttoned camisole, pink to match the skirt, and a light cotton cardigan over that, to keep out the chills. My shoes are low-heeled and quite pretty, and underneath I'm wearing my best and sexiest underwear.

I aim to please….

The marquess comes across and hands me my drink, then

retreats to his own chair. There's a moment of silence, tense for me, but apparently totally relaxed for him, and I snatch the opportunity to feast my eyes on his gorgeousness.

He sits so elegantly, even though he's totally at ease. Long legs out in front of him, booted feet crossed.

Boots? Hell, yes! They do something visceral inside me. They make me shudder and my sex clench and seem to twist and flutter with their connotations of masterfulness. They're old and soft and well polished and not all that tall, but all the same, I almost feel faint just looking at them.

And I get mostly the same feeling from the rest of him.

He's got the most exquisite black silk shirt on, full of sleeve and so fluid it seems to float on his body. The collar's fastened up for the moment, but I have the most intense urge to crawl on my hands and knees across the room and rip it open so I can kiss his throat and his chest and suck his nipples.

And not just his nipples.

His thick, black hair is shiny with a fresh-washed satin sheen and his fine-boned face has the delicious gleam of a recent shave.

Bless him, he's made as much of an effort for me as I have for him. Another reason to worship and adore him.

I take a mouthful of my drink. It is gin, as I mostly suspected, and it's a strong one with very little tonic. The balsamic kick of the uncompromising spirit almost makes me cough, but I'm glad of its heat as the first hit settles in my stomach.

"So…here we are," the marquess says pleasantly, eyeing me over the rim of his own glass. As he takes a long swallow, his throat undulates, pale and sensuous.

"Yes…er…here we are," is all I can manage in reply. The gathering tension in my gut renders me all but speechless.

"Have you been thinking about what happened here the other day?"

I nod, dumbstruck now with intense lust. I don't know

whether I want him to spank me or fuck me…probably both. But I want whatever's on offer as soon as I can get it.

"So how do you feel about being spanked a little? Does that interest you?" His lips are sculpted, but somehow also soft and sensual, and when they curve into a little smile, the way they are doing now, they make me want to wriggle and touch my sex to soothe its aching. So much for wearing my best knickers. They must already be saturated with juice, I'm so turned on.

"I think we could enjoy ourselves together, you and I," he continues. "I'm not offering eternal love and devotion, but we can share a little pleasure and perhaps expand your horizons in a way that doesn't involve flying thousands of miles."

Those crazy notions caper around my mind again, taunting me with the prospect of what he *isn't* offering rather than what he is.

"Rose?" he queries, swirling his glass in the face of my continued dumbstruck silence.

I want it. Oh, how I want it. And even just the mutual pleasure if I can't have the other thing. But I'm scared. I feel as if I'm stuck between reality and some kind of weird dream. I still can't speak, but I take another swig of my gin.

The marquess frowns. It's not a cross frown, just a sad little frown, sort of regretful. "I'm sorry. I've come on too strong, haven't I?" He tips his head to one side, his dark hair sliding across his shoulders as he lets out a sigh. "Look, don't worry about it. Don't think any more about it. Just finish your gin and we'll say no more about it. It was wrong of me to ask."

I don't know whether I'm relieved or disappointed. I felt so close to him for a moment, and God, I wanted it all so much. My heart thudding, I swig down my gin and get to my feet on wobbly legs.

The marquess rises immediately, perfect manners second nature to him. He comes forward as if to escort me to the door, and does so as I make my way toward it, my heart sinking at my own craven lack of daring.

With one hand on the door handle, he touches my face. The contact is so gentle yet so meaningful, I feel quite faint.

"Don't worry, Rose, there'll be no hard feelings. It's just a might-have-been." He sounds so kind, so ineffably kind that it's almost like a knife in my heart. "I may have lost all my money and be a poor excuse for an aristocrat, but I do try to behave like a gentleman. We'll speak no more of this and just go back to a friendly working relationship."

"No!"

He stares at me. The frown is a puzzled one now.

"No…I mean…yes, I am interested. Definitely. It's just something that's completely out of my experience…. Yes," I repeat, aware that I'm babbling. "I'm definitely interested."

His stern, elegant face lights up as if the sun's just come out. He looks happy, genuinely happy, in a way that seems quite astonishing in a man so obviously worldly and experienced.

"Splendid!" He sets down his glass, and leans forward. "I'm so glad."

Without any warning, he leans down and dusts my lips with a tiny, fleeting kiss.

"For luck. To seal our agreement." A wry, strange smile flits across his face. It's almost as if he's surprised somehow, but not by me. "Come then."

He takes my hand and leads me back toward the fireside.

When he reaches his armchair, he sits down in it, all elegant, languid grace, and draws me between his outstretched thighs. I suddenly feel very small. Like a naughty little girl, and as that registers, I realize it's exactly what he wants me to feel. Suddenly, I'm staring at my toes, too embarrassed to look at him, even though he's the most beautiful thing I've ever seen.

"Ah, now then, my Rose…" He reaches out, lifts my chin with the tip of his finger and makes me look at him. His brown eyes are electric, gleaming and wickedly dark. Just for a second his tongue tip flashes out and licks the center of his lower lip, and it's as if in that instant someone's thrown a switch and changed everything in the room.

We're playing.

"So, do you normally go around prying into people's private belongings? Or is it just me that you spy on?"

I don't know how to answer. I don't even know if I should answer. But he prompts me.

"Well, Rose?"

"Um…no, not normally, but I was interested. I wanted something to watch."

"And you didn't think to ask first?"

"No, my lord…sorry, my lord…."

His title slips perfectly off my tongue, so sweet and so dangerous in this context.

"I think I should be punished," I add rashly, suddenly wanting to move on and get to the heart of the game.

"Really?" His voice is arch, slightly mocking, but I can still hear the joy in it. "In that case, my dear, bold Rose, I think we should oblige you, shouldn't we?" He's still holding my hand, and unexpectedly he brings it momentarily to his lips before releasing it.

For several long moments, he just watches me, peruses me, looks me up and down as if he's planning something demonic, and then he says simply, "Undress."

Oh, God, I wasn't expecting this. I thought it might come afterward—after, I suppose, my first spanking. I'd been picturing myself across his knee, maybe with my skirt up and my knickers down…but not totally naked and exposed.

When he says, "Did you hear me, Rose?" in a soft tone of remonstration, I realize I'm just standing here dithering.

I peel off my cardigan, and to my surprise he takes it from me and places it over the arm of the chair. Nothing too frightening there. But next, it's my little buttoned top, and I fumble with the fastenings as if I have five thumbs.

The marquess sighs softly, gently puts my hands down at my sides and then undoes the top himself, divesting me of it with precise efficiency as if he undresses clumsy women all the time. Maybe he does. Well, not necessarily clumsy ones…but who knows whom he sees when he's not here at the manor overseeing the renovation.

Now, on top, I'm left just in my bra, and the marquess studies it, doing that little head tilt thing of his again, as if he's grading me on the quality of my underwear. I swallow hard, wondering how my choice stands up. It's a delicate white lace number, my best…I hope it passes muster. I hope my breasts do as well, beneath. They're not big, but they're perky, and right now my nipples are as pink and hard as cherry stones. Something the marquess takes note of by reaching out to squeeze one. I moan like a whore as he twists it delicately through the lace.

Lust and blood and hormones career wildly through my body. It's as if I've got too much energy to fit inside my skin. I close my eyes tightly, ashamed of my own wantonness as my hips begin to weave in time with the delicate tweaking. But the marquess says, "No," and with his free hand he cups my chin. "Look at me, Rose. Give me your feelings. Don't deny me them."

I open my eyes, aware that they're swimming, but it's not from the pain. It's that overflow again, that wild abundance of emotion and sensation; it's welling over in the form of sudden tears.

The marquess's eyes are amazing—deep as the ocean, unfathomable and yet on fire. He reaches for my other nipple and as he plays with that, I wriggle anew as if my pelvis had a wicked life of its own.

"You're willful, sweet Rose," he purrs, tugging, tugging,

first one nipple then the other. This simple punishment is far more testing than any amount of smacking or spanking, I sense, and suddenly I'm proud to be put to such a test.

The marquess's eyes glitter as if he's read my sudden thought, and he permits me the beneficence of a slight smile. Then he draws a deep breath and leans back in the chair, abandoning my breasts.

I feel bereft until he tells me, "Continue."

Slipping off my bra, he gives my breasts and my rosy, swollen nipples a swift once-over, as if without covering they don't interest him quite as much. I hesitate and he nods to indicate I should take off my skirt.

First I slip my feet out of my shoes and kick them away, then I unfasten the button and zipper of my skirt. For a moment, I clutch at it, suddenly nervous despite everything. Then I let it drop, and kick it away, standing as proudly as I can in just a very tiny G-string.

I keep my own smile inside, but elation geysers up inside me as the marquess can't disguise his grin.

"Oh, how splendid…how splendid…." he murmurs, and that naughty pink tongue of his slips out again, touching the center of his lush lower lip. Reaching out, he runs the backs of his fingers over the little triangle of lace and over the fluffy pubic hair that peeks out on either side. Fleetingly, I wish I'd had a chance to visit a salon and get a Brazilian, then I change my mind as his fingertips coil in my floss and gently tug it. He seems to like me *au naturel,* and whatever the marquess likes, I like, too.

He tweaks a little harder and the tension transfers directly to my clitoris. I'm so excited I almost come; I'm so close to the edge. As it is, I let out a groan, I just can't help myself.

The marquess pulls again, making a tiny pain, a little hurt, prick and niggle at the roots of the little curl he's playing with. But at the same time, he reaches up with his free hand and places his fingers across my lips.

"Now, now, Rose, you must learn to control yourself," he reprimands quietly, but without rancor. "A good submissive is quiet and still, bearing discomfort—" he twists a little more tightly "—with perfect grace and fortitude. You have a long way to go yet, my dear, but I hope that you'll learn."

The tears trickle down my face. This isn't quite what I expected, and somehow I feel reduced to some kind of wayward little girl for a moment. But this excites me, and inside, deeper than my confusion, is a brighter glow. It's a game, and my body loves it even though my mind is still learning.

It isn't only my tears that are trickling.

As if he, too, has detected my welling arousal, the marquess's nostrils flare eloquently. His deep chest lifts as if he's breathing in my foxy, fruity smell. A slow smile curves his lips and I half expect him to lick them again, savoring my aroma.

A moment later, I'm gasping, fighting for breath, desperate to obey his wishes, and at the same time on the point of shouting out and jerking my hips.

In a sly, deft, sleight-of-hand motion, the marquess has abandoned my pubic curls and slid his fingertips into my cleft beneath the lacy triangle of my underwear. One finger zeroes in like a guided missile and pushes right inside me. He presses in deep and lifts his hand, and I rise on my toes, speared and fluttering.

When he rocks the digit inside me, I grab his shoulders, almost fainting as I come. My resolution crumbles when he squashes his thumb down flat onto my clit and I groan like an animal, lost in pleasure.

Pulsing, sweating, burbling nonsense, I lose all strength as my knees turn to jelly. The marquess's free arm snakes around my waist to hold me up, while between my legs, he both supports and manipulates me, his finger lodged inside me while his thumb presses and releases, presses and releases, presses and releases…tormenting me by lifting me to orgasm again and again.

I hold on. My body clamps down on him again and again. Time passes.

Eventually, the tumult ebbs and I flush with shame and a strange, tangled happiness as I regain the ability to stand up straight.

The marquess's strong, straight digit is still inside me.

And it stays there, his hand cupping my mound, as he speaks to me.

"You have so much to learn, sweet Rose, so much to learn." He looks into my face, his beautiful brown eyes gleaming with sex, yet somehow almost regretful. "And we have so little time, you and I, don't we? Just a week or two."

What the hell is he talking about? I could stand here forever, possessed by him, my sex his plaything.

And then I remember that all this is temporary. There's my dream job of a lifetime waiting for me in the Caribbean in a few weeks, and I'll be thousands of miles away from the marquess and his hand, his eyes, his body.

The shock must show on my face because he smiles kindly. "Don't worry, my dear. All the more reason to make the most of things while we can." His finger crooks inside me and finds a sweet spot, forcing me to grunt aloud, flex my knees and bear down. "Usually, I start with a little pain before the pleasure. But in your case, I couldn't resist handling your delightful pussy and making you come."

He flexes his finger a little more.

I cry out, "Oh, God!" and come again.

It's quick. It's hard. It satisfies, yet primes me for more. But instead of either working me to more orgasms, or just pushing me down on the rug, unzipping and thrusting into me, the marquess withdraws his finger, suddenly and shockingly, and offers it to me.

My head whirling, I wonder what he means, but then it dawns on me that he wants me to clean it off.

My face flaming, I suck my own musk from his warm skin as more flows between my legs to quickly replace it.

I feel bereft when he withdraws the digit and then dries it methodically with his perfectly laundered handkerchief.

"And now to business," he says briskly, as if implying that I've deliberately kept him from it with my orgasms. "I think I'd like to bind you. Are you okay with that?"

Speechless, I nod like an idiot as he reaches down the side of his chair and pulls out a length of soft, silky cord. I feel it slide over my hip and flank as he turns me to face away from him, and then, bringing my hands behind me, he fastens them at the wrist.

I think that this is it, but suddenly he produces another length of cord and, pulling my arms back tighter, he winds it around my elbows, drawing them together.

Twice bound like this, I start to sweat even harder. While not really painful, the position is uncomfortable, and what's more, it forces my breasts to rise and become more prominent, vulnerable and presented.

When he spins me around again, I feel almost faint as he leans forward and slowly licks and sucks each of my nipples. His silky hair swings and slides against the skin of my midriff and the scent of an expensive man's shampoo fills my nostrils.

As he torments me with his tongue, I feel his fingers at my thong. He plucks at the lace and elastic and tugs the thing up tight into the division of my sex lips. When the sodden cloth is pressing hard on my clit, he reaches around behind me, working beneath my shackled wrists, and makes a little knot somehow at the small of my back, to keep it taut.

He licks at me a moment or two more, then leans back, almost indolent in his great chair as he cocks his head to one side and regards his handiwork.

I feel like a firecracker in a bottle, an explosion of sexual energy and need contained by my bonds. I'm desperate to come again, but I'm reaching and yearning for more than just simple gratification. The marquess smiles as if he understands me completely.

"And now we really begin," he says softly, taking me by the waist and pushing me from between his knees. Then, settling himself more comfortably in the chair, and setting his booted feet more squarely on the floor, he nods to me, his eyes dancing with lights and a subtle smile on his handsome face.

I know what he's indicating. That I should assume the position.

It's difficult to settle elegantly across his lap with my hands tied, but I do the best I can, not wanting to disgrace myself. Even so, he has to more or less grapple me into place, setting me at precisely the right angle and elevation and disposing my limbs and torso in the optimum position to present my bottom to his hand.

I wait for the first spank. The first real one...the tap the other day was nothing, I suspect.

But it doesn't come yet.

"Mmmm..."

It's a low, contemplative sound, and as he utters it, the marquess gently cups my bottom cheek, testing its resilience. The feeling is entirely different this time; his fingers on my bare skin feel like traveling points of electricity, sparking me and goading me as they rove. He grips me harder and I have this sense of some kind of computer in his brain calculating, calculating. How hard to hit. How high to lift his hand for the downstroke. How many slaps is optimum.

"Ready?" he asks, to my surprise. I'd expected him to just take what he wanted. He's in charge, after all.

And yet, is he? I bet if I said "no," even now, he'd immediately desist and help me restore my clothing to decency and propriety. But no way would I do that. I want what I want, and it's what he wants, too.

"Yes," I whisper, barely able to hear my own breathy voice over the bashing and thudding of my heart.

"Good girl."

And then he spanks me.

Oh, dear God! It hurts! It hurts so much!

What a shock! I'd expected a tingle, a little burn…something that's as much pleasure as pain.

Bloody hell, how wrong can you be?

It's like he's slapped me with a solid hunk of wood rather than his strong, but only human, hand. For a moment, both mind and bottom are numbed by it, but then sensation whirls in like a hurricane, I shout out loud—something indistinguishable—and my left buttock feels like it's on fire.

And that's just one blow.

As more and more land, I realize in astonishment that in that first shot, he was actually holding back….

Slap! Slap! Slap!

Spank! Spank! Spank!

The whole of my rear is very quickly an inferno, and the heat sinks like lava into the channel of my sex, reigniting the desire, the grinding longing I felt before my orgasms, and rendering it slight and inconsequential.

I know I should be quiet and still and obedient. I know I should just accept my punishment like a good little girl. Instinct tells me that a master appreciates that in a supplicant. Perfect poise. The perfect ability to absorb the punishment with grace and decorum.

But me, I'm rocking and wriggling about, struggling against my bonds, plaguing my own clit with my wild pony bucking and jerking that makes my pulled-tight thong press and rub against it.

I feel as if I'm going out of my mind, and yet I know, in some still-sane part of it, that I've never been happier in my life. Despite the pain and the strangeness and the sheer, unadulterated kink of what's happening to me, I know that this is where I should be and who I should be with.

The marquess lands a particularly sharp blow, and I let out a gulping, anguished cry. But it's not from the impact, or the raging fire in my bottom cheeks.

No, what pains me the most is that in two weeks I'll be thousands of miles away from the hand that's spanking me.

Still squirming about, my backside still in torment, still almost about to orgasm, I begin to cry piteously, completely out of control and racked by raw, illogical heartache.

As if he were plugged right into my psyche on the deepest level, the marquess stops spanking me immediately.

Strong and sure, he turns me over as if I were as light as a feather across his lap. I gasp as my sore bottom rubs against his denim jeans, but he takes the exhalation into his own mouth as he swoops down to kiss my very breath.

With his tongue still in my mouth, he unfastens my hands and elbows, then, with a swift, sharp jerk that snaps the lace like a cobweb, he wrenches the thong from between my legs and replaces it with his fingertips. His gentle fingertips that love me to a swift, sweet, pain-stealing orgasm.

I moan into his kiss, pleasure sluicing through my loins, rising through my body and my soul and soothing my aching heart. He touches me so tenderly, coaxing me to the peak again and again. As I twist beneath his touch, I realize, distantly, that I'm clinging on to him for the dearest life, yanking at his dark shirt and digging my nails into his back, perhaps inflicting a tiny percentage of the pain I've just experienced.

Finally, we both lapse into silence and stillness. He holds me. I hold him. We're two breathless survivors of a whirlwind.

How long we sit like this, I have no real idea. My entire world is his strength, his scent, his sure, steady breathing and the beat of his heart in his chest where I huddle against it. After a while, though, another physical factor begins to impress itself on me.

I'm on the marquess's lap, and in the cradle of that lap there's the hard knot of an erection.

I start to feel hot again. My cheeks flush with shame at my own selfishness. This spanking was something he wanted to do, but it was really as much my idea as his…and I've had the pleasure of it—several times—and he's had nothing in the way of sexual release.

He's been stiff all through this strange interlude and I've made not the slightest offer to do anything about that. Even though he's seen to *my* satisfaction…repeatedly!

I wonder how to broach the subject. He seems to be quite content for the moment just to hold me, despite the fact that he must be in a fair degree of discomfort. Something that's dramatically illustrated when I shift my position slightly and he draws a swift, sharp breath.

"Um…Your Lordship…er…shouldn't we do something about that?"

Not exactly eloquent, but I drive my point home by moving again, cautiously rubbing my sore bottom against the solid bulge that's stretching his jeans.

If I've been expecting a positive response and an enthusiastic segue into the next delicious stage of the proceedings, I'm completely wrong. He remains silent, perfectly silent, for several long moments, and when he does utter a sound it's a soft, regretful sigh.

"That's a sweet offer, my lovely Rose, and I'm very tempted." I gaze into his face and suddenly discover that he looks quite sad. "But perhaps it's not the best idea…not really."

"Why not?" I demand, my submissive role suddenly a thing of the past. His eyes widen, and for a moment I wonder whether I should apologize and grovel a bit, but then he smiles and shrugs, the movement of his shoulders transmitting itself to me more through his erection than anything else.

"I…" He looks away, distant for a few seconds, and then returns his gaze to me. He looks rather sad, almost wistful, and then he smiles again. "I prefer to just touch and play and give pleasure, rather than receive it."

What?

"But…um…don't you need to come?"

He laughs. "Of course I do. But I'll deal with myself later, Rose." He tips his head back, as if looking heavenward for inspiration, his night-black hair sliding away from his face with the movement. "It's hard to explain, but basically, if I get too intimate, I want too much…and I'm not really a good prospect for relationships." A heavy sigh lifts his chest. "I'm a widower, but I wasn't much good as a husband. Or even a boyfriend. Too wild…too selfish…. I've settled down a lot now, of course—" he makes a vague gesture as if to encompass his responsibilities at the manor "—but now I'm saddled with debts and commitments, and anyone who takes me on takes all that on, as well."

I can see what he means, but suddenly, in the midst of that thought, a bright revelation shatters the gloom.

Oh, God, even though he's expressing his shortcomings and his wariness of relationships, the fact that he's actually mentioned a relationship—marriage even—must mean that he feels more for me, and sees me as more than a temporary employee and a casual spanking playmate.

Mustn't it?

"Look, please, let me…let me touch you…or maybe we can even fuck? I won't expect more than just that. All it'll be is a bit of pleasure with no commitments. Um…just friendship with a little bit of extra, really, nothing more."

It's out before I've really thought about it. But thinking about it, I know I do want more, despite what I say.

Even though it's possibly the stupidest thing I've done in my life, even crazier than agreeing to be spanked by my temporary boss, I've only gone and fallen head over heels in love with the marquess, haven't I?

And he's right, there's no future in it, is there? None at all…
Soon I'll be leaving for the Caribbean, to take up my chance-
of-a-lifetime job.

He looks at me, and his dark eyes are still sad, but strangely
yearning. It's as if he's just read my thoughts, and feels the same
bittersweet emotions that I do.

"You're a wonderful girl, Rose." He touches my face, the
same fingers that punished me now a tender, caressing curve.
"You're far too wonderful for me. If I take more from you,
I'll just want more than that. And more…and more…and
that's not fair of me."

I could weep and scream. He *does* bloody well care!

Acting on impulse, I turn my face into his gentle hand and
kiss his palm. He groans and mutters, "No!"

But I know I've got him. His whole body shakes finely, and
beneath me, his cock jerks and seems to harden even more, if
that were possible.

"I shouldn't…I shouldn't…"

"It's all right. It'll be 'no strings,'" I whisper against his
palm, then inscribe a little pattern, a promise, with my tongue.

"Oh, hell," he almost snarls, and then he's kissing me,
tilting me back on his lap and going deep with tongue and
lips…and heart?

I embrace him, writhing on his knee again, the discomfort
of my spanked bottom forgotten. Wrapping my arms around
him, I try to silently say all the things that are too difficult and
irrational to say.

Like…

To be with him just a little while, I'll pay any price, do things
his way and never ask for more.

Like…

I'm prepared to take my chances on his lack of prospects
and commitments.

Like…

Who needs a fucking job in the Caribbean, after all?

This last one shocks me, but just as I think it, the marquess deepens the kiss even further. His arms slide around me, holding me tight, and yet with delicacy, as if I'm precious to him.

And then, somehow, we're on the rug, and he's lying over me, great and dark, like a shadow that's so paradoxical it's also light. The light of revelation…

His hands rove over my body, exploring with reverence this time, and great emotion. And the touch is a thousand times more sexy than when we played. With a gasp, he straightens up momentarily and rips open his shirt, sending buttons flying in his impatience. Then he embraces me again, skin to skin.

His body is hot, feverish and moist, with a fine sheen of sweat that seems to conduct electricity between us. I moan, loving the communion, almost feeling that this might even be as good as sex in some mysterious way. But then my cunt flutters, reminding me I want more.

Still kissing me, the marquess deftly unbuckles his belt and then unfastens his jeans. But just as he's about to reveal himself, and allow me to feast my eyes on that which I've been fantasizing about since the moment he cordially and quite impersonally welcomed me to the manor and the work team, he lets out a lurid, agonized curse.

Then says, "I don't have a condom. I wasn't expecting to need one."

A part of me thinks, whoa, he really did mean all that stuff about not fucking! But another part of me gives thanks for the fact that hope always springs eternal.

"Er…I've got one. It's in the pocket of my skirt."

He gives me a look that says he thinks I'm a saucy, forward minx, but he's more than glad of the fact, and then he scoots gracefully across to where my skirt landed, and locates the contraceptive in my pocket.

Back close again, he hesitates, and gives me a beautiful,

complex look, full of hunger, compassion, yearning again…
and a strange fear. I nod. I feel just the same.

And then he reaches into his jeans and reveals himself.

Involuntarily, I make a little "ooh" sound.

He's big. Stunning. Delicious. His cock is as handsome and
patrician as his face, magnificently hard and finely sculpted.
He's circumcised and his glans is moist and stretched and shiny.
I've never seen a prettier one, and it's almost a shame when he
swiftly robes it in latex.

I reach for him, expecting him to move between my splayed
thighs. But with all the authority of his centuries-old title, he
takes hold of me and moves me into his preferred position.
With his arm around my waist, he scoops me up and places
me on my hands and knees and moves in behind me.

It's not what I would have chosen, but I'll take what I can
get. And I understand his reasons. This way is more impersonal,
not too intimate and less dangerous to his emotions and to mine.

At least I think so, until he moves in closer, pressing his
condom-clad penis against my still-tingling buttocks while he
leans over me and molds his bare chest against my back so he
can reach to give the side of my neck a soft kiss.

I sway against him, loving the kiss, loving his skin, loving
his scent…and loving him. His weight is on one hand, and
with the other he strokes me gently and soothingly, hot fingertips traveling over my breasts and my rib cage, then skim-
ming my waist before finally settling over my sex. He cups me
there, not in a sexual sense, but in a vaguely possessive way that's
almost more intimate than a blatant attempt to stimulate me.

Then his long finger divides my labia and settles on my clit.

I moan, long and low, already fluttering as he rubs in a
delicate, measured rhythm. He's trying to make me come first,
I realize, and perversely I resist for a few seconds, holding out
for our union. But he's far too clever and too skilled, and I
crumble, coming heavily and with an uncouth, broken cry.

As I'm still pulsating, he pushes in, the head of his cock finding my entrance with perfect ease.

Oh, God! He's big! He feels even bigger than he looks, so hot and imposing. I pitch forward onto my folded arms as he ploughs into me, making a firm foundation from which to push back at him.

The impact of his penetration shocks my senses for a moment, and pleasure ebbs while I assimilate what's happened to me.

I've got the marquess's cock inside me. I'm possessed by this strange, elegant, deeply personal and mysterious man that I work for. We are one, for the moment; joined by flesh.

But when he starts to move, I'm back in my body and the pleasure reasserts itself.

We rock against each other and he thrusts in long, easy, assured strokes. At first he grips my still-tingly bottom cheeks, but as things get more intense, he inclines right over me, taking his weight on one hand again while with the other, he returns his loving attention to my clit.

Somehow he manages to stroke me in exactly the way that suits me, a firm rhythm, devilishly circling, but not too rough. God alone knows how he manages it. Maybe it's pure instinct or something? Because, judging by the way he's gasping and growling, he's just as out of it as I am.

Sublime and miraculous as all this is, I can't hold out for long. And I don't. Within moments, I'm growling, too, like some kind of she-wolf, and climaxing furiously. Dimly, I sense the marquess trying to contain himself, conserve himself as long as he can, to increase my pleasure. But I'm not having any of that—I want *his* pleasure, too!

I milk him hard with my inner muscles, and he lets out such a string of profanities—in his immaculate upper-crust accent—that I find myself laughing just as wildly as I'm coming.

Then he laughs, too, pumps hard and fast and shoots inside

me. I feel the little bursts of his spurting semen even through the condom, and despite it being very stupid, I suddenly wish the rubber protection wasn't there. As we both tumble forward in a gasping, sweating, laughing, climaxing heap, I have fleeting but dangerous thoughts about one or two or three little marquesses or honorables or whatever, all running around the place looking as dark and aristocratic and beautiful as their daddy.

Lying on the rug, wrapped in his arms as he cradles me spoon-style—his still partly clothed body warm and protective against mine—I fight with a huge case of genuine post-coital tristesse this time.

This is all there is, Rose, I tell myself. A couple of weeks of this. A bit of naughty spanking and sex play by mutual consent. Maybe a friendly, but not too personal, fuck or two.

And then you're off to your lovely new job and a new life of opportunity.

While he stays here, in the heart of England, tending to his great house.

Outside, I hear it start to rain again.

Two weeks later, it's still raining. In fact, there's a raging thunderstorm outside and it's really scaring me.

But in a way, this is a good thing. It's taking my mind off the fact that tomorrow, I'm supposed to be leaving. And though I won't miss this cold, English rain one bit, there are a lot of things I am finding very hard to leave.

This funny old house has really grown on me, and I wish I was going to be here to see it finished.

I'm going to really miss being spanked and tied up and given mock orders in a mock-stern, beautiful cut-glass English voice. Oh, I'm sure there'll be a man somewhere in the Caribbean who'll oblige me, but it won't be the same. It won't be the same.

And pleasure, oh, how I'll miss the pleasure. Not just any

pleasure, but the bliss gifted to me by a man who seems to know my every thought, my every response, inside out.

I'll miss the sex, too, even if I never do get to see his glorious face as he comes inside me. But even if he won't face me, I still don't think I'll ever find anyone with his finesse, his strength, his sweetness, his consideration…and his mastery.

Yes, it's the marquess. I fear he's irreplaceable.

And it's our last night.

Lights flicker along the passage as I make my way to the little sitting room, and just as I knock on the door, as I always do now, the lights dim and then go out. There's still some rewiring to do and this happens now and again, but this is the first time the power's gone out in a storm.

There's a loud crack of thunder, and lightning flashes almost simultaneously.

I shriek with fear and the door to the study flies open.

If I wasn't so terrified of the storm outside, I would laugh out loud. It's just like a Dracula movie, with a venerable old house, a wild storm and a beautiful, dramatic aristocrat dressed from head to foot in black.

I squeak again as he gathers me to him and hustles me into the softly lit room.

"I didn't think you'd come tonight, Rose. I thought you'd be down with the others in the kitchen, all seeing out the storm together."

I would be annoyed that he'd think that of me, except that the joy in his eyes at the fact that I did come is patent. He looks as if I've just given him a supremely magnificent gift, and that expression binds me to him far tighter than any length of rope ever could.

Mad, mad thoughts gather in my mind. They're thoughts that have been circling for the past two weeks, nipping at my resolutions and my every idea of what I've always wanted for my future.

But they're so crazy that I find it hard to acknowledge

them, and when thunder cracks again they disappear, along with almost all my normal ones.

The marquess wraps me in his arms, softly cooing to me in low, comforting tones, and it's only as I settle that it dawns on me that I just shouted out incoherently again.

The embrace isn't sexual, it's protective. And yet I can still feel him hard against my belly. I hope he'll make love to me tonight, seeing as it's our last time. He doesn't always. Sometimes he's still hard when he escorts me to my little room, high in the old servants' quarters, and I can only assume he deals with his own needs after, alone.

His hold on me is too nice, too sweet and tempting. I struggle out of his grip and try to sink to the floor and kneel… to begin the game.

But he holds on to me, his big, strong hands gripping my shoulders.

"Not tonight, dear. You're too frightened, aren't you?"

He gazes at me, his dark eyes full of complicated emotion. He *does* want to play. I can tell by his erection and the tension in his body that these games of ours seem to release just as much as actual sex does. But there's more, so much more on his mind.

Turbulent joy rushes through my veins. He's going to miss me! My marquess is going to miss me!

And it's for more reasons than just the obvious one— because he likes to spank my bottom…

Amazingly, for one so confident and masterful—both by birth and by inclination—he snags his lip like a nervous, unsure boy. And in this sudden, weighted moment, I sense another, far more real, chance of a lifetime.

"Where's your bedroom, Christian?"

His given name, on my lips for the first time, comes out so naturally. He looks perplexed for a moment. Not angry or confused, just amazed really. I can almost see him rapidly processing an array of new factors in our brief relationship. Then his sculpted, intelligent face lights with joy.

"Not far," he says, suddenly gruff as he grabs my hand and leads me swiftly out of the room. His long stride eats up the yards and I have to trot to keep up with him.

As we round a corner onto another corridor, a particularly violent crack of thunder seems to shake the entire manor, and I yelp again and falter, despite my eagerness to follow wherever he leads. He spins around, his long, night-black hair whipping up as he turns, and in one smooth, effortless move, he sweeps me up in his arms, and then we continue on our way, me being carried and with my arms wound tight around his neck.

The storm, his knight-errant act and his intoxicating and spicy male fragrance all make me dizzy. Everything feels unreal, yet more real than anything that has ever happened or will happen.

As he kicks open a door, there is no job, no Caribbean, no life plan…just the marquess…no…just Christian and his bedroom and his bed.

His room is big and dark and lit by just one rather anemic bedside lamp—rather gloomy. It's nothing like what one would expect in a stately home, but then it's not a public area, just actual living space. The bed isn't even made, so I guess he does his own housework up here. My gaze skitters around and I notice there's a black shirt flung across a rather saggy armchair in the corner, a bottle of gin and a glass on the sideboard and a heap of books beside the bed, all with old, well-worn bindings.

It's like the cell of some rather libertine type of monk.

But he won't be particularly monkish for much longer, if I get my way.

Christian carries me to the bed, sets me down on it and sits down beside me.

His face is still a picture of enigmatic emotions, as if there's a war going on inside him. But at least one part of the battle is quickly resolved, because drawing in a deep breath, he sweeps his hair back to one side and then leans down to kiss me.

It starts gently, but quickly takes fire, his tongue possessing me face-to-face in a way his cock never has. Adjusting his position without breaking lip contact, he stretches out alongside me, then half over me, reaching for my hand and a lacing his fingers tightly with mine.

For a long time he just kisses me as if he were fucking me, his tongue diving in, exploring and imprinting its heat on the soft interior of my mouth. I can't believe how exciting it is, as stirring in its own way as any of the naughty sex games we've played. And yet, for all its power, it's a simple kiss.

When my jaw is aching and my lips feel full and red and thoroughly marauded, he sits up again, and mutters, "Oh, God, I shouldn't do this...."

"Yes, you should!" I insist, not sure what it is he shouldn't be doing, but every instinct screaming that if I don't get it now, I'll just go mad.

For a moment, he tips back his head and looks to the somewhat discolored ceiling moldings for inspiration. His sublime hair slides back, accentuating his profile, and giving him the look of a fallen archangel contemplating his sins. And then he swoops back down again and starts undressing me, his hands working deftly at first, and then more frantically. I swear if I didn't help him, he'd probably have torn my flimsy knickers to get them off.

Thunder peals again, and though I don't cry out, I still can't help but flinch. Instantly, he's holding me to him, stroking and cherishing and protecting, his still fully clothed body creating a piquant sensation against my bareness.

But when the noise from the heavens ebbs, I spring into

action. I don't want to be just held. I want to be fucked! I want him inside me, face-to-face, possessing every bit of me.

And now it's my turn to tear at clothes, wrenching open his shirt as he first heels off his boots and kicks them away, then fumbling with his belt and his jeans button and struggling to free him from his jeans. Between us we achieve our objective and he sinuously wriggles clear of the restriction of the denim.

He's glorious naked. Utter perfection. Long and lean, yet powerful, his enticingly defined chest dusted with a scattering of dark hair. And there's more of that dark hair clustered below, adorning the base of his belly and the root of his eager, jutting cock.

He's everything I've ever wanted in a man, and I want to be worthy of him, a graceful, dexterous, intelligent lover.

But instead, I squeal like a scared kid and hurl myself at him for protection when thunder roars again, right overhead. The crack is so loud I'm convinced the manor has been struck, but it seems not to have been when all Christian does is gather me into his arms and hold me tight against his warm, hard body, stroking my back and murmuring sweet, reassuring bits of nothing.

The heavens rage and bellow, lightning illuminating the room, even though the obviously ancient and rather shabby curtains are quite thick. One powerful arm still wrapped around me, Christian tugs at the bedclothes—old-fashioned linen sheets, woolen blankets and a quilt on top—and pulls them right up and over our heads, sealing out the light show and some, if not all, of the noise.

"Better?" he whispers, his voice echoing strangely in our frowsty little nest. He tightens his arms around me again, and snuggles me close. The heat under all this bedding is really quite oppressive, but the sensation of safety, and of being cared for, more than makes up for that.

And the fact that he's still erect, and his delicious penis is pushing against my belly and weeping warm, silky fluid, makes matters infinitely more interesting and sensual.

"Yes…" I whisper, adjusting myself to rub against him and let him know that my fear of the storm hasn't killed my desire for him. In fact, the more I feel that long, hard, fabulous tower of flesh against my skin, the less I seem to be noticing the muffled booming of the thunder.

"Well, we'll have to pop out sooner or later, or we'll suffocate." He pauses, then chuckles. "And I'm going to need some air if I'm going to make love to you properly. A guy needs plenty of wind in his lungs for a good performance."

As if by magic, the next roll of thunder sounds much more muted, more distant. And the one after that even more so, far less fierce.

"I think I'll be all right now." I place my hand flat against his belly, then slide on down. When I fold my fingers around his prick, he gasps and tugs at the quilt, so we emerge.

"Are you sure? It could still come back again. We could wait a little while, if you'd like."

He's still concerned, thoughtful, caring. Even though his penis is like a bar of fire in my hand, and the satin flow of pre-come is yet more copious.

"I don't think I can wait."

It's true. My own body is flowing for him, too. I'm wetter than a river down below. The thunder chunters again in the background, and though I flinch, my need for Christian is far greater than my remaining fears.

I part my legs and he gets the message and starts to touch me, his fingertip settling lightly, yet with authority, on my clit.

The pleasure comes quickly, as wild and elemental as the storm, and just as electric. Within seconds, I'm climaxing hard, rocked by the intense, hungry spasms in my sex, and fighting a battle with myself not to grip Christian's cock too roughly.

But he just laughs kindly, and pushes toward me while I pulse and pulse.

When I get my breath back, I stare at him as he looms over me in the low light from the bedside lamp. I'm still holding his erect penis, but there's more than sex in his eyes. They're dark yet brilliant, a chiaroscuro of turbulent emotions. They seem to say so much, yet the message is still scrambled, unclear. I sense some of it, and it takes my breath away again.

"I want to make love to you." His voice is husky, low, intent. "No spanking, no mind games, no ropes or bondage. Not tonight."

I don't know what to say, but he seems to read my thoughts. He gives me a little smile, then rolls away from me for a moment and pulls open a drawer in the bedside cabinet, and fishes around in it without looking. It takes next to no searching to produce a foil-wrapped condom. He puts it into my free hand.

My fingers shake as I dress him in it, rolling the superthin latex over his silky skin and encasing the iron-hard strength of his erection. When he's covered, I hesitate.

What will he want? His usual position? Taking me from behind?

I start to roll into position, but he stops me, a firm but gentle hand on my flank.

He smiles, pushes me flat against the mattress and then parts my legs and moves swiftly and elegantly between them.

For a moment, he just rests there, the head of his cock nestling tantalizingly at my opening, almost quiescent.

"I've so been wanting to do this," he says, his eyes grave. "Wanting it, but knowing I shouldn't."

I want to say *why not?* But I think I know why.

Games of spanking and bondage are just that. Games. Beautiful and life-enhancing. Sexual fun.

But this, this is serious. This is more.

I sense a different kind of bond breaking as he enters me.

It's a restriction. An artificial barrier we've set between ourselves, and it's shattered now.

All is open. All is honest, dangerous but wonderful.

"I love you," he says quietly, then starts to thrust.

I can't speak, but I show him with my body that I feel the same. By holding him in my arms as tightly as I can while still allowing him to move. By hooking my legs around his body, and undulating my hips to press against him.

If only I could mold our two forms so closely together that we could become one, be inside each other's skin.

We rock and surge against each other, our heated perspiration almost fusing us in the way I crave. Christian's thrusts are short, shallow, urgent, almost desperate. He braces himself on one arm for leverage, and clasps me tightly to him with the other, his fingers digging into my flesh, not in cruelty but in possession and fierce need.

The joining is manic, almost animal, and yet at the same time soaring and transcendent. Holding him, being held and owned and fucked by him, I'm aware of my life changing as my flesh throbs with pleasure and clutches at his.

I gasp those three words, too, as my future changes shape.

In the morning, the park outside is fresh and clean and bright with sunshine. It's like a brand-new world after the storms of last night, a tangled paradise as I stare out from the window.

On the mantelpiece, Christian's clock reads a little after 6:00 a.m., but I'm wide-awake, anticipating a busy day ahead. I've so much to do and I don't know how to start.

So instead, I return to bed…and my man.

We said very little last night. Our bodies spoke for us. But this morning, I have to confirm not just my hopes and fears but my beloved's.

I know he probably wants what I want, but will his ancestral notions of duty and honor stop him from taking it? He might feel he has to set aside his needs for what he thinks is best for me.

Time to persuade him that he can't live without me.

Lifting the sheet that covers him, I feast my eyes on his magnificent body for a few moments, loving his tousled hair and the faintly sweaty early-morning aroma of his skin. His patrician face looks younger in repose, and his long, lush eyelashes are two dark fans against his cheekbones.

I wonder whether to bend down and take his cock in my mouth. It's already thickening, as if it's awake even if Christian himself isn't quite yet.

But instead, I try something different. Lying down against him I press my bottom against his thighs, and then draw his sleeping hand against its rounded shape, hoping he'll respond.

Yours, I think as his fingers automatically curve and cup me. *Yours until the end of time, to spank and play with at your leisure.*

"You do know what you're asking for, doing that, don't you?"

His voice is sleepy, yet still full of masculine power. He squeezes my cheeks briskly, already waking and ready for his treat.

"Um…yes, I think so."

"You know, there isn't really time, my love." There's regret there, but it's tempered with typical British stoicism. As if he's bracing himself already for what he dreads. "Isn't your taxi coming at eight? Shouldn't you be packing?"

I can't speak. Now that I have to tell him about my decision, I'm scared. I know I've read him right, and I know he cares, but still….

"I'm not going."

There's a long silence. His hands are still upon me, but they're quiescent.

And then he laughs. And squeezes again.

"You're a very silly girl. You know that, don't you?"

"Yeah, I do know it…but it doesn't change things." I press

myself back into his hold. "I've decided that I like rain, and I want to hang around here, stay on the team and see what this old heap looks like when the renovation is finished."

"Is that all?" I hear the smile in his voice as he rolls me onto my front, still palpating my bottom in a way that's utterly sensual and full of delicate, delicious menace. "I do hate it when someone I care about keeps things from me." He lifts his hand, and that's more menacing than ever. "Now, tell me the whole truth…or I shall be forced to punish you."

"You might think I'm a bit forward."

"I'll be the judge of that, Rose. Now tell me."

I hesitate again. Deliberately.

He makes a soft tutting sound, and though I can't see him, I imagine him shaking his head, and his gorgeous black hair rippling.

A little tap lands on my right buttock. It's light, barely a smack at all, but my sex ripples in luscious excitement. He barely has to touch me and I'm soaring toward pleasure already.

Another tap lands and I swirl my hips, rubbing my mound against the mattress, trying to stimulate my clit.

"Keep still. Don't be naughty."

He's fighting not to laugh, and his voice is so warm, so affectionate that I begin to melt in an entirely different way. My spirits sing as I work my crotch, happily defying him.

He smacks again and again, a little harder, warming up my hind parts to match the glow in my sex and in my heart.

"Tell me…tell me everything." He smoothes his free hand down my back and my flank, the other still softly slapping at my bottom.

It's hard to answer now because I'm so turned on I can't think straight to form words, and it's also getting difficult to keep my hips still against the sheets.

I grab at the pillows, clutching the linen of the pillowcase hard in an effort to concentrate.

"I…I've decided that I'd quite like to find out what it's like to be a marchioness!"

There's a pause, during which I hold my breath, then I feel a kiss settle on the small of my back like a butterfly.

"Well, I can tell you what that will be like." His breath is hot against my skin, wafting over my bottom, which is already even hotter. "You'll never have any money. You'll spend your life enslaved to a great monster of a house that'll never ever stop needing attention." He kisses me just one more time, and then straightens up again. "And you'll probably get your bottom smacked at least once a day, if not considerably more often!"

Spanks begin to rain down. Hard, loving, rhythmical and stirring. I surge against the mattress, my clit pulsating and my heart thudding and leaping with the purest love.

A while later, I've been spanked and I've been fondled and I've been comprehensively fucked…and I've been brought to climax again and again and again. And with each smack, each stroke, each thrust and each orgasm, I've been told that I'm cherished and adored.

Christian's gone back to sleep now, and I'm lying here savoring the peace and the closeness of his beloved body. Pretty soon I'll have to start making phone calls and explaining a lot of things to a lot of very astonished people. But for now, I'm just listening to my darling's breathing and the sound of a new, teeming downpour outside.

British weather? It's not so bad…in fact, I love it! Almost as much as I love the man who's at my side.

★ ★ ★ ★ ★

THE PRIESTESS

Elliot Mabeuse

THE SUN WAS SETTING SLOWLY BEHIND THE hills to the west, and long gray shadows were beginning to crawl along the dusty yellow streets of Thebes. The heat still lingered in the avenues and mud-brick walls of the shops and houses, but with evening came the breeze that lifted at last off the Nile and brought a welcome coolness to Tia's young face. She stood drinking in that coolness, standing in the shadow of her doorway, waiting for her brother the priest.

This was the sun as she loved him best, as Aton, old and mellow, his day's journey almost done. Soon he would sink under the edge of the west to engage in his night of struggles and tribulations with what lay in the darkness below, but Tia had perfect faith in her gods, and knew that he would emerge victorious as ever. She wished she could say the same for herself.

But already here was Kheneb, her elder brother, striding across from the shade of the other side of the street with his priestly staff in his hand, his white robe adorned with a turquoise cloth across his shoulders. He was arrayed in a fine panoply of jewelry, which explained the four armed temple servants who accompanied him a respectful three paces behind. There were always thieves about, and a priest at night was no safer than a pharaoh's tomb.

"Good evening to you, my little sister. You are all ready, then?" he asked. His eyes glowed with affection, but he only allowed himself the faintest smile. Kheneb was a powerful priest at the temple of Hathor, and he knew how to maintain a suitably grave and pious face in public.

Tia nodded her head in a small, polite bow, then smoothed her black hair back from her face. "As my elder brother wishes."

He smiled at her formal greeting and looked her over critically—her spotless white gown, the string of turquoise around her neck, the bracelets on her arms. She was pleased that he approved of how she looked, though it did little to allay the growing nervousness in her stomach. She was not really frightened, just a bit anxious about what lay ahead.

The town was coming alive in the cool of the evening, some shops closing for the day while others were just opening. The tavern owners were raising the reed shades that kept out the daytime flies and heat, sweeping the sand and dust from their establishments, setting out their signs and banners. Two boys herded a flock of geese into the shade across the road while a third led two mud-spattered oxen back from the fields by the river, giving the priest and his party a wide berth. This was a favorite time to shop and socialize, in the cool of the evening before full darkness fell, and already people were emerging from their houses, dressed in their fine linen skirts and gowns.

Out came the fine ladies of the evening, too, perfumed and oiled so that their skin gleamed, their mascara perfect, and Tia watched them as she always did, seeking to learn the secrets of their grace and charm. Tia knew how men loved beauty, and these women had that beauty that went deeper than just appearance. They moved with the grace of the river, the mysteries of the gods in them, and Tia envied them deeply.

Tonight she looked fine, as well. Her black hair had been dressed in the Hathor manner: parted in the middle and brushed out with a bit of sweet oil until it positively gleamed. The hairdressers had seen to her makeup, too, lining her large, dark eyes with powdered malachite, also sacred to the goddess, and coloring her lips with the juice of the pomegranate. Her robe was new, of the finest linen, and so were the sandals on her feet. Kheneb had even purchased jewelry for her, the first she had ever owned, and she was sinfully proud of the necklace, bracelets and earrings of turquoise and gold, colors also favored by Hathor. As the daughter of a powerful and well-placed priest, Tia had never been poor, but tonight she was dressed as beautifully as the wealthiest lady in Thebes, and for the first time her brother had to treat her as a woman and not a child. It amused her to see him struggle with this change in her, but he had no choice. The foreign goddess would only accept women as priestesses; she had no interest in flighty little girls.

It was not far from here that Tia had first known the pleasure of a man's embrace with a handsome young captain from Pharaoh's guard. Pharaoh had come down to the river to bless the Nile at harvest, and the celebration had been grand. There'd been musicians and dancing and the gods had been paraded. Beer was consumed in wild abandon and even Mother Nile had her fill. Pharaoh was magnificent and so were his guards, and Tia had been swept up in the excitement, literally, and had found herself then in Setka's chariot, held between his strong arms, racing through the streets as he lashed his horses.

And then she knew not what happened. His lips were on the back of her neck as he drove and his hands were on her breasts and she felt the hardness of his groin pressing against her. She, Tianefhet, had aroused this handsome captain of Amenhotep's guard, and he pressed her against him and his lips found hers, his hand went between her legs—and who was she to refuse him on this joyous day? His chariot left the procession and turned off into the high reeds that grew along the Nile, and even as she heard the brass trumpets sounding Pharaoh's return to the great Double House, Setka's lips were on her breasts and all around her was the green of the reeds and she was swooning under his touch.

His chest was broad and his belly hard as marble as Tia sank to her knees and worshipped him like a god, taking him into her mouth and sucking him like a starving child. Setka groaned and guided her, filling his hands with her hair and thrusting his lean hips with selfish urgency until Tia felt faint with desire to know him this way. But Setka was determined to have her as a man has a woman, and he made them a hurried bed of his soldier's cloak and quickly stripped her naked of her simple linen gown. How his eyes had glowed when he looked at her lying there in the reeds, open and waiting for him! He hurt her when he entered her, but only for a moment, and then she closed about him and held him tight with legs and arms as Setka used his strength to take her. He rode her as he rode his chariot, high and proud and fierce in his desire, his strong arms planted on either side of her shoulders, his loins slapping against her with such force that Tia cried out as if lashed with a golden whip. She'd never known such joy and it was indeed as if she were his vehicle of pleasure, taking him exactly where he wanted to go, higher and higher and faster and faster until the very earth fell away and it was just she and Setka and the green fire of the sun in the reeds. Then suddenly he had rolled them over and Tia was on top of him, on top of her magnificent lover, and it was as if she were a woman possessed, as if the horse had taken control of the chariot.

Even now she blushed to remember it, how she couldn't control her hips or the sounds that spilled from her open mouth. She'd spread her hands wide on the broad muscles of his chest and began to move with a hunger she didn't know she possessed, fucking him with a savagery that shocked them both. Setka raised his head and looked down to where his cock disappeared into her. He put his hands on her thighs and began to work her up and back, sliding her on his thick flesh, moving her like a child's toy, and Tia groaned, falling down over him and seeking blindly for his mouth, for the comfort of his kiss. It was madness divine, as if the gods themselves touched her. It picked her up and shook her to the core so that she wasn't herself and that was all she could think of, that she wasn't herself, but someone else.

The next thing she knew, she was on her back again and Setka was slamming into her, sweat dripping from his body onto her breasts as he pulled her to him. Tia could hardly breathe. She was digging her nails into the muscles of his ass and her pleasure was breaking over her in a blinding wave like Ra breaking through the morning mists, and she burned with the holy fire of the gods. She cried out and clung to him as his full body went rigid, and then he was moaning and growling, emptying himself into her, and she knew then something of what the gods must surely know, and Tia the girl became Tia the woman once and for all time.

The captain had been good to her and gentle, but she saw in the way he quickly gathered himself up to go that she'd surprised him, shocked him even. He left her alone and lonely, though by no means sorry for what she'd done. And she'd been curious ever since, certain that the gods were involved in this kind of love between a man and a woman, but not sure just how, and aching to find out. She didn't dare ask her brother—he'd never understand—but Tia knew the gods had touched her that day and she wanted to know more. She burned to know more.

Kheneb took her arm and they began walking down the street, the bodyguards falling in behind them. She could tell her brother had been cautious in choosing the number of his retinue. This was a delicate mission, and he obviously wanted to be impressive but not intimidating. He had mentioned taking sedan chairs—hence the four guards—but decided against it. Walking was more egalitarian, and they didn't have far to go.

"Stand erect, child. Don't slump like a sack of barley," he said, stopping to push on her shoulders. "Straighten your back. You want pride, little sister. You're a lovely girl, Tianefhet, and you must learn to be proud of yourself, especially tonight. This is truly a remarkable offer."

"Yes, my brother." She drew herself up and stood erect, and Kheneb looked away uneasily as her breasts came into prominence.

She did feel proud, but along with the pride was fear, even a mild dread. She knew and loved the gods of her Egypt, but this strange goddess was no one she knew, and she had the vague feeling of betraying her people. It didn't help that Kheneb was uncharacteristically nervous, as well. It was very much unlike him.

They turned a corner and came out into a plaza of food sellers. The yeasty smell of beer and the aroma of grilled fish was in the air, mingled with the earthy smell of the river carried in on the warm and fitful breeze.

"Now tell me once again," Kheneb said, deftly plucking a fresh fig from a fruit vendor's table as they walked past. The vendor looked up in reproach, but seeing that Kheneb was a priest, he lowered his eyes and said nothing. "What is the goddess's name?"

"Kheneb, really—"

"Now, now. Answer me, little sister. We want no mistakes, no slips of the tongue."

Tia sighed. They walked in the middle of the street now, and she was aware of the stares of both men and women, some who knew her, others who didn't, but all wondering what this special occasion might be that a fine lady walked in the street with a high priest and an armed escort.

"Her name is Astarte, my brother, though her worshippers often just call her the Great Lady."

"And who is she?"

"She is a goddess of the Mitanni, the hairy people of the east," Tia said, remembering to keep her back erect as they walked. "She is a goddess of love and war, and some would call her Isis, but she is not Isis."

"Just leave Isis out of this," Kheneb said testily. "This goddess is the same as Hathor. Anyone can see that. That's what this is all about—to show that this Astarte is Hathor, the Mistress of Joy, the Golden One."

"Yes, my brother," Tia said gravely. She knew how he felt about competing goddesses and had said it partly to tease him and distract him from his nervousness. "But how one goddess can embody both love and the violence of war, I'm afraid I won't ever understand."

"Understanding will come with time, once you're accepted into the temple," Kheneb said. "And that's what we must concentrate on now. I do hope you will keep in mind what an honor this is, Tia, and how important it is to us, and to all of Egypt. I've worked very hard to get you this appointment. It's almost certain now that Great Pharaoh will have Prince Nekhet marry the Mitanni princess to cement the two lands' alliance, and so Pharaoh has set his mind on making a home for this princess in Egypt, and that means a home for her gods as well, though I hear the funds for her new temple are not quite flowing as freely as could be wished, what with all the other building he is doing. In any case, it's very important that you be accepted into this temple, and that we establish once and for all that this foreign goddess—this Astarte—is our Hathor, not Isis. You know how I feel about Isis."

"Yes, Kheneb."

"I mean, I have nothing against her. Nothing at all. But she is not Hathor, and I will not have anyone confusing the two, least of all my little sister. How would that look?"

Tia didn't understand this rivalry between the gods, but then she took a much simpler view of their religion than did her learned brother. In her mind, Hathor was the goddess of joy and fulfillment, the goddess of happiness, just as Kheneb had always taught her. Isis embodied something completely different, a more troubling mixture of love and loss, altogether more human. Whereas Hathor was joy and beauty, Isis was grace and mercy. Both goddesses were ancient, and, of course, as a priest Kheneb honored them both, but Tia knew that he always thought of Isis as being something of an upstart.

"Now," Kheneb said, clearing his throat and drawing himself up. "As for the role of *hierodule* or sacred prostitute, we shall most certainly have to make some arrangements about that. Such barbarian practices are foreign to us Egyptians, we who dwell in the Happy Land. It's quite unacceptable. And I won't have you doing anything you don't want to do, or anything that will bring shame upon our family."

Tia felt a little surge of excitement in her stomach. In truth, this was the crux of the entire matter and what made her so nervous and yet strangely excited. Sacred prostitution was the rule with the goddess Astarte; Tia had known this since she was a girl, and that was already long after the time when soldiers from the army of Thutmose the Third had brought back tales of the practice. She and her friends used to tease and scandalize each other with the idea of giving oneself away to a strange man for a night. And in the name of what was holy, too! But that had been in the days before the foreign goddess had been brought to Egypt itself, back when her worshippers were still strangers far away in a faraway land. Now that she might serve as a temple prostitute herself, Tia wasn't sure if there wasn't something wonderfully exciting about it in a wicked sort of way. On the one hand she was horrified, but on the other…to be the conduit of a goddess, to feel her power and beauty in your own body— that was something she was frankly quite curious about. She didn't reject it out of hand as Kheneb thought she did.

Now, walking along with her noble elder brother, dressed in her new things and made up by Hathor's own priests, she felt very beautiful and desirable. Cosmetics and perfume were also sacred to Hathor, and there was no doubt in Tia's mind that she was one of the most beautiful women in the entire town. The thought of a tryst with a total stranger—someone strong and handsome and exotic—was not unappealing.

She knew the rumors: as temple prostitute she would have her pick of the supplicants who came begging for her services, spying on them in private as they presented themselves. Only the ones she approved of would be brought to her, bathed and perfumed and blindfolded. They would be brought to her chambers where she would recline, dressed in fine robes, and there they would make love to her, treating her as a goddess, caressing her with lips and hands and body, using all their skills to please her. And if they did, if she found them entirely to her liking, only then would Tia assent to their embrace and let them come to her. Only then, and only if she were certain of the approval of the goddess within her would she open herself to them and take them, and in so doing know a pleasure few mortal women could even imagine.

Could any young woman seriously refuse serving the gods in such a way?

They turned off the side street and headed west toward the Avenue of Osiris that ran along the banks of the Nile, just in time to see the last edge of the sun sink below the vividly green palms on the far side of the river, flooding the facades of the buildings with fiery light. The moment of sundown always moved an Egyptian's heart, and the party paused while Kheneb pronounced a quick thanksgiving and a prayer for the safe journey of Ra through the subterranean land of Duad below their feet. As always, darkness fell as quickly as the sun, and before they had gone very far, two of the guards trotted off into a beer shop to borrow a flame for the lamps they carried.

"Tia," Kheneb said tenderly. "You do not have to do any-thing you don't want to do. You know that, don't you?"

"Of course I do, my brother."

He stared at her, apparently waiting for her to tell him that she was unwilling to go through with this, but Tia just looked with perfect equanimity across the tops of the palm trees to the broad swath of the Nile, where a royal barge painted in blue and gold could now be seen racing downriver, brightly lit with numerous lanterns. From the sound of their laughter Tia knew the rowers could not be slaves. So most likely it was one of Pharaoh's sons, perhaps Nekhet himself, who, as the prospective betrothed of the Mitanni princess, was overseeing the building of Astarte's temple. He was reputed to be a dashing and fearless young man, given to acts of valor and gal-lantry and known for the reckless way he handled a chariot, as well as for taking his barque racing along the Nile. Tia watched the barge for a while, but she could not make out who was at the helm. She waited, enjoying her brother's discomfi-ture at her silence.

Kheneb finally made a sound of exasperation and turned away. More than she, he was of two minds about this arrange-ment. He wanted the political victory that would come of allying the new goddess with Hathor, and yet he feared en-trusting his little sister to the barely civilized influences of the foreign goddess. He loved her dearly.

The guards came back, bearing their lamps on poles, and the little party started out again.

"Now, you will let me do the talking," Kheneb said, bending close to her in a final inspection. "And you will remember to sit or stand erect and not fidget. The priestess's name is Illana, and she speaks fine Egyptian like a normal human being, not all that coughing and throat clearing of the Mitanni. She was brought to Egypt as a child, and has served Great Pharaoh's ministers as an interpreter and counselor. She

knows many in the great Double House herself and is not
without considerable influence. She is also a consecrated
priestess of the foreign goddess, so don't fail to show her
respect."

They at last stepped out into the wide Avenue of Osiris, the
finest in the city, running along the banks of the Nile and fronted
on both sides by stone temples and the buildings of Pharaoh's
government. There was a ceremony going on in the great Temple
of Amun, the Hidden One, and the glow from many oil lamps
spilled through the maze of pillars and out into the street where
a loose crowd of undesirables milled about, not allowed in the
temple, but eager for the god's blessing. The sight of the golden
lamplight among the blue and purple shadows stirred Tia's heart.
Kheneb ceased his brotherly chatter and drew himself up into
his priestly posture once again, taking a moment to arrange the
heavy jewelry around his neck. He glanced into the Temple of
Amun with professional interest as they passed, gauging the size
of the crowd and nodding to a priestly acquaintance on the steps,
then fixed his eyes ahead. They were almost there.

Work had already begun on the promised Temple to Astarte
on a patch of ground overlooking the river, but it was pro-
ceeding slowly, funds being as tight as Kheneb had said. The
pillars were erect and the stairs half-finished, but the wooden
scaffolding of the stone masons was still in place and there was
as yet no roof, making it hard to visualize the finished struc-
ture. While the temple was being built, the foreign goddess
was being worshipped in a large yet simple mud-brick temple
close by. An older woman and a girl of Tia's age or less stood
with two servants outside the gate waiting for them.

"That is she," Kheneb whispered out of the side of his
mouth. "The girl must be from the Temple of Isis."

"I bid you good evening, your sacred lordship," the woman
said as they approached, and she bowed gracefully. The two
servants dropped to their knees in the Mitanni fashion.

"The blessings of all the gods upon you and your people," Kheneb said, switching to the hieratic tongue used by the priests. "And upon your noble temple. How fine it is looking!"

"And so this is Tianefhet," the woman said, smiling. "What a lovely creature. A grace upon the earth." She turned to the other girl, who was dressed in a simple robe trimmed with green, the color of Isis. "This is Hafertiri, our new novice. She comes to us from the Temple of Isis the Protectress."

Tia made her bows, and looked up at the priestess Illana. She was a handsome woman of middle age, but younger than Tia had expected, and with an air of self-possession and composure that Tia had not thought a Mitanni capable of, they being such an excitable and uncivilized people. She had long hair that fell to her shoulders in the eastern fashion, in tight, crimpy waves, like ripples on shallow water, and her eyes were especially beautiful—dark and deep with long lashes, calm and knowing. She wore the clothes of an Egyptian, and in the darkness her white linen robe seemed to glow as if lit from within.

Hafertiri was smaller and, now that they could see her, obviously younger than Tia, not as womanly, and indeed seeming to violate the principle that a priestess of Astarte be a fully developed woman, for she was still given to inappropriate giggling. Her hair was plaited into braids and hung with precious stones in the Isis manner, and the diadem of the Wife of Osiris circled her brows. She had an elfin face and seemed to have some trouble holding still. Her eyes invited Tia to share her private joke, but Tia was not going to be bated. She was more mature than that.

"Please, my lord," Illana said to Kheneb, "let us go within. I must ask your pardon for this simple dwelling, but it is only temporary while the new temple is being built." Kheneb gave her some conciliatory words, and they proceeded into the temple, followed by Hafertiri and Tia, leaving the servants to wait outside.

Inside, Illana dismissed Hafertiri, sending her up to her room in the gatehouse now that the introductions had been made.

The temple had apparently once been a noble house, for the trees and vines that grew around the pond in the court-yard were well-tended and mature, and the garden itself redolent with the smells of hibiscus and water lotus in bloom, as well as the fragrance of ripe grape and orange blossom. Tia glanced into the still waters of the pond and saw the fish there stirring slowly among the stands of papyrus and water lily, and then her eyes were drawn to the back of the temple, where the actual sanctuary of the goddess stood. The building had been modified, the roofline lifted to well over twice the height of a man, and through the widened doorway she could see a portion of the large image of Astarte, the foreign goddess, standing behind a deep blue veil of the sheerest fabric and il-luminated by the orange-yellow glow of oil lamps.

"On behalf of the priests and the clergy of the great goddess Hathor," Kheneb said, beginning his formal introduction and prepared speech. But Illana's eyes were on Tia, watching her intently, and she gently silenced him, holding up her hand. Kheneb followed her gaze and they both watched Tia, who was walking toward the image of the goddess as if drawn to it, her eyes wide, her hands unmoving at her sides.

The goddess was half again as large as a person, and com-manded the space within the sanctuary. Her bodice was open, and her perfectly spherical breasts bulged forth, obviously gorged with milk. She held her hands at shoulder level, and in each was the figure of a writhing snake.

But it was her face that drew Tia. The nose of the goddess was long and Semitic and she had the same tightly waved hair as her priestess, but her eyes were soft and knowing, and much more human than the eyes of the gods and goddesses that Tia knew, the *neter* of Egypt. She stood on an altar of plain mud brick and looked down benevolently at Tia. The goddess's lips

were full and sensual, but with a smile upon them; a smile both
simple and subtle, a smile of indulgence or perhaps forgive-
ness, and yet one promising pleasure, too—the expression of
a woman who knew the ways of the world and the human
heart. It was a very human smile—surprisingly human to Tia,
whose own native gods never smiled—and it immediately
made her feel akin to this foreign goddess, as if they shared
some secret between them.

Tia stared into that face, the face of a goddess, and yet a
woman not unlike herself. The idea that a god or goddess could
smile captivated her, and she searched the image's face for an
explanation. Astarte had perhaps known pain and loss and
love, too, like Isis, but obviously she was no stranger to joy, to
the happiness and completeness of spirit associated with
Hathor. Most of all, she saw on Astarte's face a look of reas-
surance. The goddess had triumphed over all and held out to
Tia the promise that she might triumph, as well. It was an intoxicating look, and Tia was intensely curious and deeply
moved.

"She looks so familiar," she said aloud.

"Tia, you forget yourself...." Kheneb said. He started forward, embarrassed, but Illana laid her hand on his arm and held
him back. She raised her finger to her lips for silence, never
taking her eyes from Tia.

"There is incense at your feet," Illana said softly, and Tia
looked down at the faience jar standing at the foot of the idol,
containing a mixture of resin, cedarwood and rose petals.

Without a thought she bent and took a pinch of incense in
her fingers. She did not know the proper prayers, but something went up from her heart, and she knew that her offering
would be accepted. She dropped the mixture onto the brass dish
of glowing coals that sat at Astarte's feet, but nothing happened.

Kheneb cleared his throat nervously. Tia didn't know the
prayers, was ignorant of the rituals and hadn't even purified

herself; it was almost blasphemous for her to make an offering like this, even one of incense. And now what had happened? Perhaps the coals had gone out, or Tia had missed them altogether. In any case, this wasn't a good sign. The goddess had rejected her offering, and rightly so, Kheneb thought.

With a loud rush of sound the incense suddenly ignited, and a sharp tongue of orange-and-blue fire chased the shadows from the room. In the sudden brilliance, the smile on the goddess's face could be seen to broaden into a look of fond acceptance as the light of the flame flickered on her face.

Kheneb had never himself seen such a clear and unmistakable portent, and his eyes widened in surprise as the smoke began to billow forth from the brazier in thick, intoxicating clouds. Illana gasped, as well, putting her fingers to her mouth in shock, but Tia just stood there gazing at the statue as the rich clouds of sweet and aromatic smoke surrounded her.

"My Lady, I apologize for my sister's lack of manners. It is inexcusable, but the girl is nervous, so great is her zeal...."

Illana turned to Kheneb, her eyes glowing.

"If it is acceptable to Tia," Illana said, "the Great Lady and I would be happy to have her serve as a novice in this, her new home in Egypt. Never have I seen such an auspicious omen. I no longer have any doubts. There is nothing more we need discuss."

But in truth there was more to discuss, all of it tedious, about Tia's service, and Kheneb and Illana retired to a room beside the goddess's image to confer over wine and dates while Tia, uninterested in these particulars, wandered about the garden, studying the image of Astarte from varying angles. She had no doubt that this would be her new home, and the details of her service mattered little to her. There was something between the goddess and herself, something very personal that she had never felt with her native gods. She loved them, of course, but she loved them as a child loved a parent. Astarte was like the older sister she'd never had. Astarte was someone she could open her heart to, someone she could converse with, not just beseech.

And converse she did. The garden was lovely, but the figure of Astarte drew her back into the flickering oil lamps of the sanctuary, and she stood in front of the image for a long while, watching the play of light on her features. A goddess of love and war. How could that be?

Tia noticed something now about the goddess's face. Perhaps it was the light, but within that enigmatic smile there was strength and wisdom and a patience of spirit that affected her greatly. The gods of Egypt were beyond time. They rode upon it like a boat on the Nile, barely touching it. But Astarte seemed to be of this world, swimming in the same water as Tia swam in. There were things she had to teach that Tia was suddenly very eager to learn.

Kheneb came out of the temple with Illana at last, laughing and shaking his head. It had obviously gone well and, as an unusually pragmatic type of priest, it always surprised her brother when things went smoothly. He was of course a believer, but still, when the gods actually seemed to step in and take a hand in the affairs of men, he always looked baffled.

Now that the business was concluded, he was very solicitous, and touched Tia fondly as she walked him to the gate, caressing her back and gazing into her eyes, clearly looking for any hidden signs of fear or reservation.

"I will visit you the day after tomorrow, darling sister," he said. "Lady Illana and I have discussed it thoroughly, and she assures me that you are under no obligation to do anything you don't want to do. So if at anytime there is ever anything you're not comfortable with…"

"Brother, I am fine. This is where I want to be. I know things will be fine."

Kheneb nodded, his eyes down. "Lady Illana seems eminently worthy and pure in sentiment, but still…"

"My dear brother. You worry entirely too much. I'm no longer a child."

Kheneb's eyes flicked up at her, and he nodded his head in understanding. He embraced her without a word, but when he turned from her he hid his emotions in a sudden irritability with his guards. "On your feet, you worthless toads! You've been drinking beer, I can smell it! Farewell for now, little sister. Lady Illana, a thousand thanks. The blessings of all the gods upon you both!"

Illana had been standing back between the gatehouses, giving them their privacy, but now she stepped forward. "And the blessing of all the gods and the Great Lady upon you and yours, too, Lord Priest."

They watched them go, then Illana turned to Tia. "Come. There is much to discuss. You have much to learn."

"Yes," Tia said. "There is so much I want to know."

Illana looked at her, her dark eyes meeting Tia's. Something passed between them, something terribly intimate and honest, and then there was a burst of noise from the river—men's laughter, some raucous joke.

Tia looked over to see that the royal barge she'd watched earlier, all its lamps blazing, was making fast to the quay right below the temple, where the stone steps of the levee reached down to the black face of the water. She could see the oarsmen standing in the prow, bright and flushed with wine, and she could see a man's form as he stepped off the barge and trotted easily up the darkened stairs.

"Prince Nekhet," Illana whispered to her. "He is our sponsor, and it is through his graciousness that we have our home here in this land."

"Yes," Tia said, straining to see through the trees. "I saw his barge earlier."

Illana smiled. "I daresay you have. He has been rowing up and down all afternoon, eager to see our progress."

She gave Tia a knowing look, but the girl's eyes were on the stairs.

Nekhet emerged from the steps on the other side of the wide avenue. He was bare-chested, his body gleaming with a sheen of perspiration. No doubt he had been rowing, too, testing his strength against the current of the Nile, and the muscles of his wide shoulders were taut from the vigor of his exercise. Around his neck he wore a wide collar of dark blue lapis trimmed in gold, and a slim skirt of fine linen covered his loins, sheer enough that Tia could see the workings of his strong thighs as the light from the Temple of Amun shone through the fabric. He carried horsehair mounted in an ebony handle as a fly whisk and symbol of his royal authority, and he flicked it absently against his leg as he walked. As he approached, his brown eyes showed his noble blood, his ease with command, but there was nothing harsh or cruel in them. He was looking right at Tia, and there was a quiet expectancy in his gaze.

Tia drew herself up and surprised herself by staring right back at him. She knew he was coming for her. She knew it just as she'd known that Astarte had special things to tell her. She knew, too, that the goddess's magic was already working on her—that she'd never been more beautiful, and with a thrill so deep it almost made her shudder she realized that somehow this prince of Egypt was hers for the taking. It was a moment of such intense and intimate certainty that she felt her nipples harden on her breasts in preparation for the feel of his lips and, remembering Kheneb's words, she threw her shoulders back to show off her womanly form. She felt herself cast a spell upon him as a fisherman standing in the prow of his boat casts his net into the Nile.

"By the gods," Illana whispered in her ear. "The Great Lady has taken a shine to you, Tia! Already she fills your spirit, doesn't she?"

Tia didn't answer. She felt a flood of heat as Nekhet approached her, as if she had walked out of the shadows and into the noontime glory of the Egyptian sun. She knew that the spark of Ra was in his eyes.

"Lady Illana," he said, bowing his head slightly, a very unusual gesture to see from a prince of Egypt. As the fourth son of the Great Pharaoh, Nekhet was far removed from the throne, but he still bore the blood of the gods in his veins and need never incline his head to any mere human.

Lady Illana bowed, as well, and the fact that she didn't get down on her knees and press her forehead into the dirt showed that there was a very special relationship between these two. Tia should have fallen to her knees, as well, but something prevented her, though at long last she did lower her head. It didn't go down easily. Something had taken control of her and Illana was right—she was filled with a proud and rebellious spirit.

"Who is this, then?" Nekhet asked, looking at Tia with eager curiosity.

"This is Tianefhet, sister of the Priest Kheneb of the temple of Hathor," Lady Illana said. "She has come to serve as a novice priestess for the Great Lady."

"Is that right?" he replied. "Now there are two, am I right? And they will both serve as you have told me? I'm interested in seeing your religion in practice."

Illana bowed her head in agreement, but another question hung there between the three of them, unasked; they were all aware of it. He wanted to know if she was going to serve as a temple prostitute and open her thighs to any man who came along in the name of the foreign goddess. He had the courtesy and breeding not to give voice to his thoughts, but they all knew what he was thinking.

Tia felt an unexpected thrill of angry pride. She had been here but an hour or two, and yet already she knew that there was more to this than mere copulation, more to it than lying with a man like a beast of the field. He might be a prince of Egypt, but this was a holy precinct.

"Why don't you say what you mean, my lord?" Tia heard herself ask.

The three of them were all too shocked to speak, Tia not least of all, but she stood her ground.

Nekhet stepped closer to her so that he could see her face in the torchlight. She could see the sinews in his shoulders and smell the scent of his sweat—salty and with a hint of the darkness of the river. Her heart beat so in her chest that she thought she might faint, but she kept her eyes level, so she couldn't avoid seeing the whiteness of his teeth as his lips drew back in a wary grin.

"Is this what you mean by possession, Lady Illana?" he asked. "Where the Great Lady enters into her servants and makes them say foolish things? For a mere Egyptian girl would never speak to a prince of the Double House thus."

Before Illana could answer, Tia felt her own mouth move and words issued forth before she could stop them. "Perhaps not, but a woman would speak to a man thus, would she not, oh, great Prince?"

There was a moment of stunned silence and then Nekhet laughed, and laughed again. He turned to Illana so that she was obligated to laugh, as well, and even Tia then joined in, shocked at her own outrageous boldness and relieved that the prince had dismissed it as a joke.

"Tomorrow is my birthday," he said at last. He spoke to Lady Illana, though he was looking at Tia. "How long before this priestess is consecrated?"

"My lord, she is a novice. With training and prayer and preparation it would take weeks, and even then…"

"Tia, is it?" he asked. He looked over at where the temple was being built. With the builders' scaffolding and piles of stone, it looked ugly and incomplete, like a ruin in the moonlight.

"They are about to lay the lintels," he said. "The builders will be wanting stone, and money for stone. I can bring the gold tomorrow night, the night of my birthday, but only if Lady Tia is ready."

Four of his crewmen from the barge, all of them noblemen's sons, all stripped to the waist and drying off their perspiration with linen towels, now appeared on the levee and prepared to cross the avenue. They called to Nekhet and waved, impatient for him to rejoin them.

"As your lordship wishes," Illana said, bowing deeply. "And if it is acceptable to the Great Lady."

"I'm sure it will be," Nekhet said, waving back at his friends. "She does desire a temple, doesn't she? I'm sure she would make an exception for the sake of her temple."

"Place the lamp there and sit down, Hafertiri. Do be quiet. This is for Tia, but you might as well listen, as long as you can keep still." Illana smoothed her skirt and made herself comfortable in the chair, as comfortable as she could, given the sudden sense of urgency.

It could only be that the spirit of the goddess that had come over Tia. That was the only thing that would explain her shockingly forward behavior and rudeness in speaking as she had to Prince Nekhet. That the prince had only smiled and not had her head stricken from her body on the spot— which would have been entirely within his rights—was further proof that the Great Lady had plans for Tia and was therefore watching over her. That was the only reason Illana even attempted to instill in her now what should really take weeks or even months of instruction and preparation. This Egyptian girl had a connection to the goddess such as Illana had never seen before. It was uncanny. Almost frightening.

There was little time to go into the stories and mysteries of the goddess. The moon was already high in the sky and the entire city was well into its sleep. They sat in one of the small chambers that were reserved for the temple prostitutes and Illana spoke as a mother speaks to her daughters. The statue of the goddess could be seen through the doorway, facing outward as if protecting them, lit by the lamps that glowed at her feet.

"It is my prerogative to choose who has the honor of lying with a priestess of the Great Lady," Illana told them. "Though, of course, you may refuse anyone I send to you. This is not done for sport or even for pleasure, but so that the worshipper can gain knowledge and experience of the goddess. For that to happen, her spirit must enter into you, and there it must stay. You yourselves will stay pure, unsullied though touched by man, or woman—for I must tell you that women may enjoy the favors of the goddess, as well, though that is not for you. Not yet.

"She is called the Great Lady because she is great above all mortal women, and yet she is a lady. She knows the secrets of being a woman and of all you might ever feel. To take her spirit inside you is to become one with all women who have ever lived, to feel yourself as the vessel of life and the bearer of kings. Remember that even our Great Pharaoh came through the gates of life, the gates that Astarte keeps.

"But you must tell me this, Tia—are you a virgin? Or have you known a man's embrace?"

Tia just lowered her eyes, and Illana smiled indulgently at her.

"That's just as well," Illana said. "We don't want any virgins here. The Great Lady doesn't want your innocence—she wants your experience. We don't want anyone falling in love like a foolish girl might. Remember, although the Lady uses your body, she maintains the purity of your spirit. There is nothing shameful in this. There must not be anything shameful in this.

"I cannot tell you what your experience will be like, Tia. My own relationship with the goddess is so very different from yours that I doubt my experiences would shed much light on what you may expect. I have never seen such astonishing signs and portents of the goddess's favor. You are truly her chosen one. All we can do is trust to her wisdom."

Down sank the moon toward the hour of the jackal, when the door between the worlds opened and the barque of Ra made its slow ascent into the land of the living once more. Through the crack between the worlds, the morning wind rustled the palms outside and the first fishermen and farmers began to stir. The lamp guttered and Lady Illana blew it out. Hafertiri had long since retired, and Tia lay asleep on the bed she would soon know as a priestess, as a prostitute and as an incarnation of the holy goddess.

Tia slept late the next day, not arising till the sun was high in the sky. Never had Khepri seemed like such a sluggard as he pushed the disc of the sun slowly across the vault of the heavens. Never had the noontime shadows seemed to move so slowly. Tia was allowed to idle the day away around the temple, and in the afternoon Illana made her lie down for a nap, but Tia was not used to sleeping in the daytime, and besides, her heart was high in her chest thinking about the coming evening. She kept on seeing Nekhet's face, his warm eyes and broad shoulders, his air of command.

In the late afternoon she bathed, then sat in the light of the garden while Illana and Hafertiri combed out her lustrous black hair. Tia could see through the open gate, across the Avenue of Osiris and through the palms to a stretch of the Nile that was still brilliantly lit by the mellowing sun. She watched the barges plying up and down, and wondered what Nekhet was doing now, and whether he was thinking of her, as well.

"At some point the goddess will come to you," Illana told her. "If she doesn't, you must stop. Even if he is a prince of Egypt, you must. It is an abomination, a sin."

"What does 'sin' mean?" Hafertiri asked her.

"Never mind, never mind. There's no word for it in your language," Illana said. "Let us just say that it is a wrong against the goddess and it would displease her greatly. Now come inside. We must present you to the goddess and invoke her protection. There's so little time."

Tia paid little attention to the invocation and Lady Illana's hurried prayers. As she had begun to find, when she was in the presence of the goddess, time ceased to exist in its normal sense, the sense she was used to, and she felt herself enfolded in a special, protective aura from which she viewed Illana's subtle anxiety and Hafertiri's nervous foolishness with detached equanimity and a little amusement. The goddess was already with her, and Tia knew she was safe.

It's been so long since I've known the embrace of a man, Tia thought to herself, and knew that the words were the goddess's, as well. *Just as Astarte is a stranger in this land, so I am a stranger in her temple, and we both need to know the love of this Egyptian prince that we may both find our homes here.*

Tia was aware that Lady Illana had lit the coals in the braziers, and was burning incense—myrrh and cassia wood soaked in oil of rose. She stood up at Illana's urging and allowed the priestess to remove her robe, and she stood naked in the smoke of the incense as Lady Illana looked her up and down, and Hafertiri, leaning against the wall in the corner, did, as well. Illana was looking for some sign, some imperfection that would disqualify Tia from her role tonight, but she saw nothing but a girl's body at the very peak of her sexual desirability, shaved absolutely clean in the Egyptian manner. Her skin was as smooth as the waters of the Nile in flood.

Illana ran her hands over Tia's shoulders and down her arms, then took her breasts in her hands, feeling their sensual weight. She applied the juice of dates ground in oil to Tia's nipples to make them sweet for her lover's lips, then painted them with madder to bring out their coral hue. She sat Tia down and bent to her makeup, lining her eyes with malachite paste and painting her eyelids blue with pulverized turquoise. She dusted them with gold powder, then dabbed pomegranate juice on Tia's full lips. Tia looked at herself in a polished bronze mirror and saw the face of a goddess looking back at her. She wasn't surprised.

Illana had Tia stand while Hafertiri brought a special robe from the other room. Like the scrim curtain that hid the figure of the goddess in the temple, this robe was a deep sky-blue and yet so finely woven as to be transparent. Illana tied it around her waist with a sash of blue and gold, and then put all the combs and cosmetics away in their carved box, and she and Hafertiri left Tia alone with her thoughts.

Tia didn't know how long she sat there basking in the presence of the goddess. She was an offering to Astarte. More than that, she was Astarte. She belonged to the goddess now, and that gave her a peace and quietness of spirit that finally banished all nervousness. She knew she was beautiful and desirable, and the knowledge gave her a feeling of wonderful power.

By the time she got up and walked into the garden, the moon had climbed into the sky—a sickle moon, horned like the goddess Hathor, symbol of a woman's secret, the door of life. Illana had told her that Astarte often wore horns on her head as well, symbolic of the changing moon and thus sacred to all women. The breeze off the Nile cooled her face, and through the dancing fronds of the date palms she saw the flash of golden oars on the surface of the river as Nekhet came to keep his appointment.

Lady Illana came to watch with her and thought to speak but could find no suitable words.

Finally, she said, "Hafertiri and I will be in the gatehouse. The Great Lady will be with you, I am sure of it. She will see that nothing bad happens to you."

"I have no doubt," Tia said, and she meant it.

Nekhet came walking across the empty moonlit Avenue of Osiris, flanked by two of his friends. Tia watched them approach—nervous, unsure, like naughty children come to peek up a lady's skirts. When they caught sight of Tia standing outside the gatehouse, poised like a statue in the night, they paused and abruptly stopped their foolishness.

Nekhet spoke to his companions as they stood there in the road, and they left him, walking back to the river with quick glances back over their shoulders. Nekhet wore a new linen skirt, the pleats sharp as knives. Around his neck was a necklace of jet, and he carried his fly whisk in one hand, a leather purse in the other. Without his friends, his step was measured and serious.

Tia felt his approach in the pit of her stomach, and felt as though she was pulling him toward her by the force of her beauty, a beauty to rival the night. Indeed, she felt that her beauty actually partook of the night and of the moon sailing through the starry heavens, for both were ruled by the goddess and surely the goddess had already taken control of this man. She could already feel the goddess standing huge and smiling behind her. The breeze blew through the fine weave of her robe, carrying it open and exposing part of one breast to the moonlight. She felt her nakedness like a delicious warmth, like a sexual aura about her, and she knew she was irresistible.

"Lady Tianefhet," Nekhet said, clearing his throat.

Tia could have laughed with eager joy, seeing his sudden boyish nervousness, but instead she said, "My lord prince."

"I have brought a purse for Lady Illana," he said, holding out the leather bag. "For the stone. For the temple."

"She is not here," Tia said. "But I will give it to her." Nekhet handed the purse over to Tia. It was very heavy.

"It's more than I can carry, my lord. I am but a woman. Could you bring it into the temple?"

"By all means," he said, anxious to have something to do.

Tia stood by the gate to let him precede her into the sacred precincts, and as he passed she leaned subtly forward so that the petal-soft buds of her nipples brushed against his naked arm. She felt him pause just momentarily, perhaps shocked by her boldness. He was scented, his chest anointed with oil in which she could detect the masculine odor of cedar and pine and muscle that had been working in the sun.

Once inside the gate she felt a passion take hold of her like a trembling hunger in her stomach. She walked in front of him, leading the way through the shadowy garden to the soft warm glow of the goddess's sanctuary, yellow amidst the blue and deep purple shadows.

He was a prince of Egypt, and no matter how remote from the throne he might be, the air of royalty and divinity clung to him like a perfume. His father was Ra's spirit on earth, the Righteous Bull of Truth, and some of that power surely ran in his veins. Tia knew he was to wed the foreign princess, but she also knew that such things meant nothing to the desires of the heart. Great Pharaoh married all his children to foreign princes and princesses; it was how he made alliances. The heart of Prince Nekhet did not belong to this princess, and Tia knew it had never belonged to any woman.

She could feel his eyes on her hips as she led the way through the fragrant garden. The robe she wore was all but invisible, and it was the goddess who made her roll her hips as she walked, of that she was certain. She was already damp with excitement and her breasts felt full and heavy, her nipples keenly aware of the sheer cloth against them.

She stopped at the door to the sanctuary and waited for him to enter, but he stopped.

"I have heard things about this goddess," he said. "And about her priestesses."

Tia bowed her head. "And what have you heard, my lord prince?"

He kept his eyes on her as he spoke. "I have heard that they sleep with men who come to her temple. Is this true?"

"It is as you say, my lord prince." She said no more than that, although her face felt flushed and hot.

"How is this done?" he asked.

"Need you ask, my lord prince?"

He was discomfited, then laughed—a short nervous laugh. "No," he said. "I mean, what ceremonies must be performed?"

"There are no ceremonies, my lord. Not this night. When the goddess enters a priestess, she becomes one with the Great Lady. You may take her then, but not before."

For the space of two heartbeats he said nothing, then he raised his hand and laid it on her breast. Standing in the yellow light, his words were as soft as the moonlight on the plants in the garden. "Then let her take you, Lady Tia, that I may take you, as well."

Tia knew he could feel her heart, and she rang with a sudden nervousness. She knew he was hers, and that he would be powerless to resist her, and yet the goddess told her she wasn't quite yet ready. With her eyes cast down to hide her own excitement, she could see his arousal already awake in the lift of his skirt and she felt her own answering wetness. And now she knew what she had to do. She took his hand—a strong hand, with long, sensitive fingers—and led him into the sanctuary, and she watched his face as she led him to the figure of the goddess.

He stood erect as he regarded the face of Astarte, and Tia regarded him. She bent and took a handful of incense and threw it down on the coals, then she turned her face to the goddess. As the smoke enveloped them, she saw the goddess's smile and she felt a sudden surge of such need and wild passion that she almost cried out, almost fell against him. The goddess had entered her, and her need for this man suddenly overwhelmed her, sweeping all fear and reservations aside. She turned to him and put her hands on his shoulders and looked into his eyes. Of their own volition, her hips pressed against his and she felt his amazing hardness.

"Lady Tia," he began, shocked at her boldness.

"Not Tia," she breathed. "But a goddess for you."

She reached up for his hair and pulled his face down to her kiss, and he stood there, stunned by her sudden hunger, feeling her feminine softness as she ground herself against his cock. His hands went around her and felt the catlike muscles in her back, her female strength, then slipped down to cup her ass through the delicate fabric. Her buttocks clenched as she shifted her weight and rolled her hips against him. Her mouth opened and her tongue sought refuge between his lips.

Nekhet kissed her back. He'd been caught off guard by her sudden assault, but he had known more than a few professional women in his time, the best Egypt had to offer from the Nile Delta to the Second Cataract, and he quickly regained his poise. However, Tia didn't stop. There was nothing studied or contrived about what she did, or in the way she moved against him, and her breath was as hot as the smoke from the incense, hardly the cool breath of a harlot. She ground her breasts against him, her stiff nipples poking through the fabric of her gown and pressing like coals against his chest, and the way the muscles of her bottom tightened and relaxed in his hands, lewd and obscene, as if she were already trying to draw the seed from him, made him dizzy.

He knew how it went with a whore. After her first on-slaught she would step away from him and make some teasing remark, then lead him to her bed and beguile him with her tricks and techniques. But no, it didn't happen that way at all. Tia rocked back just far enough that she could grab his cock beneath his linen skirt, and the feel of her eager touch, her frantic need for him, made his own lust swell in his chest.

He felt hard and heavy, but her skin was wonderfully soft

and velvety as she began to fuck him with her fist. Her touch wasn't studied and contrived like a whore's. It wasn't expert and efficient. It was all hunger and raw passion, her fingers curling around him and squeezing with excitement, reaching under him to feel the potent weight of his balls as her kiss deepened in response to his rising excitement. She began to melt against him, as if just the feel of his virility made her weak and pliant.

Nekhet was not used to a woman taking the lead like this. Usually at this point they were on their backs, asking him what his pleasure was, eager to provide it, but Tia stood against him with no sign of surrender, one arm around his broad shoulders, shamelessly frigging his hard prick as her tongue fluttered in his mouth like a hummingbird lapping up dew.

Her hand was soft and cool, yet feverish in its ministrations. For one so small, she clung to him with wonderful strength. He had never felt such desire in a woman.

"Who are you?" he asked her at last, suddenly breaking away from her kiss.

But Tia didn't answer. She was beyond speech, knowing only a terrible ache like an urgent thirst between her legs, a thirst that now crept up into her throat, as well. She sank to her knees before him, trailing her red lips down his chest, his stomach, kissing his hips, raking her nails over his muscular thighs. She impatiently threw his skirt aside and took his cock in her hand. He was shaved and hairless, as were all Egyptian men who could afford it, and she stared eye to eye with that powerful and angry rod of Seth. She tossed her hair back, opened her lips and swallowed him into her mouth.

"Ahhh—" Nekhet threw his head back in pleasure, then looked down to watch this remarkable girl on her knees at his feet as she sucked on his prick, pulling at him with her lips. She cradled his balls in her hand, hefting them.

Nekhet was beside himself. He was used to taking com-

mand, to telling his women what to do, but Tia was too fast
and too excited for him, and there was a hunger in her like he
had never sensed in a woman before, a desperation for him that
made him tremble even as she bobbed her head slavishly over
his loins. It was as if she were indeed a goddess, a goddess of
desire, famished for him, refusing to be denied.

Finally she had to pull her face off him to breathe, gulping in
air as she continued to stroke him. She was aware that she was
out of control, but she also had never felt such delicious desire.
She knew now how the Lady could claim both love and war as
sacred to her spirit. Tia's desires were warlike; there was that same
high passion, that need to possess and conquer or be conquered.

"Come, come, to your feet," Nekhet said, grabbing her elbow
and pulling her off the ground. "Is this how a priestess acts?"

"Yes," she said, wiping the saliva from her chin. "Yes, it is
exactly how a priestess acts. I am all desire, my lord prince. I
die for you. My life is in your hands."

"Where is the nobility in this?" he asked her. "Where is the
royalty of the goddess?"

At this, Tia's passion seemed to quiet down. The flame
became a steady glow, and she felt her womanly power flowing
within her like the waters of the great river, calm yet powerful.
She knew he would be hers. She knew he could not refuse
her.

"Come with me," she said. She took his hand and led him
into the small bedchamber behind the statue of Astarte. She
lowered the curtain, so that all the light they had came from
one oil lamp and the moonlight that shone through the open
window. In the starry silence she untied her sash and let the
gown whisper to the floor and stood before Nekhet in all her
naked excitement.

Her hips were generous, her thighs lean and her breasts rich
and heavy, round like ripe fruit. But it was the way she
trembled when she pressed her nakedness against him that

made his blood rush hot in his body. He had seen deer tremble like that at the end of the hunt, when they knew their hour was up. It was her total surrender and it inflamed him.

"My lord, my lord," she whispered as he laid her down on the bed. He kissed her mouth, her breasts, her belly, as she writhed beneath him, tugging at his skirt, her fingers anxious and confused and shaking with need. He stood and removed what clothes he wore, and Tia gasped when she saw his cock, even bigger and harder now than when she'd had him in her mouth, and more commanding now that he was naked.

She spread her legs; she spread her arms. She lay back against the cushions, her breasts heaving with her heavy breathing. She could feel the tickle of her own arousal creeping from her opening and she felt all liquid inside. She could feel the night upon her skin and the goddess moving through her flesh— the need, the hunger to be pierced and impaled and possessed.

Nekhet looked down at her and felt the surge of her excitement, as well. Perhaps she was possessed. She certainly seemed to be: she was the very incarnation of womanly passion. He realized now that this was not a goddess like the deities he knew, the *neter* of Egypt. This was a goddess who embodied all the qualities of human women, all that was divine and powerful about them: their beauty and their desire, their ability to weaken a man and make a slave of him. He felt her need for his hardness inside her. He looked down at her and marveled at the power in that frail body. She was so much like him, and yet so utterly different.

Tia watched and trembled as he climbed between her thighs, and she scrambled to get herself into position in the shadow of his covering body. He reached for his prick, but she was already ahead of him, and she took him in her small hand and guided him anxiously to her opening, her palm feverishly hot. She took him and rubbed the head of his cock salaciously up and down her moist slit, getting herself ready for him, gasping and whimpering with pleasure and impatience. Once she had him in place, she wrapped her legs around him and pulled him inside with her legs and her arms, trembling as if she were a warrior impaling herself on her own sword.

They both cried out as he entered her and pushed her flesh aside as the prow of a boat cuts through the face of the waters—his a deep groan of pleasure and relief, hers a sharp cry of urgent fulfillment, loud enough to be heard in the gatehouse. It had been years since her one experience, and Tia was like a virgin again, was a virgin, in fact, when it came to making love, her one other session having been so short and hurried. Now she had time to feel his hardness going into her, stretching her open with his implacable masculine force, filling her aching emptiness with the heat and strength of his body. He touched her deep, touched her where her heart hammered in her chest, and it was better than water to a raging thirst. And, as if it were water, she lay there luxuriating in the feel of him, letting his hardness fill her.

She was certain the goddess had taken her. Certainly nothing had ever felt as divine, and what made it so good was that she was hardly herself. She had no thoughts for her dignity, her reputation, for what he would think of her when this was over. She was the incarnation of Astarte and not responsible for what she did, and so she was free—free to experience the glorious sensation of his godly prick inside her belly, the potency of this strong body on top of hers.

Nekhet twisted about, stirring his cock around inside her, and Tia responded with a loud gasp of pleasure. It hurt a bit, but wonderfully so, his cock so alive, filled with his divine essence, the semen of the son of the God-King. Excitement overtook her and she dug her heels into the bed and thrust up at him, lifting him from the bed in her sudden urge for more sensation.

"By all the gods!" he moaned as he felt her tight sheath slide over him. The girl had the strength of a lioness. She gripped him inside and squeezed him, reached for his mouth with hers and pulled his head down to her kiss. Nekhet got his knees under him and hung there suspended like the sky god, Shu, as Tia's cunt reached to engulf him again and again in feverish spasms of pure lust. There was little he could do but kneel there over her as she serviced him, her pussy drawing at him like a wet silky fist, pulling the come from his balls, urging it out, begging for it.

His thumbs found the spiky buds of her nipples and caressed them, making Tia whine in her throat like an eager puppy at her master's call. The speed of her hips increased so that the legs of the bed began to bang against the tiled floor, and Nekhet realized that this was no normal girl. He looked down at her face, clenched in erotic concentration, her fine features screwed into a mask of passionate lust, her lips swollen and parted, her breath hissing through her white teeth. He stared at her face and thought he had never seen a woman so beautiful, so transported by erotic pleasure. And then Tia opened her eyes and looked back at him.

Those eyes were sightless, dilated, seeing not him but something inside or beyond him, seeing through him and into the core of his masculine soul. It was the way the earth goddess, Geb, must have looked at Shu when he covered her and filled her with his semen, bringing forth the myriad forms of life that graced the earth. It was the look of the moon when it broke through the clouds. It was the look of the warrior with his sword held high when the enemy was in flight. It was the look of triumph in surrender, of feminine victory, and it seemed to draw him up out of himself when he felt his orgasm start, the tides of her body pulling the seed from him, from his very depths.

He was like a god reversed; the head of a man with a man's tenderness and awe for her beauty, but an animal below as he fucked her savagely with the strength of a bull, spearing her deep, sending his cock into her depths, out of control in his need to possess her. And Tia now gave up her role as seductress and surrendered to his assault, flinging her legs wide and letting him use her for his pleasure.

Nekhet had a moment to rise up on his strong arms and arch his back into her as Tia writhed beneath him, her nails like the claws of a lioness dug into the clenched muscles of his ass, pulling him tight and deep, and then Nekhet exploded into her with the brilliance of a sunrise flooding the darkness with its glorious light.

His body froze with the force of his release and his semen jetted into her. He cried out in surprise at the intensity of his pleasure and his feeling of triumph as his prick spit inside her like some striking cobra, pouring his essence and his relief into her eagerly accepting body.

And Tia, feeling her lover orgasm inside her, seeing the look of awestruck rapture on his face and hearing his cry of male triumph, felt released of any last constraint. She had done the goddess's work and she felt the divinity inside her reveling in Nekhet's hot ejaculation, taking it up and bathing in it, drinking it into her. Her triumph filled Tia with a blazing joy and lifted her up, up into the air, into the realm of the gods, into a high place filled with light, and then Astarte let Tia go, let her fall into her own sea of physical pleasure, and Tia fell until she shattered into a thousand shards of liquid ecstasy, her body trembling as her pussy continued to suck his victorious cock and she knew no more than the animal joy of being alive.

A stillness took them as they lay entwined on the sweat-soaked sheets and they trembled like flowers of the field caught in the wind. The moon rode through the mansions of the night as Tia felt her desire blossom again, and Nekhet raised himself on one arm to stare into her face. "Who are you?" he asked her again.

On her hands and knees she took him next, during the very darkest hours of the night, the hour of the ape, with her back curved down, her breasts hanging beneath her and swaying with the force of her lover's thrusts, her black hair curtaining her face, just as Seth had taken Horus in the swamp as they struggled for dominance before the gods, with Nekhet's prick deep in her own swamp between her legs. Every time he touched her, every time his lips brushed hers or sought out the smoothness of her skin, Tia felt as though she'd been lashed with whips of pure pleasure, and the tears dried on her cheeks and were wet with fresh ones as the night proceeded—tears of joy, tears of a physical and spiritual pleasure almost too intense to bear.

At some time near the awful hour of the jackal her prince left her and stole away, back to where his barge floated idly in the river, the bargemen all asleep hours before. He cast off and they drifted downriver as Tia drifted on rivers of her own, asleep and alone in her empty bed. She didn't awaken till Ra in the holy barque was well into the sky, now as Khepri, the sacred scarab, rolling the ball of godlike light through the dome of the heavens.

It was Kheneb who finally woke her, gently, his eyes wide with wonder. Illana stood behind him, looking over his shoulder at Tia with fear and concern in her eyes, wearing the long heavy dress of her native country, the goddess's homeland.

"Tia, Tia!" Kheneb whispered, barely concealing the excitement in his voice, "What happened last night? What did you say to him?"

"Hush," Lady Illana admonished. "She is not allowed to tell, nor are you permitted to ask! Such effrontery!"

Tia rolled over onto her elbow and stared about the room, now bright with sun. She was deliciously sore between her legs. Her hair was a mess and her lips felt tender and bruised, but wonderfully slaked and satisfied. She didn't know what to say, especially to her elder brother, but she could see that Illana already knew, and that Illana would tell him in a language he could understand.

"Prince Nekhet has endowed the temple," Kheneb said eagerly. "He has sworn to pay for the entire thing himself! There is to be a fine dedication, for which he is also paying. His messenger was just here—whatever did you say to him last night?"

Tia sat up, holding the sheet against her breasts, and gratefully took the jar of water that Illana held out for her.

"Never mind that now," Lady Illana said. "The prince is coming back tonight. We must prepare you. It is already late. And you are the only one he will talk to about the new arrangements."

Through the doorway Tia could see the image of the goddess, her arms raised, holding the snakes, her symbols of power, showing how she connected the earth and the sky, the world of the spirit and the world Tia lived in.

Tia only raised the water to her lips and felt her heart rise with it. She said a silent thanks to the Great Lady, and drank.

★ ★ ★ ★ ★

TAKEN

Lillian Feisty

CHAPTER ONE

MÉNAGE.

The word played in Chloe's head as she wound her way through the crowded Vegas bar. Two men, seated at a small table on the other side of the room, watched her.

Her skin heated as she maneuvered toward them, dodging her way through tourists high on that entrancing Vegas vibe. Even though she'd lived here for more than five years, she could still soak up that untamed energy; an energy that had her considering something totally mysterious, unfamiliar. Forbidden.

A shiver raced up her spine.

Just a few feet away from her now. One was tall, with shaggy blond hair and bright blue eyes. The other was fair skinned and dark haired. Both were as breathtakingly handsome as she remembered.

Ménage. That was why she was here, wasn't it? Though they'd never come right out and discussed it, ever since she'd met the two chefs six months ago at an annual culinary conference there'd been an erotic undercurrent running through all their communication.

Sexy innuendos, playful at first, now hung in the air. Suggestive. Tantalizing. Irresistible.

And now this. If she desired, she could have them. She could live out her fantasy. Experience a ménage à trois.

If she desired. Her body's response left no doubt as to what she wanted. As she walked, her pussy throbbed at the very idea of sharing a bed with Joe and Walker. Fucking them both. Simultaneously.

God, she was wet.

From the moment Walker had e-mailed her that they were coming to Vegas, she couldn't stop thinking about *it,* couldn't stop the fantasies from slamming into her head, couldn't stop her body's response to the erotic scenes playing out in her mind.

She'd masturbated every night this week, imagining what it would be like to have two men make love to her. Have *these* two men use her for their pleasure.

And now they were here. It was real, and every nerve in her body tingled with edgy anticipation.

"Chloe!" Joe was on his feet, pulling her against his lean form in a big hug. "How are you?"

She'd forgotten how comforting his voice was. She looked up into his soft green eyes and relaxed, just a bit. "Good! I'm good." She breathed him in. It had been over a year since she'd stood this close to a man, felt the heat from a male body mingle with her own.

It was ironic, really. She had twenty—mostly male—employees underneath her. But her position as head chef at a top Las Vegas restaurant required her to keep a solid distance from her subordinates—to always be on guard, and most importantly, to have a big ol' pair of cojones.

Chloe remained in Joe's embrace until he released her. Walker stepped forward. Her pulse jumped. Nothing had changed since she'd first caught sight of the tall blond with the surfer's body all those months ago. Just being next to him sent a flurry of excitement through her belly.

She was attracted to Joe, but there was something about

Walker that caused her heart to skip beats. It wasn't just his looks. Six months of online communication had revealed a caring personality and a sharp wit that drew her to him.

"Hey, Chloe." He pulled her to his chest and then leaned down until his lips brushed her ear. His voice was raspier than she recalled, darker. "You look fantastic."

Her pulse quickened as his warm breath caressed her ear. God, what was wrong with her? She shouldn't be reacting like this to the simple sound of his voice.

Fiddling with a strand of her hair, she tried to calm herself. "Thanks. You, too. You, um, look good." *Relax!*

"Here." Pulling a chair out for her, he swept his hand over the seat in a large theatrical gesture.

"Thanks," she said, grinning.

Joe leaned across the table, his green eyes sparkling in the candlelight. "What can I get you to drink?"

"A cosmo, thanks." She couldn't keep her eyes off them. Six months was a long time, long enough to forget how straight Walker's nose was, or the way Joe's hair fell charmingly over his left eye. The way being around them made her feel so feminine and sexy.

A flutter of excitement flashed through her chest. She couldn't believe Joe and Walker were actually *here*. In Vegas, sitting a few feet away from her. Was she really going through with this?

Yes. Her nipples tingled as every nerve in her body responded to the silent question.

Yes! For some reason she wanted to scream the word as loud as she could. She wanted to slam her hands on the table and announce to the crowd of strangers that these men were here for *her*. Chloe O'Malley, the chick who had not had sex in over a year. She wanted it known that she fully intended to get it on with these *two* men later that night.

Instead, she straightened the hem of her new black dress and took a deep, steadying breath. Okay, so she was going a tad crazy. Where was her cocktail, anyway?

Walker seemed to be biting back a grin. "You okay, Chloe? Have you eaten?"

"Yes, I had dinner earlier. Um, just leftovers but, no—I'm not hungry. Not now. Thank you." She closed her eyes. Why was she babbling?

She spoke online with these two men almost daily. They knew things about her no one else did. But to have them actually here, where they could *see her,* was so much different. All safety through anonymity was gone. Risky.

Isn't that what you wanted? To take a risk?

"Here you go." A waitress in a feather ensemble placed a Vegas-size cocktail on the table before her.

"Thank you." Chloe brought the oversize glass to her lips and took a sip of the syrupy red liquid. It wasn't a proper cosmopolitan—it was too sweet. But she was thankful for the chilly drink and hoped it would help take the edge off.

She looked up to find Joe and Walker staring at her and suddenly she realized it would take a lot more than a sip of alcohol to calm her nerves. And surprisingly, she discovered there was a part of her that was enjoying the slight rush of adrenaline thrumming through her veins.

She lifted her chin. "What?"

Walker glanced to Joe. "She's nervous."

Joe nodded. "Yup."

She shook her head and waved her hand at them as if to say, *oh, stop!* But her shaky fingers belied her protest.

Walker took her trembling hand in his dry, warm palm. "It's just us."

Just us. Her gaze shot between the men, each looking at her like she was a delicious crème brûlée and they were ravenous for a sweet dessert.

"Just you!" A laugh burst out of her throat.

Joe grinned back. "Just two guys who think you're the smartest, wittiest, most lovely female on the planet."

Coming from anyone else the statement would have sounded false, cheesy even, but she knew Joe meant it. Both he and Walker were true to their words, true to themselves.

When she'd met them at the conference in Dallas, it hadn't been obvious at first that the men were together. It had been the subtle things, like the way Walker looked at Joe when he placed a spoonful of béchamel sauce on the other man's tongue. The way they stood just a fraction too close together in the elevator. A definite sexual undertone was present in the men's interaction. However, she'd never been able to pinpoint the exact nature of their relationship. Joe had once said he didn't believe in monogamy. Walker hadn't taken a stance on the subject.

"You are, you know."

She looked up to find Walker's gaze boring into hers. Her palms dampened even as desire shot through her. An intimacy passed between them and she was sure that, had she been standing, her knees would have buckled.

He didn't look away and she gave in. "What? What am I?"

"Gorgeous."

Her face may have flushed, but she grinned and glanced toward Joe. "You guys aren't so bad yourselves." Yes. *Calm down, you ninny!* She could do this playful banter. After all, they'd been talking this way for months.

And now they were here.

It was perfect. She'd have one night of sexual exploration to get this longing out of her system. Then they'd go home, and she'd go on with her life. If things went well maybe they'd do it again. After all, she'd see them again in six months at the annual conference. And she couldn't imagine it not going well. Not with these two.

She took a lingering drink of her sugary cocktail and smiled to herself. Yes, this was the ideal situation. She'd learned the hard way that her schedule left no time for a traditional relationship. A naughty tryst a couple times a year was just what she needed.

A sense of excitement took flight in her chest, and when she looked up to discover Walker's direct gaze still on her, her breath caught. She wondered if Joe picked up on her strong reaction to his friend. She wondered if he would care.

Joe drained his beer and plunked the bottle onto the wooden table. "It's early yet. What's the plan for the evening?"

Her sex gave a clench at the question. An image from last night's fantasy popped into her head. A picture of herself, naked, in bed, lying on her side, squeezed between their two hot, smooth, solid bodies—

"Chloe?"

She gave a start. "Um, sorry. What were you saying?" She took another sip of her drink. *Get a grip!*

Joe grinned. "I hear they have a nightclub right downstairs. You're a local, is it any good?"

She nodded. "Yes. I love House of Blues—what's wrong?" Walker was shaking his head at her, making a slicing motion with one finger across his neck.

Joe rolled his eyes. "He hates dancing. But it's two to one, right?"

"That's right. Two to one." For some reason the words sent wicked goose bumps tingling up her arms.

Joe stood and extended his hand. "Shall we?"

She glanced over at Walker's unreadable expression then looked back at Joe. She nodded and gave him her hand. "Yes. Let's."

Because Chloe was a local, her Nevada driver's license allowed them to bypass the long line of people waiting to shake their thing inside the House of Blues.

Once they passed through the entrance, the steady beat of a catchy tune lured them down into the heart of the club. Flanked by the men, she held their hands as they descended the wide staircase.

She looked sideways to Joe. "I'm so glad you thought of this! I haven't been dancing in forever."

Joe just smiled as Walker grumbled something. They landed at a table on a platform overlooking the dance floor. At eleven o'clock things were just beginning to get started, and the club wasn't too crowded yet.

They each took a seat and Walker placed an order with the cocktail waitress. As they waited for their drinks to arrive, a fresh wave of excitement washed over her.

Drinks, dancing, and after that who knew what could happen? But one thing was for certain; she was more than ready to go with the flow. Every minute she spent in Joe's and Walker's presence elevated the anticipation thrumming through her veins, and she couldn't stop snippets of her fantasies from flitting through her head, keeping her on edge like a talented lover.

Joe took her hand in his tight grip and she gasped. "Wanna dance?" He grinned as if he knew what she'd been thinking.

She looked at Walker. "What about you? Are you coming?"

He shook his head. "I'll watch."

Her pussy tightened. Such a simple statement, and yet…

She gave herself a mental shake. "You sure?"

He nodded. "Yes. You two go."

This was a test, a challenge. She could see it in his sharp blue eyes. Well, she was ready for the trial. More than ready.

Two stairs down to the dance floor. Joe led her to a spot not too far from where Walker sat. She glanced up just in time to catch Walker's nod of consent. Interesting. But she couldn't dwell on the subtleties of the boys' dynamics, not when Joe was pulling her into a rhythm with him. Not when he was leading her with such command it melted her a little.

The music blurred together, one continuous pattern that freed her mind beat by beat. Joe never broke physical contact, even if it was just their fingers touching.

When a tall redhead got too close to him he subtly turned his back on her and pulled Chloe tighter. "You're the prettiest girl here. You know that, right?"

She smiled against his neck, soaking it all up.

Strong. She had to be for her job. Her position required total dominance. She needed to be stronger than the most overbearing man working for her.

Every day she covered her long brown hair in a handkerchief and dressed in unflattering chef's pants. She wore hideous black, nonslip shoes that felt heavy and awkward, masculine. She played her part, a role that made it too easy to forget she was still a woman.

She glanced at the black stilettos on her feet. She'd bought them just for tonight. The things were killing her, but they made her feel sexy, alluring.

Joe pulled back to look into her eyes. His expression was dead serious. "I'm not lying. You're amazing. Walker and I discussed it at length. Discussed *you* at length."

She peeked over Joe's shoulder and caught a glimpse of Walker. Her stomach dropped at the way he was staring at her. At *them*. Her legs trembled when she caught the spark of desire burning in his eyes.

Joe's hand was on the small of her back as he pulled her against the length of his body. She closed her eyes and took a deep, calming breath.

This was it. It was happening. When she felt his lips softly brush against hers, she welcomed it, opened her mouth and met his tongue.

Her knees went weak, but he held her steady. They kissed that way for what must have been minutes, exploring each other's mouths, knowing all the while Walker was watching them.

Walker. His gaze on their mouths set her sex on fire. For some reason being watched by Walker turned her on even more than the actual kiss between her and Joe.

Joe. He was walking her backward until she hit an obstacle. It was the half wall, topped by a scrolling iron rail that separated the bar area from the dance floor. Although her back was turned, she knew Walker was sitting just on the other side, only inches from her.

And still Joe kissed her, deeper now as his hands went gliding over her rib cage, her sides, until he gripped her hips.

Her limbs went liquid when she felt Walker's hand caress her head, petting her hair for a minute before he gathered a handful and pulled. She gasped, astonished at how the abrupt pain made her sex pulse.

Joe released her mouth to skim his warm, moist lips over her neck, her collarbone. Her heart hammered in time to the steady beat of dance music as he continued to taste her skin.

Walker tugged her hair, forcing her head to tilt back over the railing. The diffused lighting was dim, but anyone could see them. Anyone could see her melting under the touch of these two men. Anyone could see the way she spread her legs so Joe could step between them. Anyone could see the way her chest rose and fell in a rushed rhythm.

For a second Chloe worried that someone she knew would catch a glimpse of her behavior, but she pushed the concern aside. In the dim light, no one was likely to recognize the woman in the flirty dress and teased hair.

And it was sinful how the idea of people watching them encouraged her behavior. Lowering her lids, she imagined eyes on her, aroused by what they saw. Two men making love to one incredibly fortunate woman.

She moaned aloud as she felt Walker's free hand encircle her throat, holding her tight with the grip he had on her hair and her neck.

"Chloe?" Walker's voice was a warm question in her ear.

"Yes," she panted.

"Is this what you want?"

Last chance. If she was going to walk away, this was the time to do it. She took a deep breath, exhaled.

Joe looked at her, his green eyes dark and serious and wanting. She jerked a nod. "Yes. I want you. Both of you."

And she did.

CHAPTER TWO

SHE DIDN'T HAVE TIME TO CHANGE HER MIND.

They exited the club and entered the casino, Walker leading her by the hand and Joe strolling along on her other side.

Despite the fact that she wanted this, she was still nervous, and as they approached the elevator her heartbeat sped faster and faster until pure adrenaline raced through her veins. She had no idea what was going to happen, no idea if this would affect their friendship. She hoped not. But this desire had been building and there was no way she could turn back now.

Later. She would worry about consequences later.

Then they were in the elevator, standing on a swirling red carpet, and Walker was pushing floor 35. The door was closing and soon they'd be alone—

But a hand shot between the elevator doors, pushing them back open. Her toe tapped an impatient beat as a crowd of people pushed their way inside. Walker and Joe inched closer to her, surrounded her.

She was shaking.

Hurry up! she wanted to scream. But the fucking elevator seemed to be stopping at every floor. Damn tourists!

The three of them stood at the back of the mirrored elevator car, listening to the Muzak. Her pussy throbbed. The lace of her bra teased her sensitive nipples. When she felt Walker's fingers on her skin, she jumped.

He smiled down at her. "You okay?"

She nodded. "Yup, great." His touch burned a circle around her wrist.

He drew her hand behind her back. In her daze, she didn't notice Joe doing the same thing with her other hand, but seconds later Walker held both of her wrists, pressing them against the brass rail lining the back of the elevator.

Restrained. Walker's grip was as solid as a metal handcuff. She glanced at Joe, who was smiling at her like the handsome devil he was. And she couldn't say anything because there were two gray-haired women in front of them talking about the value of the ninety-nine cent buffets.

They stopped at another floor and one of the old ladies exited. Then there was just four of them. The remaining woman turned and smiled.

Chloe tried to return the gesture, but it must not have worked because the woman looked downright alarmed. As soon as the elevator doors opened the elderly woman bolted as fast as her Easy Spirits could take her.

"Finally." Turning toward her, Joe reached into the neckline of her dress, slid his fingers beneath her bra and brushed her nipple. "You're ours, aren't you, Chloe? Our girl now, so beautiful like this."

She gasped as Walker's grip on her wrists grew firmer. He pulled her arms tighter, straighter. He leaned down and placed a soft kiss on her clavicle. "Isn't she?" he murmured, his voice a rich breath on her skin.

Biting her lip, she tried not to moan as Joe pulled her nipple between his fingers and pinched. "Just as lovely as we thought."

The elevator continued to rise as Walker's other hand moved over her lower body. She closed her eyes, trembling as his hand lightly skimmed her waist, her hips, her thigh. He reached under her skirt to glide his fingertips over the elastic of her panties. "Hmm," he murmured against her skin. "What color are these?"

"Red," she gasped.

"Nice. My favorite color." His hand slid inside the lace and finally! Finally his finger, his knuckle, so strong, so warm, was touching her, fingering her. She was so wet she was almost embarrassed. But that didn't stop her from widening her stance a bit, urging him on. She bit harder on her lip before she begged him to finger-fuck her. Not yet. She wouldn't beg yet.

The elevator stopped. Walker withdrew his hand from her panties, but did not release her wrists. With a firm hold he directed her down the hallway, their footsteps silent on the thick carpet.

He hadn't straightened her panties; they were still twisted to the side. The discomfort rubbed at her hypersensitive flesh as the men marched her toward their room.

The casino was huge, the hall seemed never ending. By the time they reached the door to room 3525 she was in a daze, ready for anything. She wanted to come right *there* in the hallway. It would have been so easy for Walker to lift her up, push her against the wall and dry-fuck her. Even through his jeans, the feel of his cock against her sex would send her over the edge, she was sure of it.

But Joe was pulling a card out of his pocket and then they were inside. The minute the door shut, Walker released her, pushed her back against the heavy wood and slammed himself against her body.

His mouth was on hers, his lips devouring her in a way that seemed primal, hungry. She responded by wrapping her hands around his neck and urging him deeper. Everything seemed to fade away under Walker's touch.

Want coursed through her and she pressed against him. His

erection was rock hard and pushing at her thigh, just inches from where she wanted it—

"Isn't she remarkable?"

Walker pulled away and took a deep, ragged breath. For just a second she had forgotten about Joe, and as she watched Walker run his hand over his shaggy hair she wondered if he had, too.

But that was impossible.

"I had to kiss her." He smiled at her, took her hand and led her from the door.

Joe grinned. "I know exactly how you feel. She's as good as we imagined."

Fuck, but she loved it when they talked about her like this, like she was theirs. After all she'd done to prove her worth in a chauvinistic field it seemed monumentally wrong to get off on letting them treat her like a possession. And yet, right then it was exactly what she wanted. Shaking the thoughts from her head, she followed Walker as he flipped a light switch, led her deeper into the room.

Or suite, she marveled as she took in the spacious accommodation. Through a set of French doors she saw a dark leather sofa and a coffee table. The space in which the three of them currently stood housed the bed, one upholstered wingback chair and a few bland accent tables.

What struck her was the glaring lack of clothing, suitcases or anything else that would indicate someone was actually staying there. So. They'd booked this room just for this. It seemed like such a sordid thing to do.

An erotic thrill washed over her.

She stared at the bed. Covered in a loud floral brocade duvet, it was enormous. It seemed to take up the entire room. She stood there for a minute, staring at the king-size invitation.

Now what? Should she start stripping? Get on the bed? Wait for them to kiss her? Kiss each other?

Would they kiss? The thought stilled her. Thrilled her. In all her fantasies she'd been the center of attention, the star of the show. She hadn't thought about them, what they would be doing to each other.

But then Joe had her in his arms, was kissing her, directing her backward toward the bed. He followed her down onto the mattress, covering her body with his.

His kiss was so much different from Walker's. Softer, less demanding. Slow and sensual. The contrast made everything real somehow, solidified what she was about to do.

Out of the corner or her eye she caught Walker on the blue chair. He was watching again. Watching as Joe pulled up her dress, exposing her legs, her thighs and the twisted red panties.

Her pulse beat a steady rhythm in her ears as he tugged the fabric up over her hips. It should have been strange. It should have felt odd to have Joe lifting her dress over her breasts, her shoulders, taking her nipple into his mouth through the lace of her bra while another man sat in a chair, looking on. But as he pulled her dress over her head, she thought back to previous lovers and realized she'd never felt so at ease, so comfortable. So excited. She wanted them, both of them. She wanted to be filled with them.

"Take off your bra." Walker kicked off his shoes, leaned back in his chair.

Her hands shook as she obeyed. Lying on the polyester duvet, the soft glow of the chandelier illuminating the fact that she wore only damp panties and come-fuck-me shoes, she felt beautiful. Beautifully flamboyant.

Leaning over her, Joe kissed her rib cage, his soft lips tickling her skin. He went lower to her panties, pulled them down her thighs, her calves, over the black pumps. He threw the scrap of silk onto the floor.

Shivering, she locked her gaze on Walker's. Joe spread her legs wide, opening her. "Stunning," he murmured.

She jumped when she felt his fingers on her damp flesh,

exploring her pussy lips. Instinctively, she wanted to close her eyes, but Walker would not release her from his stare.

She began to squirm as Joe stroked her cunt, played with her until she was bucking against him, gasping. Then he was sliding his fingertips across her sex to the part of her body that was begging to be filled.

She wanted him to fuck her, to ram his fingers into her as Walker watched. But she bit her lip, quivering as she held back. She wanted to plead, but she wasn't there; she couldn't let go like that. Not yet.

But she was so close.

She was losing herself to Joe's touch and her skin burned under Walker's gaze. Sensation overwhelmed her, possessed her. When Joe tapped her clit with a flick of his finger she writhed on the bed, kicked out her legs, silently begged him to put his mouth *there*.

He didn't. He flicked her again, a prick of pain that she welcomed. She took her breasts in her hands, pinched her own nipples.

Walker's eyes went dark.

Finally Joe put his warm mouth to her needy clit, licking and sucking until her head swam from pleasure. She had to tear her eyes off Walker as she moaned. "Oh, my God!"

She was going to come, right there while Walker looked on.

She grabbed her knees, spread her legs wide, as wide as she could. She came with a guttural scream, her entire body shattering nerve by nerve.

Joe didn't let her go until her breathing had slowed. When she opened her eyes she found both men staring at her. If she thought they looked hungry earlier, it was nothing compared to now. Now they wanted to devour her. She understood their need. Spasms still shook the very center of her, yet she was not satisfied. She wanted more.

"Joe?" Walker raised a brow at the man between her legs.
"Yeah?"

"We're not done with her."

A tremor ran through her. *Yes. Talk about me like I belong to you because I do, tonight I do.*

Joe's green eyes glistened up at her. "No. We definitely aren't done with you." He stood, faced Walker. Her heart pounded as she watched the men come together.

She couldn't breathe. *Walker.* Every inch of him radiated control and domination. The clench of his fist, his unblinking gaze, the way he ordered Joe to stand.

Shaking, she watched as Walker closed in on the other man. He grabbed Joe's head and lowered his mouth to his. They kissed. Her pussy ached, her breath caught. A rush of envy ripped through her; she didn't want to be left out of their interaction a second longer.

And yet her voice failed her. She'd never seen anything like Joe and Walker's kiss. Tender yet harsh, beautiful and strong. Her hand fluttered to land on her belly and she itched to go lower.

Watching this intimate act between them sent a powerful erotic thrill through her; brought forth an incredible desire to reach between her legs and relieve herself. Because she knew how Joe felt; she knew exactly what it was like to succumb to Walker's command, knew firsthand what it was like to melt under his touch.

And then Walker stepped back, releasing Joe.

Joe looked slightly dazed as he dropped into Walker's abandoned chair. He yanked his black T-shirt over his head and threw it onto the floor. Her face heated. How strange to see his naked chest after all these months, after what they'd done. She couldn't stop herself from staring. He was too beautiful.

"Chloe?"

She turned her gaze to the second man in the room. He'd also removed his shirt. While she appreciated Joe's beauty, Walker took her breath away. So masculine, with his broad shoulders and ripped torso. Built in that way surfers were, long and lean, his sinewy muscles moving under his tanned skin as he approached her.

And he was Walker. That simple fact made her heartbeat quicken.

"Come here."

Shivering, she scooted down on the bed. She wondered if this was how it was going to go, if they were going to take turns with her. Fine. She wanted them to use her, to pleasure themselves with her body. She didn't care how they took her. She simply wanted to be *taken*.

Walker flipped her over onto her stomach. He pulled her down a few inches until her knees dropped nearly to the floor. She felt his hands on her skin, her lower back, her ass.

"You're so fucking beautiful."

His words and his touch went right to her gut. *So beautiful.* She believed him.

She heard a zipper and the sound of Walker shedding his jeans. Then the tearing of foil. A condom. She lifted her ass a bit, giving herself over because she needed to feel him inside of her. Fucking her. It was Joe's turn to watch.

Then another sound, this time liquidy. When she opened her eyes she saw that Joe had removed his pants, too. He was palming himself slowly, taking his time. And he was staring at Walker, at Walker's hands.

She felt Walker's fingers along the cleft of her ass, slick with lubrication. Her legs began to shake, her pulse went crazy.

"This is what you wanted, right?"

She nodded.

His touch became unyielding, circling her anus. "Tell me. Tell *us*."

"Yes," she breathed. "It's what I want. Both of you."

"You want both of us to what?"

Her sex ached from what she craved. "I want both of you to fuck me." The words hung in the air.

She watched Joe's fist, the way he stroked his cock up and down, caressing the taut, pink skin. His eyes were dark, dilated. The sight of him was stunning, made her moan.

"Good." Walker's fingers were gone, replaced by something bigger and rock hard. His cock was pushing at her, pushing inside of her. Filling her.

"You okay?"

She fisted the covers beside her head. "Yes."

His hand was soft yet solid on her hip. "That's our girl."

Deeper. A wave of erotic ecstasy washed over her as he stretched the very inside of her body. Full. So strange, this feeling. So good, better than her fantasies. She cried out as he went deeper still, his legs firm and strong behind her thighs.

Her gaze drifted back over to Joe. His hand was a blur of motion as he stroked himself. She listened to his breathing, fast and getting faster. Their eyes met and she wanted to come from the intimacy of it all. It didn't matter that he was a good six feet away; Walker controlled Joe as he did her.

She groaned as Walker's fingers snaked around to her clit, rubbing her until she was screaming for him to fuck her harder, fuck her harder in the ass.

A sense of relief flooded over her. Now she could let go, Walker made it safe. She wanted to feel him in the deepest parts of her body.

"Please." She'd never begged like this, never given herself over. He had total control of her. And Joe.

"Hold on." His hands gripped her around the waist. Then he picked her right up off the floor, lifting her as though she weighed nothing. He held her against his chest, her back sinking into his solid torso. He shifted until his hands supported her beneath her thighs. Her feet dangled in the air as he pulled out then slid back into her. He did it again and again. They faced Joe, gave him a wide-open show.

Her mind descended into a dreamlike world where fantasy melded with reality. She was totally exposed and yet so completely free. It was easy, too easy. She never wanted it to end.

Throwing her head back against Walker's shoulder, she let him spread her, his arms under her knees holding her wide open as he fucked her ass, held her up, spread her apart. So much strength in him, to hold her like that.

Joe groaned as he kicked his legs out, brought his palm to the glistening tip of his penis and rubbed his fingers into his pre-come. He used his own natural lubrication to ease his hand down over his rigid erection, pumping himself, and she couldn't keep her eyes off his cock because she wanted it, wanted it inside of her. Now.

Joe rolled a condom onto himself and stood. That pounding want in her core increased with each step he took toward them. He was coming to her, to them.

Stepping between her legs, he pressed his erection between her legs. She groaned when the hardness of him connected with her wet pussy, and was thankful for Walker's secure stance.

Joe took her chin in his fingers and kissed her. The room spun as he nipped at her lips, licked her.

Then they were sinking. Walker lay back on the bed, and she straddled him. A powerful erotic rush overcame her as she lifted herself up, then sank her ass back down onto his cock. She could barely believe what she was doing, riding a man like this as another man watched.

She met Joe's eyes and a rush of power came over her. She loved knowing that at *that* moment she was the one in charge, that the control had been given to her.

She wanted more. "Come here."

A thrill coursed through when he obeyed.

His eyes were bright as he climbed onto the bed and joined them. He kissed her clit, her pubic bone, her stomach. Walker leaned back on the bed, and she lifted her hips a fraction, watched as his long, strong legs tensed at the movement. Her own legs shook around his steady thighs. She moaned when Joe kissed her breast, took a nipple between his teeth and bit. She gasped at the sharp pain and silently begged him to do it harder.

She could not believe this was happening and yet she'd never experienced anything so genuine, so real.

"Please." She couldn't wait. So much leading up to this minute, she couldn't delay one more second. *"Please."*

Joe climbed higher until he was between her legs, his beautiful cock pressing against her swollen cunt, his legs settling between her wide-open thighs. She tilted her pelvis, encouraged him in. Walker gasped beneath her, his skin slick on hers.

She cried out when Joe thrust himself into her, filling her. The sensation of being penetrated by two men at once made her scream from pleasure, and when Joe pulled out and slid into her again she nearly came.

"Not yet," Walker whispered into her ear.

Taking a deep breath, she watched as Joe braced his arms on either side of Walker's shoulders. It was then that Joe found his rhythm, and she wanted to come so badly each time he drove into her, but Walker held her hips still.

Joe's gaze was locked beyond her shoulder. He was watching Walker's face as he fucked her. *Oh, God.*

"I'm going to come." Her limbs went liquid, tears stung her eyes. It was too intense, too much. She couldn't take it….

Walker brushed her hair behind her ear. "No," he murmured. His voice was soft and commanding all at once. Yes, he'd taken charge once again and she loved it.

She closed her eyes, fought the tremors that swam just outside the very core of her body. The men moved inside her, she felt their balls meeting between her legs, coming together each time they drove into her.

Her voice. It didn't sound like her voice at all. It was low, throaty and moaning as she begged.

Her skin. Slick, shiny. Hot.

Too much…

Walker had her nipple between his thumb and forefinger, was twisting and tugging. And when Joe leaned down and took her nipple into his mouth, sucking the tip that Walker held out for him, her body went rigid.

"Please, Walker. *Please.*"

"Okay, baby. Come for us now."

She threw her legs open, so wide, until her heels skirted the edge of the bed.

"Yes. *Fuck.*" She could barely believe that raspy voice was hers.

Walker's fingers were still on her nipple as Joe reached between their bodies to her clit. He pulled on her sensitive flesh and it was over. The climax rolled over her, and even as every nerve exploded the men continued to fuck her, harder, until she lay between them, limp and exhausted.

She loved them like this, using her for their pleasure. Loved watching Joe's green eyes as he thrust one final time into her. Loved feeling the slick skin of Walker's chest against her back as he bucked beneath her.

The three of them were like one fluid piece. And when they were inside of her she'd never felt so whole.

CHAPTER THREE

A MONTAGE OF BLURRY SOUNDS AND IMAGES
swirled before her heavy-lidded eyes: a faucet turning, steam
from a shower, the low murmur of male voices.

Joe threw off the duvet while Walker laid her gently on the
soft sheets. She smiled as she felt Walker's weight sinking into
the mattress beside her body.

Then sleep washed over her.

And now. She knew it was Walker lying next to her before
her eyes drifted open, knew it was his arm slung over her side.
Somehow she knew they were alone, that Joe was gone.

"Hey, baby."

Her nipples went hard at the sound of his voice. He brushed
her hair back and placed a warm kiss on the back of her neck.
She shivered as his dry lips skimmed her bare skin.

"Hey," she managed. She wanted him. She was barely awake
and she wanted him.

He rolled her onto her back. She glanced at the bedside clock.
The red LED light glowed 3:48 a.m. She'd been sleeping for just
over an hour and was groggy. Stretching, she smiled up at him.

A lamp from the next room dimly illuminated his blond
hair. It was messy, and for some reason that little thing made
her chest ache. When would she see him again?

He was so beautiful, so kind. She was glad they had a moment alone, but could not ignore a prick of guilt for wanting this time to themselves.

She cleared her throat. "Where's Joe?"

The corner of his mouth turned down. "Why?"

She shook her head. "Oh, no reason—I was just wondering."

He climbed on top of her. She gasped as his erection pressed into her hip. "Am I not enough?"

"No. I mean—*yes.*" Edging her legs apart with his knee, he pressed his cock against her, nestled himself between her pussy lips. She welcomed him, spread wider for him.

Her face flushed as images from last night blasted into her head. The experience had changed her, freed her. She wasn't afraid to ask for what she wanted, not with him.

She met his gaze. "I want you."

"Do you?"

"Yes." Her pussy throbbed where his cock pressed into her.

Yes, something had shifted. Before, it was an experiment. Now it was real. He was real.

She pushed the thoughts from her head. Too much thinking; she'd have plenty of time for that later. Now he was on top of her, his smooth, bare chest rubbing against hers as he fumbled with something on the nightstand.

He kissed her. Kissed her until she was melting for him, around him. She bent her knees beside to cradle him between her legs.

Then he was reaching between them, sliding a condom onto his erection.

"Am I enough for you?" He asked again, and thrust into her, so deep it bordered on painful, but she welcomed it.

"Oh, God, Walker."

He pulled out and rammed her again. "Am I?"

"Yes. Please, yes." Every nerve in her body lit up as he drove into her, again and again, her breasts swaying with each thrust.

She was so close to climax already, need swelled through her, shutting down her brain.

"Chloe, I…"

Her eyes fluttered open. "W-what?"

"You're just…amazing." He took one of her ankles and brought it over his shoulder. "I just had to tell you that."

She smiled as he continued to fuck her, his hip bones slamming against the insides of her thighs. Her sex throbbed, her breasts ached. His words sank into her head as his cock sank into her body, penetrating her everywhere.

She closed her eyes, moaning as he angled himself even deeper. She shook her head; she wasn't ready yet. "Walker…"

"Yeah, baby?"

"Fuck!" But the climax overtook her in wave after wave of unreal bliss. And he was next, his grasp on her ankle tightening as he rammed into her one final time, his body going rigid as he ejaculated.

Panting, she lay on the bed as he climbed off of her and rolled onto his back. He took her hand and held it to his chest. His heart pounded beneath her touch as she waited for both of their pulses to slow down.

She listened absently to a drunken shout echoing through the hallway, the clanking sound of a cart being pushed down the corridor. The muffled beat of a nightclub. In Vegas, the party never stopped, not even at four o'clock in the morning.

Pushing herself onto her elbow, she looked down at him. She took a deep breath; she had to know. "What's the deal with you and Joe?"

He had his arm over his eyes and he kept it there. "Joe's probably fucking some handsome blackjack dealer in our room right now."

"W-what?"

He sighed. "Last night was phenomenal."

Her skin heated as she remembered just how amazing the

experience had been. "Yeah. It really was." So why was Joe off with someone else?

And why did the thought not bother her? It should have, but she found herself more curious than jealous.

But so much had changed in the past twelve hours. She had a feeling she'd be looking at many things differently now.

He removed his arm and met her gaze. "Joe doesn't do phenomenal. In fact, the minute he cares too much about anything he finds the nearest piece of ass and helps himself."

She sat up cross-legged and pulled a sheet across her naked body. "What about you?"

"We've never had a commitment."

"Do you love him?" Her heart hammered as she awaited his reply. *And why does it matter so much?*

"Yes."

Her mouth went dry. "Oh." *Brilliant reply, Chloe.*

He rubbed the pad of his thumb over her wrist. "But I've never asked him to be faithful. And he's never asked it of me. What we have now works."

Her pulse quickened as she remembered the way Joe had looked at Walker over her shoulder as they'd both made love to her.

She cleared her throat. "He loves you, though."

"Yes. But he's not capable of monogamy."

"And you?"

"Maybe." He shrugged. "I might want that one day."

Her heart was going crazy, but she had no idea why. "Really?" And why was she thinking about those things, too? Why was she picturing a scene from *Leave it to Beaver,* only starring her and Walker as June and Ward?

That was *so* not what she wanted. Maybe one day, but not now.

She shook her head. "That's going to be hard with a boyfriend on the side."

His grip on her hand intensified. "Is it?"

Her throat constricted, her gut twisted into a mess, but there was no logical reason for her body's response. Surely he wasn't suggesting *she* was that woman.

Was he?

He pulled her down to lie on top of him, settling her into the crook of his arm. "It's way too late for such heavy talk. Sleep now."

As she breathed in his spicy scent, her chest went tight. They only had a few hours left and she knew one thing for certain: she did not want to wake up with either of them. She couldn't take the chance of harsh morning light tainting this life-altering experience. She wanted to leave before the sun came up.

Walker settled her closer to him and placed a soft kiss on her forehead. "I don't know if I can wait six more months to see you again."

She closed her eyes as grief settled in her heart—she'd miss both of them. But the thought of going six months without seeing Walker especially was downright painful.

But she *would* see him again. Both of them.

And she couldn't help smiling to herself because when Chloe O'Malley went to work on Monday she'd be a different woman. A woman who'd lived out her naughtiest fantasy.

A woman who'd been part of a ménage à trois.

And the best part was she knew that six months from now she might just do it again.

Running her hand over Walker's broad chest, she sighed. She knew she should get up, get dressed and go home. But one of his strong hands was caressing her back, the other was twisting a lock of hair rhythmically around his finger.

Maybe just a little longer. She had a few hours until the sun came up. A few more hours to enjoy lying in Walker's arms.

"'Night, baby."

She nodded, already half-asleep.

Another kiss placed at the top of her head, followed by a soft whisper: "See you in six months."

She woke up alone. She didn't need the sliver of sunlight slicing between the dark drapes to illuminate the fact that Walker and Joe had gone. During their short time together she'd become accustomed to the powerful energy the men exuded, and now that it was absent everything seemed horribly empty.

She missed them.

As she stretched, her body gave a trembling reminder of her escapades from the previous night. Her muscles ached from the unfamiliar positions she'd executed with Joe and Walker.

She couldn't believe what she'd done.

She wanted to do it again.

A small piece of paper on the nightstand drew her attention. It had her name on it. She picked the note off the table, and as she read, her heartbeat skipped.

Smiling, she sank back onto the pillows and held the card to her chest. Five little words. How could five little words fill her with so much excitement? How could a note bring her alive like this?

She read it again.

Dear Chloe,
See you in six months.
Love,
Walker and Joe

Exhilaration raced through her veins. She realized she was looking forward to every minute of every day that would pass between now and then. Six months of expectation, of waiting. Six months of fantasies. Six months of having the men always in her thoughts, anticipation at seeing them building and building....

Yes, she thought as she ran her hand across her rib cage, over her belly and past her pubic hair. She sighed as her fingertips reached her clit, and she spread her legs wide beneath the covers.

She watched the bump of her hand as she slid her fingers across her pussy lips, raw from last night. It had made the flesh ultrasensitive, and just a few strokes had her moaning out loud.

Closing her eyes, she imagined Joe's tongue on her clit, licking and sucking as he had done the night before. Fucking her with two of his long, strong fingers.

She imagined Walker kneeling beside her, and she was taking his cock in her mouth. Rubbing herself hard now, she bucked against her hand. Fuck, but she hadn't tasted either man's cock. Oh, how she wanted to. She wanted to take Walker deep into her mouth, until he pushed against the very back of her throat. Wanted to suck his cock while Joe fucked her....

She came against her hand, her body shuddering as the climax washed over her. Not nearly as satisfying as having two men fuck her simultaneously, but for the next six months it would have to do.

Tomorrow she'd go about her routine, complete with ugly shoes and head scarf. But they'd never be far from her mind.

She flopped onto her side and closed her eyes. For the next six months, every thought in her head, every fantasy that entered her mind, would center on Joe and Walker. For all intents and purposes she was theirs.

For the next six months she was taken.

* * * * *

FAVOR ME

Jenesi Ash

WHEN YOU'RE GOOD AT SEX, PEOPLE THINK
that the only work you're capable of is a blow job.

I don't waste my time trying to clear up that misconception. I'm good in bed, and as far as I'm concerned, sex is not an amateur sport. If you do it for payment, you need to be smart about it. People might think I trade my body because I can't use my brain, but the truth is that I simply don't want to work any harder than I have to.

If my long-term plan works out, I will never have to get another job. There were times when I had two, sometimes three jobs at once, and I would still have trouble making rent. That all changed when one of my coworkers offered to pay my bills if I had sex with him whenever he wanted.

I probably should have been offended, but honestly, I was intrigued. I liked the idea of a man spending his hard-earned money to be with me. He must have known he couldn't get me any other way. And how could I possibly say no to paying my bills without having to roll out of bed?

It turned out to be a pretty good arrangement—my credit rating was great during that year—but I soon realized that if I wanted to be a full-time mistress, I needed a wealthier lover.

I thought it would be tough finding a guy who was willing

to keep me in style. Who knew that job hunting would turn out to be the easiest part of becoming a mistress?

My lover is Leon Richmond, one of Seattle's many millionaires. Leon is sexy, creative and richer than anyone I know. He's also heading toward fifty, on his fourth wife and is insatiable when it comes to sex.

I've been with Leon for just a couple of months. I should have known that for the astronomical amount of money he offered me, he was going to have a few bents and kinks. I thought I had seen and done it all when it came to sex. Ha! Leon has proved me wrong.

Sex with Leon is a lot like training camp. What I did with my friendly coworker was a lot different than being a full-time mistress. Leon doesn't seem to notice that I'm learning on the job, or maybe he doesn't care as long as I fulfill my part of the agreement.

As much as I appreciate the opportunity Leon has given me, I'm not going to stay with him forever. He's the richest guy I know, but after living in a million-dollar condo he bought for me in downtown Bellevue, I've seen a higher level of wealth that could be mine for the taking. Leon is my starter benefactor, and when I get a better offer, I'm going for it.

I feel something bump at the foot of my bed. I'm fully awake and alert, but I keep my eyes closed. I sense the bright morning light filtering through the curtains and all I want to do is burrow into the tangled sheets. Maybe if I fake sleeping, Leon will get dressed and go make a couple more million at the office.

Leon cups my bare shoulder and gives it a good shake. "Amaris?"

Aw, man. I hear the excited rough edge in his voice. He wants to play some more; I should have known. "Hmm?"

"Smile."

Shit. He has the camcorder on again. My skin immediately starts to tingle.

Leon enjoys taping us having sex. We never watch them together once the filming is complete. I don't know why, but Leon won't show them to me no matter how nicely I beg.

Maybe he keeps them for his own private home collection. I like to think he plays them when he can't be with me, but for all I know, he makes the videos to show them to his friends. Hell, I wouldn't be surprised if he posts the tapes on the Internet.

The thought sends a flash of heat to my pussy and I squirm as my clit begins to swell and throb. My nipples pucker and rub against my nightgown. The satin suddenly feels like it binds my breasts and I can't wait to get it off.

I recently discovered that I have an exhibitionist streak as strong as Leon's. I like to imagine countless strangers watching these homemade movies, their faces almost pressed against their computer screens. I want to be naked with my legs splayed and have everyone watch me come. I want to be seen, remembered, desired.

Rolling onto my back, I stretch my arms over my head, doing my best to appear open and vulnerable. I purr low in my throat as I arch my spine, thrusting my breasts out. I bend my knees slightly, letting my green satin nightgown hike up my legs. I feel it strain against my thighs and I hope the fabric drifts and settles in all the right places. I want the nightgown to hint at my full breasts and shaved mound.

I blink my eyes open and offer a dazzling smile. "Good morning, Leon."

He towers over me. His skin is still wet from the shower and I inhale his scent. It's masculine and very expensive. His dark blond hair is slicked back and the morning sun reveals every line on his harsh, craggy face.

"Come back to bed," I suggest as I reach out for him.

He dodges my fingers. "Convince me," he challenges softly as he holds the camcorder up to his eye.

Most women would probably squeal and hide, but I revel

in the spotlight. I look straight into the camera and rub my hands along the satin. The sound of the fabric sliding over my hot skin is the only thing I hear.

I cover my breast with one hand and pinch my nipple through the nightgown. Sure, I could strip off, but where's the fun in that? I want to tease Leon until he can't think straight, and I want that on tape, too.

I cup my mound with my other hand and I feel the steamy heat through the satin. I caress my clit, keeping my nightgown as a barrier. The friction has me biting back a moan.

It doesn't take long before Leon gets impatient. "Take off your clothes," he says in a husky voice. I follow his order, bunching the hem in my fists and inching it over my hips and waist. He focuses his camcorder on my pussy as I wiggle my way out of the nightgown. Knowing that he's taping me makes me wetter.

I toss the green satin to the side and slide my hands over my body. I feel tight, flushed and swollen, ready to burst out of my skin. I pinch my nipples harder until I gasp out loud. Leon leans in closer, his camcorder almost brushing against my breasts and he watches my nipples turn an angry red.

"Oh, yeah," he says in almost a growl. "Give me more."

I keep playing with my nipples with one hand as I glide my other hand down between my legs. Pressing down on my hard clit, I stroke small circles that send a crackle of fire through my bloodstream.

"Wider," Leon says gruffly as excitement hitches in his voice. "Go wider."

I spread my legs as wide as I can. I feel Leon's warm breath on my inner thigh and the cold touch of the camcorder as I rub my fingers fast against the slick skin. I smell my arousal as my juices drip down my slit.

Most of all, I ache for Leon to cover my mound with his mouth and lick the wet, sticky folds until I come screaming. The thought alone has me rocking my hips, but I don't ask him. I know he'll deny me, and I'm not willing to let that be caught on tape.

Dipping my fingertips into my pussy, I roll my head back and let out a long groan as the pleasure rips through my body. My vaginal walls clamp onto my fingers and draw them deeper. I start pumping my hand, desperate for relief.

I finally rub my clit with one hand and pump inside me with the other. I dig my heels into the mattress as I go harder and faster. My moans mingle with Leon's harsh, uneven breaths. With every rise and fall of his chest, I know he's going to make a grab for me and take over.

Leon retreats and gets on his knees to get a full picture of me. I wonder if I look as wild as I feel. I must look good by the way he's licking his lips. A shudder sweeps through me and I have to pause to ride it out.

Bright sparkles and dark spots dance before my eyes and drift away. I watch him stroking his cock as he tapes me. I continue to stroke myself, my hips bucking and twisting from each touch.

Leon's skin takes on a ruddy complexion and a muscle above his jaw begins to bunch. He can't fight the desire he feels for me. Soon he's going to need me more than his next breath. And it will show through on the tape.

That's what I like the most. I close my eyes as another wave of sensations laps over me. I enjoy being desired more than the act of sex, believe it or not. I want men to lust after me and wish I were theirs. I dream of women envying my sensual world. I want people to know that not many women have the ability to expose the elemental beast behind the layers of Leon's cosmopolitan facade. This is when my power is at its highest, and I find it addictive.

Leon decides he has had enough of being a spectator. I feel the bed dip beside me as he lies on his back. I turn to see him and find that that the camcorder is still trained on me. But what

I really notice is his cock pointing straight to the ceiling. It almost curves toward his stomach, and the tip is already wet and shiny.

"Get on top of me," Leon says through clenched teeth.

I'm so ready for him, but I try to mask my eagerness as I get up and straddle his hips. The truth is, I can't get enough of his cock. I love tasting it and taking it any way I can. I curl my hands around his length and squeeze, enjoying the feel of his heat and power pulsing beneath my palms.

But he flinches at the touch of my hands. He's past the point of being teased. "Now," he bites out.

I slowly lower myself onto his cock, pressing my lips together as he stretches me until I feel like it's almost too much. I lean forward, pleasure rippling through my pelvis, and rest my hands on his chest. I'm so close to going over the edge.

I look at the camcorder and slowly smile. I trail my fingers down my long brown hair, then slide my hands over my neck and shoulders before cupping the underside of my breasts.

"Ride me," Leon orders hoarsely. "As hard as you can."

I swivel and grind my hips, slowly at first until I build up speed. My breasts bounce as I rock against Leon. The slap of skin and his groans fill the air.

I ride him with a driven intensity and heat coils deep in my belly as shivers run up my spine. A delicious sensation builds inside me, winding tighter and tighter as I ride Leon harder and faster. It presses against my skin, and I think I'm going to shatter.

I can feel the changes in Leon's body. He's going to come any second now. But I don't watch his face. I tilt my head, toss my hair back and look straight into the camcorder.

I imagine an audience of thousands behind that lens. It's time to show them what they're missing. They're panting for me and jacking off. They are waiting to hear my startled gasps and satisfied moans. They wish they were in my bed, but deep down they know this is as close as they're going to get.

A hot jagged climax rips through me. I stiffen, unable to

move as it whips my flesh, tears me inside out and sucks away the last of my strength. I dimly hear Leon's hoarse cry of release as I sag and collapse onto his chest, my core still clenching his hard, pulsing cock.

I swear, this is the best job ever.

After breakfast, we're riding in the limo to his office when Leon tells me about his change in plans. "This afternoon I have to go on a business trip."

"Oh?" I ask as I inspect my manicure. This is the first time Leon has taken a trip since I've been with him. "When will you be back?"

"It's hard to say." He rubs his hand along my thigh. I'm tempted to cross my legs and trap his hand. "Meet me at my office after your shopping."

Uh-huh. He's going to get all the sex he can before he leaves. I like that he can't get enough of me, but he probably just wants to get his money's worth. "What do you have in mind?"

His smile was positively smug. "You'll find out."

I probably should question him more, but I'm a little distracted because I'm late for my appointment at Vincent's, my favorite lingerie boutique. Vincent is one of those designers who will drop you from his books if you miss a fitting. I usually can't stand people like that, but this guy is my secret weapon. Every time I wear one of his creations, Leon is putty in my hands.

Vincent's shop is in the main lobby of the office tower where Leon works. There's also a fancy restaurant on the top floor that offers amazing views of the Seattle skyline and an expensive menu. I've been there with Leon on many occasions, although we haven't done the private dining rooms. He always gets a table where we are seen, and I never understand that. If he's having an affair, wouldn't he want to keep it quiet?

It's almost as if he wants to get caught. Our limo pulls up to the entrance and Leon helps me out. It's raining hard and I'm wearing spiky heels. I slowly get out of the car, making the most of my black seamed stockings and a flirty black satin raincoat. Leon's look of appreciation brings a spring to my step.

He guides me into the building, his hand resting low on my back. He greets another businessman as we go through the revolving door. I don't recognize the man, but I like the way his gaze lingers on me.

As the man gives me one last covert glance, Leon's hand slides down and squeezes my ass. I hide my surprise at this public display of possession and I hold my instinct to swat him away. Who cares if the gossip reaches his wife's ears? Leon is obviously willing to risk another expensive, messy divorce to show he can get someone like me at his beck and call.

We step into the main lobby and once again I'm struck by the layout. The banks of elevators are in the middle, and there are four shops in the far corners: a florist, a chocolatier, a jeweler and a lingerie store.

I am not kidding. If this isn't a red flag that most of the guys in this building are having extramarital affairs, I don't know what is. Sure, they might buy all this stuff for their wives, as well, but those would be guilt purchases.

If all of these businessmen have a woman on the side, I wonder if there's a hierarchy in how a man maintains a mistress. I bet it's not good enough that you can afford one. If you can get the most infamous, the kinkiest or the highest-priced one, then you are the most envied.

If that's the case, I'm going to go for all three and become the most sought-after.

We head straight for Vincent's and the front door swings open. Usually I have to ring the bell to gain entrance. I heard they had to install that and start taking appointments after one too many run-ins between mistresses and wives. But today,

Brianna, the stunning beauty who works the front desk, is waiting for me.

"Good morning, Ms. Martin," Brianna says and she motions for me to come in.

"I'm sorry I'm late."

"My fault," Leon apologizes. To my surprise, he steps into the shop. "I hope I didn't cause you any inconvenience."

I don't know what's going through his head. I know Leon doesn't care one way or the other if he causes a hiccup in their schedule. Nothing is more important than his own time. But Brianna smiles and lets him know that it isn't any trouble at all.

For a brief moment I feel a spurt of insecurity. Is Leon checking out Brianna? She is younger than me and her exotic looks make me feel pale and boring in comparison. I have no idea if she would indulge a lover's fetishes, but Brianna oozes sex appeal.

I'm actually feeling envious of her kimono-inspired dress when Leon reaches for one of the expensive black bustiers in the store window and strokes the lace. "This is nice."

I can hear the burr in his voice and I want to breathe a sigh of relief. He didn't notice Brianna—he has plans for the bustier.

"Excuse me for one moment," Brianna says, casting a curious glance at Leon. "I'll let Vincent know you're here."

She hurries away, her stiletto heels clacking on the floor. Leon reaches for the sash of my raincoat and pulls me close to him. I can feel his cock pressing into my stomach. He's already aroused from imagining me in the bustier. I know I would look good in it, especially with my black heels, seamed stockings and garter belt.

Leon brushes his mouth against my ear. "Meet me in my office in one hour."

An hour? I can't do that! Vincent is going to have a fit. "But I—"

"Wear the bustier under your raincoat."

There's an edge of warning in his voice. Who would I rather displease, my lover or my lingerie designer? I hate to admit that I hesitated. I give a reluctant nod as Vincent hurries out. "Amaris! So good to see you again."

Vincent is exactly what I think a designer should look like, from his bald head to the gold signet ring on his little finger. Today he wears a long-sleeved pink shirt with a burgundy scarf tucked in the collar. The tailored gray pants and polished shoes show his attention to detail and love of fashion.

I give him a kiss on both his wrinkled cheeks, inhaling his familiar scent of eucalyptus and mint. I turn to introduce him to Leon, but apparently they already know each other. I catch Vincent's wince as he shakes Leon's hand. Glancing down at his fingers, I notice the designer's knuckles are swollen and red.

"I won't take up any more of your time," Leon says as he goes for the door. He pauses and gives me a hot, smoky look. "I'll see you in an hour."

Vincent turns and looks at me in horror. "An hour? We have too much to do!" He tosses his hands up in the air. "I need you fitted for the negligees you ordered."

"I can come back again later in the day," I promise and I glance at the appointment book on Brianna's desk. Apparently, I am the only client today. Now I don't feel so guilty.

But Vincent seems to think this is reason enough to carry on. "You can't give genius a time limit!" he continues as he takes me into the fitting room. "I can't be held responsible for the results."

I see his assistant, Denise, getting everything ready for my fitting as Mary, the seamstress, waits for me by the raised dais. They greet me warmly and Vincent immediately gets to work.

As Denise and Vincent discuss the selection for me, I notice that the assistant looks more pulled together today. Usually she's frazzled and messy, too busy handling a million things for Vincent. But today her blond hair is styled in a smooth blunt cut. Her business pantsuit is a bright shade of blue and shows off her athletic figure. She looks sexy, which can only mean one thing. She has a new man in her life.

The first thing I try on is a champagne-colored negligee. It fits me like a glove and I can't help but preen in front of the mirror.

When I step out of the dressing room, the seamstress is the only person waiting for me. I don't hear Denise or Vincent, and the cup of hot tea on a side table is the only sign that Brianna has been here.

"Where is everyone else?" I ask Mary as I step onto the raised dais.

She shrugs. "They are fighting over creative differences." Mary studies my appearance with an intensity that borders on scowling.

I turn and look at the three-way full-length mirror. Why does Mary disapprove of my nightgown?

"It doesn't fit," she announces.

"Are you kidding? It fits perfectly!" What does she know about fit? Sure, she's a seamstress, but her gray uniform is baggy and does nothing to show off her petite figure. I bet she's a size two just like me, although you would never know it.

She purses her lips. "Your hips are wider."

My mouth drops open. "I beg your pardon?" I flatten my hands on my hip bones as if I can hide them from her.

Mary glares at me. "Have you gained weight since the last time we measured? I hope not. That makes more work for me."

Oh, yes. I want to ruin my figure for the sole purpose of giving Mary extra work. It's been my evil plan all along. I look around for Vincent, ready to hear some soothing words about how wonderful I look.

"And the hem is all wrong," Mary decides. "It's supposed to be beveled."

I frown at her through the reflection.

"That means the front is supposed to be shorter and slope down to the back."

"I know what beveled means." Sort of. Mary reaches for the hem and I take a step away before she does something drastic. "Shouldn't we wait for Vincent to decide that?"

"He trusts my instincts," she says with a smug smile. "Turn toward me and I'll pin it up."

I don't want to. I want Vincent's opinion first. That's why I'm paying him the big bucks. But he's nowhere to be found. I slowly turn and face Mary. She kneels down in front of me and measures the hem.

Looking around the fitting room, I wonder where Vincent went. Is he still mad at me for being late? I wouldn't put it past him to have a hissy fit.

Did he leave completely? I hope not. I glance in the direction of his office and notice that the door isn't fully closed. I see something move in that room. It must be Vincent.

Correction! It's Vincent and Denise. He is leaning against his messy desk and she is standing close to him. Really close. I squint, trying to see what's going on.

Vincent is holding something that looks like a letter, only it has a pale blue paper backing. I wonder what it is because it's making Denise really happy. She is smiling as she links her hands around his neck and gives him a deep kiss.

My mouth drops open. No. Way. Denise and Vincent have hooked up? When? More importantly, why? I glance down at Mary, who is measuring my hemline with her usual methodical approach. Does she know about her coworker and her boss? I'm dying to ask, but I don't think that's a good idea.

I look back in the room and see Vincent pushing Denise's shoulders, the paper in his hand brushing against her hair. I squint harder, and realize he's not pushing her away. He's motioning her to go down on her knees.

Denise willingly kneels down in front of her boss and palms his cock through his gray pants. I don't have to squint hard to see he has a big erection. Wow. And all this time I pegged Vincent as gay.

I know I should look away. I'm already getting aroused. My breasts feel heavy and full and my clit is beginning to swell. But I can't ignore what's going on in the next room. I have to watch.

Denise has already pushed Vincent's clothes past his knees. She grasps the root of his cock with both hands and starts to lick him with the tip of her tongue. A low, insistent throb gathers deep in my belly and I shift my legs. I immediately stop, surprised Mary didn't reprimand me for moving. Is she watching, too? I glance down and see she's pinning the hem with her legendary focus.

I tense up when I hear a groan from Vincent's office. I can't help but glance in that direction. Vincent looks like he's either in pain or in ecstasy. His hand crumples against the paper. He bucks against the desk before he plunges into Denise's mouth.

The wooden desk is squeaking and Vincent is not being quiet about his pleasure. Denise is slurping loudly against his cock. Am I the only who hears this?

"Try on the next one."

I jump and give a startled look at Mary, who is still kneeling down in front of me. My heart is racing and I feel flushed. I'm aroused and I wonder if she can tell.

"I'm sorry?" I ask weakly.

Mary makes a face and it's clear she's fed up with me. "Go put on the next negligee."

I gesture at the nightgown I'm wearing. "Vincent hasn't seen me in this."

She gives me this look, and I know I'm pushing my luck with her. I want to hold my ground, but Vincent may be a while. Since I still have to meet with Leon within the hour, I decide to surrender gracefully.

The phone rings in the fitting room and Mary gives an impatient sigh. She rises from her position and heads for the phone that is on the desk next to my dressing room. I step into my room and firmly close the door.

I'm so horny right now, but I can't do anything about it. I try to focus on anything else.

The first thing I wonder is how long does it take for a man as old as Vincent to reach an orgasm. I decide that I have no envy for Denise. One day I might have a lover as old as Vincent, but what kind of setup did she agree to? If I was sleeping with the boss, the first thing I would do is cut my hours. I'm sure Denise gets amazing fringe benefits, but what's the point of doing someone if you also have to work for him?

I slide on the next negligee, this one shorter and the color of coffee. When I step out of my dressing room, the designer and his assistant both are out of his office and acting as if nothing unusual just happened.

It's hard not to miss Vincent's smile. It's a little bit naughty and carefree. I see that look on men all the time. Vincent's complexion is rosy and he's rubbing his hands as if he's coming up with a devious plan.

"Amaris, you look very sexy," Vincent says in a booming voice. His hands flutter around me as he takes in my appearance. "My creation is going to be ripped right off your luscious body."

I smile, but I see Denise flinch. She needs to work on that. Sure, it's never easy to have a man show appreciation to another woman right after you had his cock in your mouth, but Denise should be used to it.

As Denise picks up a notepad and pen, Vincent gives a few suggestions, all the time describing my body as "scrumptious" and "delightful" and "made for sin." I feel like a goddess. And not once does he mention I gained weight. I glare at Mary, who doesn't try to share her opinions this time. She keeps her head down as she takes in the lace bodice.

Brianna comes in to see if I needed my drink refreshed. I glance at the clock, noticing that I'm cutting it close to meet with Leon. "Brianna? I need to wear one of the bustiers from the window display. Can you get one for me? I need it right away."

"Of course!" Brianna says with a smile. She doesn't question the urgency and hurries out of the room.

Vincent and Denise are still coming up with ideas on how my negligee can look better when Brianna rushes in, clipping the sales tag off the bustier with a pair of scissors. She puts it in my dressing room and I glance at the clock again. I can't hold it off anymore.

I turn to the designer and brace myself. "Vincent, I'm sorry, but I need to take a break. I have to meet Leon."

"But we've just started!" Vincent clutches the top of his bald head with both hands and gives an outraged huff.

That's not my fault, but I barely hold my tongue. "I'll come back. This is unavoidable."

He tosses his hands in the air. "We have so much to do if you want the last Vincent original!"

That stops me in my tracks. "What do you mean the last?"

He waves away my question with the flick of his wrist and abruptly stops. "I haven't announced it yet," he says quietly, almost sadly, "but I'm retiring."

"Retiring!" The word hits me like a punch in the stomach. I look at the other women in the room for verification, but they look as stunned as I feel.

This will not do. Vincent can't quit. The man is my secret weapon. I can't go back to buying chain-store lingerie.

"Don't worry, my dear." He gives me a pat on my bare shoulder. "I'm staying on in an advisory capacity."

Relief crashes through me and I feel so much better. What Vincent is proposing is essentially what he does now, whether he knows it or not. He tosses his arms around and makes declarations, but I have never seen him work up a sweat.

I hurry back into the dressing room and grab the bustier. As I carefully remove my negligee, I hear a harsh whisper outside my room. I press my ear to the wall, wondering if they're talking about me.

"Why didn't you tell me you're retiring, Vincent?" Brianna asks, her voice shaking with anger. "I'm your heir."

Heir? My fingers still on the hooks of my bustier. Is she his daughter? Why haven't they mentioned that? Maybe Vincent doesn't want people to know he had a grown daughter.

"I never decided that," Vincent says.

"I may only be your niece, but you told my mom you wanted to keep the business in the family. I'm the only one who's showed an interest in it."

I'm adjusting the bustier as I hear Vincent say, "You still have a lot to learn."

"Bullshit!" she whispers fiercely. "You've been using me. You got cheap labor and dangled the possibility of me owning this business."

I didn't hear what Vincent's response was to that. I could say he lowered his voice, but frankly, I lost interest once I caught sight of myself in the mirror.

I look freaking fantastic! I stand straight and notice how the bustier plumps up my breasts while making my waist look smaller. I put on the garter belt and then my panties. I learned this trick after the first time Leon wanted me to keep my garter belt on while we had sex. I carefully slide on my stockings and put on my black heels before I look at my reflection in the mirror.

My stomach gives a naughty flip and my heart starts to pound with anticipation. Leon is going to go crazy when he gets a look at me.

I put on my satin raincoat and tie the sash firmly against my waist, then open the door to my dressing room. No one is around. I guess they decided to do their fighting out of range.

I check my watch and hurry out to the reception area, barely managing a goodbye to Brianna, who is definitely making a personal call as she speaks angrily on the phone while I make my exit.

Once the elevator arrives, I'm the only one who gets on. That's kind of a disappointment. What's the fun of wearing next to nothing if you can't tease anyone with it?

When I get off the elevator, I march straight to Leon's offices. I get past the snobby receptionist only to come toe-to-toe with his loyal secretary. From the disapproving look on her pinched face, I can safely say she knows all about me. I'm tempted to open my raincoat and flash her, but I don't give out freebies.

I'm immediately escorted inside Leon's office. He greets me with a smile, but doesn't rise from his chair as he would for any other visitor. Instead he asks his secretary to hold his calls.

The minute we're alone, I untie my raincoat and allow it to fall to the floor. I lean against the door, my hands flat against the wood. I jut my hips out, silently inviting him closer.

Leon doesn't move. He's mesmerized, and I've never felt this kind of sexual power.

"Come here," he says in a gruff voice.

I should have known he wouldn't grovel for me. I walk over to him, letting my hips roll provocatively until I reach his desk. I perch on the edge close to where he sits. Tilting my head back, the sunlight gets into my eyes.

That's when it occurs to me that the shades aren't closed. I glance outside and see men and women in the high tower across the street. They are working intently, but if they were to look out their window, they would clearly see into this office. Anyone could get a good view of me seducing Leon.

I get wet just thinking about it. I rub my thighs together as excitement rushes through me. I want an audience see me take Leon and watch me go wild. I widen my legs, drawing Leon's attention to my pussy. "I'm going to give you a lap dance."

Leon's eyes gleam with approval. "Make it slow," he suggests, propping his chin in his hand as he watches. He isn't as relaxed and indifferent as he tries to appear. I can see his cock pressing against his pants. "And take off your panties. Nothing else."

He really loves seeing me in this bustier. I wiggle out of the panties and kick them off. I'm aroused and ready for action, my core pulsing and greedy for Leon's cock.

I glance out the window. Not one person has seen me yet. Damn. I want to catch their attention. Make them press against the glass, their tongues hanging out of their slack jaws, panting for me.

I grab the headrest of Leon's chair and straddle him. I grin as the chair rocks and swivels with every move I make. I know each sudden motion is going to add to the feel of his cock inside me.

My knees dig into the cushioned seat and my breasts are level with Leon's harsh mouth. I feel the heat emanating from him as my wet slit hovers above his aroused cock.

I look down at Leon and meet his gaze. He grabs my breasts and squeezes hard. His eyes darken with pleasure and he drags my bustier down, slowly unpeeling the fabric from my breasts. His face tightens as he exposes my tightly puckered nipples. Leon groans deep in his throat before he takes one nipple in his mouth and bites down.

I give a little scream and arch back. The chair tilts wildly and my pussy rubs against his cock. I hiss when his cold belt buckle presses against my hot skin.

Deciding I've been patient long enough, I let go of the headrest and grab his belt. My hands fumble as Leon continues to tease my breasts with his fingers and tongue. When he draws me deep into his mouth I almost orgasm right there.

I tug his belt free and lift myself up just a little to unzip his pants. Leon skims his hands down my hips and holds me still. "Stay like that," he says softly against the underside of my breast.

I can't think straight with his hands squeezing and massaging my ass. He flattens his palm and my knees start to tremble. I know what he's planning just as he gives me a hard smack.

I gasp as the spank echoes in the room. Sizzling heat spreads through my buttocks and he smacks me again. I swallow back a whimper as my clit pulses for attention.

Leon spanks me again, only harder. I glance at the shut door. Can his secretary hear Leon spanking me? The idea drenches my pussy.

I need Leon's cock now. I drag his zipper down and he raises his hips so I can push down his pants and underwear. This time I don't stop to fondle his cock and balls. Heat streaks through my pelvis as I lower myself onto his cock. I bite my lip as he slowly fills me. I rock against him, the chair tilting as the small of my back tingles. I sway my hips and the world spins.

White-hot lust claws my insides, desperate to break free. I grip Leon's shoulders and meet each of his thrusts. The chair swivels and squeaks as I stare over his head. It bucks, tilts and turns and I can't fight the feeling anymore.

I feel dizzy, but I can't climax. I don't know what's wrong. And then someone in the other building looks out the window. A businesswoman frowns as she watches me. My pulse quickens as her brow clears and understanding hits.

Leon's fingers press into my hips as he thrusts deeper. Harder. My breath snags in my throat as the pleasure breaks free, whipping through my body as Leon's release triggers my own.

I stare out the window, gulping for air, my heart racing. The woman from across the street guiltily looks away and my satisfaction evaporates. I gingerly disentangle myself from Leon. "I take it you like this outfit."

"Get one in every color."

I adjust the bustier until it covers my breasts while Leon reaches out and spans his fingers over my mound. His possessive touch makes me shiver. I almost sink to my knees when he strokes my clit with his thumb.

A firm knock on the door gives me a jolt. I don't have time to jump back as Leon tells the intruder to enter.

My eyes widen as the door opens and a gorgeous man in an expensive suit steps in. He's looking at a file in his hands and doesn't notice that he steps on my discarded raincoat. My heart is stuck in my throat, waiting for the inevitable.

He looks up and pauses. His face tightens for the briefest moment and then his expression turns blank. "Sorry, I thought you told me to enter."

"It's all right," Leon says, as if he's not concerned our encounter has been disrupted. "Kyler, this is Amaris Martin. Amaris, this is Kyler Thorn, my new assistant."

This is his assistant? There's something about this tall man that would intimidate his enemies and comfort his allies. And it is more than his impressive height, the ruthless cut of his hair or the aggressive lines of his face.

Kyler Thorn doesn't look like a guy who takes orders well. He looks like someone who would take heart-stopping risks and violate a few ethics to get what he wants. The intelligence shining in his dark eyes shows that he has the mind of a scholar, but his lethal grace and muscular body makes me think more of a warrior. Then again, the commanding way he stands and the power pulsing from him is better suited for a ruler than a follower.

I step away from Leon. My skin feels hot and my legs are wobbly, but I'm excited. Someone is seeing me half-naked and enjoying an afterglow. If only he'd walked in a few minutes earlier.

I stroll toward him, my heart racing. I try to appear casual as my state of arousal zooms up to another level. I offer him my hand. "It's a pleasure to meet you."

He takes my hand and I swear I feel a zing that goes straight to my core. I give him a startled glance, but he shows no emotion whatsoever.

Damn. I want him to be shocked. Aroused. Even disgusted or confused. Anything but this indifference.

His lack of emotion is like a splash of cold water. I withdraw my hand and look at Leon, who continues to sit back in his chair, his desk hiding his unzipped pants and softening cock. My panties are probably under his feet.

I decide it's time to go. "I'll get out of your way, Leon." I give his assistant a curt nod. "Kyler."

I walk to the door, which is still open, but no one is in my line of vision. I pick up my raincoat and put it on as Kyler tells Leon to sign some document.

I give the satin sash one final tug and quietly leave. As I close the door behind me, I look over my shoulder. Leon's attention has already turned back to business. His head is lowered as he scrawls his name on the document.

But it's Kyler who is watching my every move with a hot, dangerous intensity. I feel the power of it hitting me with the force of a sledgehammer. My lips tug into a knowing smile as I pull the door shut.

Kyler wants me. Badly. It's a shame he can't afford me.

I stride out of the office and back to the elevators, shaking my hair loose as I feel more masculine gazes and a few feminine ones. The ride down to the lobby goes by fast and I glance at my watch. I've been gone for barely a half an hour.

I march to Vincent's boutique. Brianna hurriedly rounds her desk to open the door. "That was quick!"

"Vincent wasn't happy that I had to leave," I explain as I walk toward the fitting room with her. "What kind of mood is he in?"

"I don't know," Brianna confesses. "I haven't seen him since you left."

Great. He's probably sulking in his office. I decided to go

play nice even though Vincent is acting unreasonable. I go to his office and the door is closed shut. I give it a knock, but there's no answer. "Vincent?" I call out. "I'm back now."

He still doesn't reply. I knock harder and raise my voice. "Vincent?"

Wow, this guy can take sulking to the extreme. That's the problem with dealing with creative types.

"Let me talk to him," Brianna offers, looking embarrassed by her uncle's childish behavior. She opens the door. "Vincent?"

He's sitting at his desk, but I don't understand what I'm seeing until I hear Brianna's scream. Then it's as if all the pieces suddenly fit.

Vincent is slumped forward, his head lying on his desk, almost as if he's taking a nap. But his eyes and mouth are wide-open. A pair of stainless steel scissors have been plunged into his back, and blood seeps into his crisp shirt, leaving a crimson stain.

I grab Brianna as she moves to touch him. "Call the police," I tell her. I almost say the ambulance, but it's clear that there is no saving Vincent. The guy is definitely dead.

There goes my competitive advantage, I realize with the cluck of my tongue as I stare at Vincent. I'm going to be wearing Victoria's Secret like everyone else. Damn.

Brianna hurries to her desk to call for help and I grab my cell phone. My fingers shake when I hit the speed dial. I'm not sure why I feel the need to call Leon. Probably because he is the most powerful person I know and my world just went belly-up.

I get his voice mail and that irritates me to no end. I'm there whenever he wants me. Can't he be there the one time I need him?

I wait for the beep. "This is Amaris. Vincent is dead." I pause and then look away from the body. "Murdered, really."

The police get here faster than I anticipate. In fact, I'm still walking around without panties because I decided to do the nice thing and inform Mary and Denise, who were wondering why Brianna was bawling. That'll teach me.

So I'm stuck wearing a raincoat, bustier, garter belt and stockings and black heels. I have a feeling I'm going to be fined for indecent exposure by the end of investigation. It's been that kind of day.

Mary and Denise are not taking the news any better than Brianna. The crying and screaming is getting on my nerves. I can't stand drama, unless it's mine, of course. I especially hate the waterworks when they're hypocritical. These women weren't fond of Vincent and they hate each other. So why are they sobbing over the man while clinging to and hugging each other?

The doorbell rings and Brianna blots her eyes to deal with the uninvited client. Imagine my surprise when moments later I see Kyler Thorn enter the room.

"Kyler?" I hurry over to him and pull him to the side. "What are you doing here?"

He doesn't look at me, too busy scanning the room. "I'm here for you."

Those words give me an odd buzz until I realize he doesn't look too happy about it. "Where's Leon?"

"He asked me to come in his place. In fact—" Kyler leans down and I get a faint whiff of his cologne that makes my mouth water "—it would be best if you don't mention Leon's appearance here earlier today."

Oh, I get it. I pull away from Kyler and try to hold back my anger. Leon doesn't want his appearance in a lingerie boutique questioned or revealed. He can do me in his office in front of a window for the world to see, but he can't have our association detailed in a police record.

"Kyler," I say sweetly as I bat my eyelashes, "are you asking me to obstruct justice?"

A ghost of a smile tugs at his full lips. "No, I want you to use discretion and good judgment."

"In other words, you want me to lie."

He finds no reason to answer that. Instead, Kyler strolls over to the crime scene. He unflinchingly assesses Vincent's body. "Did you do this?"

His casual tone almost shocks me as much as his words. "Hell, no!" I put my hands on my hips and glare at him. "Why would you think something like that?"

He shrugs. "Why else would you call unless it had something to do with you?"

Hmm. The guy only met me for a minute and he thinks he knows me. "Vincent was killed with a pair of scissors. Does that sound like me?" I ask with a tight smile.

Kyler looks at the body again. "I guess not. You're more of the stiletto-heel type of killer." He surveys the little group of boutique employees. "Which one do you think did it?"

I look at the women huddled to the side. "Mary," I decide. Anyone who suggests that I'm getting fat deserves the death penalty.

A police officer steps out of the office and gestures for us to move away. "This is a homicide scene. I need everyone out of the area so we can rope it off."

"Great," I hear Denise mutter. "That's really going to drive clients away."

"How long do you think they'll close us?" Mary asks.

I'm beginning to believe that they aren't crying so much for the passing of Vincent as much as from worry over their next paycheck.

Brianna dabs her eyes with a tissue. "I think we should close the store for a week in respect to Vincent."

Mary rolls her eyes. "Oh, please. When did you ever respect Vincent?"

"Excuse me?" Brianna clasps her hand to her chest. "Vincent was my uncle."

"So? I was his protégée," Mary says.

"Not quite," Denise interrupts. "You were his employee. I was his lover."

Brianna gives an inelegant snort. "I'd hardly call you lovers, Denise. You only fucked him so you could gain favors."

To my surprise, Denise doesn't take offense to that accusation. Her smile is downright triumphant. "And it worked, didn't it?"

Mary frowns. "What do you mean?"

Denise stands tall and proud. "He left the business to me."

"Whoa, whoa, whoa." Brianna waves her hands to halt the conversation. "That's not right. I'm his heir."

"Think again."

"You don't get it," Brianna says, and I can see she's going to fly into anger again. "He told my relatives that he wanted to keep the business in the family."

Mary and Denise look at each other and share a bitter laugh. "He says what he thinks you want to hear," Denise informs Brianna.

"You can say what you want. I'm his next of kin."

"So what?" Mary says. "I worked for him longer than the two of you combined. I'm the one who did all the work here and Vincent knew it."

Denise scoffs at Mary's claim. "That's no reason to reward it. You can get cheap labor anywhere. I'm the one who came up with all the designs."

I stare at Denise. *She's* the one who came up with the designs? Hope flutters in my chest for the first time since the moment I found Vincent dead. Maybe I didn't lose my secret weapon after all.

No, what am I thinking? I rub my forehead as if I can purge the thought. I might be mercenary, but I still have my limits. Denise may have murdered her boss.

Then again, I have to admire her level of commitment and ambition. This is the kind of passion I want in my lingerie designer.

"He promised me the boutique," Brianna says, her voice rising.

Denise folds her arms across her chest. "Did you get that in writing?"

Brianna thrusts her chin out. "Yeah."

Mary does a double take. "You did?"

"Today?" Denise asks.

Brianna's smugness wavers. "What are you talking about?"

"Because he showed me this today." Denise walks over to a desk by the dressing room, pulls open a drawer and retrieves the blue paper with a flourish. "I am the new owner of Vincent's."

Mary puts her hands on her hips. "Vincent's body is still warm and you're claiming the business?"

Denise glares at her coworker, obviously trying to hold back a few choice words. "This boutique changes hands upon his death."

"Excuse me, miss," the police officer in charge is suddenly at Denise's side. He points at the paper in her hands. "Where did you get this?"

"Vincent gave it to me today. Over an hour ago."

The officer skims over the words and turns to Brianna. "Do you have anything like this?"

"Yes, but it's in my safety-deposit box."

The officer turns to Mary and gives her a questioning look. She shakes her head. "First time I've seen it. What is it?"

"It's a legal document that promises me the boutique," Denise decides to answer for him. "It's signed, sealed and makes all previous agreements null and void. And there is nothing you can do about it."

"What?" Brianna yells and she bunches her hands into fists.

"It comes into effect when Vincent dies?" Mary asks, her eyebrows arching high. "You hurried up that time line, didn't you?"

Denise blinks and takes a step back as if she's just been slapped. "No, I didn't. I wouldn't. I loved Vincent."

Okay, I'm not too sure about Denise's claim on that. I never saw any gestures of affection or secret exchanges. I didn't know they were intimate until I saw her giving him head. It makes me wonder if she just realized she has shown her hand too soon and is now backtracking.

"You need to come with me, miss." The police officer takes the document from Denise's hands and guides her to a quiet corner in the fitting room.

They pass me and the officer stops. He looks at me like he just realized I'm there. His reaction doesn't do wonders for my ego. "And you?" he asks me. "Who are you?"

"I'm Amaris Martin. I came for a fitting and found Vincent's body."

He glances at Kyler who stands at my side. "And you are?"

"Kyler Thorn." He takes a step forward, blocking me with his shoulder. I can't tell if he's trying to hide me or protect me. "I'm a...friend of Amaris's."

Friend? I bite my lip. As in my benefactor? On his salary? Oh, he wishes.

But in order to keep Leon's visit a secret, we need to play pretend for a few minutes. I glance over at Brianna. For a moment she looks confused and then her eyes widen. That's when I know she understands why I'm lying.

Not that she's going to disagree. If you're selling luxury goods, you follow the one golden rule: The customer is always right. Even in a police investigation.

"I'll have someone take your statement."

The fact that the officer in charge doesn't plan to do it personally makes me think we aren't suspects. The questions they ask me seem routine. It's like they've already decided I'm a waste of time. For once, I'm perfectly happy not to be the center of attention.

The detective flips his notebook closed. "You're free to go."

"Thank you." I can't wait to go home and take a nice long

bubble bath. I hesitate and look over to where Denise is still being interrogated. If she is the true creative force of Vincent's, then I want to remove her from prime suspect status.

But how? It really hits home that I have no skills and no real ability to help myself or others. I may feel powerful and protected, but it can be taken away from me in an instant.

Kyler is suddenly in my view, getting into my personal space as he clicks off his cell phone. "Amaris, we need to leave."

I don't argue and we leave without talking to anyone. It's only when I walk into the lobby that I realize I'm still wearing the bustier and garter belt under my raincoat. I look over my shoulder at Vincent's boutique. "I need to go back and get my clothes."

Kyler grasps my elbow and propels me to the revolving doors. "There is no time."

"There is when it's a Chanel dress." And Mary is also a size two. The woman better not touch it. I saw firsthand how grabby the seamstress can be.

"Leon is waiting for you in his limo out front. He wants to talk to you on his way to the airport."

He can send me a postcard. It's so tempting to say that out loud, but I made an agreement with Leon. I don't get to take a break because I'm having a bad day. "Thanks for helping me out."

He does a double take. Does he think I'm completely without manners? "You didn't need any help," he finally says.

"You sound surprised."

His mouth slants in a smile and my heart does a funny flip. "You aren't what I expected."

He opens the back door of the limo and lets me slide in the car. My raincoat is really too short for such a maneuver. Kyler gets a glimpse of the lace tops of my stockings. As I sit down, my raincoat parts and reveals my naked pussy.

I swear, that was totally accidental. I keep my eyes straight ahead and oh, so casually cross my legs, but it's too late. I feel the tension shimmering from him. He shuts the door quickly, but he doesn't walk away. His hot gaze could sear through the smoked glass.

It's only when the limo pulls away from the curb that I exhale slowly.

"I trust everything is in order?" Leon asks as he shuffles through a sheaf of papers.

He doesn't care. If he did, he would ask for details. He would ask how I felt. "Kyler and I made sure your name didn't come up."

"Good." He tosses the paper in his briefcase and clicks it shut before leaning against his seat and studying me. My legs are crossed and my arms are folded tightly against my chest. "Take off your coat."

I bristle at his command. I hate how my body goes into full alert and I want to deny him. I want to go back home and purge the murder scene from my mind.

"Amaris?"

I reach for the sash of my raincoat and shrug it off. I look out the smoked windows and watch us zigzag through downtown Bellevue traffic. I try to act like it's no big deal that I'm sitting in the back of the limo wearing a sexy black bustier. Or that I'm wearing stockings and a garter belt without the panties.

I hear the changes in Leon's breathing. He's getting turned on. I'm glad I have the power to do that by just sitting next to him. It's good to know I can arouse him while I'm still pissed off.

Leon slides next to the center of the backseat and caresses my arm. I shiver from the soft touch, but I still look out the window. His hand brushes against the top of my breasts and my nipples tighten in anticipation.

It's really hard to focus on how we're merging onto the highway when Leon dips his hand in my bustier and cups my breast. He knows just how to fondle me to get a strong reaction. Sometimes I think my capitulation gets him aroused faster than my sexual appeal.

I close my eyes as he pinches my nipple. It sends a white-hot sensation down my body and straight to my clit. I press my lips together, determined to ignore him, but a gasp escapes from my throat when he captures my earlobe with his teeth.

"Sit on my lap," he tells me softly.

I move to straddle him, but he stops me. "No, face away from me."

Face away? What is he up to? I want to ask, but that might make it sound like I'm hesitant to turn my back on him. I do trust him—to a point.

I get up and straddle him, facing away. I lean forward, putting my hands on his knees for balance. Leon murmurs with approval as he places kisses along my bare back.

As I look forward I suddenly realize that the privacy window isn't closed. My heart stops as all the blood rushes from my skin as I stare at the back of the driver's head. I have no doubt he can hear us. All he has to do is turn his head and he will see me.

I keep my eyes trained on the driver as Leon rubs his hands over my body. He splays his fingers against my mound and slides one along my wet slit. I dip my spine and sink onto his finger, gasping as my body sucks him in.

The limo swerves into the carpool lane. I almost lose my balance and clench onto Leon's knees as he finds my clit. I can't hold back a moan as he captures the nub between his fingers and gives it a sharp pinch.

The musky scent of arousal and sex fills the limo. Every rasp of clothes and breath echoes in my ear. The cars around us are a blur as Leon fingers me.

I feel him struggling with his zipper. My core clenches with anticipation. I am so ready for his cock. He grabs my hips and guides me to the wet tip. I arch my back and take his thick cock with one thrust. Our groans mingle.

Now that Leon has a good hold on my hips, I take my hands off his knees. I grab my breasts and knead them through the bustier as I rock against him. Leon's breath snags in his throat and his fingers pinch into my skin. I would love to see his expression.

As he thrusts into me, I continue to look straight ahead. I glance in the rearview mirror, but I don't see my reflection. Instead my gaze collides with the driver's. His eyes are dark, wide, stunned.

Heat blooms into my skin. My heart pounds in my ears. The driver can see me. A wicked sensation ripples through me. How much can he see? Just my eyes? My face? My chest?

I want him to see everything. I reach for my clit and watch the driver's gaze follow my movement. I caress my clit slowly for him. Soon I'm rubbing with lightning speed as Leon pounds into me from behind. My hair spills in my face as I perform. Not for Leon, but for the driver, whose gaze keeps darting to the mirror.

I ride Leon so hard I'm breathless. My heart feels like it's going to burst from my chest. It's as if all of my senses are heightened. Each move Leon makes electrifies me. My groans are deeper and longer as the pleasure shimmers to a breaking point.

My climax comes out of nowhere. I hear my high, mewling cry as my mind tumbles. I would have lost my balance, but Leon holds me tightly as he drives his cock into me, deep and hard.

I can't catch my breath. I feel dizzy and lethargic as Leon shows no sign of slowing down. I look straight into the rearview mirror, my gaze connecting with the driver. I see the crinkles around his eyes and I know he's smiling, enjoying the show.

I see the sign welcoming us to the airport. I can't believe we're already here. I have to get Leon to come or we'll still be going at it like bunnies at the drop-off point.

As I hold the driver's gaze, I squeeze my vaginal walls tightly around Leon's cock. Leon rears back and bellows. His fingers tighten against my hips with such force it hurts as he gives one final, brutal thrust.

Leon and I don't move as the limo slows down. We're gasping for air. I feel hot and sweaty and my legs ache. I see we're approaching the airport terminal and I carefully withdraw from Leon's cock. I tumble back onto the seat, sitting on my satin raincoat.

I watch Leon readjust his clothes and smooth back his hair. The high color recedes from his face and he transforms from lover to businessman. You would never know that he just had sex in the backseat of his limo.

As the limo slows to a stop at the drop-off section of the airport, I decide to be nice. "Have a good trip," I tell Leon as he opens the door to step out.

"Be good while I'm gone."

I watch him close the door and walk away. Be good? What the hell is that supposed to mean? Is he still worried I'll mention him to the police?

I shake my head in disgust and look away. My eyes rest on the rearview mirror. I then glance at the back of the driver's head.

I return my gaze to the mirror. The driver is watching me intently. He looks like his attention is straight ahead, but his focus is all on me. What? Is he waiting for an encore?

My body jerks to attention as I remember the mirror in the fitting room at Vincent's. Nervous energy flutters in my stomach and I don't know what to do.

"Driver?"

The man pauses. "Yes?" he asks hoarsely.

"Take me back to the office," I order, and push the button to close the privacy window. I need the peace and quiet to get my thoughts together. I think I have an opportunity to save Denise, but I have no clue what I'm doing.

Once the driver drops me off at the office, I hurry through the lobby and make a beeline to the boutique. I come to a screeching halt when I see Kyler leaning next to Vincent's door, his arms crossed against his chest.

I immediately realize that the driver and Kyler were keeping tabs on me. Were those Leon's orders? No, it doesn't sound like him. Kyler has me pegged as trouble. He's probably right.

"Don't you have work to do?" I ask as I walk toward him.

"Don't you have *anything* better to do?"

"I'm not going to mention Leon," I insist as I press the doorbell. "I figured out who killed Vincent."

"*You* did?"

Okay, that might be a big, fat lie. I don't know who killed Vincent, but I know who lied. I can only see one reason why she wouldn't tell the truth, and that has to do with Vincent's death.

Then again, I could be totally wrong.

A uniformed police officer opens the door. "You can't come in. This is a crime scene."

Time to use my charm, which is really just a euphemism for my sexual allure. "I'm aware of that," I say with a friendly smile. I press my hand against my chest, drawing his eye to the plunging neckline of my raincoat. "I'm the one who found the body. I forgot something."

He lets me in and I hurry through to the fitting room before anyone gets the bright idea to stop me. The room is still packed with the criminal investigation unit. No one is on the raised dais and I step on it, facing Vincent's office, just like I did when I saw him getting a blow job.

"What did you forget?" Kyler asks.

"My clothes are in the dressing room." I say as I stare at the door to Vincent's office. "Be a dear and get those for me."

He scoffs at the idea of playing errand boy. "I don't think so."

I hop off the dais, turn to face the mirror and crouch down. Not a good thing to do in a room full of men. If anyone looks in the reflection, they are going to get a really good look at my pussy.

The investigating officer approaches me. "Ms. Martin, you are not supposed to be here."

"I understand, but I think Mary lied to you."

Mary tenses and I suddenly feel jumpy. I'm not sure if I should be doing this. I'm not one to get involved and it feels foreign to me. I rub a hand over my stomach, hoping I have this right. If either Denise or Brianna is the one who killed Vincent, then I am screwed and will never be able to shop here again.

"Can you elaborate on that?" the officer asks.

"While I was getting fitted, I saw Denise and Vincent having sex in his office."

I hear Denise's gasp and turn. She stares at me, blushing furiously. "You saw us?"

"Oh, get over it. This is going to save your ass."

"What does this have to do with Mary?" the officer asks impatiently.

"I saw him show that document to Denise. So did Mary."

Mary takes a step forward. "I did not. I was facing away."

I gesture at the mirror. "You saw it in the reflection."

She shakes her head. "I was concentrating on your hemline."

"No, you weren't. I realized this while I was in the limo and watching the driver. You were facing forward and never moved your head. You were acting like you were working when all the time you could see what was going on in the back."

"I didn't see anything."

"I thought it was strange that not once did you look back with all the grunting and animal noises going on." I give Denise an apologetic look before I continue. "But you didn't have to look back because you had a full view."

"Even if I did—which I didn't—it has nothing to do with Vincent's death."

"It has everything to do with it," I declare, hoping I'm right, "because you saw him give Denise that document with the blue paper covering. You knew what he was giving her because you have one, too."

Mary stands very straight as everyone's attention zooms in on her. Her gaze darts around the room. "No, I don't."

She couldn't make eye contact—just like a cheating boyfriend confronted with an accusation. "All it takes is a quick call to Vincent's lawyer," I remind her.

Mary presses her lips together. Is she going to call my bluff or start to backtrack? I don't have enough to prove her guilt, but all I want is to get the suspicion off Denise.

"You knew that Vincent doubled-crossed you," I say, trying to sound confident in my findings. The truth is I'm guessing. "He'd already doubled-crossed Brianna."

"And if anyone deserved the boutique," Kyler arrogantly interrupts, "it's someone who is his own flesh and blood."

"Deserves it?" Mary whirls around and glares at Kyler. "Brianna doesn't deserve it and neither does Denise. I'm the one who worked years for this man. I stayed late at night, I gave up weekends and holidays so he could meet these impossible deadlines."

"And all Denise had to do was sleep with him," I comment.

"It wasn't fair!" Mary hunches her shoulders as if Vincent's decision was too much for her to bear. "He promised me, but he took it back."

"When did he take it back?" I ask. "After I left?"

"He didn't think he did anything wrong," she says in a growl. "He stabbed me in the back, so I returned the favor."

Whoa. My eyes widen. Did she just say what I thought she did? I turn to Kyler. "That counts as a confession, doesn't it?"

The police officer seems to think so. He takes out his handcuffs and tells Mary, "I'm arresting you on suspicion of murder. You have the right to remain silent."

Oh. My. God. It actually worked! I feel a little light-headed. I think I might need to sit down, but Denise is suddenly in my face.

"Thank you, Amaris." Denise clutches my hand with hers and shakes it vigorously. Her relief is overwhelming. "I was really sweating bullets there for a moment."

"You're welcome." I lean forward and whisper, "Are you really the creative force of this boutique?"

"I am, and have been for a couple of years. I hated that Vincent took credit for my designs. He didn't do anything for the last couple of years. No paperwork, no designing. The man didn't even pick up a pair of scissors."

"Because he had arthritis in both hands?"

"How did you know?"

"It was kind of obvious." Okay, so I didn't recognize it until he shook hands with Leon today and my powers of observation aren't always great, but Denise doesn't need to know that.

"We all worked together to hide that from the clients. I don't know how we managed to share the secret. Vincent probably dangled the possibility of owning the boutique to each of us so we would keep quiet."

"And you came out on top."

"Thanks to you." Denise's smile couldn't get any wider. "And I want to show my appreciation. Take anything you want from the boutique. It's on the house."

"No, no. I couldn't." I try to decline gently. I'm not being nice. The truth is that the gift of lingerie isn't good enough. Anyway, as of now, I'm her favorite customer. I want more, and I want to see what Denise can offer.

"Then tell me how I can repay you," Denise urges me. "Name your price."

To my surprise, I don't know what to ask for. Money can

only go so far. And, after Leon's defection during my time of need, I realize that power is a nebulous, nontransferable thing. "You know what? When I need a favor, I'll call you."

I immediately know that this is the right way to go. Denise is now obligated to me. She will treat me well until I call in my favor. It's tempting never to cash it in.

Kyler walks over to me and casually grasps my arm. His touch makes me tingly, but I don't pull away. "We've overstayed our welcome, Amaris. It's time to get you home."

"Fine. Let me get my clothes." I step into the dressing room and grab my dress before leaving the boutique.

We walk into the lobby, our stride matching. We have nothing to say. I keep my eyes focused on the revolving door and I see the limo waiting at the curb. But I have one more thing to settle. "Don't tell Leon, okay?"

"Why not?"

Leon thinks all I can do is give great sex. He trusts me in his bed because he doesn't think I have the power to hurt him. It's always best if Leon underestimates me, but I don't want to say that out loud. "He didn't help and he doesn't deserve to know."

Kyler gives an impatient sigh. "Drop the attitude, Amaris. Leon can offer limited protection. If your trouble puts him in jeopardy, or if it causes him inconvenience, he won't help you."

"He sent you."

"This time."

He doesn't need to spell it out for me. I get it. If anything, the women at Vincent's have taught me a lesson. Blood and loyalty means nothing.

If I want to protect myself, I need to create my own power base. Something that is all my own and not based on being Leon Richmond's mistress. I have Denise under my thumb, but really, how much good can that do me?

"You did good back there," Kyler says, almost begrudgingly. "You're very smart."

Translation: he's surprised I have a brain. "I'm a regular Sherlock Holmes."

"I don't think he solved a crime wearing a black garter belt and bustier."

I smile and push my way through the revolving door. I don't think Kyler realizes his slip. He can't stop thinking about my outfit under the raincoat. I hope the image is branded on his mind.

"Why are you with Leon?" I don't know why I'm curious, but the need to know has been poking just under the surface since I've met him.

It's the wrong question to ask. His eyes shutter and it's like a shadow drifts across his face. "The same reason you are. For the money."

"Fine, don't tell me."

I study Kyler. He really is gorgeous. I don't care that my senses are warning he's dangerous; I want him. I could do him right here and now, but I don't offer sex for free. And I'm not screwing someone who works closely with my provider.

It's a shame. Kyler has a bright future ahead of him. I know that one day he's going to be the most powerful man I'll ever know.

I can also tell that Kyler and I are cut from the same cloth. I bet he grew up dirt poor just like me. His tailored suit can't hide the hunger inside him. The kind of hunger and fear that will never go away no matter how much power and wealth you accumulate.

And he sees it in me, too.

He opens the door to the limo for me. I slide in and my raincoat parts, revealing my naked pussy.

And this time, it's intentional.

He doesn't close the door right away and I look up at him. His eyes glitter with lust and I smile back. Kyler shuts the door with more force than necessary.

I wonder if he knows that I get him. I understand what

makes Kyler tick. He wants what he can't have. It won't matter how powerful he becomes. He is not a man to be denied.

So he will pursue what he longs for with a single-mindedness that borders on obsession. He will hunt it down, corner it and pounce. Once he gets his treasure in his grasp, he will savor it and never let it go.

I lean back in the leather seat and close my eyes as strategies and ideas bombard my mind. I need to prepare now, because one day that treasure will be me.

* * * * *

MEDUSA'S FOLLY
Alison Paige

MEDUSA LOWERED HERSELF ONTO THE STONE-hard cock, slow and easy as the smooth granite split her pussy, pressed cold and solid inside her.

In all her centuries she'd never seen a gargoyle positioned quite like this one, mounted to the corner of the castle wall, leaning over the city below. Its legs bent at the knees, muscled arms back, thick, clawed fingers and toes gripping the wall, erect penis pointing straight from its body. In fact, it was rare to find them with penises at all.

And this time she hadn't questioned her good fortune, racing from the dark Paris streets below to the barred rooftop of the ancient castle. Her pussy was already creaming her thighs as she climbed the long spiraling steps, anticipation heating though her body.

It wasn't easy getting to the thick-muscled creature. Never mind the metal gates humans erected to keep mortals from exploring the top floors of the castle—laughable. The hard part had been climbing over the edge between the battlements and scaling down to where the gargoyle clung at the corner.

Though it leaned at an angle from the building, the gargoyle's stone lap made a solid ledge beneath her ass, her feet wedged between its calves and the building to give her

leverage. The gargoyle's cock was a tight fit, the stone unfor-
giving inside her. The artist had no doubt compensated for his
own shortcomings by enhancing his creation's endowments.
Men. Her sex muscles twitched and squeezed in protest.

A moment's pause and her body adjusted, fresh juice
washing through her, creaming over the stone to slick the way.
She pushed, her arms holding around his hard neck, lifting
herself. The thick cock slid from between her legs, rippling
sensation in tiny, delicious jolts through the walls of her pussy.

The smooth, round head of its cock held her open. She
stilled, teasing her needy body, her sex muscles clenching for
more. Medusa flicked her gaze down her body to the hard
shaft poised between her legs. The gargoyle's rippled stomach
glistened with her spilled cream; the stone was darker where
her juice had stained it.

By inches she lowered herself again, driving the granite
cock inside her, impaling her body. A hundred million little
tingles vibrated through her nerves as it went, squeezing
through her chest, tightening muscles, stretching and filling
her so she could scarcely breathe.

Her ass settled on its cold lap again, its cock filling her so
deeply a sweet mix of pain and pleasure tingled at the feel of
it pushing against her cervix. Medusa took a heated moment
to admire the artistry of its body, her sex squeezing and flexing
around the stone.

Muscles ripped over the gargoyle's arms and legs, defined
its chest and thickened its neck. Its face was squarish, with a
wide nose and cat-shaped eyes. Its mouth gaped open in a
joker's grin, flashing long canines and a devilishly pointed
tongue. Its ears were pointed, as well, but not so much as others
she'd seen, and the wings molding along the wall behind it
were large and batlike.

She was fucking a stone-cold monster, but she knew of little
else fit for the task. It's not easy fucking without catching your

lover's eye, and that, for a male inside Medusa, was fatal. Not that she cared.

In her experience most men deserved the punishment of her gaze. How many had she turned to stone statues over the years? They deserved it. All of them.

Medusa banished the thoughts, and with them, the anger prickling up the back of her neck. This was not the time for revenge, for hatred. This was the time for lust and sex and sweet satiation.

Though, she thought, it would be nice to feel the warm give of male flesh inside her, the firm press of lips against hers, the spicy sweep of a tongue inside her mouth. Medusa pulled close and teased her tongue against the frozen grin of the gargoyle. She traced around the upturned corner of its lips, then down to its teeth, feeling the sharp points of its canines. She drew back, the gritty mix of dirt flooding through her mouth.

Bitter disappointment and the sour taste of loneliness coated the back of her tongue. Medusa gulped it all down, shifted her thoughts once again. She arched her back and lifted her body, brushing her excited, hard nipples against a cold granite chest.

A luscious chill raced through her breasts, sent a shiver quaking all the way down to her pussy. Her sex muscles flexed, squeezing tight around the stone cock sliding through her body. She wiggled when she reached the end, stroking her sensitive folds along the smooth head, teasing her clit with chilly touches of stone.

Medusa rocked her hips, bringing her ass in line with the slippery tip of the gargoyle's cock. She rocked back and then again, spreading her juice, wetting her tight opening. With one hand still hooked around its neck, she dropped the other to her sex.

She fondled her fingers over the swollen nub of her clit, making her breath catch as she pushed her fingers deep into the drenching heat of her pussy. Her muscles clenched around her. A building sensation coiled in her belly, tightening her muscles, squeezing through her chest.

The gargoyle's cock pressed at her anus and Medusa pressed back. Her ass clenched, both wanting and resisting the cold invasion. The promise of wicked pleasure was there. She could feel it wetting the channel of her ass, slicking her pussy, tightening the muscles of her groin. But she'd never managed to push through the sharp press of pain, the instinctive resistance.

She tried, settling her body over the hard cock, leaning back, angling her body with no concern for the precarious perch she held on the side of the castle. The fat head stretched the puckered muscles of her ass, broke through the outer rim and Medusa gasped, frozen by the quick stab of pain. She couldn't do it, not on her own, no matter how exquisite it might feel.

A shift of weight, a push of her legs and Medusa dislodged the cock from her body. Aftershocks rippled through her bottom, clenching and relaxing muscles, the pain slowly easing to nothingness.

Pleasuring herself with the rarely found stone cocks, or with less firm toys she could purchase, over the centuries had its fine points. Namely, the inexhaustible hardness. But it could also be frustratingly limiting in the way of variety.

A stone carving couldn't hold her, couldn't kiss her, couldn't press its mouth to her pussy, tease and wet her ass, coax her to relax enough to drive deep into every wanting orifice of her body. A statue couldn't speak to her, couldn't flatter her with adoration of her beauty, of her thick auburn hair, her jade-green eyes, her ample breasts and slender waist. A man carved in stone couldn't love her…and he couldn't betray her, either.

The last was all that mattered. Medusa refocused her thoughts, banishing once and for all the melancholy nonsense of her heart. The only good man was a man of stone—hard to find and good to find hard.

She rocked her hips, slid her pussy along the slick head of its cock, centering herself. Her toes curled as the hard shaft pressed inside her, smoothing between the tight clench of her walls, zinging sensation to every corner of her body.

The chilly hilt of its sex touched her outer lips. She pushed up, drawing the long cock back through her, a slow build of pressure welling through her groin.

A night breeze tingled over her breasts, cooled the exposed lower portion of the gargoyle's cock. The icy feel of stone slipping inside her as she came down again only added to the breath-stealing tingle of pleasure.

She filled her pussy with the fat, hard shaft, stroked it in and out of her body. Her juice flooded through her, each thrust churning more from her body until the granite cock was greased slick. Medusa pumped her body faster, her pussy hugging tight so every carved ripple of stone skin sent a new wave of sensation shooting through her.

Her back arched, she rubbed her breasts and her tingling nipples against the stone chest. Faster, deeper, harder, she slammed her body down onto the pillar of stone until each impalement brushed her clit against the hard curl of pubic hair at its groin. The bite of sensation ripped through her, making her rock her hips to feel it again and again.

She writhed on top of the stone monster, fucking its hard cock, tossing her head, arching her back, propelling herself faster, faster. Wicked pleasure tightened every muscle in her body, zinged along her skin, coiled deep in her belly. Her pussy tightened and flexed, adrenaline building, pressing against her flesh, pushing her to give in to the need squeezing through every fiber of her body.

Not yet. She wanted more. She wanted to ride the stone monster's cock all night.

But without warning her resolve faltered, and a gush of hot release flooded through her. Her breath caught, then shuddered from her mouth with the flutter of muscles pulsating in her sex. Her orgasm drenched the stone she pumped between her legs as she rode the last sweet spasms of her body. But just when she finally slowed to a stop, the stone cock between her legs…twitched.

Uphir's hands latched onto the feminine hips straddling his lap on reflex. The sensation of her wet pussy muscles quivering around his cock was so mind-numbing he nearly let them both plummet to the sharp slope below.

He pumped his massive wings, set the two of them aloft again. The woman clung to him, a ghostly reflex of her old, mortal life, no doubt. Uphir knew her for what she was—a goddess. No mortal woman could undo a goddess's curse. No mortal woman could undo him. He sent them higher, his cock still hard as stone—or nearly—inside her.

Hell's bells, she felt good around him, tight and wet, her pussy muscles still milking his cock with quick little spasms. He rocked his hips, lifting her as he did, so his sex slipped through her walls, stroked his shaft. Her pussy clenched, hugging him so tight he nearly blew his control right there.

Uphir pumped in and out of her again, creating an odd rhythm with the flap of his wings, but no more difficult than walking and chewing gum. By the fourth stroke, her desire loosened the knot of her arms around his neck and the lock of her ankles around his waist. He drove into her again, ramming his cock as deeply as he sensed she'd taken him in stone.

The woman reeled back, nails digging into his shoulders, arms straight, angling her body to drive his sex deeper. Her long auburn curls spilled over her shoulders, and her breasts were offered up to him, their pert tips accented by rosy circles and hard, puckered nipples.

His next hard thrust ripped a gasp from her throat, set her straight again so those magnificent green eyes opened wide on him. Their gazes met, but a moment before she focused, her brows drew tight.

"Bastard." Her eyes clouded to milky white even as the word hissed from her lips. All that beautiful hair began to twist and writhe about her head, snakes slithering, forked tongues darting in and out.

Uphir snatched her chin with one hand, wrenched her head so that lethal gaze cast out into the night. "Uh-uh, little goddess. I've already felt a stony gaze such as yours. We'll finish what you've started before another of you curses me to granite again."

But he couldn't take her body as he wanted while one hand held her aloft with him, and the other kept her gaze aimed in a safe direction. He lowered them to the castle keep, pinning her back to one of the higher projections of stone circling the top of the tower like a crown.

Breath huffed out of the woman when her back hit the stone and he rammed his cock deep, hard, mercilessly. How long had it been—centuries, aeons, an eternity? Uphir could hardly remember when last he'd felt the soft, feminine embrace of a woman's body on his.

He was beyond restraint, beyond gentleness. And, as she was a goddess with a proclivity for turning men to stone, he felt little guilt in his rough abandon. He'd met her kind once before, and found nothing pleasant in the remembrance of it.

The goddess struggled against him, but only served to wiggle herself lower onto his cock. Her protests be damned, the female enjoyed his cock inside her.

Uphir tucked his head beneath her chin, his eyes safe from her angry gaze, his hand free to do as he liked. He spied her breasts, flush and full, white creamy flesh quaking with each hard thrust. He raised a hand, then remembered his thick, clawed appendages. He didn't have the concentration or strength of will to alter his form to human.

"Forgive me, m'lady," he said, though his words were more a growl. "It's been too long, and your immortal flesh is resilient enough to risk."

He took her tiny, pebbled nipple between his fingers, careful not to nick her flesh with his razor claws. He twisted and rolled the hard little nub, and even in this thick-skinned form the feel of her was an erotic appeal that triggered everything male inside him. His hips thrust hard on reflex, driving his sex deep, ramming her body against the stone wall.

She gasped, though her body softened, her sex stretching, taking all of him. His enormous hand engulfed her breast, his long, pointed tongue flicking over the sensitive tip. She wiggled against him, pushing her little hips into him, coaxing his pace.

"Ah, the little minx likes when the monster fucks her back," he said. He pumped into her again and again, churning sensation through his body.

His heart shuddered, filling his veins with the hot sear of lusty blood. His chest squeezed at the feel of his cock sliding through the tight hug of her pussy. Her cream spilled over his balls, wetting his thighs. Her wriggling and rocking quickened, grew frenzied, as though she'd pleasure herself with his body, his pleasure be damned.

Like hell. He wasn't stone now, to be used, to be ignored. He'd fuck her better than she'd ever been fucked if not for her worrisome gaze.

"What is it you want, my little goddess?" he asked, without risking a glance at her face.

"More," she said on a shaky breath. "More. Faster. Do it."

His muscles snapped tight at her plea. "Close your eyes, you vengeful wench, and I'll fuck you raw."

"Yesss…" She leaned back, flattening herself to the wall, giving him space to move.

He straightened slowly, holding her with one hand under her

ass, the other crushing over her breast. Her weight was nothing to his supernatural strength and he pinned her to the spot.

Good as her word, the goddess kept her eyes squeezed tight, though her hair still writhed and hissed about her head.

"That's my good little minx," he said, leaning close to trail the long point of his tongue up her neck to tease her ear. Her body shuddered, the spasm vibrating all the way down through her pussy and over his cock.

He gasped at the unexpected sensation, his muscles snagging through his balls, jerking the swollen flesh of his sex inside her. *Enough of these games.*

Uphir leaned back, his gaze dropping to the connection of their bodies. Her slender legs stretched wide around his waist, the small lips of her sex open on him, his penis buried deep inside her. He pulled back, watching the long length of him slip from her body, the shaft glistening.

He knew his sex was big by human standards—longer, fatter, more that of a beast than a man. But she took him to the hilt when he thrust into her again, and hugged him tight through the backward draw. He pushed into her again, the snug fit of her body rippling sensation through every square inch of his, from the point of his ears through the quaking muscles of his thighs to the very tips of his wings.

He clenched his jaw, fighting hard to resist the tide of pleasure swamping over him, pushing him to the edge of release.

Not yet. Not yet. He'd waited too long, suffered too much to let it slip through his grasp with a few fluttering hugs from the first pussy he tasted.

But the sensation tightening through his gut, tugging muscles along his thighs, squeezing through his chest, was not easily refused. Uphir rocked his hips, thrusting deep, his skin tingling with the feel of her body clutching hard around his cock. He pushed again, and then again, going faster, watching as his shaft drilled through the tight, wet entry of her body.

She opened wider, allowing him to go deeper, faster, and Uphir's heart shuddered with the spike of excitement her invitation sent surging through his veins. Pressure swelled too fast within him, tightened his body beyond his control. The tempting call of release was too sweet, too needed, to resist, and his body toppled over that imaginary edge, the rush of his surrender exploding in a gush of liquid heat from his sex.

But the wicked little goddess wasn't finished with him. She writhed and squirmed at the end of his cock, pumping her slender hips, her pussy milking his semihard cock for all it could.

He pushed into her, filled her with the softening meat of his sex, and she squirmed for more. He rolled his hips, stroking her as best he could even as her eager little jerks and wiggles teased his cock into stirring again.

She stopped suddenly, and huffed a frustrated sigh. "Enough. I can't allow this. You've enjoyed more than you deserve. Time to return you from whence you came."

Uphir had a moment to puzzle out her meaning through the fog of his blood-starved male mind. It wasn't enough. The lithe goddess opened those milky eyes of hers and turned them upon him.

Their gazes met and Uphir gasped at the sharp stab to his heart. But it wasn't the hard freeze of stone that squeezed through his chest upon seeing her…it was love.

CHAPTER TWO

LOVE AT FIRST SIGHT. IT WAS THE ONLY WAY
Medusa could ever know the elusive emotion. She never had.
She never wanted to.

"Unhand me, you beast," she said, her tone acidic.

"It's not my hand that holds you, m'lady."

Medusa tried hard not to squirm with the feel of his penis
quickly swelling inside her, filling her up to bursting. The
wicked impertinence. He'd take her again. She'd see that he
paid dearly for his brazenness—never mind how glorious it felt.

Did he not know who she was? What deadly, stone-cold
power she wielded? She'd turn him to—

"Why aren't you stone?"

"Give me a minute, goddess, it's getting there."

Oh, that wicked joker's grin on his beastly face incensed her
last nerve. "Not your penis, you dolt. All of you. Why have
you not turned to stone?"

He shrugged, an easy roll of his massive shoulders that made
his black wings bob behind him. "Perhaps I'm already stone
and it's only the sweet nectar of your pussy that keeps me flesh.
I was made of flesh once. Long ago."

"Clearly you've mistaken me for someone who cares," she said, noting the stone-gray color of his skin. "If it's my pussy that keeps you flesh then the lack of it should return you to form."

She raised a leg, the shift of muscles over his cock sending a warm tremble through her sex, and wedged her foot against his hard belly. With her hands on his chest and her foot on his stomach, she pushed, using all her goddess strength to unsheathe his sex from hers.

The gargoyle stumbled back, his stiff erection wagging from his body, wet and shiny with her pussy's cream. Medusa fell the few feet to the floor from where he'd held her, landing with the grace of a goddess. She straightened, resisting the urge to snag her tunic from where she'd dropped it when his lust-filled gaze raked over her.

Let him look. Precious few before him had ever enjoyed the privilege. They were solid stone before they could even take in the full beauty of her face. Again she wondered, why wasn't he?

"Who are you, gargoyle? Who made you? Who placed you on this castle?"

"To begin with, I am not a gargoyle," he said, and his voice resonated through her body. It was truly the voice of a beast. The sound was too deep, too filled with power. It was as though his words echoed from within the massive frame of the monster, just as it echoed through her head, through her body, vibrating through all the sensitive parts of her feminine flesh.

"Then are you a god or a devil?" she asked.

He propped his hands on his hips, the roll of muscle across his chest distracting her gaze. "Tell me your name before I take that sweet body of yours again. It's been a long while and I've not had my fill by half."

"What are you?"

"What's your name?" he insisted.

"How did you come to be frozen in stone on the side of this castle?" she asked.

"Your name?" he snorted. "Glare at me all you want with those ghostly eyes. I'll not turn back to stone. I'm flesh now and you see how this flesh strains for yours." He glanced at his erection and back at her so she couldn't help following his gaze.

Her mouth watered, her body warming at the sight. "Medusa."

"Medusa," he said as though the word had form and substance he could feel and taste on the tip of his pointed tongue. "Daughter of Athena, are you?"

She blinked. What did he know of the goddess who'd gifted her? "How dare you speak her name, beast? To hell with you."

"To hell indeed." He laughed, and the sound rolled through the air like thunderclouds, stealing her breath as it engulfed her body.

The laughter stopped like a thing unplugged and his face turned hard and cold. "Trust me, little one. I've damn well earned the right to speak her name. I spit it from my lips as I would a bitter poison. And yours right along with it if your loyalty lies with her."

It did, but she hesitated to admit it.

His sex hadn't wilted one bit for his anger, and the memory of it stiff between her legs still tingled through the muscles of her pussy. He was as thick and hard as he'd been in stone. Only now that stone-hard erection was gloved in velvet-soft skin and made of flesh and meat that would give and bend and twitch inside her.

A warm shiver tingled up her spine at the thought and her gaze shifted to the creature's face. He flashed that joker's grin again, reading the lust in her eyes as easily as a picture book.

Having her gaze met eye to eye unnerved her. Having her thoughts exposed and read from her face was just damn annoying. "I've told you my name—now tell me yours. Tell me what you are and how it is that you meet my gaze and not have your flesh and innards turn to stone."

"I cannot tell you what I don't know," he said.

"Then tell me what you do know, and quickly. For you are right. I am a goddess and by all that I am I *will* find a way to end you should you displease me." She stiffened, chest out, chin high, knowing full well her body was a form to be proud of.

His narrow brows hiked high on his wrinkled, hairless head. His long, pointed tongue flicked along his lips, the very tip resting for a tantalizing second at the corner of his mouth. Lord, what he must be able to do with that tongue.

Medusa banished the thought before her blasted face betrayed her again.

"Then I shall make every effort to please you, goddess." His voice lowered. "In every way."

She shuddered as the thought and sound warmed through her body.

"My name is Uphir. And I am, as you suspected, not of this world." His big, fisted hands dropped from his hips as he took one casual step toward her, then another and another. His progression was slow but sure, closing the distance between them.

She swallowed hard, feeling his growing nearness as surely as if he'd reached out to her. Her body tensed, her pussy slicking, readying for the cock that wagged before him.

"Not of this world? That's as helpful as describing a particular star as bright. What are you, Uphir? Is this your true form?"

"I am demon," he said. "And yes, this is my birth form. But it is not the form in which I once walked this plain. It is not the form in which I drew the goddess's curse."

"Athena?" What could he have done to bring her mother goddess's wrath? "Show me your alternate form."

"So you're not frightened by the term *demon?*"

Medusa scoffed. "Certainly not. I've not been human for aeons. Human religion, zealots, ignorance corrupted the word long after I became what I am. No," she said. "I know there are as many races of demons as there are humans, and one no more predestined to evil than the other."

He circled behind her, his breath a faint, warm breeze across her shoulders. The sensation set her skin on fire, lust tightening every muscle, coiling low in her belly. She closed her eyes to better withstand it, to better enjoy it.

"I see. Clever little goddess." His lips brushed her ear, breath hot on her neck and smelling of warmed brandy. The head of his cock nudged the top of her ass, made her breath catch. He flicked his tongue, teasing her lobe, and again her mind flashed on all the erotic possibilities.

She fought her body's treacherous reaction, cleared her throat and forced a strength into her voice she didn't feel. "What passed between you and Athena? How did you draw her wrath?"

"How?" He laughed, and it was the same rumbling thundercloud laugh as before. But this time his chest pressed against her back and the sound rumbled straight through her, filling her from head to toe.

"I was too pretty. That's how," he said.

Medusa snapped her gaze over her shoulder. "Too pretty?" She couldn't fathom it.

Uphir was tall, broad-shouldered, thick-muscled, with a cock fit for the most insatiable of female needs to be sure, but pretty? His face was not so much ugly as frightening. A mix of beast and man. Devilish, mortals would call him.

He reached up and traced her cheek to her chin with a gently laid claw, razor sharp. "Your eyes are stunning when not clouded white with fury."

She jerked her chin back around, ignoring how his touch sent a thousand tingles rippling through her belly. The monstrous creature made her body ache for his. What must his alternate form be like?

"Show me," she said, her voice too weak, too breathy with need. *Curses.* She loathed such vulnerability.

"What? My true form? To you, daughter goddess to she who cursed me to stone for all eternity?" He snorted a laugh. "I think not."

Uphir snagged her in a breath-stealing hug, pulled her back tight to his body, his cock thick and full along the crease of her ass, the small of her back. His clawed gray fingers splayed across her belly, sliding warm and heavy toward the apex of her thighs. His other hand kneaded her breast, teasing the hard, sensitive nipple.

"Besides," he said, hot and breathy against her ear, "I can bring you far more pleasure in this form. A truth which your dear mother failed to consider. I am Uphir, the handsome, renowned lover of woman, who refused to bed a goddess at her command. She froze me in stone, captured me for all eternity in a form she thought hideous. Forever ready for a woman, but never again to be desired, to be loved, to be fucked." He squeezed his arms around her. "Until you, Medusa, her daughter, mounted my ugly, stone-hard cock."

Medusa's breath caught, her exhale shaky, shallow, as the hot point of his tongue caressed along the sensitive flesh behind her ear. A tidal wave of pleasure zinged over her skin, crashing through her body, flooding her sex.

Her knees buckled, but his hold, and her pride, caught her, firmed her legs. She swallowed against her arid mouth, licked her lips. "You're free now. By whatever means, you *are* free. I've no further need or want of you. Release me and let us both go our separate ways."

He laughed, that deep, rumbling belly laugh that left her weak and breathless. "No further need of me? Little goddess, I can smell the sweet cream of your pussy from here. I can feel the wanton heat of your womb through your belly, warming my palm. If you wish to go, to be free of me, then leave. You're a goddess. I am but a lowly demon. It's not my strength or will that holds you."

It was true, she knew. He'd be no match for her goddess strength, but mounting the will to break his embrace required far more of her than simple physical ability. She squirmed weakly, a pathetic display. And Uphir's hold on her snapped iron-tight.

"I'm impressed. You'd deny your body to spare your pride?"

"I'm not ruled by my body," she said, finding the will to squirm again, though the way her body warmed and softened in his embrace, she scarcely believed her words. Medusa had vowed long ago never to allow a man to rule her in any way. But tonight, for the first time in aeons, with this man, this creature, she wanted to be ruled, to be dominated. And that, more than anything, made her squirm again.

Uphir's hold tightened once more. "Fascinating. I can't say I've ever met a woman with such inner strength. I like it. More than you know. Very noble. I, however, am not so noble. At least not tonight. Tonight I am a slave to my body's needs, and to yours."

He bent his knees, dropping lower, and rocked his hips up so his cock slid hard against her, spreading the cheeks of her ass. "And your body needs mine."

The powerful demon spun them both, turning her to face the low opening at the top of the castle wall, where warriors of old had peeked to shoot their arrows and spears. Even this low wall came to her waist, so when Uphir bent her over along the thick ledge her legs were straight, her feet firm on the floor.

"Mmm, such a lovely view," he said, then traced a clawed finger over the wet lips of her pussy and along the long crease of her ass.

She glanced over her shoulder, watched him lower to his knees behind her and knew, instinctively, his plans. Her breath caught in her chest, her sex muscles flexed and slicked. She looked away, squeezing her eyes tight, her heart thundering in her ears.

With one swift stroke, she no longer had to imagine all he could do with that long, pointed tongue. It pressed between the sensitive folds of her pussy, licking straight up to her ass. A powerful quiver shook her body in its wake, from her toes up her legs, through her pussy and up her spine, leaving her body in a hot rush of breath.

"Mmm, the taste of a female. It's been too long." And he licked again, the firm point of his tongue fondling over her clit, pressing up to the entrance of her body. He drove his tongue inside her, its length and width and firmness like a tiny cock that could wiggle and curl inside her.

Her sex clamped around that long, wicked tongue. She gasped, pressed her hips back against his face on reflex. His fingers clenched on her buttocks, the razor points of his claws denting her flesh. He spread her wider, held her open even as she pushed her feet farther apart.

His tongue slithered in and out through her walls, sending ripples of pleasure to every corner of her body. He flicked the tip deep inside her, finding the spot that made her writhe like a thing gone wild against his face. He brought her over, her release flooding into his mouth, spilling down her legs, wetting her from clit to anus. He drank it in, coaxed her sex for more.

Medusa's breath came in ragged heaves, her knees weak, her head low between her shoulders as her fingers white-knuckled over the edge of the castle wall. Uphir withdrew his lascivious tongue from her pussy, lapping up her come, slicking his way to her anus.

But when he flicked the firm, moist tip over the puckered opening, her whole body tensed. Heat flooded through her, her mind doing more to ready her body than anything Uphir could accomplish. For the first time in her long life she'd know this pleasure. She wanted it, feared it, relished it.

"Relax," he said, pressing a warm kiss to the cheek of her ass. "No other man can give you this as I can. I was made for this."

He swiped his firm tongue over her anus again, then swirled the tip, teasing the tight hole. Her body shuddered at the feel, muscles pushing, opening on reflex. He'd moved a hand to her clit without her notice, so when the round of his knuckle stroked over the sensitive nub she flinched, then arched her back, pressing into his touch.

Uphir tasted her again, his knuckle working her clit while his tongue pushed and teased against her ass. Liquid heat gushed through her sex, and her muscles flexed, eager to be filled. The wet press of his tongue pushed through the puckered outer rim of her ass, and Medusa's breath caught.

Sensation swelled within her, like the constant pluck of a cello string, building and humming through her clit, vibrating within the muscles of her sex, pulsing down the channel of her ass. Uphir stroked in and out of her anus, going deeper as her body opened, his tongue never too large, never too hard, filling her perfectly.

Her legs spread wide, opening her to him, her hands tight on the castle wall, Medusa's body caught the rhythm, rocking faster, driving Uphir's wicked tongue into the forbidden depths of her body. Her pussy gushed hot and wet, muscles clenching air, mimicking the tight grip of her ass.

He tugged her clit between his knuckles, sending jolts of pleasure sizzling through her body again and again. Her chest tightened, skin humming from the top of her head to the soles of her feet. The tiny spasms mixed and mingled with the filling thrusts in her ass, and the maddening emptiness pulsing through her pussy.

As though he were pulling the trigger of a gun, Uphir stroked the back edge of his claw against the gaping, needy entry of her sex and Medusa's body exploded in a tidal wave of liquid heat. Her release pulsed threefold through her sex, her clit and her ass, each response slightly different, each one enhancing and propelling the others.

Her orgasm washed over her, roaring through every fiber of her body, exploding through muscle and meat, tweaking sensitive nerves. Pleasure hummed along her skin until every part of her gave way to it, and her knees buckled beneath her.

Uphir moved fast, catching her, hugging her to his hard chest. They crumpled to the floor, Medusa resting on his lap, leaning her head against the stone wall, her breaths ragged, shallow.

A smile bloomed from the very depths of her soul. "That was...dear goddess, what was that?"

He kissed the back of her shoulder. "Your future...if you wish it."

Medusa managed to raise her head to glance over her shoulder. She scoffed at the earnest look on his face. "Years of living as stone have affected your brain, demon. Or perhaps your brain has always been thick as stone."

His brow knitted along his ashen forehead, and then before her eyes that forehead flushed with color. His head sprouted rich golden hair. His eyes rounded, turned a pale sky-blue, and the claws hugging around her shrunk to thick fingers, meaty hands. Within seconds it wasn't a monster that held her, but a man, big and breathtaking.

"You are a goddess who cannot love or be loved without turning your lover to stone," he said. "And I am a creature that cannot live but for the touch of you. We were meant for each other, Medusa. End my imprisonment, end your years of bitter loneliness."

"And if you turn to stone again?"

"I'm filled to overflowing with your sweet nectar, little goddess. If the cream of your pleasure is indeed my magic elixir, I'll not be turning to stone anytime soon."

The thought streaked through her mind and stabbed her heart. She'd never even considered the possibility of a companion. Not once since the day she'd become what she was.

Why? Why now, why him? She'd felt something strange the

moment she'd seen him from the dark Paris streets below. Something that had called to her, propelled her up those long, twisting stairs, over the high edge of the castle wall and down to his cock. Something that had made her want to feel him inside her, to touch him, kiss him.

Was it simply that she'd never gazed into a man's eyes before and had him gaze back? Or was Uphir able to gaze back because no other man was meant to?

A strange heat pressed through her chest, squeezed around her heart. It warmed her, filled her up so she could scarcely breathe. Was this…love?

Ice raced up her spine.

No. Panic.

"YOU ASSUME TOO MUCH, DEMON. I'M NEITHER lonely nor desirous of love. And stone is how I like my lovers best," Medusa said, her expression suddenly as hard and cold as Uphir had been before she came to him. He didn't believe it for a second.

He hiked a brow, tried to temper his smile. "And when was the last time one of your stone lovers licked you from clit to ass and sent you crashing over the brink into bliss?"

"Approximately the same time one of them bored me with male boasting and insipid talk of love and loneliness. I'm not convinced the pleasure of one is worth the torture of the other." She stood, shedding his embrace, and strode the short distance to where her white dress lay in a crumpled heap.

She bent, giving him a heart-clenching view of her ass, then straightened as she readied the garment to slip over her head. "What is it about the male ego that requires every little ac-complishment be applauded?"

"Little?" He nearly choked. Uphir swallowed his pride and crossed the distance to her.

"Give a woman a simple orgasm and you'd think he snatched a star from the heavens." She raised her arms, letting the dress slip down her arms and over her head. "Honestly, I've had toys that accomplished as much, and their greatest request was that I flip a switch and spare the battery."

Uphir snagged the silky fabric just as it fell to her breasts, and whipped it back off her before she had the chance to lower her arms. "Careful, little goddess, or I'll begin to think you don't like men at all."

Medusa seemed to tamp back her surprise, masking the shock that flashed through her eyes by narrowing them to slits. She knotted her arms under her breasts. "No bruised egos or cries for accolades? No concern for a man's selfish needs or what little care he'll give to me in order to satisfy those needs? Synthetic or stone, with Zeus as my witness, I'd choose either to spare the pain and bother that comes with a flesh-and-blood man."

"And a woman is any less of a bother? Any less selfish or careless?" Uphir snorted.

"Of course women can be troublesome," she said. "But I'd wager the last woman you bedded before me didn't blather on about her carnal skills or propose a lifetime together after one hearty release."

"You'd be surprised."

"I'm certain you never once feared for your life in the face of a woman's desire. Or had your virtue ripped away because to gaze upon you filled your lover with such beastly passion she couldn't temper her lust."

His thoughts flashed to the goddess Athena. "I must admit, my virtue was offered up willingly aeons ago, and I've never feared for my death. But my life…? A woman's *beastly* lust kept me frozen in stone for centuries. Trust me. I'm alive, but I haven't been living. I have your mother to thank for that."

She stiffened at his comment. "Athena is not my mother, but she did gift me the life I have now. She made it so no man can be lost to his passion at the sight of me again. She made it so no man can survive my gaze."

"Save for me," he reminded her.

Medusa exhaled in a sniff through her nose and looked away. "Yes. Save for you, it seems. And you're all the more treacherous to me for the talent."

"Treacherous?" Uphir laughed out loud. He couldn't help it. "This coming from a woman with not only the power for stone-cold vengeance, but a taste for it? Much like your malicious benefactress, I might add."

Medusa's ghost-white eyes snapped to his, her auburn hair suddenly slithering and hissing about her head. "No more malicious than the men who seek to dominate her."

He scoffed. "Rot. No one dominates a goddess. No one dominates you."

"Indeed. Not for centuries." Medusa closed the small distance between them, her nipples brushing his chest, snakes snapping and hissing at his face, making his body war with itself for the proper response.

"But once, long ago, a young girl entered the house of Athena in worship, in reverence," Medusa said, "and was brutally attacked, *dominated* by a man, a god."

"Poseidon," Uphir said.

"Yes." The word hissed from her lips like the snakes slithering on her head. "That girl will never be dominated by another. Never."

Uphir had remembered, the moment Medusa spoke her name, the sad tale of her creation—beauty igniting lust, lust driven to rape, sparking centuries of unspeakable vengeance.

His chest squeezed as he now realized her story was true. "And how long will you permit him to rule you?"

Medusa flinched as though he'd slapped her. "No one rules me. I'm a goddess. I am endless."

"Yes. And aeons ago you were a helpless girl on the floor of Athena's temple, violated, alone, consumed with anger and pain. From that day to this, what has truly changed?"

"I...I am not the girl I was." She blinked and when her eyes opened again they were the color of new spring leaves—green and bright. Her hair coiled in soft wine-colored ringlets over her shoulders and down her back, and her voice lost its unearthly wrath. "I am powerful. Untouchable."

"You're still filled with anger and vengeance, lashing out at the man who wronged you by striking down all things male," he said. "But even a goddess can't end a god, and in the absence of that you cannot, and have not, moved on. He dominates you still, Medusa."

She shook her head, staggered back a step. "No."

"Yes. In all these years what have you done that hasn't been because of him, because of what he did to you? What have you done for yourself, for your pleasure rather than to spite your pain?"

She shuffled back another step, confusion glazing her all-too-human eyes. "I am a goddess."

"Through your pain and fear and rage, he's kept you the same scared young girl you were all those years ago. Forever alone. Forever unable to love or be loved." Uphir reached for her, pulled her to him. "You have the power to thwart him once and for all, Medusa...by letting go. By feeding your pleasure, instead of your pain."

Her eyes focused, connected with his, and then a familiar determination wrinkled her brow. "My pleasure? To feed my pleasure I would feed on you."

Uphir's heart pinched, his body again at war with itself, unsure of her meaning. His cock twitched as a chill raced down his spine. But when those determined green eyes dropped to his sex, he understood her intent.

"I've never tasted a man." She licked her lips, her hand reaching for him. "So soft. Like velvet."

A wash of tingles raced over his body and up his cock, following the tentative stroke of her fingers. His whole body shuddered, the gentle touch a torturous tease. He was hard as steel in an instant, filling her small hand so she could scarcely touch finger to thumb around him.

She slid her grip along his shaft, from head to root and back again, stopping beneath the thick mantel of its tip. She brushed her thumb over the tiny cleft opening, spreading a bead of come he hadn't realized had escaped. His breath caught at the wicked sensation, a jolt of pleasure shooting through him, snapping muscles tight.

His thighs trembled, need swelling fast and hot through his gut, tugging through his balls. As a man, Uphir wasn't as large as he was in demon form, but he was still more than most mortal women could endure. Despite her long life, Medusa was inexperienced, and suckling a man his size called not just for experience, but for practice.

"I'm afraid I'm not sized for learning, little goddess," he said. "And having you try and fail might prove more maddening than having you not try at all."

Her gaze met his and she hiked a brow, her expression mischievous and sexy. "I'm willing to take the risk."

Hell's bells, so was he.

One hand gripping tight around his cock and the other slipping down to cup his balls, Medusa lowered to her knees before him, her bright green eyes still locked with his. "My mouth waters for want of this, though I must admit, it irks me that this may please you as much as me. Old habits. But you're right. In denying you to spite Poseidon, I deny myself. I won't give him that power over me any longer."

"I shall endeavor to temper my enjoyment, if it helps."

"That's a good demon," she said, her breath warm over the head of his cock. Electric tingles rippled down his back, tightened muscles through his chest and gut and legs. His breath caught when her moist red lips parted over him, and his knees trembled as she drew him deeper and deeper into her mouth.

Sultry heat surrounded him, and he realized suddenly that with all her inexperience, his last experience had been so long ago as to make the simple feel of her enough to shred his tenuous control. His hips rocked forward, pushing his sex deeper, the tip nudging the back of her throat. Medusa withstood the press, holding him for a brief instant before drawing her lips up his shaft.

Sweet suction tugged along the sensitive skin, her fingers rolling and squeezing his balls. Uphir dropped his hands to her wealth of auburn hair, gripped her head and rocked his hips back until the mantel of his cock slipped through her lips. And then he pushed into her again.

Medusa fell into the method and rhythm by the third thrust, her free hand slipping around to latch onto his ass, taking control, setting the pace, the depth. His cock filled her mouth, drove down her throat, and still his little goddess milked him for more.

Sensation roared through his body, heat sizzling through his veins, racing toward his cock. The mix swelled within him, tightening through his balls, pulling his muscles, pushing him closer, harder, toward the edge of release. Uphir closed his eyes, clenched his jaw, fighting to make it last.

Each second he succeeded only heightened the wicked pleasure, made it harder to resist. A mind-numbing circle of denial, rewarded by pleasure, built upon itself inside him until he could barely breathe, could scarcely think.

And then his cock slipped from her mouth, a cool night breeze scattering his thoughts. He opened his eyes, but his brain couldn't reason as he watched her lean into him again, lower. His breath exploded from his lungs when the moist heat of her mouth engulfed his balls.

White-hot pleasure slammed through his body, knee-buckling jolts surging up his cock, pounding mercilessly at his control. His chest squeezed so tight his breaths came in short, shallow gasps, and still Medusa toyed with his body.

He fisted his cock, stroking himself hard, fast, the way he wanted to fuck her mouth. His muscles flinched and twitched each time she rolled her tongue, tugged him harder. It was too much. He was too sensitive, too close to the edge. He couldn't take it, wouldn't last. He could hardly stand.

Uphir rocked back, pulling his tight sack from her mouth. "Enough. I've not waited centuries just to cream my own hand."

He tried to pull her to her feet, but Medusa resisted, her eyes meeting his, lids low, sexy, gazing up the length of him. His stiff penis nudged her cheek, her lips wet, glistening.

"I'll say when it's enough, demon. You'll hold your seed until I draw it from you. How and when is for me to decide."

Hot blood rushed his cock at her commanding tone. Precious few women could keep their wits about them while indulging in carnal pleasures with him. He was made to drive a woman insane with lust. But Medusa's focused desire was a wholly unexpected delight and so strangely satisfying. He hiked a brow, felt the tremor of a smile at the corner of his mouth. "Yes, my goddess. As you wish."

Medusa's simmering green eyes stayed locked with his, watching as his mind fogged. She licked the very tip of his sex, sending a warm shudder straight through his groin. She opened wide, devouring him, taking his cock all the way to the hilt.

Uphir rocked his hips forward, his hands fisting her hair, and together they drew apart, her cheeks hollowing with her hard suction.

Like the stirred embers of a low-glowing fire, Uphir's lust flamed to life. All at once he fought the strong pull of release again, teetering on that titillating precipice, fighting not to tumble too soon. His skin hummed, sensation vibrating over every inch of his body. His heart thundered in his ears, his muscles trembling with restraint.

He thrust his cock deep, just as her nails dug into his ass, tugging him to her. The exquisite suction of her mouth never faltered, drawing his release closer and closer to the surface, like the swirling pull of water through a drain.

There was no way to deny the tow toward orgasm, only delay it. Pressure built, the sensation fogging his head, swirling through his groin, coiling his muscles, pulsating along his cock. Until he couldn't delay a moment longer.

"Goddess…" He meant to warn her, but the thought occurred too slowly, and his release exploded from his body too swiftly for words.

She drank him in, his seed filling her mouth, spilling down her throat. Medusa luxuriated in him as though he'd been filled with sweet wine, suckling his softening sex, eager for more.

"Is my goddess pleased?" he asked when she let his sex slip from her lips.

Her gaze flicked to his, her bottom lip plump, almost pouting. "No," she said, radiating confidence. "I've been so consumed with making men pay I had no idea how glorious it could be to collect." She straightened, rubbing her soft, feminine body up the length of his.

Uphir's heart shuddered then pounded faster. Blood rushed hot through his veins, filled his sex. Medusa was in complete control, and Uphir struggled to wrap his brain around the thrill of it. Not even the goddess Athena had been able to rule him sexually. Why was he so excited to find that Medusa could?

"My body calls to you, demon. Tend to me." She slipped a hand between them, gave a firm squeeze to his cock.

Suddenly he didn't care why she could rule him, but only that she never stopped. "As you wish, little goddess."

THE EMOTIONS TWISTING THROUGH HER HEART were unlike anything she'd ever known. Even in her mortal life she couldn't remember feeling this way, feeling so...safe.

Medusa took Uphir by the hands and tugged, encouraging him to follow as she led him across the castle keep to a small stone box along the wall.

"Sit," she said, and he obeyed.

What use did she, a goddess, have for these feelings? Nothing could harm her. She was immortal. She was always safe. So why did this sensation warming through her chest stir her notice? Medusa didn't want to think on it.

Uphir's deep blue eyes gazed up at her, so human, so male.

"Change to your true form, demon."

"Why?" His brows knitted. "You don't like this form?"

Human? "No."

His smile flashed across his lips until he seemed to realize she wasn't joking. He stiffened, cocking his head to the side, his confused expression making him all the more adorable. "But women have always found me stunning—irresistible."

"I'm not a common woman. I am a goddess, and I prefer your birth form. Now do as I command," she said. "This is for my pleasure, after all. Isn't it?"

"That's not the reason."

Medusa blinked, her brain scrambling to understand. Was he asking a question or making a statement? Either way, how dare he? "It's not for you to say, demon. Now, shift forms."

"No." He stood, bringing his mouth level with her eyes. "You want this body, just as it is. I can feel your desire, the energy sparking between us."

She couldn't help watching his mouth form the words, the way his bottom lip caught under his top teeth for an instant when he said "feel." A warm shudder shook across her shoulders, sending ribbons of heat straight to her center. She wanted to feel those strong, soft lips on hers, to taste him, to kiss him.

A mental shake brought her back to her senses. She flicked her gaze to his, hardened her heart. "Impressive, demon. To say no to a goddess epitomizes bravery. To do so twice, however... Perhaps Athena's punishment has done more damage than meets the eye."

"I only refuse your request because I know it's not really what you want."

"Typical man," she scoffed. "So consumed with your own wants you can't fathom a woman's would be any different. I've seen hundreds, thousands, of beautiful men during my life. Trust me. Your beauty is not so enticing to a goddess. You're merely...human."

"Human," he repeated. "*Your* birth form. The form you're predisposed to find appealing. The same form Poseidon took when he came to you in the temple all those years ago."

His hands smoothed up her arms, made her shiver. She squirmed away from his touch. "Make your point."

"You're still doing it. Still denying yourself to punish him."

"Or perhaps Poseidon's actions have simply destroyed my appetite for the human male. And now you have destroyed my appetite for everything else." She turned to walk away, escaping, she knew, but Uphir snagged her arms, held her.

"I don't believe you. Your face is flushed, your skin is hot to the touch and—" he inhaled deeply through his nose as though savoring her aroma "—I can smell how your body's creamed and ready for me."

Medusa twisted her arms, but Uphir's grip tightened around them, tugged her to his chest, crushing her breasts against him. She could've broken free, but the feel of his warm flesh on hers, his hard cock pressing a line along her belly, made her heart race, thundering in her ears. Her chest squeezed. She didn't want to be free of him.

But she couldn't let him have her, not in that form. If she gave in to the swell of heat he sent flooding through her body, it would be like saying that Poseidon in human form had appealed to her, as well. How could she justify the difference? Why did one human man make her body melt and so many others freeze her to the core with disgust? What was the difference? They were all men, all human. What was wrong with her?

"I won't hurt you, Medusa." His thumbs stroked small circles on her arms, his grip still firm. "Poseidon was only interested in what he could take from you. That's not me. I want to *give* to you, Medusa, everything and anything you need. I want to help you, the same way you've helped me."

The warmth stirring in her chest spread, heating through her body with his words. He met her eyes, held her gaze confidently, earnestly. And then suddenly she knew what was different.

Uphir actually meant what he said…and she believed him.

The steel line of her shoulders eased, her body softening against his. A cool breeze washed over her skin and she breathed it in, let it cleanse her, then blew it out. With her exhale went the sharp edge of fear and mistrust she'd been clinging to for centuries.

"What then? You plan to take me to bed and make sweet,

human love to me?" Her words dripped with sarcasm, but her heart fluttered at the thought. She was no virgin, but never in all her life had a man made love to her.

"Yes," he said, then chuckled. The sound was low, more a rumble in his chest. "At least I would…if I had a bed to take you to."

Medusa couldn't help the smile tugging at the corners of her mouth. "Foolish demon. I am a goddess. The universe bends to serve my will."

At that, she stretched out her power, calling on the winds to bring her the materials she desired. She commanded molecules to part and reform, the earth and sand to mold to her need. She watched Uphir's eyes widen as he took in the magic swirling around him.

The thick layer of dirt and fine stone coating the roof of the castle rushed like water beneath their feet until not a speck was left unmoved. It gathered in front of them, piling up to form a circle eight feet around and two feet high.

A moment later the night sky filled with downy white feathers, whirling on the breeze like falling snow, spinning and churning their way toward the circle of earth. Many of the downy flakes caught in the strings of pure raw silk streaming through the air, weaving together as they watched, binding the feathers in a mattress as soft as clouds atop the earthen bed.

She glanced over her shoulder at the bed when she knew all was done. Her belly rolled, uncertainty fighting with the need inside her. "There's your bed, demon…human."

"What luck," Uphir said, and Medusa swung her gaze back to his. Uphir's eyes were no longer wide with awe; they were intense, hungry and focused on her.

The look in his eyes sent a shudder quaking down her spine. She could almost feel the primal need radiating through him, tightening muscles, making his body hard as flesh over stone beneath her hands.

He scooped her into his arms, cradling her. Her arms looped around his neck. Three steps brought them to the bed and Uphir braced a knee on the edge before lowering her. The silken feather mattress cushioned her, but the earthen pad beneath ebbed and flowed, rolling like water. The resilience would add a spring normal packed dirt would not.

Uphir's brows hiked, his delighted smile lighting his handsome face, sparking in his human blue eyes. Her breath caught at the beauty of him, and the sound seemed to refocus Uphir's intent. His smile didn't fade, but the light in his eyes warmed, heat smoldering deep within.

He centered her on the silken cushion, spooning his body beside her, his elbow braced so he could gaze down on her. "It is truly a blessing of the gods that to give you pleasure I must taste heaven, as well."

Medusa swallowed, her mouth suddenly dry as a desert breeze. Her exhale shook from her lungs, and a wash of goose bumps raced down her body. "A perfect world would have every pleasure given returned in kind. Too often it's not."

"Be mine, and every pleasure you gift me will be returned tenfold." Uphir shifted beside her, his hard cock pressing against her hip and thigh. The sensation triggered a reflexive pulse through the muscles of her sex, liquid heat flooding the spot.

"Tenfold?" She tried to scoff at his boldness, but just then he reached up and tenderly brushed a strand of hair from her forehead, tracing its length to tuck it behind her ear. Another tingling shudder shook across her shoulders. She couldn't speak. It was all she could do to lick her lips, trying desperately to moisten her arid mouth.

Her chest tightened and her gaze caught his, the earnest look in his eyes so clear her heart pinched. He lowered, drawing nearer to her lips, and Medusa held her breath. It wasn't her first kiss, but the sensation roared through her like no other before. She let her eyes close as his tongue slipped between her lips, gentle but firm, sweeping her mouth, tasting her.

Muscles along her belly fluttered as his hand feathered over her skin, his palm warm against her, cupping her breast, squeezing, possessing. Uphir shifted as though he could lie closer to her, though their bodies were flush—his chest, the firm muscles of his stomach, the hard line of his sex all pressed along her side, imprinting on her brain. His fingers rolled the pebbled flesh of her nipples, tugged and toyed, made her back arch in response.

His low, grumbling approval filled her mouth, rumbling down her throat a moment before his hand tightened on her breast and he moved to taste her there. Sultry heat, delicious suction and a pinch of sharp teeth—the feel of her breast in his mouth shot a vivid mix of pain and pleasure shooting through her body.

She gasped at the sensation, squirmed, tugged and pushed at his arm, trying to worm her way beneath him. She wanted him centered atop her, his sex pressed to hers. Uphir offered no help, and only bent his knee across her hips and shifted his chest to better trap her, hold her still.

A stab of panic iced through Medusa's veins; her entire body went rigid, despite the way this new position brought his stiff cock closer to her entrance.

Uphir lifted his head, met her eyes and seemed to read her thoughts. He smiled, his lips shimmering from his kisses. "I want to make this as pleasurable and enduring for you as possible, goddess. But once I have you beneath me, my restraint will be close to spent. So if you don't mind...hold still and stop rushing me. Please. Your wiggling is driving me to distraction."

Medusa huffed, her frustration tingling over her skin. "We'd be halfway done by now if you'd let me help."

"Exactly." He kissed her quickly. "Which is why you won't

be helping…yet." And then he kissed her again, pressing long and deep, opening to her when she pressed back.

Muscles low in her belly heated, tightening. She rocked her hips, feeling the solid line of his penis press over her belly, nudge through the hair at her sex. She slipped a hand to the leg he'd draped across her, gripping the back of his thigh.

Thick, hard muscle and skin brushed with wiry hair warmed her palm as she felt her way to the firm curve of his ass. She squeezed, dug her nails in and thrilled at the way his glutes tightened, his hips rocked into her side. Medusa pulled at him again, encouraging him to mount her, opening her legs to give him room.

Uphir didn't budge. His sweet kisses left her mouth, tracing her jaw and moving back to her ear. He found her lobe and suckled it into his mouth. Medusa gasped. Her eyes rolled back as a rush of glittering pleasure rippled from her ear down to her neck, over her chest and belly and straight to her sex. No one had ever done that…ever. Stone statues and rubber toys aren't much for nibbling on earlobes. Good goddess, she liked it.

Excitement, hot and wet, gushed through her, spilling over the lips of her pussy, slicking the tops of her inner thighs. Her hips bucked as Uphir nipped the sensitive flesh, then released her lobe to lavish kisses on the sensitive spot behind her ear.

She writhed beside him, her need sizzling through her veins, tightening muscles, coiling in her womb. She slipped her hand between them, fisting his cock. She squeezed, pulled, desperate for him to center his body on hers. But Uphir only rocked his hips, stroking his sex along her belly, coaxing her for more.

His mouth found her breast again, flicking a wicked tongue over her nipple, toying with the hard, sensitive flesh and sending waves of pleasure rolling over her body, pooling deeper and deeper at her core. Her thoughts fogged as he slid his hand down her belly, tunneling his fingers through her tiny curls, following the curve of her body.

She lifted her hips on reflex, rising to meet him, spreading her legs as her own heat warmed her thighs. Her pussy muscles opened, flexed, needing his touch. He didn't disappoint, slipping his thick finger between her folds, stroking the tender nub of her clit.

Electric sensations swirled up through her chest, humming along her skin with each soft brush, each purposeful stroke. Medusa moaned, her hand latching around his wrist, holding him to her. Uphir pushed lower, teasing her pussy with his finger, drawing out her cream, slicking her entire sex and then diving in for more.

Her body clenched around him, making the most of his finger, closing tight so each stroke in and out of her body filled her, tantalized her every nerve. Uphir angled himself better, driving deeper, faster, his heavy body an exquisite weight against her side. His blue eyes glanced at hers, watching her impassioned response to him.

Pressure built inside her, the sensation winding tighter and tighter, pushing at her skin, squeezing her lungs. Medusa caught her bottom lip between her teeth, closed her eyes and rode his hand like a piston. Each pump of his hand drove her closer and closer to the brink, to a release she both ached for and resisted with all her will.

Her thigh muscles trembled, her toes curling. Uphir leaned close, so close his lips brushed her ear. "My goddess, my love, I live only for you."

The warmth of his breath on her skin, the deep vibration of his voice through her chest, the words he spoke all worked to ignite the explosion that suddenly roared through her mind and body.

She arched back, thrusting her hips, riding the waves of hot release crashing over her body, pulsing through her sex. When the last spasm of her orgasm rocked through her, Uphir caught her mouth in a kiss. His tongue teased hers, his teeth nipped her lip and his inhale stole the breath from her lungs. He mounted her, sliding his manly weight atop her, pinning her.

Medusa clenched her fingers on his sides, nails digging into his skin. Uphir showed no sign of it, lifting his upper body, locking his arms on either side of her shoulders, his hard cock heavy on her belly.

"This is for you, as well," he said. "Do you refuse it?" He pushed his groin against hers, the lips of her pussy opening against his balls. He rocked back and then in again, stroking her too-sensitive flesh with his, squeezing his cock between their bellies. The wiry curls on his sac chafed against her, a maddening mix of pain and pleasure.

Lust overpowered the small flash of panic. Her legs opened wider, his knees coming up to spread her further. "If it's a gift then give it to me."

"It is a gift. But you'll have to take it," he said, his eyelids low, his voice a heated whisper.

Medusa glanced down her body at the hard shaft of his sex pressed between them. Uphir raised his body, rocked back as she reached for him. She caught him. Her fingers wrapped around his fat cock. She stroked him once, and then again, watching how his eyes fluttered each time, how his hips rolled to help drive the motion.

She angled the thick shaft toward her entrance, and teased the velvety smooth head through her folds. So soft, so perfectly made to touch her there. She closed her eyes, enjoying the zing of sensation tingling through her sex.

Uphir moaned, then gasped when she nearly slipped his cock inside her. "You mean to torture me?"

"To torture us both. And what sweet torture it is," she said, then pulled his cock to her pussy and thrust herself against him.

Such a shocking difference from his finger. His cock filled

her, stretched her and drove deeper still. She could hardly breathe for the tight fit of him, for the fast pull of pleasure drawing from every corner of her body down toward her womb. His body met hers, the juice of her sex wetting his belly, his balls, and Uphir pulled back.

His long, muscled body set a rhythm, pumping in and out of her, growing fast, going deep, thrusting harder. She reached up to feel the roll of muscles on his arms, the flex and pull across his back, over his ass. Such pure male power, pounding into her, claiming her in the most primal way, just as she claimed him.

She was a goddess, stronger than any man, human or demon, but still he could wound her. He hadn't. He'd given her what no other man had: himself…willingly.

Uphir's breaths grew shallower, and a fine sheen of sweat slicked over his skin. His locked arms bent, dropping to press a kiss to her lips, his hips still pumping his cock in and out of her body. Salty-sweet, the taste of him filled her mouth, swam through her senses as the musky scent of their lovemaking dizzied her brain. So human.

She wrapped her arms around his neck, her legs around his thighs, and rode the earthen waves of the bed beneath them. That familiar pressure swelled inside her, tightening the muscles of her sex. She squeezed hard to feel every bump and vein along his cock. His thrusts came hard and wild, his balls slapping against her ass, so that the sound of flesh smacking flesh filled the night air.

Her heart pounded a frantic beat in her chest, filling her ears, rocketing red-hot blood through her veins, electrifying her senses. She held her breath, squeezing around every part of Uphir she could. And then suddenly…she let go.

Like a cup overfilled, her release spilled over her, washing through her body, fluttering through her sex. Uphir gave a breath-stealing thrust, ramming deep inside her, then held himself there, riding the spasms of her body, letting her sex milk his, bringing him over with her into bliss.

His body relaxed on top of her and she could feel his exhale shake through him. He wrapped his arms around her, pushing under her, hugging her as his cock slipped from her sex and he slid to lie at her side. He buried his face in the crook of her neck, her hair a tangled blanket around his head.

"You smell so good, little goddess. I'd be a happy man to live the rest of my days swimming in the scent of you." He kissed her neck warmly and gently, and Medusa let go of her last thread of concern.

If ever two creatures were meant for each other it was them. She knew it the way she knew the sun would rise within the hour, the way she knew the ocean would ebb from the shore. It simply was as it should be, as it must be, as they were meant to be.

Medusa closed her eyes, luxuriating in the feel of his powerful male body against her, his steady breaths warming her skin, slowly lulling her to sleep.

HER FACE WARMED BENEATH THE MORNING sun, and Medusa opened her eyes, stretched the sleep from her body across the hard earthen bed. While she slept her will had faltered, and the magical, liquid quality of the dirt had returned to its natural state. Still, the silk-and-down mattress remained as it was, blissfully soft beneath her.

And what a sleep it had been—sated as never before, in the arms of a man she trusted. The feeling was wonderfully new and brought a smile to her face before she'd finished stretching. She rolled toward Uphir and only then realized she was alone...as always.

Her stomach twisted, soured, and she pushed up to sit. The cushion was empty beside her; not even the warmth or impression of Uphir's body remained. How long ago had he left? Medusa blinked at the empty bed, her mind scrambling to understand. Where was he? She scanned the rooftop, the morning sun peeking between the battlements. There was no sign of Uphir.

Had he really sneaked away while she slept? She'd given herself to him and he'd taken her greedily, made her trust him. Then he'd left her?

She swallowed down the clog of emotion at the back of her

throat, reality seeping into her brain, banishing her silly romantic thoughts. *Of course he did. He's a demon. He's a man.*

Medusa turned away from the emptiness he'd left, swung her feet to the floor. How could she have been so blind, so easily seduced? Was she truly so desperate? Had she learned nothing over the centuries?

She reached for her dress, still crumpled in a pile on the castle roof, and stood. Her belly rolled, and her chest ached as though a blade pierced straight through to her soul. She clutched her tunic to her breast, closed her eyes and tried to will her frantic heart to calm.

A sob pressed up through her throat; she clenched her jaw, refusing it. Her lungs burned, her breath coming too quickly, too shallowly. She shut her eyes tight against the sting of tears welling behind her lids. She would not give him the satisfaction. She would not allow herself to crumble so easily.

Medusa was not so fragile, not so female, as to allow a man to bring her to her knees with a simple slight. She sucked in a deep breath, gazing toward the bright blue morning sky, blinking away those wretched tears. She reclaimed her composure inch by inch. She was a goddess after all. What need did she have for a man—demon or not?

She straightened the fabric of her dress, slipped it over her head and smoothed the lines past her hips until it hung loosely to her ankles. With a flick of her wrist she dismantled the hideous bed, a reminder of a weakness she hadn't known she possessed. The materials melted into the floor, molecules shifting, bending to her will. The layer of dirt thickened, spreading evenly beneath her feet.

Medusa watched, unaffected by the working of her power. There was a time she'd marveled at her abilities. Not today. Not anymore. She was alone and her power was a cold comfort when she was faced with the eternity of her existence.

A chill iced her spine at the thought of the years upon years that stretched before her. Her stomach sank inside her, making her feel ill and hollow at once. Such thoughts had never occurred to her before last night. If only she could take back the last few hours.

A hard pinch squeezed her chest at the thought, and she knew that, despite herself, she wouldn't want to give back her time with Uphir. Goddess, what was wrong with her?

Medusa pulled another breath of crisp morning air into her lungs and took the few steps to where her leather sandals lay. She slipped them on then moved farther toward the edge of the roof.

It wasn't a conscious decision to follow the same path she'd taken last night as she climbed between the battlements and down to the erotic gargoyle. But this time, when she leaned over and saw the great stone expanse of his wings, the hard round of his head, the dull points of his ears, she mentally chastised herself for waiting so long to check.

Her heart pounded, the beating so fast she was dizzy with it. He hadn't left her. Just like her will, whatever power had made him flesh must have waned during the night and returned him to his cursed perch on the side of the ancient castle.

Medusa kicked off her sandals again and scurried over the wall. She wasn't sure what power or will had worked its magic last night to free them both from their lonely prisons, but she'd find a way to unlock its secrets and take back the only real happiness, the only true pleasure, she'd ever known.

She made it down to him in seconds, straddling his bent knees, finding the tiniest bit of room beyond his stone-hard cock to sit. The cool shaft pressed along her belly, stirred memories of the night before and sent them warming through her pussy.

Her hand cupped his cheek; his mouth was frozen in the same joker's grin, and she gazed into his stone-gray eyes. "Come back to me, demon. I command it."

Seconds passed without so much as a flicker of life. Her

belly clenched, her mouth going dry. She licked her lips, caressed a hand over his head. "Turn flesh for your little goddess, demon…please. Uphir…*please.*"

Nothing. His cold eyes gazed wide and empty; his clawed fingers and toes stayed as they were, clutching the corner wall behind him. Her thumb traced over the hard ridge of his lips, following the curve of his grin, touching the dull points of his teeth.

Medusa leaned close, ignoring the stab of his stone erection against her belly, and pressed her lips to his. She tried with all her heart to soften his mouth on hers, to will him to return her kiss, but nothing happened. She drew back, licked the grit from her lips, ignoring the cold chill of stone on her skin.

Her throat tightened, sorrow squeezing through her chest. She blinked back the sting of tears and dropped her gaze between them. There was one more thing she could try. Even Uphir had believed her nectar, the cream of her body, had brought him to life. She had to try.

Far below, Paris was slowly waking. The distant sounds of car horns, of merchants opening their shops for the day, edged at the corners of her consciousness. At any moment someone could look up and see her clinging to the side of the castle, fucking a stone monster. She didn't care.

One arm wrapped around his neck, holding her to him, Medusa used her free hand to hike up her dress. She pushed up, her feet wedged between his calves and the wall, and centered her sex over his. She didn't care how dry she was, how harsh the invasion of cold, hard stone would be. It didn't matter.

Her lover's cock pushed inside her, spreading the lips of her sex, stretching her muscles, chafing her most sensitive skin. She dropped lower, impaling herself with the stone shaft, forcing it deeper and deeper. Her pussy clenched in protest, her inner walls burning against the rough friction. She lowered herself another inch, then another, until her ass met the cold chill of his stone lap.

Medusa exhaled the breath she'd been holding, tried hard to relax, to loosen her muscles, to want Uphir in stone as much as she had once before. Impossible.

How could she? Now that she knew what it felt like—velvet flesh, firm but giving, sliding in and out of her body, stroking her in ways nothing else could. He fit her perfectly. His body was made for hers.

The stone shaft was a poor substitute. How could she live an eternity without feeling him thick and alive inside her? She wanted to feel him now, warm and firm, filling her, his body flexing to fit her, stroking through the subtle contours of her body.

Medusa rocked her hips, the memory of his warm flesh pressing into her, clouding her thoughts, sending a wave of heat washing through her veins, slicking her sex. She rocked again, lifted from his lap and slid down again. Breath-shaking tingles rippled through the sensitive walls of her pussy, coaxing her to move again and again.

Sensation hummed along her skin, coiling through her muscles, forcing her heart to beat faster. Her womb clenched, holding for a few minutes more. She pumped her body harder, faster, losing herself to her memories, finding pleasure in so much less. Pressure built inside her, like the fast rise of a rain-drenched river, pushing at her skin, promising a gushing release.

She gave in to that need, that promise, letting her memories do as much for her as the rough friction stroking through her pussy. Medusa squeezed her thighs against the hard waist of the gargoyle, her sex muscles fluttering through the rolling waves of her orgasm. Her come streamed down the stone shaft plunged deep inside her, wet her thighs, creamed the cheeks of her ass.

But Uphir remained unchanged. It didn't work. Her body's craving for him was not the magic elixir they'd thought. Medusa framed his catlike face in her hands, her sorrow teetering on the edge of anger.

"Uphir, why is this happening? Why let me taste what I cannot have? Why show me the loneliness of my existence, if only to make the coming eternity more poignant? Are you so cruel, Uphir?" Her voice trembled. She struggled with all her will not to cry. She leaned her forehead against his, the stone chilling through her skin.

"Daughter, why do you offer this stone beast the magic of your body?"

Medusa snapped her head up and met the eyes of the goddess Athena, gazing over the edge of the castle at her. Even knowing the power of Athena's beauty, Medusa gasped in the face of it.

Raven-black hair spilled over her shoulders, so stark against the white of her robes every strand seemed luminous. Her eyes were like pools of blue sky, bluer than anything on earth. And when she smiled, her rose-red lips curved soft and moist. A sweet flush warmed her skin down her slender neck and colored the pale skin of her ample breasts. She was woman personified—beauty, grace. She was a goddess.

"Mother. You've come. Oh, blessed are you to have heard my cries."

"Of course I heard your cries, child, as well as the mewling prayers of that beast whose cock you've plunged into your womb," she said. "Unsheathe yourself from that creature, daughter. You've played enough havoc with my punishments for one day."

Medusa, so thrilled to see the powerful goddess, obeyed without question, scrambling up the wall, slipping between the battlements to stand before her. "Sweet goddess Athena, it's a miracle. I'm in love. Love at first sight. There could be no other way for me. We were meant for each other." She clasped her hands together at her chest. "Oh, please, Mother. Free him. Give him to me and me to him."

Athena rolled her beautiful eyes and shifted her weight to one hip, her slender arms crossed beneath her bosom. "Not you, too? All night that daft fool's prayers battered at me. 'Keep me flesh, goddess. I cannot bear to leave her. She won't survive it, nor will I.'" Athena scoffed. "He dares to swear his love to you when he refused me a simple poke? The impudence."

Medusa blinked, understanding dawning slowly. "But surely it's as you planned. No other man can gaze upon me without turning to stone. You wouldn't deny me such a perfect match, perfect happiness, to spite him."

"No?" Athena strolled to the edge of the castle, peering down at the creature she'd frozen there. "I make you a goddess, gift you with immeasurable power, and how do you thank me? By freeing that selfish, cocksure demon. I was not at all pleased at having to spare him a thought so as to return him to his punishment."

"You took him from me?" Medusa's gut twisted.

Athena's narrow black brows knitted. "Of course. He wouldn't have gone on his own."

"But…why? Mother, I love him."

The goddess scoffed. "You can't. You are vengeance, daughter. Flawless in your design, untouchable, unswayable by the seductive influences of men."

"Save one," Medusa said. "Uphir. And he loves me."

The goddess glanced over the edge again, then back to Medusa, her brows high. "Love? Him? He's a selfish, womanizing hedonist. He can't love anyone or anything more than he loves himself. Women swoon at his feet with the slightest crook of his finger. He has no respect for the female gender."

"I didn't swoon at his feet," Medusa said, closing the distance between them. "I tried to turn him to stone."

The goddess laughed and the sound was like the tinkling of tiny bells. "Oh, Medusa, my daughter. You do lift my spirits. But you are a goddess, and he is a lowly demon. Oil and water, my dear. You cannot mix."

"Then I don't want to be a goddess anymore. End me now. I can't bear the thought of eternity unloved."

Athena huffed. "Such drama. Shall we first see if your sacrifice is appreciated?"

The raven-haired goddess flicked her wrist over the edge of the castle and an instant later, Uphir stood at her side. His massive stone-gray wings flapped once, twice, before he folded them neatly behind him.

His dark, gargoyle eyes took in the scene. "Athena. It's good to see you again. By good I mean, seeing anything is better than being locked in stone."

"My daughter wishes me to free you from your punishment," Athena said, ignoring his snide remarks. "She's dear to me, demon, so I'll warn you to choose your words wisely. I offer you a choice. Freedom to return to the life you had before. Or an eternity more on that castle wall."

His eyes narrowed on her. "What's the catch?"

"You can never see, speak to or touch my daughter, Medusa, again. If you do, you will turn to stone like any man who looks upon her."

Uphir sucked a breath through his nose, his chest swelling as his back stiffened. His gaze shifted to Medusa, the sorrow in his dark, demon eyes almost palpable. "The choice is the same. A life spent in yearning. Set me back on the wall. At least there time passes unnoticed. But first, I beg you, one final kiss from her lips to savor."

The beautiful goddess rolled her shoulders, a delicate gesture that seemed both innocent and sexy at once. "Granted."

A clap of thunder rocked through the sky, shook the castle beneath them, and a strange tingling wave washed over

Medusa. She looked at Uphir who, in an instant, shifted to human form, his handsome, sun-kissed face creased, his brows wrinkled as he studied himself.

"You may be together or not. Your future is your own from this day forth," Athena said, strolling between them toward the other side of the roof.

Medusa glanced from her to him and back again. "What happened? What have you granted?"

Athena stopped, glanced over her shoulder. "You're both human, of course. There's no other way you can be together." She shrugged. "Well, there is. But this was the first that came to mind."

"Thank you, Mother," Medusa said.

"Life, mortal life, isn't easy, Medusa. There's no going back if things aren't always as sweet as you'd like," Athena said. "This is your wish, Medusa, your folly or your salvation. The decision was yours. Remember that. You are a goddess no more."

"No." Uphir closed the distance between him and Medusa, scooping her into his arms. "She's more. She's woman. Her desire defied the gods. And our love will span the ages."

Athena laughed as she turned and walked off the edge of the castle wall, each step taking her higher and higher into the clouds. "Indeed, Uphir. Now, imagine what her daughters will be like."

* * * * *

PRIMAL INSTINCTS

Cathryn Fox & Lisa Renee Jones

FLASHLIGHT IN HAND, DR. OLIVIA MARKHAM pushed through the vines and vegetation as her glance scanned the tall palm trees fringing the overgrown footpath. With the setting sun unable to penetrate the thick canopy of leaves overhead, she had to rely on artificial light to find her way. Not that she knew her way—she didn't—which was why she, along with her best friend and fellow research partner, Dr. Jordon Brooks, had joined a local tour group that had just embarked on a weeklong safari.

The heavy, humid atmosphere closed around her, making it difficult to fully inflate her lungs with air. She swiped her damp bangs from her forehead, hardly able to believe that her research into aphrodisiacs had landed her smack-dab in the middle of the Mayan jungle—a far cry from her research lab at the University of Texas, she mused.

The tour group had been traveling from sunup until sundown. Judging from the grumblings coming from the other group members up ahead, it was clear they were ready to stop and set up camp for the night. So when Olivia's stomach started to grumble, she stopped midstride, twisted around and spoke to Jordon in whispered words. "How much farther do you think it is?"

Olivia waved her flashlight toward her friend, momentarily blinding her. Without warning, their bodies collided with a thud, and the air rushed from her lungs.

Gasping, Olivia stumbled backward, her heavy backpack throwing her off balance. With her hands flailing, her flashlight tumbled to the ground; unable to right herself, she landed with a thump a few feet away from her light.

Jordon dropped to her knees. Panicked, she reached for Olivia and gushed out, "Olivia, are you okay?"

"I'm okay, but... I can't speak for the damn bush I fell on," she said, lightening the mood. "If I didn't know better, I'd swear it was a cactus."

Jordon crinkled her nose and panned her light, taking in the flattened foliage. "Not a cactus—just the exposed roots of a Pacaya palm tree," she said.

Olivia pushed her damp bangs back with her palm. "Oh, yeah? Tell that to my ass."

She shimmied forward to retrieve her flashlight and then looked around. Sure enough, Jordon was right. It was merely Pacaya palm roots—they'd done enough research over the past few months to know the foliage intimately.

Stifling a chuckle, Jordon shook her head and reached out to her. "Need a hand?"

"I think I need a minute to catch my breath first." Olivia gripped her chest and wheezed loudly to emphasize the point.

Laughing at Olivia's exaggerated antics, Jordon plunked down beside her and went to work brushing dirt and insects from her camo jacket.

Olivia pulled off her rucksack and took a moment to compose herself. The hard truth was that Olivia and Jordon were both strong, streetwise city girls who'd trained emotionally and physically for the weeklong excursion, but despite their preparedness, they somehow found themselves a little vulnerable and a whole lot out of their element in the primitive jungle surroundings.

While they rested and filled their lungs, Olivia knotted her long auburn hair at her nape and then glanced around. She swept her flashlight over the flora, scanning the area from ground to treetop as she searched for the bright ivory petals of the estela flower.

Rumor had it that the estela, which meant "star" in English, could actually glow in the dark—hence the name, no doubt. Rumor also had it that the leaves, when ingested, had very potent, very magical aphrodisiacal powers. This was the only reason Olivia and Jordon were fighting their way through a jungle at this particular moment, instead of working at their private laboratory.

Unfortunately for them—and their research—rumor also had it that the flower was merely a legend, and no proof of its presence had ever been found. Even the townsfolk, including their tour guide, had been pretty closemouthed about the flower's actual existence.

Jordon angled her head to peer into the dark path. "We'd better get moving before we lose the others."

Olivia glanced behind her, and flicked her light over the untamed path. "Shouldn't there be a guide following up the rear to ensure no one gets lost?"

"I guess it's up to us to keep up." Jordon climbed to her feet. "Come on."

Olivia stood, threw her rucksack over her shoulder and then stilled. "Listen."

"What am I listening for?" After a quiet moment, Jordon turned in a circle, hearing only the crunch of twigs and underbrush beneath her hiking boots. "I don't hear anything."

"Precisely."

"Oh, shit," Jordon said as understanding dawned. "Let's move it. We'd better pick up the pace before we really get left behind."

Pushing through the vines, they rushed forward, searching

for their tour group. A few moments later they came upon the others, who were already setting up camp.

Following Jordon's lead, Olivia dropped her bags and hooked her flashlight onto her belt. She was grateful that they'd finally reached their destination.

Olivia went to work finding a spot to set up the tent, while Jordon rooted through their bags for food. The minute they were both rested and fed, the two had plans to scope out the area.

Before she had time to secure a spot, their guide approached with two lit lanterns and spoke to them both in rough English. "Follow me." As he handed Jordon a lantern, Olivia took that moment to study him. Splashes of colored paint, with symbols she didn't understand, covered his dark skin, making him look wild, fierce and...*carnal*. Long black hair fell forward as he dipped his head to meet Olivia's gaze straight on.

He made a low guttural sound, and lowered his voice for their ears only. "Come and learn."

Marveling at the turn of events, Olivia cast Jordon a skeptical glance, her expression conveying her disbelief; a heady mixture of concern and anticipation whipped through her blood. After refusing to even discuss the flower's potent powers, or even its mere existence, could he really be guiding them to it?

Moving with grace and agility, he turned his back to them, and stepped from the beaten path into one that appeared less traveled. Jordon held the lantern high, lighting the dark jungle before them.

Olivia stood stock-still and said in a whisper, "What do you think caused his change of heart?"

Jordon's frown deepened as she slowly shook her head. "I really have no idea at all. But I think we should at least follow him to find out." With that, Jordon picked up her rucksack and stepped forward cautiously. Olivia scooped up her own pack and followed closely behind.

Without speaking, their guide led them deep into the jungle interior. Despite their hunger and sheer exhaustion, they trekked onward, following in silence, anxious to discover the magical flower—a flower that would take them from obscurity to making their mark in the scientific world.

What felt like hours later, but in reality could have been only twenty minutes, Olivia and Jordon found themselves overlooking a tall cavern. From their elevated position, they couldn't see into its depths, but they could hear the rustling sound of water below. They both crouched down and peered into the darkness. They could see a faint light deep below. A fragrant scent curled around her, and Olivia inhaled, pulling the unique aroma into her lungs; she wondered if the scent was coming from the estela flower, and if the faint light was from its glowing petals.

When a twig snapped behind her, Olivia stood and turned to face their guide. Jordon placed the lantern near the cliff, and moved in beside her. Their guide waved his hands forward, gesturing to the thick rope dangling over the edge. "It is what you seek."

Her heart racing, Olivia narrowed suspicious eyes and said, "You want us to go down there?"

Their guide nodded. "It is safe. I will follow."

Jordon twisted around, hunkered down and grabbed the rope. She tugged, testing it. Always the risk-taker, Jordon tossed Olivia a reassuring look and shrugged. "It seems safe enough."

Was it really possible that they'd find the estela flower in the belly of the cavern?

The guide answered Olivia's unasked question. "What you seek you will find, down there. *Auga,*" he added in his native tongue, bowing his head.

They'd find the flower in the water?

Olivia noted the moment of hesitation in Jordon's eyes

before she quickly blinked it away. "What do you say, Olivia? Are you game?"

Olivia knelt beside her friend and tried the rope. She drew a fortifying breath, gathered her bravado and shot Jordon a glance. "I say we've come too far to back down now."

JORDON JUMPED TO THE GROUND DEEP INSIDE the wonderfully cool inner cavern and immediately grabbed the flashlight hanging from her belt, flipping it on. She held it up and stared in awe at the glorious sight she found around her. The light reflected off the sparkling water of a pond, which was in the center of a magnificent cavern. She quickly scanned for animals or other hidden dangers, and thankfully found nothing that represented imminent risk—only obscure beauty hidden in darkness. Drawing a breath, she tried to calm her racing heart. The idea of finding that flower had her pulse pounding at double-time. A flower as potent as legend foretold would do more than offer pleasure; it might deliver alternatives to addictive pain medications. She was dreaming big, but she couldn't help herself.

Despite her excitement, Jordon couldn't fight her uneasiness. Shouldn't the guide have come down first and ensured their safety? And why the change of heart about helping them? Why show them this secret location? Up until this point, he had acted as if their quest for the secret estela flower was some sort of great taboo. And quite truthfully, even now, she felt nervous. Could they trust him?

Before she could consider those questions any further,

Olivia landed on her feet beside Jordon, discarding her heavy backpack. Immediately, Olivia's flashlight flipped on, showing she shared the same jitters.

"Oh, my God," Olivia whispered. "It's beautiful. Or what I can see of it is."

"I know," Jordon said, following her friend's lead and sliding her pack off her back. "Easy to believe something special like that flower would be down here, isn't it?"

"Oh, yeah," Olivia agreed, not quite suppressing a sudden shiver. "And about ten degrees cooler. Gotta love that."

"I bet the water's a little chilly, though, and that's where the flower is supposed to be," Jordon warned. "We can't go in without proper gear. We'll freeze."

Abruptly, the rope jerked, and Jordon assumed the guide was headed down to join them, but instead it began to climb upward.

"Hey!" Jordon screamed, instinct kicking in as she dropped her flashlight and jumped—four years on the college track-and-field high-jump team being put to use as she leaped upward, trying to grab the rope.

"Oh, crap!" Olivia exclaimed as Jordon's fingers merely grazed the tip of the rope. The rope slid farther out of reach, and Jordon plummeted to the ground with a hard thud and scrambled for her flashlight again.

"Hey!" Olivia shouted at the guide. "What are you doing up there? I thought you were coming down, too?" No response. "Are you insane? We need that rope."

Jordon pointed her light upward at the entrance as she pushed to her feet. "This is so not good," she murmured, not bothering to yell again. At this point, it was pretty obvious they were screwed.

As if in confirmation, the guide's head appeared at the opening of the hole and he grinned. "You will get the rope back," he promised. "When the shaman, Donato, says you get it back."

"What?" Jordon gasped at the same time that Olivia demanded, "Who is Donato?"

Suddenly the cavern lit with flames; fire flickered at several corners and then followed a path around a ridge. Within seconds the entire cavern was alight, and Jordon and Olivia found themselves surrounded by natives. And not just any natives—tall, muscular men in barely-there loincloths stood in various parts of the cavern.

"To say this isn't an ordinary cavern in the middle of the Mexican jungle would be an understatement," Jordon murmured, swallowing hard as three loinclothed, godlike natives stepped closer, forming a line. She flicked a split-second glance over at Olivia and then back over the rock-hard abs and broad shoulders of "the gods." "Tell me I fell and hit my head, and this is some sort of erotic fantasy, because I really don't want all of these hot men to be cannibals about to kill us."

"Not unless you pulled me down with you, and we both hit our heads," Olivia said, delivering the hard truth. The two friends took a step closer together at the same moment. "You think one of them is Donato?"

The three men who'd formed the line eased apart, and a gray-haired man wearing a bright, floor-length robe of yellow and orange stepped forward. "I am Donato, and I possess the answers you seek. I can give you the estela." Though he spoke English, his words were heavily laced with a native accent.

Jordon gave the man a cautious once-over. "Why do I think there is more to your offer than simple generosity?"

"Exactly," Olivia inserted, her arms crossing protectively in front of her chest. "Why are we here? It's clear you planned this."

A hint of a smile played on the older man's lips, a bit of appreciation in his eyes at their astuteness. "There are certain terms to my willingness to help you."

"Terms," Olivia said flatly. "Why would we accept your terms?"

This time the old man openly smiled. "Because we both know how badly you want the estela. Why else would you be in the middle of a jungle, hunting for what many believe to be only myth?"

"But it's not a myth," Jordon countered. "Is it?"

"The estela is real, as is its power to deliver great pleasure." He held out his hand, closed his palm and then opened it. A glowing flower lay in his palm.

The two women shared a gasp of surprise. "How did you do that?" Olivia asked.

"With the same kind of magic found inside these glorious petals." He held the flower between his fingers and threw it in the air. A second later it disappeared in a sprinkle of gold glitter. "Magic I can show you." He paused. "If you are willing to meet my terms. For we are the guardians of estela. No one touches it without our approval."

Jordon and Olivia exchanged a nervous look, silently agreeing they should at least hear the man out. Olivia wasn't one to walk around a subject; she took the direct approach. "These terms you mention. Be more exact. What do we have to do to get to the flower?"

"To leave with estela in your possession, you must first understand the true magnitude of her abilities. You must experience her great powers. You must sample her essence, here with us. Learn of her seductive magic. Then you will know what she will do to your world."

"Do to our world?" Jordon asked, not sure she followed where this was leading and certainly not keen on taking the equivalent of a drug, especially outside a controlled lab environment. "What will it do to our world?"

He fixed on Jordon a deep, soul-searching stare, his gaze almost inhuman, his eyes emitting an odd quality, almost a glow. "The flower's magic must be managed," he finally explained. "Once freed into your world, her powers would become invasive, controlling. Your world would forget all it knows, living for nothing but all-consuming passion." His voice was low, yet foreboding. "You must experience this power here, where I can control estela's reach. Then, and only then, will you understand why we guard her so closely."

Olivia snorted. "Please. We have plenty of drugs in our country. None of them have consumed our world. Besides, we mean the flower to be used for medical purposes."

The old man stared at Olivia as he had at Jordon, and Jordon felt Olivia shiver under his attention. "Estela decides how she is used," he commented with eerie certainty. "If you want the flower, you will accept my terms. Sample the flower under my supervision."

As scary as this was to Jordon—testing the flower here, outside a lab—the science it represented was more important. "And if we do this and still want the flower, you will give it to us?" A slow incline of his chin followed, but nothing more. No words. No promises. Yet she understood his agreement; she also understood that he believed they would not take the flower once they tested it.

Abruptly, Olivia grabbed Jordon's arm, pulling her aside, turning Jordon so that their backs were to the man and his followers. "We can't do this," she whispered urgently. "It's insane. I like to consider us smart women. For all we know, he plans to drug us and kill us."

"Then why talk to us at all?" Jordon countered, knowing Olivia was the rational thinker, the one who advised caution, whereas Jordon took risks. Their differences made for balance, and a good team. "No one knows we are here. He could easily have already killed us. We said we'd come too far to turn our backs on this chance when we came down into this cavern. And now that is truer than ever. We know the flower is here. We're so close, Olivia, I can taste it. Think of what this discovery can do for science."

Olivia wasn't finished reasoning. "What if we die? What if we're allergic? And who says they will let us go when this is all over?"

Jordon had to smile at that. "If we have to die, doing it in the arms of a few hot men sounds like a good way to go."

An appalled look flashed across Olivia's face before she chuckled. "I can't believe I am considering this."

"I can," Jordon insisted. "We both know we can't leave without knowing we did all we could do to take this flower home with us."

Seconds ticked by as Olivia fretted. Suddenly the rope dropped from the hole above them, giving them an exit route. The girls turned to face the gray-haired man. "You are free to leave," he offered. "*Without* the flower. Or you may stay and sample estela."

Jordon looked at Olivia, her brow raised in question. Olivia drew a breath and let it out, then clasped Jordon's hand. "We're staying."

The man's wrinkled face showed no signs of response. "Then we begin." He turned without waiting for their reply, the expectation clear that they would follow. The sexy native men, who Jordon suspected would soon be their lovers, stood like statues, staring forward, eyes averted.

Hand in hand, Olivia and Jordon started forward, follow-ing the old man past the loinclothed "gods." The instant they passed those glorious bodies, Jordon felt warm all over. She continued to be aware of the men, who now walked behind them. A brief moment of fear and panic overtook her, but those feelings were quickly smothered by a growing sense of excitement and more than a hint of arousal. Even without the flower's influence, these agreed-upon "terms" were erotic and daring. They'd agreed to let that flower lead them to sensual places, to perform erotic acts with complete, utter strangers. And even if she wanted to claim it was for science, a part of her thrilled at the excitement of exploration, of an excuse to let her inhibitions go and escape into pleasure. If she felt this now, what would she feel with the flower influencing her?

Donato led Jordon and Olivia into a smaller cave within the cavern, only it looked more like a room with stone walls. Gorgeous stalactites hung like icicles, and the walls were covered in primitive erotic art. Rugs draped the floors and a small black wood-burning furnace sat in the corner, though there was no doubting the floral scent that seemed to seep from the smoke. The essence of estela, perhaps?

Jordon barely had time to consider that idea when her attention was riveted to the three chairs before her, two of which held the most gorgeous twin males she'd ever seen in her life. Long sable hair brushed their broad shoulders, while lean muscle glistened beneath olive-colored skin, their loincloths doing nothing to hide their perfection.

"If, by chance, you indeed hit your head and this is your fantasy," Olivia whispered beside her, "thanks for including me."

Donato sat down in the open chair between the twins. "These are my sons." He waved to the right, to the male directly in front of Olivia. "Chale." He inclined his head at Olivia. "And this is Amador." Amador inclined his head at Jordon.

Donato continued, "My sons are masters of estela's magic. If you accept them as your protectors and guides through this experience, you will show them so. You will fall at their knees now and submit to their rule."

OLIVIA'S EYES MET WITH CHALE'S, STUDYING THE hard angles and planes of his face, and registering every delicious detail of the broad man seated before her.

The way his intense gaze locked on hers was both erotic and unnerving. She shifted restlessly and cleared her throat, working double-time to marshal the lust that saturated her mind as unease segued to lust. There was nothing she could do, however, to bank the unfamiliar heat and need spreading through her body.

Chale stood and took one measured step closer, and she briefly closed her eyes against the flood of heat. The way his hard warrior body moved toward her with such confidence, and the way his primal scent closed around her—he weakened her knees and brought on a shudder. With just one look, this godlike warrior had her body turning mutinous.

Dear Lord, what had they gotten themselves into?

He held out one large hand, palm up. Without hesitation, Olivia placed her palm on his. When he curled his fingers around hers, her small hand was swallowed by his enormous strength. The warmth of his skin seeped into her flesh, and in that instant she just knew that what she was about to experience would somehow change her future and alter her life forever.

She shivered. Almost violently.

Chale inclined his head, and the slight curl in his lips told her that not only had he read her body's responses, he was pleased by them.

Long, sable hair fell forward, veiling his bare chest. "Do you accept me as your guide, Olivia?" he asked in near-perfect English.

Heart racing, she nodded. Knowing she had to submit to him before she began her erotic journey, she sank to her knees, coming face-to-face with his hard cock, the loincloth unable to hide his impressive magnitude. She almost wept from pleasure. Out of her peripheral vision she watched Jordon submit to Amador.

"Then I offer you estela." His voice was softly seductive and worked some mysterious alchemy on her soul. Chale twisted sideways, accepted a small bowl-like crock from a young woman and offered it to Olivia.

A pause, a quick moment of hesitation, and then Olivia drank from the crock. The sweet syrup was as delicious as it was fragrant. She could feel her body warm, feel estela racing through her bloodstream, heating her from the inside out.

Chale took the empty crock from her hand and pulled her to her feet. Feeling so small next to his large body, Olivia tilted her chin upward, bringing them face-to-face. His hands cupped her cheeks; his warrior features softened. The sudden flare of heat deep inside her made her body tremble.

Dark eyes probed hers, as though assessing her, reading her every hidden desire, her every secret fetish. His glance slid over her skin, a rough caress. She should be afraid, she knew. But at the moment, with estela racing through her veins, she felt anything but fear. Her breathing quickened; her chest was rising and falling in an erratic pattern.

A strange primal sound crawled out of Chale's throat. Raw desire flitted across his face. He bent his head, positioning his lips close to her ear, and spoke in whispered words. "You are very passionate, little one."

A moment later his warm mouth touched her skin, and she became instantly aware of the desire rising in him. He inhaled her, and then brushed his lips over the erogenous zone just below her ear. His movements were slow, deliberate, his touch going right through her.

Olivia drew in air, but couldn't seem to fill her lungs. She felt a little dizzy, a little disoriented. Sexual hunger churned inside her, prowling through her body, drawing her into a current of need and desire.

Chale inched back, his fingers brushing over her heated cheek, her neck. His nostrils flared. "Come with me now, little one, and learn."

Strong hands encircled her waist, guiding her to a smaller cave. She caught a glimpse of her friend being scooped up and carried in a different direction, and wondered where Amador was taking her, but all thoughts of Jordon were forgotten as Chale led her into his inner chambers.

Eyes alive with curiosity, she took a quick moment to catalog the unfamiliar surroundings, momentarily stunned by the beauty. Soft candlelight bathed the room in a warm, erotic glow, the arousing, aromatic scent of estela saturating the air. Although the underground lair was primitive by her standards, what it lacked in modern luxury it made up for in sensuous delight and earthy appeal. A large, cozy-looking white fur rug blanketed the circular floor, estela's leaves sprinkled on top. Flanking the rug, two handsome warriors stood guard. To her left, a round tub drew her eye, with more white leaves floating on the water's glistening surface.

She glanced at the shadows dancing playfully on the stone wall. The erotic art from the large chamber spilled inside the smaller room. Olivia touched the limestone, the tip of her index finger tracing a couple in a tantra position. She wondered if the sketches were images re-creating the sexual activities that took place in the cave. Would she find her own spot on the wall when this was all over? And if so, what erotic position would she be captured in? Suddenly her imagination kicked into high gear, her mind conjuring up sexy visuals. As a bevy of fantasies rushed through her mind, her body responded with a shiver.

With his muscles rippling and pulling her focus, Chale walked to the center of the room and turned to face her. He gave a wave and a slight nod, gesturing for his men to bring her to him. When the warriors moved in beside her and escorted her forward, away from the archway, two more men took up guard at the door, locking the world out and her inside, making escape impossible. But she didn't want to escape. She wanted to stay here with Chale and experience estela's magic in all its aphrodisiacal glory.

When she reached Chale, her eyes raked over his taut torso. Deliberately he leaned over her, his scent assailing her senses, his primal essence completely overwhelming her. She stole a glance at the two loinclothed warriors still at her side, and the male-dominated space closed in around her.

Would they be staying while Chale guided her in estela's magic? Would they be *watching* while he took her to intimate, sensuous places? Would they be *participating* in this scandalous yet so damn titillating encounter?

"What you want, and *need,* requires them to stay, little one," Chale murmured into her ear, answering her unasked questions.

Olivia sucked in a tight breath. Had estela's magic put him in tune with her desires, her *needs?* Needs that she knew she had, but never had the courage to vocalize.

Chale fingered her camo jacket, toying with the material, seductively rubbing it through his fingers as if he'd never felt anything finer. "It is what you wish, yes?"

She suddenly felt very wild, very bold, everything in her urging her to open herself up to him. And really, she'd be crazy to deny herself what she really wanted. Because what she really wanted, and what she secretly needed, was to have the warriors stay, to watch and play.

Without any censure, she gave a slow nod, and said in a breathless voice, "Yes, it is what I wish."

Her unabashed certainty seemed to please Chale, and deep down, she suspected he knew her needs and desires better than she knew them herself.

With that, Chale removed her jacket, and then stood back. His eyes fixed on her breasts, watching the way her nipples hardened and poked through her thin T-shirt. When he wet his bottom lip, everything inside her screamed to feel his mouth on hers, his wet tongue on her breasts, between her legs. Her pussy moistened in anticipation.

"Undress her, and prepare her for her journey." Chale gave the command to his warriors.

Her flesh quivered as the men expertly removed her clothes and boots. Gaze riveted, she never once tore her glance from Chale's powerful, virile physique. Her nipples quivered as her body ached to join with his. A craving she'd never before experienced swamped her. Oh, God, she needed him, under her, over her, inside her. Liquid heat lubricated her pussy and dripped down her thighs.

After they had undressed her, the men led her to the bath. She glanced at the water and suppressed a shiver, wanting to try it with her finger before climbing in. Would the water be cold, like the pond at the foot of the cave?

"Estela keeps it warm," Chale said softly.

His low voice played down her spine and moved through her like an aphrodisiacal drug. Trusting him completely, instinctively, in a way she'd never trusted another, Olivia nodded and slipped into the steamy, silky water.

Pure luxury. It was a befitting description for what she was feeling. The fragrant scent of estela swirled around her. The men dropped to their knees, each picking up one white petal.

She wondered what they had in mind. She shot Chale a glance, curious, yet excited just the same.

He angled his head. "My men will service you, and prepare you for me."

The tips of the petals flicked over her breasts, scenting and cleansing her skin while filling her nipples with heated blood.

Oh, Jesus…

Her body began vibrating, her clit swelling, clamoring for attention.

As though reading her needs, one of the warriors trailed the petal lower, over her stomach, to her legs, fueling her desires. She rested her head against the porcelain tub; her lashes fluttered shut against the erotic assault, and her thighs automatically widened. He stroked small circles over her pubis, before brushing the petal over her twin lips.

At this first touch, sparks shot through her body. Her hips powered upward, purposely placing the soft tip of the petal where she needed it most. Lust filled her and her body grew ravenous, tension building inside her.

With deft fingers, the warrior whipped the petal over her clit, while the other man turned his attention to her breasts, circling her nipples with accurate precision, seducing all her senses and raising her passion to never-before-known heights. Deep in a haze of arousal, she moaned in ecstasy and writhed as they worked her into a state of euphoric bliss.

One thick finger slipped inside her and all coherent thought was lost. In and out, in and out, he pumped into her, taking his time to caress her bundle of sensitive nerve endings. Her cunt spasmed, sucking him in deeper. Heat and desire flushed her skin.

Pleasure resonated through her, and her muscles clenched with the approach of a powerful orgasm. Her shaking hands gripped the tub. She bucked her hips forward, giving herself over to her needs. With that first sweet clench, her blood raced, carrying estela to all parts of her body, warming and stimulating her darkest corners.

Feeling euphoric, intoxicated, delirious with pleasure, she erupted, shattering all over him, letting herself go in a way she never had before.

"Oh, damn," she cried out, then bit down on her lip, riding out every delicious wave, every sweet pulse of fulfillment.

A moment later she blinked her eyes open and met Chale's glance. As her body called out to him, she realized that she was far from feeling fulfilled. Her passion hadn't even begun to recede; in fact, it was growing at an insurmountable rate. She knew, after that intense orgasm, she should have been sated, but she felt anything but. She wanted more, *needed* more. The lust rising in her was almost too much, too intense to bear. She sucked in a tight breath and sank back into the water. A low moan escaped her lips, her body shaking with sexual frustration. She tried desperately to manage her over-whelming urges, but failed miserably.

As though sensing her distress, Chale came to her, lifted her from the tub and carried her to the fur rug, giving her a tender look.

"Breathe, little one," he commanded in a soft voice. He stood her before him and put her hand on his heart, letting her follow his slow, steady beat. In the span of a moment, her racing pulse settled. "That's a girl," he murmured. "Learning to control estela's power takes time." His voice dropped to a whisper that sensuously caressed her body.

Chale's lips brushed along her cheek, making a slow pass over her mouth before settling there for a deeper exploration. The soft blade of his tongue slipped inside for a gentle kiss that grew in passion and intensity when she moved restlessly against him. Her hand slipped between their bodies. She gripped his thick cock, wanting it inside her. It jumped beneath her intimate touch.

He stepped back and met her glance. They exchanged a long look. His dark eyes gleamed with sensuality, and before she realized what was happening, Chale captured her hands above her head, tying them with a dangling rope, and then quickly inserted his knee between her legs, widening them, while his men shackled her feet to the floor.

Omigod!

He'd secured her in an erotic position straight from her fantasies.

"Chale…" she murmured. He shot her a look of intimacy and promise. A shudder overtook her, and she was ready to explode just from the smoldering look in his eyes.

She twisted sideways to watch Chale's warriors circle her, like wild animals in heat, touching her body, exploring her curves, her heat, her most private parts. She gave a broken gasp and closed her eyes, not wanting to think, wanting only to feel.

The room became charged with sexual energy, her scent filling the heavy air.

One large palm slapped her ass. It stung, but she liked it. She moaned, and arched into his touch. Another hand moved in to soothe the sting left behind.

One warrior moved to her side, bent forward and encircled her areola with his tongue. His mouth felt like fire on her skin. Chale stepped in front of her and inserted a thick finger into her sex. Her cunt throbbed, begging for him to relieve the ache.

Voice full of want, she cried out, "More."

Giving her what she wanted, Chale pushed another finger inside, stirring her desire, and filling her with his girth. God, he was touching her in ways that drove her wild, made her feel feral. Ways that she'd only dreamed of a man touching her.

"I need—" Her voice broke off when one of his warriors widened her puckered passage. Heat engulfed her. Lust consumed her thoughts, blistering heat welling up inside her. Never before had she felt so ravenous.

Behind her, the other warrior dropped to his knees, a warm tongue made a pass over her ass, and then she felt a slight pressure as he slipped a finger inside, penetrating her tight passage. Her breath hitched, her orgasm building. The room began spinning before her eyes. She gave a sexy moan, letting them all know how wild and wanton she felt.

Chale continued to pump his fingers in and out of her, plunging deeper while sensuously circling her clit with his thumb. The other men pleasured her ass and her breasts simultaneously. The triple assault brought on a fever. Her cunt muscles clenched with the approach of a climax.

Working together, the three men took her to a place she'd never been before, pleasuring her beyond her wildest imagination, while the guards stood at the door and watched the erotic show.

Nostrils flaring, Chale leaned into her and whispered, "I want to taste your cream." His voice rough with anticipation. With that, he sank to the floor and pressed a hot kiss to her pussy, his tongue burrowing deep, pushing her to the precipice once again.

His teeth scraped over her inflamed clit, stroking her with expertise, burning her flesh. She whimpered, her body going up in a burst of flames.

"That's it, little one. Come in my mouth."

She began trembling against Chale's mouth as he ravished her with dark hunger. Sparks shot through her body and she started to pant.

Chale changed the tempo. His fast, steady thrusts brought her to the point of no return. Giving her no reprieve, he made another pass with his tongue, showering her with pleasure beyond her wildest imagination, driving her into a state of aroused euphoria, making her feel wild, dizzy, feverish. As he continued with his mind-blowing erotic assault, an explosion tore through her and she nearly blacked out.

Her sweet cream poured endlessly into Chale's open mouth. He lapped at her liquid heat, moaning his approval.

When her tremors subsided, Chale slid up her body and pressed his mouth to hers. She could taste her sweetness on his lips. He pushed his cock against her midriff, his aroused scent calling out to her. Her mouth watered, and she wanted to lave him with her tongue.

Desperation fueled her. With single-minded determination, she gyrated against him and whimpered. "Please," she begged. "Let me taste you."

He nodded to his warriors, a silent command, and they went to work removing her shackles. Once the task was completed, Chale discarded his loincloth, then gripped her shoulders and guided her downward.

She settled on her knees before him, taking pleasure in his beautiful cock. She sheathed his shaft in her hands and then licked the juices pearling on the tip. A low moan welled up from his throat.

Olivia pulled him into her mouth, going as deep as possible, with no chance of ever swallowing his entire length. He was far too big for that.

She began working her tongue over his cock, one hand going to his balls, cradling and massaging his heavy sac. Chale's body began moving urgently against her mouth.

Standing beside her, the two warriors began to masturbate, arousing her even more. The entire scene was so wild, so erotic.

Her body grew tight, screaming for her to impale herself on his cock. The need to fuck this virile warrior pulled at her. She wanted him so much she couldn't even think straight. The need to ride him, to feel his gorgeous, engorged cock deep inside her, destroyed her ability to form a rational thought.

His cock swelled in her mouth, filling with heated blood, and she knew he was close. His body trembled. He pulled in a breath, and then, taking her by surprise, gripped her head and tugged her off.

She blinked up at him, not understanding. But when her glance met his, she read his intention. A shiver skipped down her spine.

Chale dropped to the floor and pulled her on top of him. He gripped her hips and guided her onto his erect cock.

"Fuck me, little one."

She moaned in acquiescence and impaled herself on him. "Yesssss…" she cried out, her voice a strangled whisper as her pussy swallowed his entire length. She rocked against him, unable to think about anything but the pleasure. A barrage of sensations closed over her and her body convulsed. Her mouth opened in a silent gasp.

Her hips pitched forward, driving him impossibly deeper. He powered upward, and together they reached a fevered pitch.

As she rode him furiously, nothing mattered. Not time, not space and not even her future. All that mattered was this man, and the pleasure he was giving her. It was addictive, all-consuming. Potent.

And in that instant, she knew it.

She was hooked on estela.

Chale's hands bit into her hips as he slammed into her. She wet her lips, needing desperately for him to ease the escalating tension inside her.

Perspiration speckled their skin; their bodies fused as one. Chale plunged deeper, drawing out the pleasure. Olivia's heart raced, making her breathless. She leaned forward; their tongues joined and tangled. She felt fierce, out of control. She cried out in ecstasy.

Her hands raced over him with aroused eagerness. Her erotic whimpers filled the room as the rippling waves of an orgasm took hold. When Chale pulsed inside her, she stilled her movements and let go, coming all over his cock. He threw his head back and came with a growl.

A moment later she collapsed against his chest in a rumpled heap. Although her body was bruised and sore, her blood was still pulsing hot, her libido aching for so much more. "I don't want to stop, ever," she whimpered, completely overwhelmed by what she was feeling. "I don't ever want this to be over between us."

After a long moment, Chale broke the quiet. "Now do you understand, little one?" A warm palm cupped her chin, bringing them eye to eye.

She nodded, completely understanding: she could never, ever introduce estela to her world. The flower was far too powerful, all-consuming and addictive for that, especially if it landed in the wrong hands.

When Chale's hand traveled over her back and stroked her flesh, she trembled against him.

As though sensing she still had unsatiated needs, Chale found her mouth and kissed her slowly, passionately. "No worries, Olivia. I will keep fucking you until estela works her way out of your system."

JORDON INHALED THE SWEETNESS OF THE ESTELA flower lacing the air, its magical scent the only urging she needed to act, to show her submission to the man called Amador. She went into action, never looking at Olivia or seeking her friend's approval. Perhaps Jordon feared one look at her friend would deliver them both to sanity and reality, would root them both in the logic and conservative actions of two scientists, rather than the desires of two women. She didn't want conservative, didn't want logic—Jordon wanted fantasy. And so she acted, moving forward and falling to her knees in submission before the dark-haired warrior meant to be her protector, acclaimed master of estela, which translated into master of her desires.

"Teach me," she whispered, her hands settling on his strong thighs. His muscles flexed beneath her palms, and electricity raced up her fingers, her arms, her shoulders.

Jordon's eyes locked with Amador's darker ones; the connection sent a sizzle of awareness through her body as if she had been touched—everywhere. Jordon sucked in a breath, shocked by the unnatural reaction to this man; her nipples tightened, her mind conjuring images of his lips brushing them, his tongue teasing them. Her breasts grew fuller, her core aching and wet. How was this possible? Was the incense of the flower enough to send her senses into overdrive, or was it simply this man called Amador? In a far corner of her mind she reminded herself how deprived she was, how needy. It had been two years since her divorce—two years of abstinence. Sex had seemed complicated. Until now. This was the perfect deliverance from a complicated past.

Someone offered Amador a crock. Jordon didn't look away from him to see who, nor did she care. She was lost in the deep, dark depths of this man's eyes, the fantasy of where they would deliver her—where he would deliver her.

Amador eased the bowl into her hand, wrapping her fingers around it as he covered her hand with his. "Drink," he ordered, his English laden with a sexy accent. With words low and resonant, he added, "Let the flower take you beyond your inhibitions, beyond your fears," and his words sent a shiver down her spine.

Fear. Was that in her eyes? Fear? Is that what he saw when he looked at her? She wasn't afraid. Was she? Was there fear behind her charge forward into submission? Had she denied herself satisfaction because of fear? No. She wouldn't go there—to a past bad relationship and a lot of pain she had buried deep below the surface. So why was she even thinking about it now? The here and now was about science, not emotion, not her life. Jordon shoved aside the personal thoughts. She didn't want to think about the past, or even the future—only the opportunity the present moment offered her, the secrets of estela.

"Drink," her warrior urged again, gently prodding with his sensual voice, lifting the cup to her lips.

Yes, please, she screamed in her mind, doing as he ordered. She sipped the sweet beverage, hungry for exploration, for the answers to the questions burning in her mind about estela, about herself. Hungry for the satisfaction her body craved already with a mere inhalation of the flower's incense.

Seconds later, contents of the cup emptied, Jordon gasped as Amador pushed to his feet and scooped her into his strong arms, that broad chest like a wall against her body.

"What are you doing?" she whispered, barely able to find her voice, her arm wrapped around his neck, his dark hair tickling her cheek.

"Protecting you," he declared. "I thought you would be more comfortable elsewhere when the heat consumes you."

"Heat?" she questioned. "I don't feel hot. I feel—" Suddenly heat rushed through her veins. She could barely breathe for the intensity of it. Her skin tingled. Everything tingled. "Oh, God." She had on too many clothes. Needed them off. She reached for her shirt, tried to tug it off but couldn't. "I feel, I need, I—"

"I look forward to finding out exactly what you need, *cariña,*" Amador murmured, continuing forward, taking her into a room she barely glanced at—a fire burning somewhere near, a bed, chairs, a room that looked nothing like a cavern. Nothing like anything but a pleasure palace. "We are here, Jordon, to the place where you will discover your every desire."

She blinked, the sound of her name on his lips erotic, enticing. This man got to her in a big way, this stranger, this warrior. The idea of having a protector was arousing—that he was her protector, her pleasure giver and taker.

"Did I tell you my name?" she asked, realizing she wasn't sure she had. Her mind was foggy with lust, though, and the question was dismissed as soon as she spoke it, the demands of her body taking over.

Jordon curled into him as he carried her; this sexy warrior meant to satisfy her, and that is exactly what she wanted—satisfaction. The desire to touch and be touched controlling her now, ruling her mind and body.

Her hands traveled Amador's perfect body as he took several more steps, his sleek dark skin feeding her need, taut muscle flexing under her command. "What I need is you," she whispered, her gaze traveling to his neck, his lips, meaning those words in a soul-deep way. He called to her beyond understanding. The reason was unimportant. The demand imperative. "I must kiss you. And touch you. I need—"

But she never finished the sentence. Suddenly she was in the center of a massive round bed. She scurried to sit, her fingers curling behind her into the black silk covering of the massive mattress beneath her. Two gorgeous naked men appeared by her side, knees on the mattress. There was no time to think, hardly time to register Amador standing at the end of the bed watching. The men ripped her clothes away. Somewhere in a far corner of her mind she was aware of candles flickering, lining the ceilings, the floors, lighting the erotic paintings that clung to the walls in bright, brilliant colors. Except these things, these images were distant; her burn, her ache, was ever-present.

She wanted to scream out and say she wanted Amador, and him alone, but her body betrayed that inner thought. The touch of these two men's hands on her skin inflamed her with desire. She was naked, with one naked man behind her, one in front, their hands exploring, caressing. They touched her everywhere, yet she couldn't feel enough of them. She arched into them, begged and pleaded for more. Her skin sizzled with each touch; her nipples ached as fingers teased them, tongues flicked the hardened peaks. And her core dripped, clenched, ached. Her legs spread, her fingers touching her sensitive flesh, her eyes seeking out those of Amador. "You," she managed to whisper urgently as one of the men tweaked her nipple with his teeth. "Not them."

Amador stared at her several seconds, his gaze traveling her body, stroking her with heat before finding her gaze again. Holding her stare, he spoke. "Come here," he ordered, still at the end of the bed.

The men sauntered away from her as if the words Amador

spoke had staked a claim—his eyes certainly did. They showed possessiveness, ownership. And it aroused Jordon. Aroused her to the point of damn near making her orgasm just thinking about him taking her.

Jordon had always fantasized about a strong, dominant man in bed, one who knew how to take a woman in all the right ways. But until now, she'd never given herself to one, fearful he'd take more than she was willing to offer. Here and now, though, there was no denying her wants and needs. Nor was there any fear of facing the morning and finding that her submission had come with a price. Desire, perhaps desire driven by estela, demanded she submit as she wished to. It demanded she allow herself to live the fantasy of being submissive. She'd felt it from the moment she fell to her knees before Amador. He was her master of the moment. Jordon swallowed hard, excitement lodging her breath in her throat.

Slowly Jordon repositioned herself on the bed, crawling toward Amador, then rising to her knees in front of him. She resisted the urge to touch him, her instincts telling her she must wait.

He stared at her, his dark eyes intense, hot. "Tell me what you want."

"You," she whispered, unable to find her voice, desire heavy in her limbs. "I want you."

A long pause, then, "I'm not sure you're ready for what I require of you." His eyes brushed her nipples, and her core spasmed in response.

"I am," she insisted, wanting him, needing him, ready to beg, which was beyond what she would expect of herself, but no less true. In a stronger voice she repeated her declaration. "I am."

He studied her for a few long, intense moments. "Turn around and face forward." Jordon hesitated, a tiny slice of her mind hanging on to the need for control. Amador's expression softened. His hand caressed her cheek, and goose bumps shivered their way up her spine in reaction. "You are truly strong, *cariña*. Estela is powerful, yet your fears still linger. Release them. Release them to me. Trust me. I will not hurt you."

She let out a shaky breath; his touch was gentle, contrasting with his powerful body, his warriorlike appearance. Jordon did, indeed, trust him, she realized. Why? She didn't know. She didn't give trust easily. It scared her that she wanted to now, but it was also extremely erotic to give herself so completely to a stranger.

Without a word, she acted, turning to do as ordered, giving him her back. She heard movement behind her, the swish of cloth, and Jordon knew he was now naked; her mind conjured images of what he must look like, aroused, ready for her. Images that had her dying to turn around, to see for herself.

But before she could cave in to that desire, he was there, his hands on her waist, pulling her back against his body, settling his cock between her legs, his hands palming her breasts. Jordon whimpered at the feel of his body, his touch. Her body arched into him. His lips brushed her neck, and then his teeth.

"Lean forward on your hands and knees," he ordered, his voice low and taut.

"I can't," she replied, not able to bring herself to pull away from him.

"You can and you will," he quickly said, his voice terse now as he pressed her forward, insistence reinforced with words and actions. When she was on all fours, his hand settled on her lower back. "Do not move until I give permission." His hands slid over her backside, palming it, possessive aggression in his touch. "Understand?"

"Yes," she hissed as he pressed her thighs farther apart, his fingers probing between her legs, teasing the sensitive flesh there, rewarding her for submission. Seconds later the long, hard length of him was there, stroking her, teasing her, but never giving her what she wanted—him inside her. Yet release crept up on her; her body threatened to orgasm without him entering her.

As if he sensed how close she was, he pulled back, taking her away from the ultimate sensation she sought, only a moment before she tumbled over into it. "Amador, please!" she cried out, trying to turn.

His hands held her hips, keeping her in place. "Patience, *cariña*. The best comes to those who wait."

But she needed to come, with an urgency that hurt—the ache of desire thrusting through her, as she wanted his cock to. She would have said as much, but he was suddenly on top of her, pushing her flat against the mattress as he settled carefully over her, framing her with just the right amount of delicious weight.

His lips were near her ear. "Is this what you want?" he demanded, his erection sliding along the wet folds of her body.

"Yes," she gasped, trying to lift her hips upward, trying to make him come to her. "Inside me. I want you inside me."

"Soon," he promised, his hand sliding down her ribs, over her waist, flattening on one butt cheek.

"Now," she demanded. "Now."

But he didn't give her what she wanted. Instead, he slid back and forth along her core, teasing and teasing. She moved against him, wild with the burn, squirming, aching, begging. And finally—finally—he gave in to her pleading. Amador slid inside her with one hard, deep thrust, burying his cock inside her.

She cried out with the joy of being filled, with the relief that lasted only seconds. For one need turned to another—simple penetration wasn't enough. Nor was it for him apparently. He answered her silent cries for movement with a hard pumping of his hips. Over and over, he pounded into her, driving his erection to the hilt, driving her pleasure to the edge and then tumbling her into release. Without warning, her body clenched around his cock, spasms ripping through her with more force than she thought possible, pleasure hitting nerve endings she didn't know existed. Even her fingertips tingled.

When her body calmed, she went limp. Amador responded by turning her over and kissing her, a seduction in and of itself. For one minute she was satisfied; the next, aroused and ready again. It seemed she hadn't gotten enough of Amador. And as he slid back inside her, still erect, she was relieved to know he, too, desired more.

The pleasure was intense, overwhelming, unbelievable. How could anyone get enough of something this good? How could anyone say no to this kind of pleasure? If she had doubted estela's power, she no longer did. Estela, and Amador, had her attention…and her full submission.

What must have been hours later, Jordon collapsed on top of Amador, and amazingly, the sweet bliss of relaxation slid through her body. For hours she'd been driven to seek that very sensation, begging Amador for more and more. Finally estela had worn off, and she felt the comforting sensation of being sated.

Amador's hand stroked the back of her hair, gently, tenderly. She felt a strange connection to him, an outcome she wondered if she should credit to estela or the man himself. Wanting an answer, she pressed upward on her hands with what little strength she still possessed, her eyes seeking his, seeking answers. In them she found such intelligence, such gentleness, yet still he managed to exude that animal masculinity. Indeed, he took her by storm, despite the fading effects of the flower.

Abruptly Amador moved, rolling her to her back, his big body framing hers, his warm lips caressing hers for the briefest of moments. His weight rested on his arms as he stared down at her. "You trust me," he said, and it wasn't a question.

"Yes."

"And I am worthy of that trust, *cariña,* but what if I were another? What if I had used estela to garner your submission with dark intentions?"

She knew where he was going with this, trying to point out the dangers of estela, the reasons she had to leave without it. She'd come too far, risked too much, to accept defeat so easily. "I chose to give myself to you because I sensed I could trust you. I had my free will."

"There is nothing wrong with giving yourself to someone who deserves the gift you offer—and your body and your trust are gifts—but those things should be given freely and to a man who deserves them. You would have given yourself to my men, unable to stop yourself from seeking satisfaction at all cost. As your protector, I didn't allow them to take you. I only allowed them to touch you, as they did, for one reason—to show you how easily you would have gone to a place you didn't want to go under the flower's influence."

Jordon swallowed hard, her chest pounding with the rapid beats of her heart. He was right. She didn't want him to be, but he was. She'd needed satisfaction and would have taken it however she could have gotten it, if not for him sending the other men away.

His finger brushed hair out of her eyes. "I know how important this discovery is to you. It is to me, as well. But if the flower escapes our protection here, it will be used to manipulate people. It would control humankind, rather than help it."

Insistence and hope rose inside her. "There has to be a way to use its abilities for good."

"I have no doubt there is a way," he agreed readily. "And we've tried. What you see here is only what we've allowed you to see. We have great minds at work and labs with high-tech equipment. But despite decades of efforts, regardless of how it's packaged, how it's manipulated, the flower's ability to control desire always prevails. Until we discover how to stop that from happening, it must stay here." A smile touched his sensual mouth; his eyes softened. "There is only one way you can work with estela." He didn't wait for an answer. "You, and your friend, as well, could join us. Be a part of our research team."

She laughed at that, a bit halfheartedly. The offer was tempting, but she had a job, family, friends at home. So did Olivia. The here and now was fantasy, a detour meant to be left behind. Still, she felt regret at the prospect of leaving it behind, not quite ready to do so.

"You could come back with us," she countered, finding she meant the words, surprising herself with how much. "Study estela with us. Perhaps we have resources that would help."

"Ah, *cariña,* you know deep down that I, like estela, am a part of this jungle. I belong here."

Indeed. Part of what made him so special was the wildness beneath the surface, a wildness that could never be captive to another type of life. But she clung to more time with him. "I'm not ready to leave yet."

"No one is rushing you," he murmured against her lips, a second before he kissed her—a long, sensual kiss. His arousal became evident as his erection settled more fully between her legs, growing longer, fuller with each stroke of his tongue against hers. And when he slid inside her, filling her, completing her, she decided estela had given her a gift. A gift of insight. For now she knew she was capable of giving herself to another man—and that she could trust again despite a past that had made her doubt she could. But first, before giving trust to another, she had to learn to trust herself, to trust her instincts. Instincts that she now knew would lead her to the right place—back to satisfaction, to a new life, complete with passion and pleasure.

HOURS LATER, CHALE LED OLIVIA BACK TO THE main chamber, where she found Jordon already waiting. Olivia glanced at her friend, who looked worn, satiated and alive, a new light shining in her eyes. Olivia could definitely relate.

Olivia reached out, grabbed Jordon's hand and squeezed, happy to see her friend. Together they stood before Donato, as Chale and Amador took their seats beside him.

Donato's soulful eyes studied the two women. After a long, thoughtful moment, he spoke in a soft tone. "What you have learned here, you will tell no other." It was a statement, not a question.

They were both intelligent enough to know that estela must forever remain a secret, or at least until the world was prepared for such a powerful aphrodisiac.

"We understand," Jordon said, and they both nodded in agreement.

Donato smiled, stood and gestured with a wave. "Your guide will be waiting for you."

Chale stepped up beside Olivia while Amador moved in next to Jordon. The two men slowly led them back outside, to the larger cavern where they'd first entered the evening before.

Olivia squinted against the morning light, surprised that the night had flown by so quickly. Her gaze raked over the majestic area, soaking in all the beauty as they followed the same path out. A moment later, they came upon the rope. Olivia glanced up to see their guide. Arms crossed, he nodded his head slowly.

Olivia gripped the rope and tugged, testing it. She turned to Jordon and noticed that she was speaking quietly with Amador.

"Perhaps we will meet again," Amador said.

"You can still come with us," Jordon whispered to him.

"I belong here," Amador replied. "But perhaps one day, that will change and I will find you."

Olivia cast one longing look Chale's way, keeping the memories of his erotic touch close until they, too, met again, as she somehow knew they would.

As though reading her thoughts, Chale smiled, gathered her into his arms and brushed his lips over hers. "Until we meet again, little one."

"Until we meet again," she whispered into his mouth.

★ ★ ★ ★ ★

THIS IS WHAT I WANT

MEGAN HART

THIS IS WHAT I WANT.

Your hands make circles around my ankles. They shackle me for but a moment before your fingertips move upward over the edge of bone, the dip and hollow of muscle and flesh. Over my calves and the prickly surface of my knees, where they linger to stroke the soft, smooth underside. Those untouched places. Your fingers linger there, seeking creases.

Your thumbs move up the sun-warmed flesh of my thighs, which I part for you beneath summer's bright golden light. Like the breeze that twitches the ends of my hair, your fingers drift along my skin, moving higher.

This is what I want. You. Touching me.

You take the time to trace the faint white line, the place where once my flesh parted beneath the edge of a razor wielded by an unsteady hand. You don't ask about this scar. You ask nothing, say nothing. You have no voice but that which I grant you...and so far I haven't given you permission to speak.

You kneel in front of me, and this is where I like you. How I like you. On your knees, my body aligned for your worship and your hands smoothing a constant upward path.

This is what I want—your breath on my skin. Your fingers parting me. Your mouth finding the sweet, small pearl of my clitoris. I want

your tongue there, and the pressure of your lips. I want you to lick me
as I stand over you, you upon your knees.
I want you to worship me.

"Hold that elevator!" Eve Grant called across the lobby,
already knowing it was a futile request. The elevator was super
slow and had a cranky habit of stalling, forcing the employees
of Digiquest to trudge up and down the stairs. Nobody was
willing to contribute to a breakdown by stopping the doors
once they were closing, not even at five to nine and knowing
she was only hollering because if she had to wait for the
elevator or take the stairs, she would be late clocking in.

Almost nobody.

A hand appeared at the last second, sliding between the
slow-closing door and the wall. The elevator door bounced
against it before grudgingly sliding back open. Eve grabbed
up her bag and ran. Her sprint wasn't dignified or graceful,
but she wasn't about to let the chance pass.

"Thanks," she said as she hopped into the elevator just
before the door closed, finally. "I appreciate it."

"No problem."

Lane DeMarco, six-foot-four of gorgeous and a half inch
of fantastic, smiled at her. Eve automatically smiled in return.
Lane's smile was hard to resist.

Eve and Lane had been hired at the same time—she in
customer service and he in IT. They'd been through the bat-
tlefield of employee orientation together and two years of
office picnics and holiday parties, but it hadn't made them
anything more than acquaintances. He was just the sort of guy
who'd flirt enough to flatter but not freak out, the kind who'd
smile and hold the elevator for someone. Anyone. It didn't
make her special or anything.

Lane lifted an insulated cup to his lips and sipped. Watching
his throat work as he swallowed was bad enough, but when

his tongue slid out along his lips to swipe away the creamy coffee, she had to look away.

"That smells good," she said about the coffee, because the only thing worse than making inane conversation was standing in awkward silence.

Where were her words when she needed them? Why could she speak to strangers online, share with them her most intimate secrets, yet she couldn't do more than mumble with Lane? Why was he so…unattainable?

Lane swirled the liquid in the cup and sipped again. "It's called a Mocha Mint. I got it from the new place next door, the Beanery. Have you tried it?"

"No." Her stomach rumbled, reminding her she'd run out of the house without breakfast. Again. She really needed to get up earlier if she was going to blog before work. "I'll have to check it out."

The elevator dinged. One more floor to go. It actually might have been faster to take the stairs…but then she'd have missed out on the exquisite torture of riding up with Lane.

The door opened on their floor. Lane hung back to allow Eve to exit first, depriving her of the chance to ogle his ass. *Shit.* Was he ogling hers? Eve glanced over her shoulder, but found Lane's gaze trained on her face. Was that better or worse? Worse, she decided, but not unexpected. Lane might be the star of most of her naughty online fantasies, but to him she was just another computer to fix.

As if he'd read her mind, he asked, "Are you still having that problem with your chat windows freezing up?"

"Oh, yeah." She hadn't forgotten about the support request she'd put in. Lane wasn't the only IT guy on staff, but she'd been hoping he'd be the one to take the task.

"I'll swing by in a bit to check it out, okay?"

She nodded and gave him a little wave as she watched him saunter away. *Gah. He's all that and a bag of chips.*

In her pod, Eve tossed her bag onto the spare chair and shook her mouse to wake the computer, then logged in quickly, barely making it before the clock clicked from 9:00 a.m. to 9:01 a.m. and made her officially late. Her queue was already five customers deep, the blinking cursor an impatient reminder she was here to work, not fantasize about Lane DeMarco, no matter how tempting it was. Her fingers tapped away at the keys that would bring up the first customer from her queue. She had a minute or two of prewritten remarks to get through before she had to actually engage her mind.

Some poor sap was having a dickens of a time figuring out how to get his wireless devices to talk to one another, a problem so common Eve had no trouble solving it. She finished the chat with the last of the scripted phrases and logged off. Immediately, a new message window opened and she started all over. It was another easy chat with a simple solution. The faceless person on the other side of the Internet didn't abuse emoticons or need the instructions repeated more than once, and Eve worked her way through the necessary steps without issue. Unfortunately, just before she inserted the text asking if she'd completed the chat to the customer's satisfaction, the screen froze. She tried every key combination she knew and finally got it working again, but the customer had already logged off. Damn. It could mean a survey response of unsatisfactory for her, maybe, which wouldn't look good on her performance statistics, but she didn't have time to worry because the next window demanded her attention and she got back to work.

Lather, rinse, repeat.

Four hours later her stomach still rumbled and she desperately needed a break. She hadn't even had time to do more than take a peek or two at her blog. The comments were coming in fast and furious, but had to go unanswered, a fact that was killing her. She peeked again, satisfying herself with at least reading what people were saying before pushing away from the computer with a stretch. She headed to the restroom and then to the break room. The busy morning had kept her from pondering too much about what she'd write later tonight, but with the bathroom out of the way and a coffee and doughnut to fill the hole in her gut, Eve had time to think about what waited for her at home.

Most of the comments to her blog were one-liners or casual compliments. Praise for her writing or the ideas she'd presented. A fair number were from what she considered admirers—bloggers who got turned on by her entries and weren't shy about telling her so. Every once in a while she even earned a "troll," someone who commented with the sole purpose of insulting her or her readers and taunting them into a battle of words. Eve never engaged trolls, simply deleting their comments without reply.

Sometimes, though, she got something special. A fellow blogger, maybe, with similar tastes. Occasionally a particular comment turned into a spectacular dialogue and led her to places she hadn't known she could go—or wanted to. Other times, someone new found her online persona and left a comment that led to another, and a friendship grew out of that small, random moment.

She sipped the bad coffee and nibbled the sugary doughnut on her way back to her pod. Her pulse leaped a little, thinking of what they'd said and what they'd say, how they'd react, her faceless admirers.

Her worshippers.

Some, she knew, like Puppetboy1241, would rave about this morning's post. He always loved the ones in which she demanded homage. He'd already offered, privately, to be her slave not only online but in real life, too.

Well, not hers, precisely. Not Eve's. He wanted to be slave to Eris Apparent, the name she blogged under. It was a

tempting offer and one she might have considered but for one
small reason. A simple, silly and ridiculous reason, Eve thought
as she rounded the corner into her pod. She stopped short at
the sight of her computer screen, which she'd left open to her
queue but was now back at the log-in screen, and the Mocha
Mint cup, steam still curling lazily from the top, sitting on her
desk. An unattainable reason.

Lane DeMarco.

This is what I want.

*You, surrounded by books. They teeter in towers ready to topple with
a glance, and you've settled in the midst of them like a king looking
over stacks of gold. Papers in piles make whispering noises when you
shuffle them. The room smells of ink and paper. Of intellect.*

*You're bent over the desk, scribbling furiously. Your glasses have
slipped down to the end of your nose, and I know you'll push them
up when you think of it, but for now your tongue is caught between
your teeth as you concentrate. Your pen scratches on the paper, creating
worlds with words.*

You're lost to everything.

Except me.

*I make no noise, but you lift your head anyway, as if you've
scented me…and maybe you have. Among the smells of ink and
paper, of dust, I carry the odor of roses, because that is how you
imagined I would smell. I wear white, because that's what you
dreamed I would wear.*

*I'm the princess of every fairy tale you've ever read. The maiden in
the tower, the sleeping beauty, the cinder-smudged waif waiting for her
prince. I am your desire made flesh; my blood, the ink in your pen;
my skin, the crumpled softness of your parchment.*

*You put down your pen. I glide to you on slippered feet, silent. There
is room on your desk, when we make it. The sound of the books hitting
the ground is very loud. Neither of us turns our head to see the de-
struction. All you want to see is me.*

You reach for me. Your hands find all the places on my body you've spent long hours creating. You kiss me, soft and slow, and hold me as carefully as though I were built of glass.

I sigh, as you want me to, when you push me onto your desk and lift the silk of my skirt over my thighs. Your hands slide up my skin. Your mouth brushes the soft floss of my pubic curls and your thumbs part me to your gaze.

"You're so beautiful."

I have longed to hear your voice from your own mouth, to hear you say the words you've thus far only written. I like your voice. It's low, deep. Rough like the rasp of a cat's tongue. I shiver.

You kiss between my legs as sweetly as you did my mouth. I arch into your embrace when you slide your arms under my shoulders. Your mouth finds my throat. My fingers rake your back when you enter me; your cry of surprise urges one from my lips. You push into me, nevertheless, and fill me with heat and pleasure.

I was made to take pleasure from your touch, and I writhe under you as you thrust. I wrap my legs around your waist and hold you closer. Under my hands your shoulders tense.

Ecstasy fills me like water, overflowing. My body shakes. You hiss when I carve the evidence of my passion into your skin. You fuck me harder and we both surge into delight.

Later you stroke my hair as you murmur the litany of my many names. I am your princess, your waif, your creation. I am your desire made real.

Her latest blog entry had been live for only a few minutes before the first comment came. The rush of it swept through Eve all the way to her toes. There was nothing quite like the thrill of almost-instant feedback.

You're brilliant.

"Thanks, Puppetboy," she murmured, leaning back in her chair. It wasn't the first time he'd said so.

Depeche Mode crooned at Eve from her speakers and she adjusted the volume as she refreshed her browser to reveal three more comments. Her e-mail program dinged at the same time, alerting her. She smiled, savoring it. She'd make poor Puppet wait for a reply while she read the others.

Eva had started blogging two years ago during a messy breakup with the man she'd been certain she was going to marry. Not because she was madly in love with him, though she had been, once upon a time. No, she'd been certain she would marry Brad because he loved her.

Or at least he had, once upon a time.

For Eve, the standard, once-a-week missionary position had ceased to satisfy, but Brad had been threatened by her suggestion they explore what he called "that kinky shit." She'd long felt he didn't really listen to her, but time and time again he'd proved it when she'd tried to interest him in something beyond the plain vanilla sex life they had.

She couldn't pinpoint when she knew she no longer loved him, nor could she determine exactly the moment he stopped loving her. It would have made things so much easier if she could have. But no, convinced of the other's esteem, both had struggled in the relationship for too long, until finally they not only no longer loved each other, she was pretty sure they'd hated each other. Because someone who cares about another person doesn't try to hurt them over and over again just for fun, which was what it felt like Brad had been doing to her, and a person who loves another doesn't shut that person out completely, the way she'd done to him.

Her first blog had served as a way to relieve some of the anxiety of the breakup, which had turned ugly not only emotionally but financially. When Brad discovered what he considered a betrayal of their intimate life, it had turned ugly physically, as well.

He'd only hit her once, mostly by accident because she got between him and the computer he was intent on smashing, but once was more than enough. Eve had kicked him in the nuts and told him to get the fuck out of her house and her life. She hadn't heard from him since, and if there were times when her bed seemed vastly empty, there were more times when she considered the silence that greeted her every night the purest sort of blessing.

The experience with Brad had taught Eve the wisdom of using a different name online, however, and she'd chosen Eris Apparent as sort of a whim. The goddess of chaos had seemed a perfect namesake for the turmoil in her life at the time.

Her second blog wasn't about her real life at all, but rather the life she imagined for herself. To her surprise, for Brad had done his best to convince her she was an anomaly, she was far from the only person blogging about sex. She'd discovered an entire community where she could, for the first time, be herself.

Or someone else.

Eris liked what Eve liked, but Eris was the one with the guts to put it out there for the world to see. Eris was the one who came up with the flirty, sexy responses or snappy comebacks. She was everything Eve was inside but hadn't yet managed to bring to the surface. And also, frankly, Eris was Eve's shield, saying and living the sorts of virtual experiences Eve was afraid to tackle in reality.

Three more replies materialized, all from regular readers. She granted Puppetboy some mercy and gave him a command or two she knew would send him into a frenzy of gratitude. Hell, truthfully, knowing that somewhere he was refreshing his browser as often as she was, hanging on her every word, was a huge turn-on. For Puppetboy, she *was* a goddess.

She traded a few back-and-forths with fellow sex blogger Lavender_whiskey, mostly good-natured taunts about the alternate uses for men's ties. Lavender wrote more often about submission while Eve's fantasies tended more toward being in charge, but both of them wrote about what they wanted.

She hadn't done ninety percent of what she wrote about, but that didn't matter. That was the point of fantasy, after all. It didn't have to be practical. She'd grown to think of Eris as almost a different person. Someone bolder. Someone worshipped.

Loved.

She was getting ready to sign off for the night when one last comment came through. She didn't recognize the user name, Tell_me, but there was nothing unusual about that. Through the wonder and glory of blog lists, Technorati and search engines, Eris's blog got hundreds of hits a day.

I like what you want.

Tired and ready for sleep, she debated not bothering to reply, but it had become a point of pride with her that all comments, aside from the obvious flames, got an answer. She hated blogs that grandstanded and poked, demanding attention, but gave none in return. If you were going to blog-hop and pimp yourself, you should be prepared to reply to someone who took the time to leave a comment.

Thanks for stopping by, she typed. It was a mild answer, neither encouraging nor insulting.

It was past time for bed. She'd spent hours online, chatting and commenting and living her life as someone different, but her real life paid the bills, and her real-life body needed sleep. The ping of her e-mail stopped her in the doorway, and like any true addict, Eve gave in and checked "just one more time." It was Tell_me again.

Do you really not care who I am? I think you do.

She paused, fingers on the keyboard, debating. Was this a troll, or a sincere question? Readers like Puppetboy never dared question her entries, but constant praise meant nothing without occasional criticism to temper it. And the use of *I*...

Eve hesitated. She wrote a sex blog. She didn't cyberfuck strangers.

What makes you think I mean you?

Two minutes passed with agonizing slowness while she waited for the answer.

Because you said so.

She had to smile at that and admit it was true, at least as far as her word choice was concerned.

So who are you? She waited, tension coiled tight in her belly and had almost given up when the new comment appeared, the answer that would keep her up, tossing and turning, for most of the rest of the night.

I'm what you want.

"Thanks for the coffee." There was no way for her not to say it, not with Lane holding the elevator door open for her yet again. "It was good."

The door closed with a slow, dull thud, but the cranky elevator didn't move. Lane punched the button for the fourth floor. The elevator shuddered slightly as a grinding noise came from above them and then lurched into its ascent.

"Was it what you wanted?" The question, asked so casually, wasn't what made the breath catch in Eve's throat.

No, that was from the look in Lane's eyes.

"It was good," she repeated, her voice gone whisper soft. Hoarse.

Lane smiled. "Good."

If this was a story, she'd have pushed him back against the hazy mirrored wall and had her way with him…but this wasn't one of her stories. Nothing ever was, that was the problem. Men—real men—inevitably disappointed, and dating someone she worked with?

Not a fantasy she'd ever had, not even in her blog.

She cut her gaze from his though she sensed his eyes on her until the elevator jerked to a reluctant stop and the doors creaked open. He reached to hold the door, which had a penchant for trying to trap people, and Eve stepped through with a murmured "Thank you."

"Anytime," Lane said.

For one instant an image of Lane bending her over a smooth, polished desk filled Eve's mind. Blood lifted to the surface of her skin, bringing heat. Her fingers would be spread. His hands would lift her skirt….

"Hey, Lane, I was looking for you!" Debbie Chambers, Eve's pod neighbor, pounced. "I've got a problem with my computer. Can you come help me?"

Eve didn't wait to see if Lane gave Debbie the same slow smile he'd given her. She walked off with a small wave, not looking back.

There was one major problem with that little scenario anyway, she thought as she slid into her chair and logged in. They worked at Digiquest, home to the typical office cubicle jungle. Nary a polished wooden desk to be found, even if it was what she wanted.

Was it what she wanted?

I am what you want.

For an instant, she heard the words from last night's newfound admirer spoken in Lane's voice. She knew how he'd sound, how his voice would dip low and gravelly, even though she'd never heard it that way. Her belly tightened and her fingers hovered over the keyboard, itching to open her blog. To see if Tell_me had commented again.

Surfing the Internet for personal use was officially forbidden, even though she knew many of her colleagues spent as much time online shopping, paying bills or chatting with their friends as they did on their queues. She'd never heard of anyone getting in trouble as long as they met their quotas and didn't do something stupid, like download porn. She didn't consider the stories she wrote as Eris Apparent porn, but they were certainly skirting the issue of what was or wasn't work-safe.

The long, dull hours of fairly mindless work had always provided the perfect time for her to think of what she wanted to blog about. She often spent entire days locked deep in her fantasies, perfecting and honing the words she'd later use to describe her imaginary sensual exploits. Her blog was a beautiful addiction, the rush she got from writing and commenting as compelling as the ecstasy brought on by drugs or booze. The interlude this morning and the conversation with Lane in the elevator had merely amplified her desire, but with the problems her computer was having, she didn't dare do anything about it.

It was a very, very long day.

By the time she got home, her body ached from tension caused by the hours of sexual fantasy. She had her entire entry plotted out, with no more than the most minor of changes needed to create the perfection she owed her readers. Hell… owed herself.

The computer screen flickered to life when she tapped the keyboard, waking from its sleep like a lover lifting his head from the pillow to greet her as she came home. The comparison gave her a moment's pause, but only a moment's. Her computer was more of a lover to her than any man had been in months. It certainly gave her more of what she needed in a partner. Always ready, always available, always faithful. She opened her browser, then her e-mail program, and smiled as the *ping, ping, ping* alerted her to a full in-box.

Twelve new comments and a few extra e-mails, too.

She savored the anticipation. Had he commented? Though the anonymity of the Internet meant it could have been a woman, she knew it was a he, a man. It had to be.

She deleted several messages offering to enlarge her penis and skimmed the comment notifications, none of them from him. But the second to last e-mail was from a user name she recognized.

She let out a breath she'd been unaware of holding.

"Well, hello," she murmured as her fingers on the keys stroked open the message.

Two words only, but they hit her like a tsunami.

I'm waiting.

I should be angry by the time you come through the door, because you're late. Instead, the waiting has only made me hungrier for you. I wait until you set down your briefcase, close the door, shrug out of the charcoal-gray jacket of your expensive suit. I wait as you hang it carefully, so it doesn't rumple. When you reach to loosen the knot of the tie at your throat, I can't wait any longer.

It makes a nice leash by which to lead you. A handle I can use to open you for me. I pull it, hard, silk fisted in my fingers, and your mouth comes down to meet mine.

You smell of cologne and newsprint, of expensive lunches and hostile takeovers. Your clothes cost more than some people's car payments, and your body beneath them is sculpted from hours in the gym.

Do I care who you are behind your wide, smooth mahogany desk? Behind your contracts and your Montblanc pen? Do I care who you are in the office? No. Because you're here now, and you're mine, and that's what matters to me.

"Take off your shirt, but leave the tie."

Your look, quizzical, doesn't stop you from obeying. You tug the knot harder, widen the loop and ease it from the prison of your collar. You strip yourself of pink linen and toss the shirt to the floor, careless with it in a way you were not with your jacket.

"And the pants."

Oh, you enjoy this, and the pants are down around your ankles and kicked to the side in minutes. Socks come next, but I don't tell you to take off your briefs. Not yet. I like to watch the shape of your cock beneath the soft, heather-gray cotton. I like to watch you get hard for me.

This is what I want, to be on my knees in front of you. I want to run my hand over your prick and watch your hips bump forward against my caress. I want to nuzzle the crisp, curling hairs of your thighs and inhale your scent. I want to close my eyes and bump at the front of your boxer briefs with my face, the way a cat will bump at its owner's hand to encourage petting.

I wet the front of your briefs with my mouth, my breath hot and seeping through the fabric to cover you. I want to feel the outline of your erection with my lips and teeth and tongue blunted by the material. I want you to thread your fingers in my hair and tug to tip my head so I look up at your face.

I want to hear you say "Please," as if my mouth on your cock is a gift you're not certain you deserve.

I want to give it to you.

Down go the briefs, over your thighs, knees, calves, ankles. Now there is nothing between my mouth and your cock but desire, and soon enough not even that, because I engulf you.

That sound you make, that low, startled moan, never ceases to amaze and arouse me. I am on my knees before you and sucking your dick, my hand on your balls, and you whisper my name.

That is the gift you give me, the sound of my name in a rough rasp. You give me your need, your desire, your passion. You give me your ecstasy, too, the taste of you flooding my mouth.

I want to come with your cock lodged in my throat and your hands pulling my hair. I want to come to the sound of my name, shouted, and the pulse of your prick against my tongue.

Eve was almost late to work again, but this time she couldn't blame the slow elevator. She'd stayed up too late the night before, replying to comments and e-mails from her mysterious new admirer. They'd both been online, his replies to her coming nearly as fast as instant messages.

She hadn't been quite ready to offer that next level of communication, somehow more intimate than simple e-mails and yet not as personal as the telephone. The barrier of time between replies allowed her the luxury to think of what she wanted to say. It was easier to remain Eris when she could make each message almost a mini blog entry of its own, when she could take her time to form her words. Real-time conversation intimidated her.

She hadn't signed off until that point in the night just before it would have made more sense to stay awake until morning. She'd fallen asleep almost at once despite the fever of blood pulsing in her veins and dreamed exquisitely of hands, mouths, tongues and cocks. She'd woken as orgasm rippled through her, twenty minutes after her alarm had rung unheard in the erotic landscapes of her dreams.

Today coffee wasn't just a want, it was a physical need, and not poofy designer coffee, either. Eve gripped an industrial-size double espresso as she rounded the corner to her pod and stopped short.

"Morning." Lane bent over her desk. "I'm here to fix your computer."

His tie, patterned with a long, ceaseless stream of numbers, fell over her keyboard. She couldn't stop staring at it. She didn't think she'd ever seen him wear a tie before. "Oh."

"Routine inspection." Lane worked the mouse to bring up a scrambled bunch of files Eve couldn't interpret. "Apparently management wants to replace some of this equipment, rebuild some of the databases. Yours was logged as one of the ones having trouble."

Eve leaned against the padded wall of her pod. "Have you figured out why my chat connections keep dropping?"

"Let me bring up your directory." Lane pointed to her monitor. "I'll be able to figure out what's going on from there."

He straightened. Eve watched his fingers stroke the smooth material. Over the past two years she'd watched those hands dismember a hard drive and fly over a keyboard with the precision and genius of a piano virtuoso playing a concerto. Lane had very, very nice hands. Strong and nimble, yet gentle enough to coax a recalcitrant computer back from death or force it into submission.

Eve had spent hours thinking of Lane's hands.

"Nice tie," she said abruptly, when he caught her staring.

"It's pi."

"Pie?" Eve's brow furrowed momentarily as she imagined cherry or blueberry, only after a moment realizing he meant the number. "Oh. Pi. I get it. Clever."

Again Lane's long fingers smoothed over the satiny material. "Yeah. I felt like wearing a tie today."

"I like it," Eve said.

Silence.

Lane smiled.

An inferno burned in her cheeks as Eve busied herself suddenly with a stack of paperwork. She'd never considered herself shy by any means, but she wore her lust for him in the quirk of her lips and flutter of her lashes. She didn't want him to see it.

"Here's your problem." He pointed to her monitor. "Someone's been playing around online."

"It wasn't me," she said a second before his teasing smile told her he hadn't meant her. "Must be the night shift."

"I know. I can tell who it is," he said with a lift of his chin at the long list of files. "The time they logged in, what sites they're surfing. All of it."

Eve thought of the day he'd brought her coffee and was very glad she'd resisted blogging at work over the past week. "The night shift must have a lot of free time."

"Yeah." Lane bent to peer at the screen. "And someone likes to hit the personals sites."

"Is that what's screwing up my computer?" Not that she cared, actually, because as long as her chat connections kept dropping she'd be paid to watch Lane work.

"Yep. But don't worry. I can fix it." He shot her another grin and heat flared again…this time, much lower down. "Just call me Dr. DeMarco."

He was killing her. Absolutely killing, she thought as he bent back to work, fingers caressing her keyboard with as much intimacy as if he were touching her body.

And he didn't even know it.

This is what I want.

The lines around your eyes and mouth should make you look haggard, but they only remind me of how beautiful you are. Even exhausted, rumpled, smelling of bad cafeteria coffee and clad in crumpled scrubs, you are lovely.

You lean over the desk to hand the charge nurse your clipboard. She smiles at you and bats her lashes, and I want to laugh. She thinks she has a chance at you, her own personal Dr. McDreamy, but she has no idea. Not a clue.

You are mine.

You are weary from hours on your feet, hours in the operating room. You've put on clean scrubs, but I know you want to shower and shave, sleep for a few hours, maybe grab another cup of disgusting coffee. I know that's what you want, but instead you'll have me.

You look up from your place on the hard cot they give the on-call staff to use when I close the door behind me. I lock it. When I smile, you smile, too.

I don't ask you how long we have. At any moment the black box clipped to your waistband can bleat. People will need you. You fix them with your scalpel and your knowledge. At any moment someone could need you more than I do…but for now there is only me.

I don't like the smells of antiseptic and despair that fill the air here, or the metallic scent of blood we can't seem to escape. I miss your clean scent, soap and hot water, but there's no time for that.

Your head tips back when I thread my fingers through your hair and pull, and you moan. You might be a god to that nurse at the desk and the people who you heal, but I know you're no god.

You're a man.

I know you're bare beneath the scrubs, a habit surgeons have to prevent their personal clothes from becoming soiled. I know if I reach between us I'll find your cock half-hard already beneath the thin, soft cloth. I know if I slid onto your lap I'll feel that heat against me, that hardness, and my body clenches at the thought of you filling me; my nipples tighten.

I brush your lips with mine, the barest hint of a kiss. When your mouth reaches for mine I pull back. I'd like to make you beg for me, to hear you say my name in that low, deep, grumble-growly voice, but I know we don't really have time for those sorts of games.

"Touch me," I say into your ear.

You do.

One of those hands, those big, strong hands, slides between my thighs up high, against my heat. I push forward, into your touch. It takes only seconds to lift my dress, to push down my panties, to ease your scrubs off. To straddle you. We rock together, your cock sliding against me without friction or effort. I'm so wet for you it takes only one small shift of hips and limbs to settle you inside me.

"Fuck me," I say, and you do that, too.

It's slow and easy, the way you roll your hips to push your prick up inside me. You slide one of your hands that make so many miracles between us and use your knuckles on my clit. Your other holds my ass as we move, silent, biting our lips. I clench your shoulder so hard my nails leave half-moons in your flesh, but neither of us cries out.

Someone might know we're fucking in here, and I don't care, but there's pleasure to be had from pretending we do.

Your throat works as you swallow your groan. I lick you and bite you softly. Beneath my lips I feel your pulse beat, beat, beat. The steady throb is echoed between my legs.

I come forever and you follow me with an intake of breath and a murmured curse. We rock together slowly, finishing, and the bed under us creaks.

From the puddle of clothes on the floor, your beeper buzzes. You close your eyes, briefly, though your lips open under mine when I kiss them.

"I have to go," you say without moving.

I'm the one who gets up, who gathers the clothes, who lifts the small black box and places it in your hands. "You go," I say. "Someone needs you."

They all need you.

But you're still always mine.

Why would anyone want to be anything else?

Tell_me had replied even before Puppetboy. The thought he'd been waiting for her to post caused Eve's heart to skip a couple beats. Eve would've made a self-deprecating comment, but it wasn't Eve who answered.

I can be a demanding mistress.

Endless minutes passed while she refreshed her browser and replied to a few other comments. When the familiar user icon—a hundred-by-hundred pixel square photo of a single red rose—appeared, she actually clapped and bounced a little in her seat.

Please. Demand.

This time, she laughed aloud. Puppetboy might have offered to be her slave, but Tell_me's genuine sense of humor only added to his appeal. Puppetboy, perhaps sensing he was losing his place in line, had graduated from sending her shots of his cock to attaching photos of his entire body, each including a small hand-drawn sign with PUPPETBOY BELONGS TO ERIS inside a lopsided heart to prove it was really him and not some stolen shot of an abs and pecs model.

Eve didn't care what Tell_me looked like…well, okay, maybe she did a little, but only because in her mind he looked like every single one of her fantasies, and she couldn't pretend that every one of them didn't look quite a lot like a certain IT guy from work. Still, while Puppetboy's body was impressive and his willingness to debase himself for her pleasure intriguing…Tell_me had stolen her heart.

They'd only been corresponding for a week, but it felt like a lifetime. He commented on her blog; he e-mailed her privately. Their conversations in public had been light and flirty, the way she was with everyone who left a response to her entries, but in private he dug deeper. He didn't just fawn over her. He asked her questions about what she wanted and why. He answered them, too. He'd managed to give her a clear picture of himself without ever resorting to sending a blurry snapshot of his erection.

They'd graduated to instant messaging, a privilege she'd granted to so few of her readers she could count them on one hand. His conversations in real time were as easy and sexy as his e-mailed replies had been.

Now, though the hour had once again grown late, her fingers flew over the keys as her eyes stayed locked on the computer screen, watching for his next words.

You like fantasies.

Who doesn't?

But not everyone can express them as well as you can. Or else they stick with clichés.

You don't think a doctor fantasy is a cliché? She'd had a record-high number of comments after that one. They were still trickling in. *Some people want me to write about a cop next. Or a fireman.*

Are you going to?

Eve paused. *I don't think so.*

Because it isn't what you want?

Because I don't take requests.

She imagined a bright smile and the low rumble of laughter, a pair of dark blue eyes.

I don't think you should write about a cop or a fireman.

What do you think I should write about?
Surprise me.

This is what I want.

At the base of my throat, where my pulse throbs in unsteady rhythm, blood pools. The wound is fresh, but numb. The monster's kind in that way. It doesn't hurt when he comes to suck my life from me.

I don't know how long I've been in this hole. Time has ceased all meaning. I stopped counting the minutes against the steady, slow drip-drip of water from an unseen pipe long ago. My eyes stare, wide, into darkness, but I see nothing. The cold has raised gooseflesh on my arms and legs, but I don't feel that, either.

When your light shines on me, I don't even throw up a hand to block it though it stings my eyes worse than anything else has, lately. I look at you, a dark silhouette behind the golden circle from your flashlight, and my mouth forms the shape of your name. I'm not sure I've even spoken. I'm not sure if I remember how.

I thought I'd forgotten the strength of your arms, but when you gather me into your embrace, your breath warm on my cold flesh, I remember all of it. You. Me. The promises you made, and broke, and the one you've finally kept.

You take me home, to the house in which you refuse to live but visit often. You bathe me. You dress me. You put me into bed and stand guard at my door until I sleep.

I think you're afraid I won't wake, but I do. I open my eyes and wince at the sudden stabbing sensation in my wounds…but I welcome the pain. It means I'm still alive.

You open your eyes at once when I touch your face. The chair jerks as you do, and your hand comes up to catch my wrist hard, not quite flinging it away. You see it's me within a second and the embrace softens. I frown when you let me go.

"Go back to sleep," you say, as if I could. As if all that happened can be put behind me the way you so often have done.

But I'm not you.

Days pass this way. I wait for you to leave, and one day you do. You come back stinking of blood and garbage, your hands in fists, and I know you've killed it. Hunted it down and taken its life the way it tried to steal mine.

I would be happy but for the fact that this means, at last, you'll go for good.

"Stay." It's the first time I've ever asked. I know the score, the rules, what to expect from you. Your life circles mine and only sometimes intersects.

You shake your head, your back to me, the duffel bag I've grown to hate thrown over your shoulder. Outside your car awaits. I don't want to see the taillights. I hate them, too.

"I can't."

"You can. If you want to."

Your shoulders hunch. I want to touch you. To offer comfort. But you don't want my comfort, do you? You don't want me.... And too late, I realize I've spoken aloud.

I'd be frightened at the way you turn and the fire in your gaze except that now I've faced much, much worse. You grip my arms and I love your touch, even as it bruises. I can see you want to shake me, but you stop yourself. You let me go. You step back.

I step forward. "Stay. Please. I want you."

I open the buttons of my shirt and offer myself. Shameless, ready to be embarrassed when you refuse me, but not caring. I want you so badly I shake. I need you.

"I can't." But I see in your eyes that you can.

I touch myself as if my hands were yours. Your gaze follows my fingers as they caress my body. Your hands are shaking.

"I promised to keep you safe." Your voice is thick with loathing.

"You promised to find me," I remind you and let my shirt fall to the ground. "And you did. You came for me. You saved me. Please don't go. I need you."

You shake your head. "It's my fault you were in danger."

I know you think this, and maybe you're right, but I would not trade the safety of being insignificant to those who stalk the night for one single moment in your arms. A year ago I wouldn't have believed the monster under the bed was real; now I know better. And I know that you're the man who keeps us safe.

You keep me safe.

"Stay," I say, and hold out my hand.

You are a man, after all, and you take it. When I kiss you, your sigh shudders out of you like the wind through trees. I undress you carefully but without hesitation, and trace the pattern of your scars with my hands and mouth until your breath comes fast and harsh in your throat and you wind your fingers in my hair to pull my mouth from your cock.

"No," you say, and haul me from my knees. "Not like this."

We've fucked on my kitchen floor before. We've done it in my bed, too, and in the shower, on the counter, in the backseat of your car. This time, you take me out into the grass of my backyard, under the stars, and you spread out the faded quilt I keep on the porch for picnics. You lay me down and follow my lines and curves with your hands and your tongue, your lips reading the entire story of my body as easily as if I were made of words.

I'm already coming by the time you slide inside me, and it's as if the stars themselves have descended to hover around us, dancing. They fill me with fire. I lift my hips to take you in deeper, eager to hold on to you as long as I can. You thrust into me. Your mouth finds the scar at the base of my throat and you whisper against it.

"I'm sorry..."

Your voice breaks. Your head dips to press against me. I hold you tight as your body shakes and mine shudders beneath you. I don't have to forgive you. I know you won't forgive yourself.

You give me the night, but when the morning comes you're gone. But I know you'll be back.

"Eve?"

She turned with a smile on her mouth, lost in thoughts of

what story she would tell when she got home tonight and what Tell_me would say. When she saw who'd said her name, she smiled. "Well, hello."

Lane held up his cup. "Mocha Mint?"

She nodded and held up her own. The new place next door to Digiquest had become something of a tradition for her over the past few weeks. "Yes. Thanks for turning me on to it."

"My pleasure." Lane gave her his slow, easy grin. "I'm glad you were turned on."

Sweet, holy mother of pearl, his voice really did dip low and growly. Eve took a sip of hot, sweet coffee and watched him over her cup. She'd spent the night revealing her most intimate sexual fantasies in intricate detail, but far from being sated, her body only wanted a real-life taste of what she'd put on the screen. He was flirting with her, which wasn't new. She was flirting with him, which was.

There was no reason not to walk with him to the building next door, nor to hold back when the elevator opened as if by magic as they arrived. The door slid shut, enclosing them together once again in that tiny space.

It would take only two steps for him to cross to her, she mused. To push her against the mirrored wall. Her skirt today was long but loose, and he could easily get both hands beneath it. Those big, strong hands...

"I'm sorry?" He'd said something she'd missed, lost in her erotic musings.

"I asked if you watched the monster marathon last night."

Eve paused with her coffee halfway to her mouth. "No. I don't watch much television."

"Really?" Lane cocked his head to give her one of those damned slow smiles. "Too bad."

The elevator shuddered to a stop. The door opened with a creak. Lane held it open for her and she stepped through. All normal, nothing different from any other of a hundred days.

Except it was.
Lane DeMarco no longer seemed so unattainable.

You haven't demanded anything from me.
I wasn't sure you were ready for it.
I'm ready.

Eve paused, watching the cursor blink as fast as her heart was beating. She shifted in her chair, her thighs rubbing. She'd played the part of mistress, and of slave, but those had been stories. She'd never taken Puppetboy up on any of his offers of subservience. This was something new, uncharted. Delicious, but frightening.

She could log out now and blame computer problems, or make no excuses but simply refuse to answer his private messages any longer. She could, but she wasn't going to. She was going to do as he'd said, to tell him what she wanted, only this time it would be for him alone and nobody else. She typed quickly, not in her blog but in a private e-mail to him.

This is what I want.

You, in the shower. Steam wreathes your body. The sound of rushing water is almost loud enough to cover the sound of your groan. Almost.

You lean forward, one hand on the tiles. The other's on your cock. You close your eyes, lean into the spray. Head down, water streams over your back. Your muscles work as you fuck into your hand.

You're thinking of me.

I want you to be thinking of me.

Your knees bend slightly as you rock forward. Your fingers curl on the tile. Your hand strokes, strokes, twisting around the head of your prick and down. Over and over you stroke yourself.

What are you thinking of? Am I on my knees in front of you? Do I take you inside my mouth, use my tongue, my teeth, my lips? Do I swallow your cock? Are you wishing your hand was mine, jerking you? Are you imagining me on my hands and knees as you fuck me from behind?

You know best how to touch yourself. How to hold off the pleasure building from the base of your gut. Your balls tighten. You push forward, harder. Faster. Your head ducks lower until the water pounds the place between your shoulders I like to kiss.

Your hand slows. Your breathing is harsh. You're sweating from the heat of the water and your arousal. I know too well the taste of you, that salty, musky flavor. You tip your head back to let the water wash over your face and down your chest. Over your cock still gripped in your fist.

When you come, is mine the name on your lips? Mine the face in your mind?

It took him a long time to reply, all the way into the next morning, but when he did, it was worth the wait. Three words that made her grin all day long.

Yes. It was.

"It's not fair." Debbie leaned against the opening to Eve's pod. "That's the third time this week you've had computer problems."

"I'm not thrilled, Debbie." Eve gestured at the monitor, where no fewer than three chat windows hung frozen. "It's really screwing with my performance stats."

"Yeah," Debbie said, lowering her voice. "But it means you get to have Lane come and work on you."

As if summoned by the sound of his name, Lane appeared just behind Debbie's shoulder. "Problems, Eve?"

"Same old thing." She lifted her chin toward the computer, then pointed under the desk. "And the tower's making a lot of noise, too."

"I'll take a look at it." Ignoring Debbie, who sniffed and disappeared into her own cubicle, Lane moved toward Eve's desk.

He was on his knees in front of her before she knew what to do. His shoulder brushed her leg as he angled his head to look beneath her desk. Eve completely lost her breath at the sight of him that way.

He looked up at her with the panty-dampening smile and it was all she could do not to put her hand on his head to press him down between her thighs. "I think it's your fan."

"Can you fix it?"

"Yes."

They stared at each other until she looked away.

"Eve," Lane said in a low voice that drew her gaze back to him as surely as honey drew flies.

She pushed her chair back the tiniest bit, just enough to move her knee away from his shoulder. This was crazy. Crazy! His gaze went to the place on her thigh where her skirt pulled up, and his hands dug into the carpet briefly but fiercely. Heat flared in Eve's face and along her throat. Hell, through her entire body. And Lane leaned forward…

"Lane?" Debbie appeared in the doorway. "Now mine's doing it, too. My chats are all frozen."

"I'll be right there." His tone was pleasant and gave away nothing.

Eve didn't move. She couldn't. She was as frozen as her computer.

Lane didn't move, either, not until Debbie made a quizzical sound, and then he got up off his knees. Up, up and up, the entire length of him, and then Eve was alone at her desk.

Her computer chose that moment to go back online. Her queue blinked for attention. From Debbie's pod she heard the low murmur of Lane explaining something, but not what he was saying. Her hands shook a little as she started typing. She thought he'd come back to check on her, but he didn't.

This is what I want.

My dress spreads out around me in layers of satin and lace. The skirts are heavy, but when I'm seated their weight causes me no trouble. My silken stockings whisper when I rub my legs together, though it's more a feeling than a sound.

I have listened for hours to supplicants begging me for favors. To ministers admonishing me. To suitors attempting to woo. But what do I want, more than anything? I want to rid myself of the weight of this dress and the crown on my head. I want not to be a queen, but a woman.

Your hands hold clear glass globes, three in each palm, and the subtle motion of your fingers is enough to send them dancing. Back and forth they move, astonishing all who watch, though many in this court are too jaded to admit it. No magician, they sniff. It's all parlor tricks. I'm thrilled to study the ease of your movements, to lose myself in the grace of your performance.

I dismiss the others, but bid you to stay. You do, of course, for though I phrase my command as a request we both know your only option is to obey. Somehow, I don't think you mind.

You're on your knees in front of me without me having to order it. Your hands, those graceful hands, push up the dreadful heavy skirts. Your fingers make whispers of their own up my legs, which I part for you with a gasp at your audacity. Nobody touches me.

You touch me. The backs of my knees, the insides of my thighs, the small curve of my belly. And finally, you touch the soft, wet slit of my sex. Without asking and without my command, you kiss me there. You lick. You move my body forward on the chair until you can suck and stroke me with your tongue until I writhe.

The sound of footsteps should make you leave me unfulfilled, but instead of springing away you pull the folds of my dress down over you. It's full enough to cloak you entirely. Your face presses between my thighs until I have to bite my tongue to keep from crying out.

They're back again, the ministers and beggars, the suitors. I could turn them away but I owe them my time in exchange for their allegiance. Today I fail to listen properly. Today you lick me in secret until my body clenches and convulses, and I have to fight back the cries wanting to tear from my throat.

You use the thrust of your fingers as you would your cock. As you will use it later, when I take you to my chambers, but for now your tongue and hands move in tandem until I can't keep from squirming and pushing against you.

"Are you well?" ask my ministers. "You look flushed."

I climax again and again through the long hours under the attention of your talented tongue and fingers.

No magician, they say, but I know differently.

You've certainly worked your magic on me.

Eve still replied to all her comments, but she'd given up the pretense she was writing for any other reason than the replies from Tell_me. Her fingers flew over the keys as she wrote her latest entry. She sat back when it was finished and waited. Her reward came a few minutes later when her instant message icon bounced.

How was work today?

It wasn't the response she'd been expecting, and so her answer took a moment.

Fine. You?

Frustrating.

Why frustrating?

He didn't answer for so long she thought he'd gone, though he hadn't signed off. Then, *You liked me on my knees for you?*

I always like a man on his knees for me.

Another long, long pause. Eve's heart thumped and her tongue tasted like metal. What, exactly, was going on? The casual, sexy banter had disappeared. The words looked the same, black on white, but something had changed.

Her in-box filled with a few pleas from the abandoned Puppetboy. The shuffle function on her music program played her some interesting songs. Her fingers clenched into her fists as she leaned forward to stare at the screen and willed him to answer.

Any man? Or me?

Eve didn't know how to answer. She blinked at the rush of sudden, unexpected emotion. How had they gotten to this conversation?

I don't really know you.

Five minutes passed, then another five, before Tell_me went off-line without saying anything else.

In the pause between customers, Eve gave in to temptation. She'd read the memos and knew the consequences, but now…she had to. She had to see if he'd commented since the last time she'd checked, just before leaving for work.

With an eye on her queue, she logged in quickly to her blog. She didn't have access to her personal e-mail here and would have to be content with refreshing her browser. She opened her last entry and experienced the familiar roller-coaster drop of her stomach when she saw the number of comments had risen by a few, but she had to take the time to enter a new customer chat before she could check.

Back and forth she went, cutting and pasting responses to stupid questions that made her jaw ache and her head pound. Refreshing her browser. New comments but none from Tell_me.

Her stomach hurt.

She cursed herself. It was an online thing, nothing more. She had lots of comments from lots of people. What was so important about his? About him?

At long last his familiar icon appeared and she held her breath, almost too afraid to read what he'd written. The counter clicked on her queue, her response time to the current client too long. It would show up on her performance stats, but Eve didn't care. Let the moron who couldn't figure out how to hook up his printer wait a minute. Maybe he'd get a clue in the meantime.

What makes it magic?

Her fingers flew. *Magic can't be defined, can it? Or it loses what makes it magic.*

Would knowing me make it more magical?

He was replying in her blog to the private instant message exchange they'd had the night before. Eve imagined a tone of dry sarcasm, but that was the problem with written words. Without the benefit of inflection or facial expressions, they could be so easily misinterpreted. He could be angry, not amused or curious.

Part of the magic is the mystery, don't you think?

She expected him to agree. She wanted him to agree. After all, he'd always given her what she wanted.

No. I don't.

Eve didn't know how to respond. Her queue wasn't getting any shorter, and she had to finish off her open chat. She stumbled on the keyboard, making too many typos. She inserted the wrong text into the chat and had to apologize. It wasn't the first time she'd had a "no" from a client when she asked if she'd been helpful, but it was the first time she knew she deserved one.

I want it to be that way.

And it's all about what you want. How could I forget?

There was no mistaking the tone this time.

If you don't like it, she typed before she could stop herself, *you don't have to read this blog.*

Eve closed her browser abruptly so she wouldn't know if he replied, and told herself she didn't care. She got back to work, but it was a long, long day.

She wouldn't IM him. She just wouldn't. Not if her house were on fire and he really was a fireman.

She was going to ignore the bouncing yellow smiley face of her instant message program. Absolutely. In fact, Eve was going to do something unheard of. She was going to get away from her computer and do something else tonight. Read a book. Take a bath. Watch bad TV.

Anything, anything, but talk to him.

She made herself some dinner that didn't come from a box or a can. She threw in a few loads of laundry. She read a magazine, but restlessly, flipping past ads for "sexual intimacy" videos and articles on how to please her man.

When she got back to her desk, the yellow smiley chastised her. She clicked on it and read his message to her. He'd sent it hours ago. Surely he wouldn't still be waiting?

You didn't post tonight.

I didn't have any inspiration.

Because of me?

Yes.

I'm sorry. I just want you to know me, that's all. For real. Not just words on a screen.

I don't think it's a good idea.

Why not?

That was a good question. Too bad she didn't have a good answer. He didn't wait for one.

I can make you happy.

What makes you think that?

A minute passed.

Because I know what you want.

Reading a blog isn't the same as real life.

You could let me try.

But she couldn't, could she? She didn't know his name, or where he lived, or what he looked like. And wasn't that what she wanted, really? An anonymous, faceless lover who gave her what she wanted, all the time, without needing anything from her? As long as she didn't know who he was, for sure, she could still have that.

Right?

Her mouse hovered over the small X in the corner of the chat window, preparing to close it without answering him, but she couldn't do it.

I'm sorry. I can't.

What are you afraid of?

Being disappointed, she typed. *Being let down.*

I won't disappoint you.

You can't know that. Nobody can.

I can be what you want.

Eve closed the window. He didn't ping her again. She stared at the computer screen for a few minutes, then opened her blog and began to type.

This is what I want.

Far away there is the sound of machinery. A mower, or a tractor. But inside the barn the only sound I hear is the rustle of the hay as you thrust the pitchfork into the pile, the sweet chirp of nesting birds high in the rafters, the quiet snuffle of the horses pawing at the earth with sharp hooves. The occasional hitch of your breath as you work.

I spy on you from the doorway. I don't want you to turn around yet. I like to watch the easy way you move. How strong you are. My eyes follow the bunch and curve of your muscles as you strain.

You wear low-slung denim, low on the hips I want to bite. Worn work gloves protect the hands that have moved so often over my body and brought me such pleasure. You grunt, teeth caught for a moment in your lower lip as you concentrate on your task. You haven't seen me, and that's all right.

For now.

Dust dances in the shafts of sunlight, golden, buttery, that have found their way through cracks and crevices in the walls. The barn is old, made of stone quarried a hundred years before you were born. A hundred and almost thirty before we ever met.

Yet here we are, inside it, in the sunlight. A horse neighs from a stall far down the aisle and you turn.

And smile.

You straighten, bare-chested and gleaming. I could reach forward and pluck the stray piece of straw clinging to the rim of your collarbone, but I leave it for now. For now, I don't touch you.

You say my name and the pleasure in your voice is so rich I feel as though I can reach out to touch it. You're glad to see me; I want you to be glad to see me.

You lean on the pitchfork to stare, and I can guess what you see. My dress is white, sheer, with thin straps of lace that will tear when you tug them. If I let you tug them. I haven't yet decided.

You don't ask me what I'm doing here, which would be a foolish question, indeed. You already know. You knew the moment you turned and saw me standing in the doorway; when your eyes caught the shape of my body, outlined beneath the white eyelet. When your gaze traced the curve of my hip, the place your hand fits so perfectly.

You knew.

The barn is silent but for the soft chirping of nested birds and the far-off drone of the tractor, for the occasional stomp of a hoof…and now, for your breath as it catches in your throat and trips on the syllables of my name.

There is a room in the back, fragrant with the scent of leather and horses. Momentarily blinded, I blink against the shadows. I don't need to see you to know where you are.

Inches apart we face one another. Now is the time for me to reach for the single, lonely piece of straw stuck to your skin with the sweat of honest work, and I let my fingers skim up your side, over your belly. The straw bends between my fingertips when I pull it off you, and it's dropped, forgotten, to the floor.

I like the smell of you. Sweat and effort. It reminds me of how you smell when I'm done fucking you, when you can't stand, when you can only lie like a broken doll on the twisted sheets. When I've used you up and worn you out, that's how I like to smell you.

"Put your hands on the wall."

You hesitate, of course, not expecting this. The jingle of metal is like a melody to my ears as you press your palms flat to the wall between the hanging bits and bridles. You could have fisted your hands against the wood, but you spread your fingers wide. Your shoulders, those broad, muscled shoulders, hunch just a little.

Are you afraid I'm going to hurt you?

I won't, love. Not too much. I just want to see you this way, giving me what I want without asking me why I want it. I am unaccountably pleased at how you move at once to obey my request.

And it is a request, because I don't want it to be an order.

You must want this as much as I, else the point is lost. I can't make you do anything you don't want to do. You're bigger than I am. Stronger. I know because you've pinned my hands above my head, bruised my flesh and soothed the hurts with kisses and the flat of your tongue, though in truth I didn't mind the marks that served so well to remind me of how it felt to have you holding me down so tightly.

You wait for me to speak, and I hear the sound of your breath again as your shoulders rise and fall.

"Spread your legs. Wider." Impatient, I nudge them apart with my foot, though my slipper-clad toes are no match for your thick leather boots. Boots made for work. Your legs move easily enough, though.

Your head dips, emphasizing the way your shoulder blades protrude. For a moment I imagine you as an angel shorn of your wings. An angel in dirty denim.

You are an angel to me.

Behind you, my hands find a place on each side of your belt. I hook my fingers in and pull your hips back until my crotch bumps your ass. I love the sound you make. Mingled surprise and arousal. I picture your eyes closing, those straight white teeth tugging at the softness of your lower lip again.

If I were a man I could fuck you. I could fill you with my cock, make you groan, reach to stroke your erection in my fist while I moved in and out of your body until we both came. But I'm not a man, I don't have a cock to fuck you with, and I have to be satisfied with running my hands down your hips and around the front of your thighs.

You groan again when my hands find the front of your belt and undo the buckle. When I unzip you. When I ease the worn denim and the blue cotton of your boxer briefs over your thighs and down past your knees, my cheek presses the hot, damp flesh of your back, and I feel the muscles there quiver.

Yet you make no attempt to turn or move your hands from their place on the wall, and this makes me smile.

I pull my dress to my waist. I'm bare beneath. I have to go on tiptoe to press my bush against your ass, but a hand thrust between your thighs moves them apart just enough to bring our bodies together. My fingers dig deep into your hips at the places I want to put my teeth, but later. Later for that.

Now I rub myself against your ass, your back, your thighs. I rub your belly with the flat of my hand and pretend to ignore the tap of your cock on the back of it. When you push your hips forward I dig my nails deeper. The groan you make is one of mingled pleasure and pain, and my clit pulses at the sound of it.

Metal jingles again and leather swings as you lean forward. For a moment I think about putting you in a harness, a bridle. Leather crisscrossing your lean body, straps molding to the curve of your head. I could hook you to a carriage and make you pull me. I could snap the thin whip of braided leather against your thighs and ass to make you run faster.

I laugh when I tell you this, but your head turns and the look in your eye is not of pleasurable contemplation, but alarm. Yet your cock taps again on the back of my hand, pressed flat to your rising and falling stomach, and your hips jerk, just a little.

"Would you like that?" I whisper. I can't reach your ear. You're too tall. But I have no doubt you hear me.

"Do you…want me to like that?"

It's in me to say yes, that I would like to hook you to a carriage and make you my pony, but I don't. I let my hand tell you what I really want. I cup your balls. I stroke your cock. I say nothing until you shudder and groan and duck your head again, and I know that you'll do whatever I want…which is what I want, anyway.

"I want to fuck you." It's not the first time I've said it, and I doubt it will be the last.

I stroke harder and you push into my fist the way you'll soon push into my cunt. I'm still behind you. I'm still rubbing myself against you. My breasts feel heavy. My cunt aches. I want you so much it's like burning.

I slip into the small space between you and the wall. My arms go around your neck. I use the pressure of the wall behind my back to climb you like a tree. My legs go around your waist. My dress bunches on my hips.

Your cock, trapped between us, rubs my cunt. My clit. Delicious, but it's not enough. I want you inside me.

"Fuck me," I say, and you're only too happy to oblige.

With one hand still flat against the wall, you slide the other beneath my ass. I've got my arms around your neck, my legs wrapped around you, your prick so deep inside me I feel it in my belly. And you move, not bothering to start slow.

You fuck me so hard we rattle the bridles and bits; we shake the wall. We shake the fucking mountains.

I watch your eyes flutter. It's the look you get just before you come, and I come, too. Hard. Like splintering. I kiss you when I come, your mouth beneath mine sweet and open, and I steal your breath.

I swallow your shout.

You thrust again. Your body quakes and shudders; so does mine. We come together with small, sharp cries that drown out the faraway sound of the tractor and the soft, sweet chirpings of nested birds.

The first thing Eve saw when the elevator door opened on the fourth floor was Lane. Today he wore a sleek, chest-hugging black T-shirt and a pair of jeans that gave her palpitations. They wanted to ride low on his hips, those damned jeans, but Lane had belted them tight to his waist with a shiny buckled belt. He wore boots, too, scuffed and black and worn from hard work, but clean.

"Hey, cowboy." Debbie gave Lane the slow, thorough, up-and-down appraisal Eve wished she could risk, but then

Debbie was about as subtle as a wiener dog with a sock toy. "Nice buckle."

Lane tipped an imaginary hat and gave them both a grin of such blinding brilliance Eve had to look away. "Well, thank you, ma'am."

He looked at Eve, who felt the weight of his gaze even though she was unable to look at his face. "See you, Eve."

Both women stared in silence after him as he strode down the center of the pod forest and disappeared around the corner.

Debbie nudged Eve with her elbow. "I would ride him like a pony."

"I bet you would," Eve said, *but you couldn't handle him* is what she thought.

"Tell me you wouldn't? Lane DeMarco is ten kinds of sexy." Debbie followed Eve to her cubicle. "He has an ass that just won't quit. Did you see those jeans? Jesus, Eve. Tell me you noticed the jeans. And the boots!"

She'd seen them, all right. She'd seen all of it. The only thing that would have made him look any better would have been a battered leather hat pulled low over his eyes, and not even Lane could get away with that at work. He had been waiting for her to get off the elevator, she was convinced of that. His look had convinced her.

It had been a challenge, but then so had what she'd written, hadn't it?

She settled into her chair, her hands moving to her keyboard automatically, though they felt too numb to actually type.

"Thank God for the casual dress code, huh? Gawd," Debbie said with another peek around the pod wall. "Do you think he does it on purpose?"

"Does what?"

"He's a cowboy, Eve. A cowboy!"

The last word ended with a squeak that made Eve look up. "I noticed."

It would have been impossible not to.

"I don't understand how you can be so immune to it, that's all," Debbie said, proving she really was clueless. "The man is a god, pure and simple. A sex god."

He was more than that, Eve thought, her fingers tap-tapping on the keys. But someone like Debbie wouldn't ever see that. "Don't you have work to do?"

Debbie sighed. "Hell, yes. And dammit, nothing's broken." She gave a wicked chuckle. "Yet."

Eve logged in, but her fingers fumbled too often on the keys and she made stupid typing errors. She messed up the simplest tasks, had to read the same customer replies two and three times to make sense of them and was, generally speaking, a mess.

How could she have not seen this before? He'd asked her about the monster marathon. He'd brought her coffee because he thought it was what she wanted. He was a cowboy today for the same reason.

Lane DeMarco was Tell_me.

She couldn't deny it any longer. The subtle clues she'd chosen to ignore had been cast aside. He was challenging her to admit she knew it was him.

Lane was her online lover. Tears of anger or sorrow—she couldn't tell which—clogged her throat and blurred the computer screen. How could she have been so blind? And how long had he known?

"Move over." The grumble-growl of Lane's voice took her by surprise, but he didn't wait for her to obey. He pushed her chair gently so it rolled to the side. His fingers tapped her keyboard.

"What are you doing?" Eve kept her voice pitched low, but couldn't keep the anger from her tone. "Get out of here."

Lane threw her a glance. "They're doing an inspection to-day. Too many complaints about slow or poor service. They're checking all Internet usage. People who've been going online for personal use are going to get written up, Eve. Or fired."

Her jaw dropped. "Can they do that?"

He nodded, mouth set in a grim line. "Haven't you been reading the memos?"

"Yes, but—"

He typed faster. Scrolling lines of files appeared and vanished just as fast. Delete. Delete. Delete. He worked swiftly, without hesitation.

"I don't need to ask how you knew I was online this week, do I?" Eve said.

Lane shook his head.

"It's the same way you knew it was me all along, wasn't it? From the time when you left the coffee."

He nodded.

She let her gaze cover him from head to toe, every inch, and if her scrutiny made him uncomfortable he didn't show it. At last she looked him in the eyes. He was the same Lane she'd known for years, the guy with the smile, but he was more than that now.

And it wasn't what she wanted.

"Thanks," Eve said coolly and turned back to her monitor. "I'd better get back to work."

She sensed him hesitating in the entrance to her pod, but he said nothing, and when she looked up, he was gone.

Gone. All of it was gone. All the entries she'd spent so many hours crafting. All the comments, the compliments, the conversations. She'd deleted all of it with a few keystrokes, even her instant-messaging account. Eris Apparent was gone.

She hadn't been to work for the past few days. She wasn't sick, but had called in anyway, unable to face him. Unable to give him what he wanted.

"You let me down," she scolded her computer in an

attempt at levity she didn't feel. "You were supposed to protect me."

At least it would help her find a new job. Getting away from Digiquest couldn't be a bad thing. She'd already sent in applications to two other, larger support firms where the pay and benefits were better. It would be good to make a break, she thought as she clicked through to another job listing. Two years was a long time to be stuck in a job she didn't really like.

She'd ordered pizza, so when the doorbell rang she thought nothing of it. She should've known better, of course. Wasn't a hot pizza delivery boy one of those clichéd fantasies she'd never written?

"Can I come in?" Lane leaned in her doorway looking more deliciously edible than any pizza ever could.

"No."

"Eve." If he'd tried to wheedle or charm her she'd have sent him away at once, but against his quiet plea she could do nothing. "Please."

She stepped aside, granting him entrance without saying a word. He pushed past her, looking too big for her living room. He turned to face her, his hands in the pockets of his faded jeans. Damn him, the ones she liked.

"You haven't been to work," he said.

"I took some personal time." She didn't sit or offer him a chair.

"Because of me?"

She meant to deny it, but instead a sigh slipped from her mouth. "Yes. Because of you."

"You deleted your blog, too."

"You should have told me it was you!" she cried suddenly, and he stepped back.

"Would you have replied if you'd known?" Lane challenged her.

"No!"

He smiled. "I thought you'd figure it out."

"I did," Eve said in a low voice. "I just didn't want to believe it."

"Why not?" He sounded curious. For an instant she saw the words on a screen as if she were reading them. How much of a difference his voice made.

"Because…" She trailed off. "The blog…it was a way for me to be someone else. And I really wanted to be someone else, Lane."

"I like who you are, Eve."

She laughed, scornful. "You liked Eris."

"And you liked Tell_me."

"It wasn't real!" she shouted. "None of it was real!"

"Is this real?" Lane demanded, and kissed her.

She melted into him. His mouth parted, and hers did, too. He tasted exactly how she'd always known he would. He felt even better than she'd ever imagined.

"This isn't going to work," she warned, voice hoarse, but made no move to step out of his arms.

"It will," he promised, his fingers already going to her buttons. "I promise."

"How?" Eve gasped when his bare skin touched hers.

Lane's slow smile went straight between her thighs as usual. "Easy. Tell me what you want."

She gulped in a breath at hearing him say it aloud. Something flickered in his gaze when she didn't respond at once; she felt the reflection of it in her own eyes, just before she took the chance and took his hand.

"This is what I want," Eve said, and led him into the bedroom to make all their fantasies come true.

★ ★ ★ ★ ★

IMPROPER PLEASURE

Charlotte Featherstone

London, 1876

IT WAS A DAY LIKE ANY OTHER. YET THERE WAS something enchanted in the air that made Amelia think that this particular Tuesday would be very different from all the others.

Despite the real unease gripping her, Amelia looked about her surroundings, recognizing the fact that everything was just as it ought to be. There was nothing, not even a warning softly whispered through the tree branches that predicted what was to come.

Wiping away the dew on the bench, Amelia sat on the stone slab and looked around the little copse that was awakening to life after the long winter. With a sigh, she lifted her face to the cool breeze and closed her eyes, relishing the sounds of chirping birds, the rustle of the wind through the leafless tree branches and the promise of a beautiful spring day that scented the air. Even the funerary statues surrounding her seemed to glow with beauty, wonder and life.

Most would say that a cemetery in the heart of London was a macabre and disturbing place to spend a few hours of solitude. But Amelia found comfort in the quiet, in the privacy of her little spot, as if it were her very own garden.

How long it was before she heard the sound of carriage

wheels clacking against cobbles, she had no idea. Despite the dew smudging her spectacles and the black lace veil she used to cover her face, Amelia could make out a well-appointed carriage with shining black lacquered doors and an elaborate gold crest. Tassels fixed in the center of the window shades swayed gently back and forth, drawing her eye to the lavish length of gold bullion fringe that edged the scalloped contours of the cream velvet shades. She recognized the carriage and the regal crest it bore. Knew the features of the occupant as well as she knew her own.

Yes, she knew the man inside the carriage, but did he know her? Could he see her? Did he know who it was standing amid the statutes with her face veiled?

There was a flicker of darkness—a shadow—that moved across the pale interior, compelling her to look deep within the carriage. She had never seen him like this, at this time of day. It had never been just the two of them, looking at each other. And even though a lane and fence lay between them, Amelia had never felt more intimate with him than she did now.

The shadow shifted once more in the depths of the carriage interior. Then she saw him, another movement of sifting light that revealed him and his black, wild-looking hair and penetrating eyes that seemed to burn straight into her as if he could see through her lace disguise.

What she wouldn't trade in order to have him see her—to notice that she existed.

He settled back against the cushions and the carriage moved on, rolling down the cobbles. Amelia could no longer see his beautiful face, and she was glad for it. For this obsession was only one-sided. It could never be more than that—a secret, forbidden fantasy—no matter how much she wished for it to be otherwise.

Turning, Amelia walked away from the copse, toward the path that would lead her back to the gate—and the reality of her life.

CHAPTER ONE

HE COULD NOT RECALL THE PRECISE DATE WHEN
he had first glimpsed her through his carriage window, yet that
day was still so fresh, so evocative in his mind. Time seemed to
stop as she stood aglow in the center of a glittering sunbeam
that had found its way through the gently waving tree limbs.

As his carriage had bounced and swayed its way down
Swain's Lane, he watched the lone figure of the woman, her
head bent as if she were reading, or praying, or perhaps even
silently weeping. He had fancied her a mystical fairy or angel
as she sat down on a bench beneath a stone seraph, the stippled
sunlight dancing off her black bonnet and netted veil. He had
been unable to move his gaze from her, a lone figure amidst
the statues.

"Stop the coach!" he ordered his driver.

How long he had his coachman hold his team of blacks in
the middle of the lane while he watched her that day, he had
no idea. How long had he been waiting now, at the gates of
Highgate Cemetery, desiring a glimpse of her, he knew not.

Since that fateful day when he had first discovered her, he
had made the weekly trek to Highgate, hoping for another
stolen glimpse of her. That was nearly a month ago.

She came only once a week. On Tuesday mornings she

arrived, dressed in a drab woolen gray gown, the skirts of which were bustled high in the back. Her long cloak was plain and unadorned, giving nothing away of her shape. Her bonnet, a simple black confection, was tied primly beneath her chin. Black satin ties whipped in the breeze beneath the long lace veil she used to cover her face.

Once a week he saw her from beyond the bars of the iron fence. Once a week he silently watched her—studied her, never allowing himself to give in to his impulse and go to her.

Once a week he allowed himself to see her. The other six days he was consumed by thoughts of her.

The sound of his mount's reins jangling in the quiet of the peaceful morning brought him abruptly back to the present. The gelding, stepping sideways, snorted and pranced, anxious to be cantering off to Hyde Park and his morning run on Rotten Row. "Just another moment," Adrian muttered, tightening his gloved hand around the leather reins. "She has only just arrived."

Pressing forward in the saddle, he inched to the right and saw her walking amongst the seraphim that stood sentry around the grove. *Find me beyond these black bars and see me,* he whispered to her.

Somehow she heard him from across the sunlit space that separated them. Slowly, she looked at him over her shoulder. With a small nod and tip of his hat, he acknowledged her, then pressed his knees into the gelding's sides. She was aware. He would let that awareness grow into something stronger—*need.* And when he was certain her need was at least half as strong as his, he would go to her. Only then would he learn everything there was to know about this woman who made him dream such beautiful, erotic dreams throughout the night.

She was playing a very dangerous game by returning to Highgate week after week. Yet she could not stop herself from coming, from experiencing those few minutes of his undivided attention. He would never know how she clutched those memories of him to her breast. Those minutes alone with him, despite the distance, were so very dear to her—as if she were the only woman in the world to him.

Yes, but what if he were to discover what you are? the nasty voice inside her asked. What if, contrary to her beliefs, he had recognized her? Her life would be ruined. Yet here she sat, wishing to see him, feeling her blood heat at just the thought of him.

What a fool she was to delude herself that he would feel anything for her, least of all desire. She was not a beautiful woman. She was plain. She wore spectacles. She was nobody. That was her reality.

This morning, she had neglected to wear her spectacles in hope she might actually come face-to-face with him. But he had not come today, and as a consequence she had stumbled about the grove half-blind.

Grumbling over her stupidity and unusual pride, Amelia stood up from the bench and reached for the strings of the reticule that dangled from her wrist. As she looked down, a blurred image of a gloved hand resting atop her fingers swam before her. With a gasp she looked up and faltered back a step.

"At last we have come face-to-face."

"I didn't think you were coming today," she whispered. As soon as she said the words, she wanted to kick herself for being so foolish—so transparently needy.

He took a step closer to her, she felt his gloved hand encase hers before he raised it to his mouth. "I have been here all morning, waiting."

Reluctantly she turned her gaze from his face in order to watch his lips press against her gloved knuckles. "I didn't see you."

"I did not wish for you to see me. I wanted to watch you

unseen. I wanted to discover everything I could about you before this moment."

What had he discovered? Did he know her secret? Panic gripped her and her fingers began to tremble in his hand. She tried to pull away, to run, but his long fingers encased her palm, holding her tight.

"Tell me your name," he asked in a silky voice that felt like a caress—a sensual, tempting touch she felt snaking along her body.

She shouldn't be doing this. He was a lord, a peer of the realm. Again, she reminded herself that she was no one, and if he were to discover her identity and expose her secret, she would be thrust back to the same horrific world she had once crawled out from.

"Your name?"

"Emmy," she told him, using the name her father had called her when she was a small child. He cocked his head to the side and studied her with his blue-green eyes.

"I am Adrian, Emmy."

She shuddered at the intimacy of hearing his voice murmur her name; she wished she possessed the strength to say his aloud, but she couldn't bring herself to.

"Who are you, Emmy?"

"No one," she replied, savoring the gentle touch of his fingers running along the back of her hand.

How many nights had she dreamed of this, his touch, his large warm hands caressing her? So many nights. So many long, cold—*empty*—nights.

"Do you come here to write?" he asked. "I've seen you with pen and book."

"No."

"An artist, then? You study the statuary as if you were a connoisseur."

"I am just a woman."

"Not just. If you were just any sort of female I would not

be here. I would not have come every week for over a month just to see you and watch you from afar. No, not just any woman, Emmy."

"I…I must leave," she stuttered, pulling away from him, fearing her weakness. It frightened her, this unbridled response to him. It terrified her to know it was not only her body responding to this man, but her mind, her heart—*her soul*.

"Don't run, Emmy. We have both waited for this moment."

"I…I can't."

"Next week you will be here. You won't run and never come back to me?"

When she did not immediately answer, he brought her chest up to his and held her close. Her body absorbed the heat radiating from his broad chest, chasing away the dampness of the morning. "You will promise me now, that next week you will be here. You have to return, Emmy, because I have to see you. *I have to.*"

Her heart soared upon hearing his low, fervent words. Dazed, Amelia nodded, unable to do anything else but clasp his words to her breast and hold them tight. One more week, she told herself, just once more, and then she would never again return to Highgate.

CHAPTER TWO

FOG HOVERED ABOVE THE WET GRASS, SWIRLING until it wrapped itself around her body like a shroud. The light from the sun, struggling to break free of the black clouds that hung low overhead, cast her in an incandescent glow that made her appear more ghostly spectre than woman.

As if in a trance, Adrian pushed open the black-and-gilt iron gate. It protested on its hinges, but with a scrape along the fieldstone path, the gate swung open. He stepped into the cemetery, his feet carrying him over to Emmy.

The mist grew thicker, engulfing her so he nearly lost sight of her in the gloomy cocoon of fog. But then a cloud parted, revealing her as she sat on the bench, her head lowered, the long, black veil billowing softly in the crisp spring breeze.

She was holding a book and he saw that her hands were bare. His gut reacted to the sight of those small white hands. It was strange that such a simple thing should arouse him so.

As he neared her, his gaze remained focused on her delicate, pale hands; his mind filled with images of her palms sliding along his chest and traversing over his belly. Three little brown freckles lay enticingly between her thumb and index finger, spaced far enough apart so that he could kiss each one. He wanted to fall to his knees and clutch her hand to his mouth, kissing the freckles then stroking his tongue along each one, wetting her hand for the easy glide along his skin. He imagined that hand—her left hand—with its freckles, sliding up his shaft. He wanted to feel her fingers stroking him, soothing his flesh that burned. It had been too long since he enjoyed the simple pleasure of touching—of being touched.

He stood beside her, looking down at her bent head, which was covered with her plain bonnet. "I despise the dawn. I loathe it with a passion. It is only the thought of meeting you that draws me out of my bed to brave the morning light."

She raised her head and studied him from behind her veil. "I adore the morn. It is a time of peace and tranquility. A part of the day for quiet reflection and memories. It is truly the only time that is entirely mine."

What drove her here? Was she grieving for a fiancé? A lover? Had she been meeting someone else here all this time? The thought tore him apart and he was amazed at how damned jealous he felt. *She was his....*

"Walk with me?" he asked, offering her his arm while fighting to contain the riotous emotions inside him. He would not think of other men, would not imagine her waiting here in this secluded spot for any man other than him.

She stopped them before a weathered statue of a woman kneeling, her stone hands cupped before her in supplication. The statue was garbed in a long, flowing robe while a veil shielded her features.

"This one is my favourite."

He felt those words, said in Emmy's quiet voice. He felt that touch as he watched her hand, slight and freckled, skate down the length of the wind-worn sculpture. He was entranced by that hand gliding over the shoulder and waist of the statue. It was as if he could feel that same hand caressing his naked flesh. And he burned. Christ, every inch of his flesh grew hot as he imagined Emmy's white little fingers trailing along his body.

Touch me that way, he wanted to say. *Look at me that way.* But he kept silent, and instead allowed himself to become mesmerized by the sight of Emmy's gentle hands and imagining her soothing touch roaming along his aching, lonely body.

"How forlorn she looks residing over this tangled patch of overgrown shrubbery and brambles. It is as though she has been utterly abandoned—sentenced to years of loneliness until she crumbles to dust. No one will remember her and her presence here. No one but me."

Reaching for Emmy's hand, he covered it with his, watching with a sense of power how his large hand engulfed her little one. Never had his body been so hard with anticipation, with passion and simple seduction. Never had he felt a more visceral connection to a woman. It was more than lust that drew him to her.

"From the moment I first glimpsed her through the brush she captured my heart. She has been left all alone, abandoned to this beautiful but lonely spot."

Had Emmy been abandoned? Left alone in the world by a husband taken too soon, or a man who no longer cared for her? He experienced a mad, almost desperate urge to ask her, but then she spoke, her voice so quiet and without artifice.

"It is her face, I think, that draws me. It is veiled and concealed from us, yet one can imagine what she looks like beneath the veil and her crown of blossoms."

He stepped closer to her so that his coat caressed her cloak and the toe of his boots touched the tips of her half boots. "What is the purpose of the veil, do you think?"

"I know little of art." She smiled tremulously and lowered her head, as if she were ashamed of that admission. He tipped her face up and brushed the pad of his thumb along her cheek as he looked through the lace to the blue of her eyes.

"You needn't know anything of art to appreciate it, Emmy. You only need to feel it and experience the emotion the work gives you."

"Perhaps the sculptor thought her too beautiful to be standing in such a sorrowful place. Perhaps the veil is there so we do not see her lack of beauty, so that we look beyond the physical and into the heart of her, so that we may take the time to know her as something more than a physical beauty. What do you see in her?"

"Sadness. Loneliness. *Need*." He was not looking at the statue, but at Emmy, her shrouded face showing those very same things. "She needs to be understood and loved by a man who would protect her. A man who could pleasure her. A man who would guard her secrets and not allow her to crumble to dust."

A faint smile broke from her lips and she lowered her head to study her hands, which were clasped before her. He tipped her chin up once again, wishing he could lift the veil from her face to see just how beautiful Emmy truly was. For he knew she was.

She had eyes a man could drown in. Lips made to be kissed for hours and designed to provide immense pleasure to a man. Her skin was the sort men wanted to touch over and over, and each time he would marvel at the softness, the suppleness, the astonishing purity of it.

She looked at the statue once again. "'Because thou has the power and own'st the grace to look through and behind this mask of me, and behold my soul's true face.' The words of Elizabeth Barrett Browning. They're beautiful, aren't they?"

He pressed closer, felt her sway ever so slightly into him. He wanted to touch her. To feel her beneath his hands before she melted into the gray fog, leaving him alone, frustrated, yearning to see her once again.

"Emmy, you cannot know what you do to me with your honesty. It empowers me," he said, unable to control his thoughts. "I can't explain it. You give me such strength. Some-how you have been able to reach deep within me and touch the man. It is more than a physical attraction between us. It is something I have never before experienced. Something powerful and beautiful—"

"Shhh, don't say it," she begged, pressing her cold fingertips atop his lips. "Words are so very difficult to take back and forget. Memories fade with time, but words never do. They linger in our minds, our hearts, haunting us. Right now, silence and memories would serve us much better."

"What I feel right now defies words, Emmy. I have never felt so vehemently about anything as I do about you." She swayed again and he gripped her arms, holding her tight.

"You must release me," she said in a breathless sob. "You must. You don't understand. I am not who you think I am."

"Are you a widow, lonely for your husband? A scorned woman, searching for a man to make it right? Tell me who you are, Emmy. I want to know. I *must* know."

"I am nobody."

"No, you are not. When I close my eyes all I can see is you. Even now I can smell you, almost taste you…Christ, how I want you, Emmy."

Amelia allowed herself to sag against the hard breadth of Adrian's chest. The inner struggling, the war waging so deep inside her was almost over. Today she would go against everything she had ever believed—would toss aside every fear she had ever clung to. Today, she would allow Adrian to take her on a journey he had begun and only he could complete.

Only Adrian made her feel this way; like a woman in every sense of the word. In this little copse she was nearly his equal in mind and beauty. In station and wealth. Here in this little spot she was simply Emmy, and he Adrian. Nothing of their lives outside of this spot intruded.

Droplets of cold rain began to fall from the sky and Adrian reached for her hand, pulling her so that she was running behind him as he steered them toward the secluded alcove, where there was a roof of carved stones and pillars that resembled obelisks. They would be dry. It would be dark. And they would be utterly alone as the rain fell down around them.

CATCHING HER AROUND THE WAIST, ADRIAN pressed her against the stone wall as another echo of thunder rumbled across the sky. The scent of cool, spring rain and fresh churned soil saturated the air. She could also smell him—Adrian—the scent a mixture of spice and wool and a hint of tobacco. She could feel him, the heat radiating off his broad, tall body as he stood before her.

His head was bent to hers and his breath ruffled the tendrils of hair that had escaped from beneath her bonnet. "Let me see you," he asked in a whisper as the pad of his thumb caressed her lips that lay hidden beneath her veil.

Fear and pride ate away at her confidence and Amelia struggled to hold on to the only shield that prevented him from seeing how very ordinary she truly was. And even if she were a beautiful woman, she couldn't remove the veil. Her face, her name, must forever remain a mystery to him.

"I mustn't allow it."

"I must see you," he said in a hard rush of breath. *"I must."*

He pressed a kiss to her brow as his hands slipped beneath the edge of the lace. His bare fingers grazed along the column of her neck as one finger hooked beneath her chin, drawing her face up to his.

Thunder rolled once again and the sky grew dark, casting a murky, forbidding shadow. The alcove was now dark, her identity safe from discovery. Adrian's face was shielded, as well, and without her spectacles, his features were blurred and cloudy.

The rain continued to pour down from the heavens and for long, unbearable seconds only the unrelenting sound of the rain could be heard above their breathing.

Then at last, he spoke. "Tell me what you love, Emmy. What you desire. Tell me who you are. I will tell you anything you want to know about me. I will not demand your secrets and give nothing of myself in return."

"I know all I need to know about you. I can feel what I need to know while I am standing in your arms, craving the touch of your hands—*needing* your touch."

"Is it anonymity you need? If it is, I will give it to you, if that is the only way you will allow this. I will be only Adrian, and you will be Emmy, and we will come together here, at Highgate, where no other soul shall ever discover us."

Amelia closed her eyes, unable to believe she was actually here with him. It was her most secret fantasy come to life. Yet she hated knowing she was deliberately misleading him. She was not this person, this woman of mystery. She was not what he believed her to be.

"Have you ever wanted to be someone else, Adrian? To be anyone other than who—*what*—you are?"

She felt him shudder against her. "Yes. Nearly every day of my life I have longed to be anyone other than who I am. And when I am with you, Emmy, I am someone else. Someone infinitely better than who I really am."

"I…I have never done this, met a stranger and given so much of myself. In fact, I have never let another see so much of my soul."

"Neither have I, Emmy."

"I want this," she gasped, biting her lip. "I know I should not. I know what you do not—how wrong this is of me."

Reaching for her hand, Adrian brought it to his chest, flattening her palm against his waistcoat. His heart was beating hard; she would feel it. He was breathing hard; she would feel that, too. He moved her palm lower over his breast, down over the flat hardness of his belly, where it rested at the waistband of his trousers. He pushed her hand lower and made her feel his cock that was hard as iron beneath his woolen trousers. She went utterly still, but did not attempt to pull her hand from beneath his. She could if she wanted to. He barely held her hand against him now.

"Take what you want," he said, brushing her hand against the placket of his trousers. Closing his eyes, he gritted his teeth, savoring the feel of her hand on his prick, despite the fact it was still innocently covered. He was so damn hard. So hungry for the feel of her flesh against his flesh.

"I can give you what you need, Emmy. I can give you everything you could ever imagine." She whimpered, a husky, throaty sound that told him she was struggling with what she wanted to do, and what she knew she should not. "Take this, Emmy. Take what you need."

She was watching him and he saw the acceptance shining in her eyes, despite the shadows that cloaked them. "Take this for yourself, Emmy. For me. For us."

Angling his head, he captured her face in his hands as he cursed the clouds and the rain that engulfed her face in shadow. Only her vibrant eyes, the color of precious lapis lazuli, could be seen in the gloomy shadows. He could drown in those eyes.

As their gazes locked, he inched his head lower. Felt her breath caress his lips, felt every nerve in his body tense and tighten as he lowered his mouth to hers. As he clutched her face in his hands, Emmy opened her mouth to him, allowing him to search between her lips with his tongue. He kissed her long and slow, his tongue moving and tangling lazily with hers as his hands slid down the column of her neck to the little lace choker she had tied around her throat.

It was a kiss with no ending and soon she was so needy, so reckless that she was grasping him to her and rubbing her mons against his body and the large erection straining against his trousers.

Adrian tore his mouth from hers and set his lips against her pounding pulse. His fingers sought the edge of the lace she had bound around her throat. "You smell of innocence," he murmured before untying the ribbon and pulling it from her neck. "But you taste of sin. Such tempting, forbidden sin…"

Tipping her head back, Amelia allowed him to suck at her neck with his hot mouth, knowing he was going to leave marks that she would be forced to conceal, but she didn't care about any of that now. She only wanted more.

"How long, Emmy?" he asked, kissing his way down her throat to the opening of her cloak. "How long has it been?" His fingers worked on the buttons of her black cape, parting it and pushing it back over her shoulders. She felt him reach around her waist for the buttons that secured her gown. He undid them slowly, teasing her with the movements of his fingers and his breath against her neck. Her legs shook as he slid the wool from her shoulders and kissed his way down her arm, until the bodice of her gown fell to her waist.

She gasped in pleasure as Adrian's large hand reached into her corset, past her thin chemise, to cup her breast, pulling it from the harsh confines of muslin and whale boning. Once free, his hot palm rubbed the flat of his hand along her nipple, sending it straining against his smooth skin.

His gaze passed over her face, then down to where he held her breast in his hand. "It has been far too long since a man has loved you, hasn't it, Emmy? I can hear your body crying out for it." He traced the contour of her breast that rested in his palm. "Beautiful. Breasts made for a man's pleasure. Made to be drawn into a man's mouth."

Unable to stand the torture, she looked down and saw how he used his fingertip to trace the circle of her nipple; her areole puckered in response to the featherlight caress. Sharp stabs shot through her, straight to her belly, as he rolled her nipple between his thumb and forefinger, lengthening it as he gently tugged and plucked at it.

She was wet between her thighs, restless with the need to curl her fingers in his hair and guide his mouth to her breast. As if aware of her desires, Adrian lowered his head and ran the tip of his tongue along her nipple. Sharp sparks of desire ignited deep in her belly and she gasped, clinging to him, her fingers biting into his upper arms—arms that felt so solid and strong beneath his jacket.

He freed her other breast so that he could nuzzle the scented valley and bury his face between them while his palms skated down her waist to grasp her buttocks. He cupped her bottom, pulling her forward while he took her breast into his mouth and suckled her hard and greedily.

Amelia purred, called his name as she ran her hands through his hair, holding and tugging with the rhythm of his mouth. He moaned and grasped with impatient hands the fabric of her gown. Cool air suddenly kissed her buttocks as he raised her skirt and petticoats from behind. His palm glided over her bottom, squeezing and rubbing, gently slapping at her full cheek.

"You've a beautiful bottom to play with, Emmy," he said against her throat as he traced the cleft of her derriere through her drawers. "Soft and plump. The sort of bottom I like to hold and caress—and grip—in the throes of passion." His fingers skated along her crease, probing at her opening before his palm came around the front of her drawers to cup her sex. "Warm. Wet. A hungry quim. God, you're perfectly made for pleasure, Emmy. Designed for hours and hours of fucking.

Could you do it for hours? Could you fuck me for as long as I wanted with this lush body?"

Burying her face in his hair, Amelia closed her eyes, unable to bring herself to answer him. "Have I shocked you?" She shook her head and allowed her lips to trail along his neck, feeling the stubble of his morning beard brush her tender flesh. "You shouldn't be shocked, you know. In my dreams I've had you every way possible. I've seen myself between your thighs, Emmy, my mouth tasting and licking your cunt. I've heard your cries of pleasure."

What agony it was to discover that there had been times when she had been so close to him, so close she had heard his breathing and felt his warm breath against her, and he had never known, never known it was her—his lover he came to meet on Tuesday mornings. And yet he had thought of her—had fantasized about her. It was more than she had ever dared to hope for.

"Do you want that, Emmy? Hours of pleasure? Do you want me—my body?"

"Yes," she cried as he pressed his palm against the muslin of her drawers. She was aware of her hands on his arms as she pushed him down the length of her body. She moaned in anticipation as he slid down and rasped an uneven breath against her. Then he put his mouth to her sex, blowing hot breath through her dampened drawers as he held her skirts in his hands. He blew again, this time closer, harder, and she felt her womb begin to ache and her thighs begin to dampen and quiver, and she thought she might have discovered heaven then.

"Oh, God." She breathed deep as she felt his mouth press against her. She felt the firm flick over her clitoris, wanted to beg him to rip the gown from her body so that she could feel that hot, hard tongue all over her.

So in tune was he to her needs, he pulled at the opening, ripping the slit of her drawers so that his mouth entirely covered her. Wantonly she moaned, fisting her hands in his hair, rubbing her pelvis against his seeking tongue. He pulled her toward him and lifted her leg over his shoulder. Parting her with his hand, he spread her wide while his tongue lapped at her.

Writhing in pleasure, Amelia closed off all thoughts. The tension continued to build inside her. Despite her trembling legs, her limbs seemed to stiffen. Her nipples tightened and her breasts bobbed freely in the air as she rocked against his mouth. Mercilessly he drove her on, ruthlessly tasting her until she was shaking. She could not stop. Could only hold him to her, forcing him to finish her off until she could no longer stand without his help.

He tugged her gently down onto her knees, seeking her mouth with his as his fingers slipped deep inside her. He did not stretch her slowly, but gave her two of his fingers and plunged deep—so deep that she moaned into his mouth.

"I want to be inside you," he groaned. "Let me inside, Emmy."

She heard the rustling of her skirts at the same time she felt his hand moving between them. The sight of his trousers being opened made her blood hum in her ears. He sought her fingers between the layers of wool and cotton and brought them to his trousers. Instinctively her fingers curled around his length. She was stunned by the size of him, the satiny texture of him, the fierceness of the blood she felt throbbing inside his shaft.

Sliding her hand down the length of him, she stroked him, taking pleasure in his erratic breathing and the way he hungrily sought out her breasts. He sucked at the nipple and she gripped him firmer, quickening her strokes. His breath rushed out and he pressed forward, his lips nearly touching hers, his breath bathing her mouth as his breathing escalated in his excitement.

"Yes," he rasped as his hand came up to cup her cheek. His fingers, long and warm and gentle, slowly curled around her throat as he breathed faster and faster, his lips a hairbreadth away from hers. "Christ, yes, Emmy. I want your hand tossing me off," he groaned, flexing his hips and encouraging her to work him faster and harder. "I'm so close—your touch— Christ, your touch is like magic. And your breasts, God, I can see them beckoning me."

"Beckoning you how?" she purred, teasing him.

"Let me," he said, breaking off. Reaching for her hand, he pulled it away and moved up to bring his shaft to her breasts. Stroking her nipples with his cock, he watched in the thin rays of light how his cock slid up and along her milky skin. He slapped at her nipples, heard her moan, and he slapped a bit harder. Christ, he grew thicker and longer, and the sight and sounds of what he was doing was driving him mad, close to spilling. But there was one more thing he wanted, and she had the perfect breasts for it. Shoving against her, he slid his cock between her breasts while she pressed them together, cradling his cock.

"Have you ever been fucked this way?" he growled as his gaze locked with hers, and then his eyes became hooded as he felt his seed snake up the length of his shaft. "Have you ever seen hot seed coming out of a cock that you've made want you? Have you had it splash on your beautiful skin?"

Christ, what was he saying? He'd scare her with his aggression. Yet he couldn't stop, couldn't be tender. He'd waited too long, and like a caged animal, he was going on pure male instinct.

"Would you let me, Emmy? Would you let me mark these beautiful tits?"

He didn't give her time to answer. Instead, he shuddered, and Amelia felt the rushing pulse of his hot seed spilling into her hands and her breasts.

"Beautiful, Emmy," he whispered shakily. Taking her hand, he pressed a length of linen in her palm and gently wiped away the stickiness. "I did not mean for it to come so quickly. Give me a moment and I will be hard and ready to pleasure you. When I'm buried deep inside you, you'll have so much pleasure. I swear it. I'll fill you deep with my cock, and I'll penetrate your beautiful bottom with my finger and give you an orgasm you will never forget."

"I can't…I *must not* do this. I cannot be the woman you need," she said, struggling to lower her skirts and push her breasts back into her corset. Reality had settled in, chasing away the passion that had run with abandon inside her.

"You are the woman I want, Emmy."

"You don't understand. I'm not—please believe me, it can never be." She reached for her veil atop her bonnet. Pulling it forward, she covered her face.

"I never believed in fate until I met you, Emmy. Not until that first moment when our gazes met and locked—then, I believed. I knew you were my fate. I will find you, you know, should you ever decide to run from me. I will grant you your anonymity. I will not ask you for answers or anything you cannot give me. I only ask that you do not end this—not yet— not when it's only just begun."

How could she say no when he was looking at her like that? How could she deny what her heart was crying out for?

"Next Tuesday I shall bring my carriage. I will draw the shades. I will make it black as night, if only you will agree to meet me here."

Raising her veil over her mouth, she rose up on tiptoes and kissed him tenderly. He reached out to touch her, but she evaded him and ran to the entrance of the alcove. Before she stepped out into the soft drizzle she stopped and looked back at him over her shoulder.

"Promise me, Emmy, that you will come."

"I promise," she said, then ran out into the rain, and home.

AMELIA'S HEART CONTINUED ITS UNSTEADY, rapid beating, making her warm and breathless long after she had arrived back home. Whenever she thought of Adrian and what they had shared that morning, an unbecoming flush marred her cheeks. It was a flush she was certain would not go unnoticed. But how could she conceal it, that blazing heat the memories of him produced?

"Your color is very high."

Beneath her lashes Amelia saw that Lady Sophie was closely observing her from her spot by the window. She was always watching Amelia, as if waiting for the opportunity to pounce upon her for doing something wrong. Lady Sophie had the eyes of a hawk, and Amelia feared that she was the lady's current prey.

"Are you ill? Your cheeks are the same color as your hair."

Automatically, Amelia slid her hand along the strands that were pulled tight into a severe bun and secured with numerous pins. *Not a strand out of place.* She was relieved at that. No need to have her outward appearance disassembling for all to see. It was bad enough she had quite come unglued inside.

Why had she ever thought it possible to carry out this charade? Why had she allowed herself to travel down a path that would only cause her heartache? Nothing could come of this with Adrian.

She, more than anyone, knew it to be impossible.

"Well, are you ill? Speak up!"

"No, madam," Amelia croaked nervously. "I am feeling rather fit."

"You're wearing an awfully high chemisette beneath your gown. And it is positively stifling in this room, what with the fire so high," Lady Sophie observed, her shrewd eyes narrowing sharply.

Amelia's hand flew to her throat. She had worn the lace collar to cover Adrian's mark. She hoped the lace kerchief would go unnoticed, but Lady Sophie was highly observant. Nothing, not even the smallest detail, escaped her eye.

"And your boots have dirt on the toe. Where have you been, *hmm,* to soil your boots with mud?"

"I ran an errand this morning. I must have missed a spot when I cleaned them off on the boot scraper."

"Obviously," she sniffed. "Ah, here is the tea, at last," Lady Sophie announced as the housekeeper carried in a silver tray laden with a fine china teapot and matching cups and saucers.

"Is that my brother I hear in the next room?" Lady Sophie asked as she craned her neck to the right where the connecting door was ajar. "What is he doing?"

Amelia's gaze shifted to the left, to the partially opened door. One lone figure stood by the window. The figure was as achingly familiar to her as the sunlight lit the contours of his shoulders and glinted off his dark hair. For long seconds she stood transfixed by him, by his masculine beauty and the memories of having those beautiful hands caressing her.

"Well, is it him?" Lady Sophie asked impatiently.

"Indeed it is."

An image of her hands clinging to him drifted in her mind, and she shook her head to clear it, but it refused to leave. *"Take what you need."* She heard the quiet of his words in her thoughts and trembled at the memory of them. Closing her eyes, she struggled to escape the hold of those memories, but they held on, fearing to be let go.

"Inform him that I wish him to take tea with me."

Don't make me speak to him. Don't make me draw any attention to myself, she wanted to cry, even as she took a step toward the door. But God saved her the task, when his lordship stepped forward and walked toward her. Gasping, Amelia jumped back and busied herself with the tea things, trying to become invisible behind the tall silver teapot.

"Is that you, dear sister, that I hear commanding everyone about?"

The sound of his voice made Amelia melt like sugar in hot tea. She remembered how that voice had sounded in her ear when it was full of passion. She could not look at him. Could not stand to meet those hypnotizing eyes.

"Ah, Wallace, there you are. Come and join me," Lady Sophie commanded. "The tea has just arrived."

He did not look in Amelia's direction, but instead breezed past her as he crossed the Turkish carpet to where his sister was seated on the settee wearing a breathtakingly beautiful pink gown, a gown that Amelia knew Lady Sophie didn't think was half as lovely as Amelia did.

"Good afternoon, Soph," he murmured, bending down to kiss his sister's rose-colored cheek. "You look lovely, as always."

"Good day, Wallace. I didn't see you at breakfast."

Amelia could no longer think of him as Lord Wallace. In her mind, he was not an earl. He was simply Adrian.

"I had an engagement, I am afraid." He turned then, his gaze landing full upon Amelia's face. What did he see? Did he know? Suspect? She saw nothing in his eyes that resembled recognition, and her breast felt as though it was being squeezed by a vice.

Amelia could not say she was relieved by the fact he did not recognize her, and yet she should be. The truth was, what she was feeling was a good deal more complicated than any emotion she had ever felt before. It was a strange blend of disappointment and resignation. Of pain, peppered with a philosophical understanding that it was perfectly normal for him to look upon her without really seeing her.

"You may begin pouring," he announced.

Nodding, Amelia lifted the delicate pot from its silver stand and carefully poured the tea into the cups. Steam vapors fogged the lenses of her spectacles, and glancing up, away from the steaming tendrils, she caught her reflection shining in the mirror above the sideboard.

What was it she saw shining back at her? An image of his lover? A woman of mystery and beauty? A woman capable of carrying out a clandestine affair?

In those seconds as her lenses cleared of the fog, her appearance sharpened into focus. Amelia allowed her gaze to rove over her reflection, taking in the plain black dress and white lace pinafore and the starched white cap that was set atop her flaming red hair. And it was then that she knew what he truly saw.

A servant.

For it was the truth. She, Amelia Cartwright, was nothing but a maid. A servant who had the misfortune of finding herself well on the way to being in love with her employer.

He watched her through lowered lashes as she poured the tea. She had served him tea hundreds of times in the past two years. But today was different. Today he could smell her, the scent of her sex clinging to his fingers. He could taste her; the sweet remnants of her passion lingered in his mouth, the feel of her—silky and warm—gliding on his tongue as she came for him.

Miss Amelia Cartwright, he mused, watching her holding out the saucer and cup to him. He raised his gaze from her hand, the one that had tossed him off so completely that morning, only to look straight up into her lovely eyes, the sparkling in the blue iris partially concealed behind her spectacles. Reaching for the tea, he allowed his finger to brush against hers, sliding suggestively along the length of the delicate bone and over her nail, letting the touch linger. He heard her breath catch, felt her gaze fix on his face, but he feigned ignorance while his gaze slipped to the three little freckles on her hand. What would she, his maid, think if she discovered what wicked thoughts were running through her employer's head at this very moment?

"Thank you," he said, purposely lowering his voice as he searched her face. Her expression gave nothing away, not even when he broke protocol and thanked her in front of his sister. No, her iron composure stayed true, and with perfect obedience, she bowed before him, angering him.

To look at her, one would never guess she'd been half-naked in his arms, her sex pressed to his mouth that very morning. Not even the faintest flush of pink marred her cheeks when it should have. After all, he had not been the one to conceal his identity from her. She knew perfectly well that it had been *his* fingers buried deep within her, *his* mouth that had made her shudder and cry out.

Sprawling in the chair, he watched her surreptitiously as she finished serving the tea. Miss Amelia Cartwright. His exemplary employee. His secret obsession.

For two years he'd desired her, watching her when she was not aware. For two years, he'd been bound by his desires and the strictures that dictated that a man of wealth and means—a titled earl—did not fall for the hired help.

But he'd been smitten with the woman who had come to apply for the post of maid. There was something intriguing about her severe appearance coupled with her lush figure and sauntering walk. The artist in him had seen the passion and intelligence in her straightaway. The earl, on the other hand, had ruthlessly squelched those thoughts. And when the artist stared at her and began wondering what all that auburn hair of hers would look like unbound and spilling over his chest, the earl had smothered those thoughts by reminding himself that she was beneath him. She was a servant. Servants were not seen. Not heard. They certainly were not talked to, and while there had been many men of his rank who had diddled the domestic help, *no one* had ever dared to lose their heart.

And while the earl had tried very hard to distance himself from her, the artist in him continually sought her out. The woman he wanted *was* his servant, and God help him, he needed her—emotionally, spiritually, carnally. She was the woman who could satisfy him both in and out of bed. She was intelligent and well-spoken, despite what he assumed must be a very humble upbringing. She appreciated art and literature and the beauty of nature. She also appreciated the beauty of passion. She could feed his artist soul while loving the lonely earl. He had found no other woman like her in his circle, and as a consequence he'd become reclusive, spending all his time at home, wanting to be close to her.

So many nights he stood outside her door, praying none of the other servants would venture out of their rooms and see him standing in the hall of the servants' wing. So many nights he wanted to grab her out of her bed and carry her down the stairs to his room where they would roll around in his bed, indulging in whatever wicked pleasure they fancied. After, they would talk and laugh and he would feed her every delight that was denied her by her station in life. And he would paint her, lounging in his bed while she picked through a box of French chocolates, wearing nothing more than an expensive piece of jewelery he had handpicked for her.

He wanted to spoil her. Wanted to lavish attention and gifts upon her. Wanted her to see him for the man he was—not the Earl of Wallace or the artist. *Not,* he glowered, *her fucking employer.*

The longer he watched her at the tea table, the blacker his mood grew. She carried on, blithely ignoring him. He had the mad urge to ask her if she had enjoyed her morning off, just to see if she would blush or betray any hint of emotion. Had she enjoyed his mouth on her? Did she regret her hasty departure? Did she wish she had stayed for the fucking? Because God above, he wanted that—still. His mind was awash with images of her yielding her body to him, begging him for pleasure.

With an oath, he placed the saucer down hard on the table. Tea sloshed onto the polished surface. He ignored it and instead pressed his eyes shut, willing his anger and the image of him taking Emmy up against a wall to subside.

He needed to talk to her, to feel her against him. But employers did not talk to their staff. Employers were not even supposed to notice that their servants were living and breathing, with thoughts and desires—dreams—of their own.

But Christ, every nerve in his body was painfully aware of Amelia Cartwright. *Emmy*…

"You may leave us now," his sister announced. With a negligent wave of her bejeweled hand, she waved Amelia out of the salon as if she were an irritating bug that kept flying into her tea. Adrian felt his lips harden. His expression, he knew, was mulish. He did not want Amelia talked to in such a fashion. Yet, to say anything, to reprimand his sister in front of a servant would draw undue attention to Amelia and to the true extent of his feelings. So he kept quiet and watched Amelia bow and leave the room.

"You cannot be serious, brother," Sophie hissed when the door closed behind Amelia.

"What are you going on about now, Sophie?"

"That servant!"

"She has a name," he growled.

"The fact you know that is evidence enough of the danger

you're in. Adrian," Sophie murmured, her voice growing low and secretive, "I've been watching you, you know—all winter long, as a matter of fact. It is quite apparent you want her."

"I will not hear a word about this from you," he thundered, jumping up from his chair and knocking it over. "Not when you of all people know that money and position does not bring happiness. You lived through that hell we called childhood. You saw firsthand how empty a marriage based solely on profit is."

"Adrian—"

"Don't!" he demanded. "Don't tell me how wrong this is. Don't say a damned word when you don't know the first thing about love."

She gasped as if he'd struck her. When he looked back over his shoulder, his sister's beautiful face was white and stricken. Her lips trembled and she raised her hand to her mouth to hide the fact from him. "You must put an end to this…this liaison, Adrian. You must learn to live with the fact that she can never be yours."

"Do you think I haven't thought about it? I can't sleep at nights for thinking. I know what I ought to do, Sophie, but I…I can't stop," he said, his voice choking. "I can't look away. I can't stop thinking, wishing…hoping. There is nothing else—" He stopped and turned to face her. "I *have* nothing else, Sophie, if I cannot hope."

His sister's eyes grew sad and perhaps a bit wet as she looked at him. "Your reputation can weather this storm, Adrian. If it were to come out that you were intimate with your maid, it would be considered nothing but an amusing little peccadillo in your past. But think of hers…think of…"

"Amelia. Her name is Amelia—*Emmy*."

"Amelia is not of our kind. She is bound by what she is. You cannot change that, however much you wish to. If you cannot stop for yourself, then do it for Amelia. Do it because you love her enough to let her go, to save her from the cruel tongues that will talk about her—not only behind her back, but to her face. Save her from embarrassment and the inferiority she will feel when she goes out in society with you. She will never be accepted, nor welcomed. When you are together, she will always been seen as inferior—beneath you and everyone else. Think of the pain that will cause her. Think of how that will shame her, then think of what that will do to your relationship. She may even grow to despise you and your love, Adrian."

He knew Sophie was right, and he hated her for it, but he hated himself more for wishing that next Tuesday did not feel so impossibly far away.

CHAPTER FIVE

THE RAIN WAS POURING DOWN IN A BLINDING
sheet. Heedless of the bone-raking chill of the wind and driving rain, Adrian gripped the iron bars of the fence and stared
at the empty spot where he'd once held Emmy.

Stark reality slapped him in the face. She was not here. She
was not coming to Highgate today, or any other day. He had
driven her away from him.

Pushing away from the fence, he took a step back, blinking
away the rainwater that landed on his lashes. Ignoring the
forked flash of lightning and the roll of thunder, he took
another step back, then another, unable to bring himself to
look away from the stone angel Emmy admired so much.

Damn her for not returning. And damn him for being such
a pathetic fool. Christ, it was utterly pitiable, this slavish need
he had for her. How could this woman have become so vital
to his happiness? Women had never factored into his happiness before, so why now, with this one?

Goddamn her, she had made him hope. Made him feel alive.
And now he felt like he had a fucking hole in his chest where
his heart had once been.

Reaching his waiting carriage, he flung open the door only

to have his coachman lean down from his perch. "Home, Your Lordship?"

"Yes," he growled. Slamming the door shut, Adrian stretched out his legs and watched the rivulets of rainwater trickle down the glossed leather of his boots. Christ, he was in a black mood. A rage he had not felt in years was gripping him.

With one last glare at the statues of Highgate, he snorted at his foolishness and looked away, trying to run from his memories. His gaze suddenly landed on the two brown packages that sat across from him. Gifts for Emmy.

By the time the carriage rolled to a stop in front of his town house, as he reached for the packages and threw open the door, his mood was nearly murderous. He was not yet in control of his emotions. When his butler opened the door for him, he all but snapped at the old retainer as the man tried to speak with him.

"What are you mumbling about?"

"My lord," Jermyn said. "I must speak with you."

"Can it not wait?" Adrian snapped as he lifted the packages from the hall table and headed for his study.

"I am afraid that this is a matter that requires immediate attention, my lord. The Season, as you well know, begins in a fortnight."

"I don't give a fucking toss about the Season."

"But it is so very difficult to find suitable staff once everyone comes back to town. Even now the agencies are busy filling requests for maids and footmen."

Adrian stopped dead in his tracks. A god-awful feeling of dread bore heavily down on him. "What is it you're trying to tell me, Jermyn, that we now find ourselves in a position to hire more staff?"

His butler's flaccid face grew pale. "I beg your pardon, my lord. I thought you were already aware."

"Aware of what?"

"That the maid, Amelia, has resigned her post. I... Forgive me, my lord, she said she would speak to you directly."

"Send her to me," he snarled, "and do not dally, Jermyn."

"At once, my lord."

Adrian slammed the door of his study shut. Goddamn her. She was not leaving his house. He was not going to allow her to leave him. He didn't care what it took to keep her, she was going to stay. And he was going to bring their little affair out into the light. It was well past time that she discovered he'd known it was her all along. There was going to be no more hiding behind her veil.

"You sent for me, my lord."

Adrian swallowed the last of his brandy and turned to see Amelia step into the study. She was not dressed in her uniform, but the gray gown she always wore to Highgate. Her hair was pulled tightly into a bun and the spectacles she wore were sliding down the bridge of her nose.

"My lord?" she asked, her voice sounding nervous.

"Where have you been this morning?" he snapped, refilling his snifter with more brandy, despite the fact it was too early to be drinking.

"I have Tuesday mornings off, my lord. I don't begin my duties for another hour."

"And where do you go on your mornings off?" he snarled, prowling about the room.

"I...I..." she swallowed, unable to speak. "I usually walk."

"Where?"

"Different places, I suppose."

"And do you meet a lover in secret, then?"

"No, my lord."

Liar, he wanted to hiss, but he refrained, trying to curb the temper that was threatening to erupt.

"What of the odd dalliance, then? Do you engage in them?" She bristled, but stood steadfast in her denial, fueling his already irrational anger. "Did I offend you with my accusation? Are you above raising your skirts for strangers, then?"

"My lord, really—"

"As your employer I have a measure of responsibility toward you. I'm only curious, you see. What exactly do you do with your Tuesday mornings?"

"I walk, my lord, and…look at things."

"Things?" he sneered. "What things, Miss Cartwright? Do you mean men? Do you look at men and wonder what it would be like to lure them with your body? Do you offer them a sample of your abundant charms? Tell me, have you fucked any of these men on your mornings off?"

She blushed and looked away. "My lord, my duties here have always been performed with—"

"Speaking of duties," he snapped, cutting her off, "I understand that you have resigned your post here, Miss Cartwright."

Her gaze dropped to her hands, which were folded very primly and properly before her. "Yes, my lord."

"Are you not happy here? Is the position not to your liking? Have you been mistreated?"

"No, my lord," she said quickly. "I have never been hap— that is to say, this has been a very satisfactory experience."

"Satisfactory?" he croaked. "If it has been so bloody satisfactory then why do you wish to leave?"

She was breathing heavily, but seemed to be in control. And that angered him all the more. She knew who she had shared that morning with at Highgate. She knew it was him. Damn her, how could she so easily dismiss that? How could it be so easy to walk away from something that had meant so much to him?

"Is it me? Have I done something to make you wish to leave?" She shook her head, and he growled. "You know nothing of me if you think I will let you just walk away."

"It is not as though maids are not a dime a dozen, my lord."

"I don't want another maid." He came to stand before her

and she stiffened, trying to step away from him, but he reached for her and wrapped his fingers around her wrist. Brushing the cuff of her sleeve back toward her wrist with his thumb, he saw the cluster of freckles that lay hidden beneath the starched muslin.

Slowly, he lifted his gaze to her face, his stomach churning uncomfortably. *Damn her, she knew who he was.* He had not concealed his features with a veil. He had not hidden anything from her. And yet here she stood before him, acting as though they had never met, never talked, never touched.

Rage made his breathing hard and he fought it, barely able to see anything other than that day at Highgate, when he had desired her so bloody much. When he had talked of himself and allowed her the briefest glimpse into his soul. Was she amused by him whenever she thought of that day at the cemetery? Was she mocking him now, secretly laughing at him, remembering how much of a damned fool he had been?

With lightning speed, he shackled her wrist and captured it ruthlessly in his hand. Before she could think of getting away, he reached for her, bringing her back against the door, pinning her against the wood with his chest and thighs. His hand skimmed over her hip while he turned the key in the lock with a soft but determined *click*.

She whimpered. In fear. In longing. He didn't know, and didn't particularly care. Tightening his fingers on her waist, he brought her ever so slightly closer to him. He saw her eyes go round, felt the rush of hot air as she released a pent-up breath. He was aware that her fingers held a death grip on her skirts.

"I know everything about you, Amelia," he whispered darkly. *"Everything."*

Her gaze flashed to his. "Don't do this," she pleaded. "It is better left unsaid."

Ignoring her plea, he slowly ran his fingertip down the column of her neck, noticing how flushed and warm her skin was. "I know that Tuesday mornings you have some free time to spend however you wish, and that you enjoy long walks in secluded spots."

The color left her face, but she amazingly held her gaze steady on him. "I think you must be mistaken, my lord."

"Highgate Cemetery? A foggy morning, standing in the drizzling rain?" he murmured, watching as his finger caressed the pounding pulse in her throat. "You pleasured me and I came in your hands, remember?"

She started to deny it, but he pressed his fingers into her wrist. "I know, Amelia. Now I just want to know why you won't admit it."

Why didn't she want him? She was abandoning him after the most beautiful, intimate encounter he had ever experienced, and Christ, how he despised the feelings of abandonment. How he loathed to admit that weakness in his makeup.

His palm slid from her waist to her breast until he cupped her in his hand. He pressed forward so that his chest flattened against her and the side of his face nestled against her neck. His gaze flickered up from her throat to her face. Her head was tilted to the side, her eyes closed behind the lenses of her spectacles, her lips, pouting and pink, were parted slightly. He parted them more as he rubbed his finger along her lower lip. "I know what you need," he whispered. "I can give it you, Amelia. Just let me."

"No, please don't." She shook her head, whispering the word *no* again, as she pressed herself against the unyielding wood behind her. Any space that was between them he closed when he pressed his chest tightly to hers.

"I knew what you needed that day in the cemetery. I know the depth of passion you keep hidden beneath this prim veneer. I know that beneath your protests, you secretly yearn."

"Please, stop—just stop!"

"I waited for you this morning. I stood in the rain and

waited for you to come to me. Why?" he growled. "Why didn't you come, Emmy?"

She gasped at the sound of her secret name. When she looked away from him, refusing to answer his questions, he reached into his jacket and removed the slip of black lace he carried with him. The same lace he removed in order to press his lips against her bounding pulse that day at Highgate. "Tell me why you still insist on hiding behind the veil when I already know it was you. I've always known, Amelia, from the minute my carriage stopped in the lane and I saw you standing in that sunbeam, I've known it was you."

"I am a servant," she said, her voice almost inaudible. "I couldn't let you find out."

"How much will it take for you to stay?"

She tilted her head and studied him with her shrewd, intelligent eyes. Eyes that burned a hole right through him from behind the lenses of her spectacles. "Is this some sort of game to you, my lord?"

"Was it only just a game to you, Emmy?"

"I don't play games, my lord. I have never laughed at you, despite what you may think. I never intentionally set out to mislead you."

"How much?"

"I am not for sale, my lord," she shrilled, her eyes blazing with indignation. "Now, then, goodbye."

It was not merely a goodbye, excusing herself for an hour, or the evening. It felt like a goodbye that was forever. He could not stand to hear it.

"What is your price?" he rasped. "Tell me. I will pay it. With gold, with my body. Whatever it is you want."

"I may be just a servant, my lord, but I am not a whore. I won't sell my body."

"But what of Emmy? Would she sell her body? Would she

fuck me now, up against this door? Because I would have her that way. Right now."

"Is Emmy who you want?" He detected a sadness in her voice, before she steeled her shoulders and lifted her chin in defiance. "Of course, she is. Emmy is a woman of mystery, someone you can pretend is suitable to someone of your station. Or perhaps you pretended that I was beautiful, or maybe you just liked the power of getting off with someone who is beneath you."

"For Christ sake's, Amelia—"

"Is that what you meant when you said I empowered you? It made you feel strong to tumble the plain housemaid, to discover her most carefully hidden secrets? Did you laugh at me then, while I was serving you your tea? Did you find it amusing to think upon how easily I fell into your arms while you were watching me make your *fucking bed?*" His breath hissed through his lips and he dropped her wrist as if he had been burned. "Did it ever occur to you, *my lord,* that while you were getting off playing your grand game of master and servant, you were toying with the only happiness I have ever known in my pathetic existence?"

"Amelia, please, this is not how I wanted this discussion to be."

"I resign my post, effective immediately. I'll not give you two weeks notice. You don't deserve it. I'm leaving now and I'll take nothing from you. Not the wages owed to me nor a reference. I want *nothing* from you."

"You cannot just leave. Where will you go? Amelia—"

She wheeled on him, her eyes flashing fury. "Do you want to know the worst part of all this? It's the pain that comes when I think of how I allowed myself to believe in you. That I permitted myself to think that you might actually desire me. I didn't go to Highgate today because I feared that perhaps you might…have begun to care for Emmy. I could not do that to you, to engage your feelings, knowing I was just a servant. I didn't want to keep betraying you. Ironic, isn't it, how I cared for you when you obviously didn't give a bloody toss about me."

CHAPTER SIX

WATER TRICKLED DOWN HER ARMS AND OVER her shoulder, running in streaming rivulets down her back. Her nipples tightened, crinkling beneath the thin chemise. Dipping the sponge into the basin, Amelia wrung out the excess and brought the sponge to her throat, squeezing the water down her neck, soaking the front of her shift so that the fabric clung to her breasts.

The water had grown cold as she sat before her dressing table. In a daze, she repeated the motions of the sponge bath, lost in thought, drowning in pain.

What was he doing now? Laughing at her? Her, a plain little peahen, desiring someone like him, a handsome and wealthy earl. What a simpleton she had been to let him in, to speak of things she could barely even admit to herself. He had used her, had made her feel small and insignificant—*invisible*.

"Amelia?"

Jumping at the sound of his voice, the sponge dropped from her hand and splashed into the basin. The door of her room clicked quietly shut, it was followed by the sound of his footsteps on the wooden floor.

He stood behind her, and Amelia felt his heat warming her back. His hands rested on her shoulders, and she stiffened, feeling her eyes immediately flood with tears. She would not cry before him. Never again would she allow herself to be vulnerable.

"Will you not look at me?"

Reluctantly she turned her head so that she faced the small mirror that sat atop her dressing table, and there he was, his reflection shining back at her. He bent down so that his face was even with hers and she watched him close his eyes as he pressed his cheek against her temple.

"I brought these for you. I had them with me at Highgate. I...wanted you to have them."

"Another bribe?" she asked bitterly, turning away from the image of them together in the mirror.

"Amelia—"

"There is nothing more to be said, my lord. I may be a servant but I have my pride. That pride cannot be purchased. And yes, I may be poor as a church mouse, but I'm not so poorly off that I need to consider bartering my sex for your amusement."

He nodded, then slowly stood. He turned to leave, then stopped, took her face in his hands and brushed his mouth against her lips. "It was never a game to me, Amelia. *Never.* You've never been just an amusement to me."

"What was it then?"

"Perfection." Such a simple word and said with such stunning honesty. Amelia could not help but turn her face up to him in wonder. "It was everything to me, Amelia. Every day spent with you meant so much. And not just at Highgate. I have wanted you since the moment you came into my study to interview for the position. Do you think me so shallow that I would not see you behind your uniform and spectacles? I did look, Amelia. And I thought—think—you're the most beautiful woman I've ever seen. You have a gift of giving me something I could never buy myself and that makes you a woman of incredible wealth and beauty to me."

"What gift is this that you speak of?"

"The gift of being myself. There are no courtly airs with you, no pretences. I am just myself. Something I have never felt comfortable being with any woman other than you. If you don't believe me, at least open the package on the bottom. Perhaps then you might have some understanding of how I feel about you and what we've shared."

It was agony waiting for her to decide, and when Adrian feared she would not agree to his request, he turned and walked away, his heart bleeding in his chest. When he reached the door, the sound of her weeping forced him to stop. Looking back at her, he saw that she held his gift in her hands and that she was looking down at the burgundy leather, crying.

"This can never be. How can you want someone like me? I cannot even read," she choked, then looked up at him. "I only pretended to, that day you saw me in the cemetery."

"Emmy," he said, not knowing whether to go to her, or stay away. What did she need from him? What did she want?

"I am not ashamed of what I am," she sniffed. "I am a domestic. I am not humiliated that I must work for my survival. I am honest and hardworking and take pride in doing my job well. There is no shame in that. But I knew the kind of thoughts I had about you were not proper. And I knew that what I was doing at Highgate was not right. But I had to discover, you see, what it would be like to be with you. To experience what it was like to be touched by your beautiful hands. I am ashamed to admit that I willingly misled you. I let you think I was a stranger to you, when I knew I was only just your servant. You asked why I did not come to Highgate today, and the reason was that I have allowed myself to think of the future. To ask myself, 'what if?' I understand there can be no future, and so I did not go this morning, and I resigned because I felt I could not see you every day and not yearn for what we had."

He walked to her and crouched down before her. She looked away as she swiped at her tears, but he took her chin and turned her so that she was looking at him.

"If you cannot read, Amelia, how were you able to recite that poem?"

Closing her eyes, she drew in a deep breath. "I was listening to you and your sister one evening. I was taking away the tea things. I took my time so I could listen, and as I stood at the table, I closed my eyes and listened to the poems as you read them. I memorized a few of them, and when I finally opened my eyes, I saw your reflection in the mirror. You were looking at me, and I thought...that is...I fancied that perhaps you might have been saying those words to me."

"I was. It's only ever been you that has seen beneath the mask I wear."

She looked at him through her spectacles, and he smiled, his heart finally feeling as though it were done bleeding. "This book, Amelia, is a collection of Elizabeth Barrett Browning's poems."

"I am sorry I cannot read it."

He took the book from her and set it atop her dressing table. Then he reached for the bun at the back of her head and pulled a pin free. Amelia allowed him the intimacy of letting down her hair. Slowly, one by one he pulled the pins from the tight bun at the back of her head. He placed each one on the table beside him before returning to pull the next free. She felt the heavy bun begin to loosen, felt the first curling tendrils slip forward so that it tickled her ears, then her chin.

Closing her eyes, she breathed heavily as his fingers raked through her hair, loosening the bun. "Curls," he said with surprise. "I never would have guessed it, you pull it so severely back that you give the illusion that it is straight. And so long," he murmured as he brushed some of her hair over her shoulder. "It goes to your waist."

His hands smoothed over her hair, and she watched as he

studied the strands in the glow of the firelight as they slid between his fingers. When his gaze slid up to hers, she felt her breath hitch and her breasts push against the wet muslin of her shift. She was exposed, almost as if she were naked. Her hair was unbound and hanging over her back. No man had ever seen her hair down. In fact, she rarely saw it down herself.

As if she were watching it all in a dream, she saw Adrian's hands leave her hair, then come up to capture the sides of her face. His thumbs stroked her jaw, then her bottom lip, only to slide up her cheeks and rest against the arms of her spectacles.

"Please, no," she said breathlessly, not wanting the last of her armor to fall away. She did not want to feel this naked with him, this exposed. The cool metal slid down her nose, then away from her face. Unable to bear it, she looked at him, wondering what he was thinking.

"You said you were nobody," he whispered, tracing his thumbs over her lids, then caressing her lashes with the tips of his fingers. "But I see someone of worth sitting before me. I see someone worthy of being seen."

She looked away, but he caught her chin in his fingers and turned her to look at him. "Speak to me, Amelia."

"What are you thinking?" she asked, fearing his answer. "This very moment, what is running through your mind?"

"I am thinking how much of a challenge you are going to be to paint. How any artist would love to be able to re-create the brilliance in your eyes. I am wondering how I will be able to capture the intelligence, the sensuality I see in them." Pressing forward he tilted her face up to his and looked down into her eyes. "I am thinking how easy it would be for a man to become obsessed with you—how very easy it would be for me to be consumed by you."

Pulling her close, he raised their hands to his mouth and pressed a kiss to the soft flesh above her thumb. Closing his eyes, Adrian inhaled the scent of them together—hers the clean, pure scent of lemon, and his, the warmth of eastern spice. Together, it was an erotic, heady scent that went straight to his head.

He pressed another kiss to her hand and watched the line of her throat move up and down as she swallowed. He trailed his fingers along that smooth skin and felt how fast her heart was beating for him.

"Come to me, Emmy." He pulled her closer. "Come to my bed. It's been waiting a long time for you."

Her breath caught, and the sound wreaked havoc within him. Nodding, she took a tentative step closer to him. He swore he could hear Emmy's heart beating from deep within her chest. He could smell her—lemon and feminine arousal, and his cock stirred.

"Come," he whispered. "Come to my bed where I can spoil you."

This was not a dream or an illicit fantasy while she was making beds and dusting furniture. This was real. His hands truly were on her flesh. It was really his breathing she heard, his lips she felt kissing her cheek. His soft sheets and feathery mattress she felt beneath her.

He followed her down, his body pressing hers into the bed. She saw his hot gaze travel over her face, then lower, to fix on the bounding pulse in her neck. Leaning toward her, he inhaled once, softly, almost imperceptibly, then again, deeper. Then his lips were pressing against the quivering pulse that leaped with his touch.

"You smell so good to me, Amelia. So right."

Closing her eyes, Amelia tilted her head farther back, her lips parting just enough to allow the barest movement of air between them. He sighed and she felt the smooth tip of his finger trace her mouth. "Innocent, perfect lips," he whispered darkly, stroking his thumb along her mouth. "I want to feel them sliding along my body. I want them hard and soft, savoring and hungry."

She couldn't think, her mind was a whirlwind of thoughts and emotions, as if she were drugged, disembodied. She was conscious of the moan that escaped her when he slanted his mouth against hers, encouraging her to open for him. He parted her lips and slid his tongue deep into her mouth. He groaned, and his hand left her face to cup her breast. Hungrily he kissed her, his mouth moving over hers, faster and faster. His tongue drove into her, and she could do nothing but reach for him and wrap her arms around his neck and hold on as he swept her away.

He kissed her for what seemed like forever, before he moved his mouth from hers and whispered, "I need to touch you."

His big hand, with its long, elegant fingers, slid along her waist, curving over her hip and skating over to her belly where he kneaded her until her womb ached. When he sat up, she whimpered and forced her hands to lie limp at her sides. She wanted to reach out to him, to beg him to come back to her. He smiled, as if he could read her thoughts, and reached for her, tugging her up from the mattress. When she was kneeling before him, he took the hem of her worn chemise and pulled it up over her head, letting it fall from his fingers to the floor. He sat back and surveyed her with his hands and his eyes.

Strong fingers gripped her thighs, pulling them apart with the barest of pressure. His fingers trailed up the inner facings. "Beautiful, Emmy," he said as he came around behind her. His palms swept up her thighs to her bottom. He gripped her in his palms, stroking and kneading as he kissed his way up her spine. With his tongue, he licked a path down her spine at the same time his finger smoothed between the crease of her bottom and stroked her, his fingertip circling her slowly, teasingly, until he rested the pad of his thumb against her and pressed.

"Adrian," she pleaded.

"Say my name again, in that same breathless way."

"Adrian," she whimpered.

His hands came around to cup her breasts and toy with her nipples. The sensation of his hands at her front, and his lips on her lower back made her feel boneless. He was cherishing her as if she were a fragile figurine he was terrified of breaking.

"With other women, it was only ever sex for me, Amelia. But now it is so much more. It has become about us. You have made me see beauty where none existed before. You have made me yearn, when I only ever had a need. I yearn for you, Amelia. I yearn—need to be inside you—everywhere."

"I want this, Adrian. I want you."

"Do you?" he asked. She heard the bedspring creak. Felt the mattress dip as he shifted behind her. Then she felt the warmth of his palms on her outer thighs, it was followed by the slow, steady glide of his wet tongue along her inner thigh. He stopped just short of her sex and she groaned in expectation.

"You accused me of playing master and servant with you. I swear, Amelia, I never did. But I would give anything to play that with you now."

Her unbound hair spilled down her back. She looked over her shoulder, watched him trail his tongue up her thigh once more, then he licked her slick sex, tasting her. His eyes closed as he made love to her with his mouth. Unable to resist, Amelia reached out and ran her fingers through his hair.

"Which you do want to be, Amelia? Master or servant?"

She waited until he looked up at her. From this distance, his was a bit foggy without her spectacles, but she could still make out the desire in his eyes. "Servant," she said, watching as his pupils seemed to widen.

"Dutiful little servant," he said, reaching for her hands. But she brushed his hands aside, turned and reached for his trousers. Opening them, she slid them along his hips and reached for his erection. Bending to him, she took him in her mouth, closing her eyes as she listened to his sounds of pleasure.

Gathering her long hair in his hands, Adrian lifted it up from her neck so he could watch her working his cock. He adored the way she played with him, sucking and pulling him into her mouth until he could barely stay balanced on his knees.

He pulled out, grasping his shaft, milking it, tracing the wet tip around her swollen lips. "I like to watch, you know," he said darkly. "It's a compulsion of mine. Will you indulge me, Emmy? Will you let me watch you sucking my cock?"

Her eyes flared and he grunted in satisfaction as she made a great show of sliding her tongue along him. The pointed tip of her tongue slashed across the opening of his cock, and she put it inside, tasting a drop of him. He brushed the tip along her mouth, dominating her with his hand along her neck. He was beyond aroused, and, heightening his pleasure, he gripped himself, masturbating before her as she sucked and pulled him deep in her mouth.

"That's it," he hissed, "take all of me in." She worked him hard, gripping him, and the sounds her mouth was making drove him wild. "Will you swallow it?" he asked, feeling it rushing upon him. "Will you take me inside you?"

She did, and he literally saw stars.

"Emmy," he said, falling back on the bed, "come to me."

He didn't wait for her to answer, but pulled her on top of him. She placed her hand palm up against his and they stayed like that, palm to palm for long seconds before he entwined his fingers through hers. "I thought I could wait. I thought I could make this the most beautiful hour of your life. But I can't, Emmy."

Flipping her over onto her back, he held their entwined fingers above her head. Catching her gaze, he thrust once, deeply inside her, feeling her body stretch to accommodate him.

"Fuck," he growled, watching himself enter her. Slowly he retreated, then thrust forward, repeating each stroke with slow determination, deepening every thrust. Her body met his, undulating beneath him. He thought it was the most amazing, most erotic thing he'd ever seen, watching himself making love to her.

Amelia had never felt this—this oneness of mind, body and spirit. As they looked into each other's eyes, Adrian's hand gripped hers tightly while his body slid into hers. Amelia knew, as her body took him in, that she would never, ever, feel this connection with anyone else.

He looked so beautiful, so peaceful as he made slow love to her. Tears began to fill her eyes, and she closed her eyes, not understanding why she had started to cry.

He kissed her, nipping at her lips until she raised her lashes and looked into his eyes, which were now unguarded. A tear crept out, dangling on the edge of her lash. She blinked, letting it slide down her lashes till it splashed onto her cheek. He took it between his lips, kissing the tear away before he whispered, "This won't be the only time for us, Amelia."

How did he know? How could he have seen through to her heart to know the fear she clutched inside?

"It is just us here in this bed, Amelia. No master or servant. Emmy," he growled, nipping her neck, "come here."

Lifting himself off her, he rocked back and brought her up until she straddled his thighs. His arms came tightly around her, pulling her close to him until there was no space between their bodies. As he brushed the hair from Amelia's dampened cheek, Adrian paused and looked down at her. He'd never before been struck by the beauty of lovemaking—the graceful movement of a female body in motion beneath him. He'd never taken the time to savor every sound, to watch as lips parted on a silent moan, or a plea for more. He'd never studied how lashes glittered in the candlelight or fluttered open and closed.

He'd never felt his heart fill with emotion, or his soul come alive when eyes, glazed with passion, met and held his. He had never made love until he reached for Amelia's hips and set her back from him, encouraging her to watch him enter her body. She watched, wide-eyed, as his cock filled her, and her body took him in and loved him.

When he could no longer fight off the desire to spill himself, he pulled her to sit atop him, wrapping her thighs around his hips while he buried his lips in her hair. His hands squeezed her lush bottom, forcing her up and down, driving her to take all of him.

He'd never experienced love until she clasped his head to her breasts and clung to his hair, her hips moving instinctively as *she* made love to *him*.

"What?" he asked, laughing as she looked up from where she was kissing his belly. Licking her lips, she smiled sheepishly.

"I think I ate the entire box."

Together they looked at the empty pink box and the ruffled wrappers that were strewn about the bedclothes. The black ribbon that had been tied around the box was still wrapped around her wrist.

"Did you enjoy them?"

Her blush grew, but she did not look away from him. "I did. I have never had chocolate before. The butter cream ones were my favourite."

"I enjoyed watching you eat them, every last one. Now, what of my other gift?"

"The book," she said flatly.

"The book."

"Would you read it to me?"

"No. I will teach you to read it, and then you can read it

to *me* while we are in bed, and *I am* eating expensive French chocolates off *your* naked body."

She laughed and rolled off him, her long, red hair trailing across his chest and belly. He watched her, laughing and rolling about the wrinkled white sheets, and thought about how he had wanted this all along. This easy contentment. The peace that came with being nothing more than a man.

"I've changed my mind," he announced. "Hand me the book."

He watched her rise from his bed and fetch the book he had brought from her room. When she handed it to him, he reached for her wrist and brought her down to him.

"What's this?" she asked, pulling out the white strip of canvas he had tucked between the pages. When she saw what it was, she looked up at him with glassy eyes.

"This is…is this…" she swallowed, unable to finish.

"It is you, standing before the angel that morning I first saw you at Highgate."

"You painted this for me?"

When he nodded, she began to cry in earnest. She looked away, flustered that he was witnessing her in such a vulnerable state. She busied herself by opening the book to the page where he'd tucked the scrap of canvas.

He stayed her hand. "I know this passage off by heart, Amelia."

When she looked up at him with her watery eyes, free of her spectacles, he needed to touch her. Trailing the backs of his fingers along her cheek he recited the poem. "'I love you not only for what you are, but for what I am when I am with you. I love you not only for what you have made of yourself, but for what you are making of me. I love you for the part of me that you bring out.'" His voice was broken by the time he finished. "Elizabeth Barrett Browning might have written it, Amelia, but I mean every damn word of it."

★ ★ ★ ★ ★

CAUGHT IN THE ACT
SASKIA WALKER

WHY WAS IT THAT HER SCENT REACHED HIM ALL the way across the room? Liam O'Neil glanced over at the pretty blonde software engineer on the far side of the open-plan office. Wherever he was, he could smell her perfume. He could also invariably see her, and feel her intense scrutiny.

Mostly it was because she was stalking him.

Chrissie Stanfield crossed his path whenever she got the chance. Apparently she had to check out what he was up to numerous times a day. Even when he was under a desk installing new cables, he'd see her stroll by, and he'd have to pause whatever he was doing to admire her legs.

He lifted his head and smiled at her when he caught her looking his way. Ruffled, she looked away without acknowledging him.

Too late, you little minx, I caught you.

Right from day one, Liam knew she was onto him—or thought she was. His current post was undercover, investigating security and a possible leak from a top-notch banking software design company. Someone was stealing and selling their code. It wasn't Chrissie, much to his relief. It certainly livened up the job having her to look at, though.

Right now her annoyance at having been caught showed.

Her lower lip projected ever so slightly, giving her the cutest pout, and it made him want to hold her. Preferably in a long, slow, horizontal grind. She was petite and blonde, her body physically compact in a way that suggested he could put her on his lap. Naked, ideally. She was also tough as old boots and fiery—hellish fiery. What would she be like in bed, with all that fire and sass on full throttle? It gave him a hard-on just thinking about it. He shook his head. Just as well he was on top of this project already, otherwise she would be a dangerous distraction.

Despite his preoccupation with her sexual personality, he could also tell she was annoyed there was something between them; the fire in her eyes told him that. So did her annoyance when he tried to chat with her. There was no hiding it. It was the sort of clash that flared up when you wanted someone you didn't want to want. He bided his time. He had his job to do, but it was fun watching her stake him out. They were two of a kind in that respect. If she wanted to stalk him around the office, he wasn't about to argue, because she was closing in, and he was waiting for her to pounce, just so he could turn the tables on her.

"He's got a great body, the new IT bloke, hasn't he?"

Chrissie looked up when she realized someone was speaking to her. Theresa, her boss, stood over her desk, glancing down at her with an amused expression.

Theresa nodded her head in the direction Chrissie had been looking. "Or were you admiring his brain power?"

"I hadn't noticed," Chrissie lied. "But there's something about him that bothers me." She was annoyed, because she had hoped she was being subtle. Even so, she couldn't stop herself looking back at Liam again. He was squatting at a PC base unit next to a desk some thirty feet away from hers on the other side of the office. His position gave her a perfect view of his physique under the soft cotton long-sleeved T-shirt and tight black jeans he wore. Some part of her instinctively knew he'd be well worth having, doing the business between her thighs. What on earth was wrong with her? She didn't normally notice whether a man's rear end was fit or not, but the rear end she was currently looking at was fit in a way that grabbed her attention. The very shape of it made her hands itch to touch him. She ran a finger beneath the neckline of her top, allowing cool air to circulate underneath the fabric. Where the hell were these thoughts coming from?

"You got the memo from head office," she added, "we need to be vigilant."

Theresa gave a knowing smile. "He's too new."

Chrissie flashed her eyes at her boss. "Maybe not—I've checked out the dates, and I don't trust him."

"You're very observant." Theresa winked. "You just go right ahead and keep your eye on him."

Chrissie pouted at her boss's back.

She couldn't deny he was an attractive man, though. What did that prove? He was up to no good, she was sure of it. Something about him was suspicious, and more annoyingly, something about him was vaguely familiar. If he was the software thief—and she was pretty sure he was—then maybe she'd seen him somewhere else, maybe at a convention. He'd want to see the people who worked here before he infiltrated the workplace.

They'd been asked to be vigilant. A rival company had put out code suspiciously like theirs only days before theirs went on the market. The board couldn't be sure, but someone on the inside might have stolen the software in production. It had to be Liam. First she'd had her eye on Ted Warburton as the possible thief. He'd always been a quiet, secretive type. Liam had quickly replaced Ted on her list of possible suspects. She glared at him, her annoyance multiplying when he smiled over at her, casual as anything. Damn cheek. She looked away, both suspicious and hating the effect he had on her. It was hot in the office today, that's what it was. It always made her horny. She uncrossed and recrossed her legs, squeezing her thighs together. Liam just happened to be there, that's all.

It was the fact he was out of place that magnetized her attention, had to be. The man looked as if he pumped iron for a living. In their business-park office on the outskirts of London, where the other employees tended to be geeky types, that was unusual. He was a distraction that was beginning to get under her skin. Her panties were damp, her pussy on fire. *Bastard.* Not for the first time this week she was going to have to sneak off to the ladies toilet to masturbate. It wasn't something that had ever happened to her in the workplace before.

"Can I get you something?" It was Liam.

Her back stiffened.

"I'm doing a deli run," he added.

"No. Thank you."

He put both his hands on her desk, leaning over in the most provocative way, looking her up and down as if it was her he was about to devour, not the mega-stuffed baguettes he seemed to favor. "Are you sure I can't tempt you?"

She felt herself blushing, her pale skin making her far too easy to read. "No."

He lifted one eyebrow. "Shame. I'd like to see you giving in to temptation. I bet it would be quite something, all that restrained fire…unleashed."

She hated her body for the way it responded. Between her thighs, her pussy ached for some of what he seemed to be offering, a vigorous session between the sheets. But he was the wrong sort of bloke to get mixed up with, she was convinced of it. Unable to sit still, she rearranged herself in her seat, gripping onto the hem of her miniskirt to steady herself. "Don't hold your breath, it's not going to happen."

"Don't be so sure." He grinned.

Frowning, she gave him a stern look.

"That pout of yours is hellish sexy," he added, then shook his head, still smiling, and walked away.

Pout? She'd meant to look disapproving. Apparently she couldn't even trust her own facial expressions when he was around. Feeling slightly demented, she glared at his back. He was so sure of himself, his hips rolling as he walked with a steady, easy gait, broad muscular shoulders shifting beneath his shirt. Power, he oozed subtle, intoxicating power. The man was pure machismo. That, and the way he looked back at her over his shoulder—dark eyes insinuating and filled with sensual humor—made her dangerously aroused.

It was no good, she decided, the midsummer heat had got to her.

Standing up, she headed off to the ladies', pretending not to hear what was said to her as she passed a colleague's desk. She wasn't in the mood for chitchat. Luckily there was no one else in the ladies' cloakroom. Darting into a cubicle, she shut the door and put her back up against it. Wedging one sandaled foot against the toilet seat she cursed men in general—and Liam in particular—and moved her hand between her thighs, the hem of her skirt edging up as she reached under it and her palm closed over her pussy. She squeezed tight for relief, her hips rocking backward and forward, the pulse in her core beating out erratically. Staring at the wall with unseeing eyes, she chafed her clit through her lacy undies, her mind filling with images of Liam, over her, inside her, possessing her, telling her how bad she needed it and how he was going to see to it she got it.

He'd left the building, and still he got to her. Cursing low under her breath, she shoved her hand inside her undies where the groove of her pussy was slick, and rubbed her clit. She could almost hear his voice, that insinuating tone, and she imagined him looking at her while she did the dirty deed in the loo. Latching a finger inside her sex, she pressed the palm of her hand on her clit, pushing herself closer to climax. He'd enjoy it, of course he would, he was just the sort of man who'd want to watch a woman masturbating. Her sex clenched, her standing leg faltering. Heat built inside her, a wall she had to break through for release, and when it came it spiraled through her groin then raced over her entire skin while she moaned lowly, hating the man who made her want him so.

HE'D STAYED BEHIND, AFTER HOURS. CHRISSIE saw him duck into Theresa's office after Theresa had gone, and he hadn't emerged. Her pulse rate picked up speed. Liam had the run of the place in his role as IT man, but he shouldn't be in there, not now. She took her time tidying her desk and watched as the last of her coworkers left the building. Where was the security guard? He usually came around about now, checked everyone had left the building before sealing it up for the night. He'd be here soon, which would be perfect timing.

After the last stragglers had gone and all was quiet, she stood up, picked up her phone and flicked it to camera mode. If she could just catch him… Her heart raced. If she could prove Liam was the thief, then…then he'd be gone. She paused, hesitant. She both wanted to find him out, and didn't. It was screwy, she knew it was, but something about the idea of confronting him was intoxicating, and she couldn't help herself. As she approached the door to her supervisor's office, she saw him moving behind the desk. Someone who wasn't in the know would just think he was switching off a PC, or checking it. But she was riddled with suspicion and curiosity. She stood just outside the open office door and snapped a photograph of him, then put her phone down on the table outside Theresa's office, making sure it was hidden out of sight.

Folding her arms across her chest, she stared at him. "Caught in the act," she said. She couldn't help being pleased with herself.

Liam glanced up, and then smiled, long and slow. He didn't seem surprised to see her, his posture both nonchalant and self-assured while he looked at her.

Even if he made a break for it, she had proof he was the thief. Strangely enough, he didn't look as if he was going anywhere. In fact, he glanced at his watch, as if he was checking how much free time he had to chat with her. He had the cheek of the devil himself.

"Caught?" A self-assured smile played around his attractive mouth, and it made her want to slap him. "I wasn't doing anything. Not yet, at any rate."

Why did he always look as if he was thinking about sex? *And more to the point, why am I thinking about sex?* "You aren't supposed to be in here, none of us are. Company rules. No overtime unless it's agreed in advance."

"And that's why you followed me in here?" His expression was filled with insinuation, and he looked her up and down in a way that left her in no doubt he was making some sort of intimate reference. "You're sure there wasn't some other reason why you wanted to be in here with me, alone?"

Her stomach flipped. *He's bluffing.*

She forced a dry laugh. "Get real. You are the thief, that's why we're both here. I've been onto you for days." He didn't seem surprised—in fact, he seemed to be enjoying it. He was sitting back in Theresa's chair with a lazy, confident posture that suggested he wasn't in the least concerned she'd caught him in there. Maybe he wanted her to follow him in here. The thought made her want to walk away, but for some reason she couldn't.

"I knew you were onto me, Chrissie. In fact, I was enjoying your attention."

"The security man will be here in a minute to lock up," she snapped. Her heartbeat grew erratic. Was this some sort of trap? Just as the thought struck her, the overhead strip lighting throughout the offices went off one by one in a succession of resounding clicks. They were alone. A dim security light was all that lit the room they occupied, the distant streetlights from the business park sending an eerie glow through the slats of the blinds.

He stood up and stepped out from behind the desk. "Am I the thief indeed? Well now, in that case, why would I find you a whole lot more interesting than swiping the lot and heading out of here?" He gestured at the PC.

"The PC should be password locked." Panic was rising. What was she doing here alone with this man?

"Theresa has been naughty, she's left her files accessible. This place is slack." He stepped closer. "I'd much rather look at you than a bunch of code. I like the idea of us having some quiet time, just the two of us, alone here." He lifted his eyebrows, and in the half-light his eyes glittered.

Beyond him, she could see the cars moving on the motorway in the distance. The business park was quiet. Apart from the security guard, who was now late, there wasn't another soul around. She hadn't thought beyond the accusation; she hadn't thought beyond getting him alone. But now they were here, and he was coming on to her.

Despite her suspicions, her body responded wildly to the knowledge that he wanted her, her skin racing, a fluttering sensation in her core making sensible responses seem much harder to muster. "Flattery won't get you anywhere. You're just trying to distract me."

"How can you be sure?" The insinuating look in his eyes made him look even more attractive. How was that possible?

He's aroused, she realized. Not for the first time she found herself involuntarily wondering what he looked like naked. *Oh God*.

"I can think of much better things to do than stealing computer software code, believe me. Besides, for all I know, you could be the thief. You could be the one who is siphoning off the code at night."

She faked a laugh. "I've been with this company for five years. I take pride in my loyalty."

He shrugged. "You might be dissatisfied with your pay, for all I know." He moved closer still, stepping behind her, circling her. It unnerved her, but she felt rooted to the spot.

"You might have a secret vice, something that needs funding." He touched her lightly on the shoulder and her head jerked back. His eyes were narrowed in the gloom; he was focused on a reaction. The scent of his cologne was enticing, something woodland, but sharp and earthy all at the same time. Underneath it man, sheer, absolute man.

"If that was the case," she mustered, "why would I be here, now, while you are in here?"

"I don't know, Chrissie, why are you here, now?" He smiled to himself. It was all one big joke to him. That would be his undoing, she was sure of it. What she wasn't sure of was why she'd let him get so close. Why hadn't she backed off?

She swallowed. *I do want him*.

The expression in his eyes grew serious. She could hear her heart pounding, the blood rushing in her ears as if the world were moving faster by the moment, while she was frozen to the spot. Then the reasons why they were here faded away as he closed on her and put one hand behind her head, his fingers moving into her hair as he tipped her head back. "I know the perfect way to prove to you I'm not in here after the code."

Part of her guessed what he was about to do, the part of

her that identified with it, wanted it. She met his stare directly, stripped of all facade.

"I'm going to kiss you now."

"I know." She couldn't have stopped him even if she wanted to, and she didn't want to. When his lips whispered over hers and his breath mingled with hers, she moaned softly, the last shred of resistance she'd held on to slipping away as he invited her to enjoy. Something pent up broke free inside her and she clutched at him with needy hands, the ability to think logically gone.

His mouth was warm and firm, sensuous in its exploration of her lips as he kissed her, softly at first, inquisitively. When she responded, he squeezed her against him with one large, warm hand at the small of her back, his mouth opening her up, his tongue teasing the edge of her lips until a shiver ran through her entire body. She responded without thought, reaching to press her mouth fully to his, her lips parting to take his tongue. He kissed her deeply, mastering her in an instant, claiming her. Beneath her hands, his body felt strong, warm and vital, and she molded against him. While his tongue thrust in and out of her mouth, mirroring the rocking together of their hips, he held her tight and she could feel every inch of him, including the hard bulge at his groin.

Locked together and wavering, they moved in unison toward the desk. She felt the hard surface against the back of her thighs and grappled for the edge of the desk with one hand.

"On the desk," he instructed. He sat her down, his hand stroking her shoulders. His face was cast in shadow, but she could feel his lust swamping her.

"Liam," she whispered, unsure.

He brushed his thumb over her lips, silencing her. He reached for her cardigan and pulled it down around her elbows, holding it tight there, locking her arms in against her sides. He leaned into her, breathing her in. The nerve endings under her skin went wild, her breasts tightening in response to his proximity. He nudged the spaghetti strap on her top to one side with his mouth and kissed beneath it, his breath hot against her skin. With one hand, he held on to her as if he was afraid she would run, and with the other he cleared the desk, pushing papers, discs and equipment onto the floor. Easing her back until she was flat on the desk, he stood between her thighs.

She caught sight of his intense expression when he passed through a band of light shining through the blinds. His sheer masculinity wrapped itself around her, and when he wrenched her legs apart she writhed with need. He positioned her with her hips at the edge of the desk, and her skirt bunched around her waist. Through his jeans, the bulge of his cock pressed hard at the juncture of her thighs. Her clit was pounding and the pressure was only making it worse. He pulled her top lower over her breasts and kissed her cleavage while he tugged down the cups of her bra to access her nipples, abusing her clothing to have his way with her. A sting loosed in her nipple when he touched it, and it brought about a needy echo deep inside. When his warm, damp mouth closed over her erect nipple and he grazed it with his teeth, it made her wild. She moaned aloud, her head rolling on the desk. The tension was unbearable. Her hips moved, her back arched. She wanted to wrap herself around him and take him inside.

"I want to taste you," he said and ducked down. His mouth enclosed her swollen clit, his tongue rubbing back and forth over it rapidly, driving her to distraction.

"Liam…Liam, please."

"I know," he whispered in response, his breath hot on her sticky, sensitive folds. "I know. I want it, too." He moved away and she saw him opening a condom packet.

They were going to do it—they were really going to do it.

It was outrageous, here and now in the office, on the desk. But she wanted to; she wanted it badly. She kicked off her sandals and lifted one knee against his hip, inviting him in. In the gloom she could barely see him as he rolled on the condom, and she rued that, wanting to see it all. But when his fingers ran across the lacy edge of her panties and then hauled them down the length of her legs, all that mattered was the fuck, the actual fuck, and she wanted it bad.

He nudged at her opening and she lifted up, giving him access, whispering encouragement as he thrust inside. "Oh, yes, Liam. Oh, God yes."

His cock was hard, hot and thick, stretching her open. She clung to his shoulders, levering her hips on the desk to take him, grinding against him as he hit home. She dug her fingernails deep into his shoulders as they found and matched each other's rhythm, days of sexual tension making it fast and furious, glorious and needy all at once. Each thrust filled her so completely that it took her breath away. Each time he drew back her body ached for more, her climax imminent.

When she felt it coming she turned away, unwilling to totally admit the power of this thing. Nevertheless, she whispered his name and it came out on a wild cry at the moment the climax hit. Her sex clutched, released and clutched again, seizing his cock. His body went rigid, his cock jerking inside her. She lifted up from the desk and clung to him, kissing the side of his head, even while his hips jerked again.

He sought her mouth, blindly kissing her, and Chrissie held on to him for dear life. The real world was rushing in again, fast, far too fast, interjecting old questions into her thoughts, spoiling her afterglow. But she didn't want him to be the thief—she wanted him to be the new IT man, plain and simple—and she pushed the questions out for as long as she could.

"ARE YOU THE THIEF?" CHRISSIE ASKED forlornly when he stood up to pull himself together, his thoughts shifting as he checked the time.

He shook his head and kissed the end of her nose. They'd finally breached the gap between them. He was happy, and it was perfect timing, because he'd just noticed a car purring past the window in the front parking lot of the building, headlights off. He ducked his head down. This is what he'd been waiting for. He knew who the thief was, and he'd already got the evidence he needed. Tonight was his last evening on the job, and Chrissie had made it all that much more pleasant waiting to close the case.

She was pulling her bra and top into place and she gave him a curious look.

He wanted to kiss her again, but there wasn't time for any more canoodling. Not right now. "Where's your car parked?"

She frowned. "At the back of the building, why?"

"Mine, too." The thief had pulled up at the front and wouldn't know there was anyone else in the building. Reaching for her hand, he dropped to a squat and pulled her down with him.

"What the hell are you doing?" She fell against him and

he moved her down onto the floor, pushing her onto her hands and knees.

"Quickly, crawl under the desk, I'll stay behind you."

"What's going on?" She looked so cute with her knickers still trailing from one ankle and her skirt at half-mast over her gorgeous bare ass cheeks.

He gave her a quick slap on the behind. "Get moving."

Her mouth opened in surprise and she wriggled provocatively, one hand going to the place where he'd smacked her. Interesting. She liked that. "Our code thief is about to walk in."

"Are you sure? I mean…it could be Henry, the security guard. He should be here to lock up by now."

"Nope. Henry was placed under arrest earlier this evening. Unfortunately he's in cahoots with the thief. He's been leaving the building accessible on prearranged nights." She stared at him, uncomprehending, but there wasn't time to explain his role. "Now move your sexy tush under the desk and stay quiet."

"This is what you were waiting in here for," she said, "wasn't it?"

"Move!"

Still she hesitated, a question in her eyes. Without further ado, he manhandled her under the desk and then sat in the chair. Her tousled blond head popped up between his knees a moment later. "Are you serious, the code thief is coming into the building now?"

"You're finally catching on." Perhaps he shouldn't have said that, because she glared at him. She was a fiery type, but he liked that about her. She was so keen to find the thief herself, she was bound to be annoyed. Flicking open his phone, he pressed the speed dial number for his sidekick, who was waiting to close in with the police in tow. "The target is on the way into the building now."

"We're on it," came the reply. "Saw the approach and we're moving in behind the vehicle."

He snapped the phone shut and took one last glance at Chrissie. She opened her mouth to speak, but he touched his fingers to her lips. "Hush now, it's time for the showdown."

A door clicked open in the outer office. He settled back in the chair, making sure he was shrouded in gloom. The thief wouldn't even realize he was in here until it was too late. He felt Chrissie's hand on his leg, but a shadow filled the doorway and he watched as the thief entered the room.

"Something you forgot, Theresa?" He flicked the desk lamp on.

"Shit!" She clutched at her chest. "I mean, yes, I... Something in my drawer. Why are you still in here?" She was trying to pull herself together, but it was too late.

"I'm investigating the security. That's why I'm here." The hand on his leg tightened.

"Oh." Theresa's attention flitted about the room. "Good," she added. "I hadn't realized they'd taken that step."

"Yup, they're right on the case. In fact—" he leaned forward in the chair "—I installed closed-circuit cameras on day three of my placement here. And, as you've probably already guessed, that means we have footage of the thief in action. Twice this week."

Her eyes rounded.

"You've been a busy girl, haven't you, selling out your employer?"

She backed to the door, her hand grappling for the wall.

"Don't bother running. It's not worth it. I have all the evidence I need, and you won't get far." A flashing blue light from outside the window bounced around the walls. Cursing, she turned on her heel and fled.

Hard though it was, Liam resisted the urge to pursue. He'd let his sidekick take it up, because he wanted to make sure Chrissie was okay. He was more concerned about her right now. And once he'd given his handover statement, he was thinking they'd get dinner, and then have some more of what they'd just shared a taste of.

He stood up and offered his hand.

When she emerged she pointed one finger at him. "I worked it out while I was stuck under there—I know who it is you reminded me of."

"What?" He'd been hoping she'd slip readily back into his arms, filled with awe after witnessing the reveal on the case she'd been so fascinated with.

She shook her head, hauling her skirt into place as she did so. "It kept bugging me who you look like, right from when I first saw you. Then, when you said you were an investigator, it clicked. You're related to that TV investigator bloke, that Benjamin O'Neil, aren't you?"

Man, that was the last thing he expected her to say. "Yes, but I am an official. I work for a reputable company. Ben's a… Well, he's a loose canon." Baby bro Ben seemed hell-bent on making a name for himself by breaking and entering, all in the name of uncovering the truth for some cutting-edge TV show. It wasn't going down well with the rest of the family. They were all worried about his safety when he stepped outside of the law.

"I knew it." Just then she glanced at the scene outside the window, where the police were involved in a scuffle with Theresa. Just for a moment, Liam caught a flash of dismay in her eyes. She was gutted, but she'd been pals with Theresa and obviously hadn't suspected her. A moment later she returned her attention to him, folding her arms over her chest and giving him a terse glance. "You've made a fool out of me."

What? "Chrissie! I have not. It was my job." He pulled her against him, annoyance biting into him at her accusation, his hands locked around her shoulders. Resistance poured out of her, that stubborn streak of hers rising rapidly to the surface again.

"I knew the thief had to be an insider," she declared, and she was plenty annoyed herself.

Liam tried to get a handle on her—which he was discovering was a pretty hard task. He never would have predicted this particular departure in her mood. What the hell was a man supposed to do? "Of course you did. You're a very intelligent woman."

"Apparently not." Color flared in her cheeks. "You should have told me you were a security person, instead of letting me make a fool of myself."

"Oh, come on, I couldn't take a risk like that. You might have let it slip, given her a chance to cover up and get away."

Her lips tightened, and her eyes shone with fury in the gloom. She wrestled herself free of his grasp. "You bastard. You used me tonight, to…to stay in here, and to keep yourself amused."

Oh, boy, she really was mad. He reached for her. "You didn't complain at the time. Besides, you didn't make a fool of yourself."

She backed away, hands up. "Don't you dare touch me!"

She'd gone loopy, but for some ludicrous reason it made him want her all the more. He made a move, but she was already headed out the door. He began to go after her and then forced himself to stop. Something was really bugging her, something he couldn't quite put his finger on. She needed time to cool her heels, get used to what had gone on here this evening, in every way. But he wasn't going to let her get away that easy. Not after what had gone on between them, back there on the desk. No way.

A WEEK LATER, LIAM FINALLY CAME TO THE conclusion Chrissie needed longer to cool her heels than he'd originally thought, but he was a tenacious sort. He wanted it resolved. In his line of work—late hours, moving from post to post quickly—he didn't often get the chance to spend quality time with the women he met. It was a family trait; he and his brothers had displeased their mother royally by not securing good women for her to take under her wing. Displeasing an Irish mother was a bad move, resulting in long, woeful speeches over family dinners; speeches about how hard done by she was not having daughters-in-law to nurture. It didn't bother him, or in fact any of the three of the O'Neil brothers, but Chrissie had caught his attention more than anyone he'd met in years. He wanted to see her again.

However, when he'd turned up at her workplace he found she'd taken unplanned leave. The staff there wouldn't hand over her home address. He couldn't blame them for that. She didn't respond to his voice mail, or return his e-mail, even though he knew she'd be checking them both from home. The desire to speak with her was becoming an unrelenting need. Thoughts of her filled his mind, his libido easily triggered as he thought back over what had happened between them. It didn't help that he had to prepare the closed-circuit footage for evidence. He delivered the hard drives for each of the nights that showed Theresa's nocturnal visits to the police. Problem was, the camera in Theresa's office had also caught the whole of his interlude with Chrissie. As far as Liam was concerned, it was the hottest porn he had ever seen.

He made an executive decision not to include that drive, since it wasn't strictly needed. Instead, he would wipe it before he returned it to supplies.

First, he had to watch it a few more times.

The images were hampered by the angle and the gloominess of the room, but he was able to enhance it and zoom in. He was fascinated by the way Chrissie looked, her abandonment. The raunchy way she wrapped her legs around his hips made him painfully erect. He jerked off as he watched her pulling him in, whispering his name and letting down her barriers. The noises she made during the lovemaking made his balls ache. His fist moved faster. He wanted to be inside her again, now, right now.

At the moment of climax, she turned her face away from his, and it caused him to swear under his breath as he watched her mouth opening, her fingers meshing in his hair. At the base of his spine pressure built, thudding hard as he jacked his load, cursing the fact it was a lonely emission instead of a shared pleasure. Afterward, he noticed that her arms closed around him and she kissed the side of his head. That surprised him most of all. At the time he'd been so caught up in his own release he hadn't realized she had shown any affection toward him.

He spent longer than was good for him rerunning the footage, and eventually burned it onto his own hard drive before wiping the company drive. He couldn't help himself—he wanted the memento. He also wanted proof she had been that way, she'd wanted that level of intimacy with him and she'd enjoyed it.

At the same time he knew that if he confronted her at work, she would make a run for it, just like she had that night. That's why he came up with a plan, a plan that involved enlisting his older brother's help to convince her to listen long enough that he could point out some home truths to her. Liam was a practical sort of a man, and he came up with a practical plan, albeit a bit aggressive.

Whatever it took, Liam was going to make her listen to what he had to say. There was a deeply sensual woman underlying that stubborn and headstrong exterior. If it took sex to bring it out in her, it was his duty to hunt her down and shag her senseless.

Chrissie drove her car into the driveway in front of her small suburban house, parked and sighed with relief. Well, she convinced herself it was relief. Maybe it was resignation. The important thing was she'd survived day one back at work. It was hard. Theresa had been the only other woman in the office, and Theresa had turned out to be the weak point. That made her feel bad, even though she knew she herself was a strong link. Meanwhile, Liam had filled her e-mail box and her voice mail, but hadn't, thank God, turned up to bug her in person. She'd been ready for that—expecting it, almost.

Now she was safely home and it was her haven. It had felt a bit lonely over the past few days, while she was off work, but Liam didn't know where she lived, which meant he couldn't hassle her here. He'd give up soon. Maybe he had already. Her head dropped back against the headrest. Just thinking about what had happened between them and how misguided she'd been made her feel uncomfortable, even now, a week later. She'd meant to confront him over his devious behavior around the office and get to the bottom of it. Somehow he'd got her on her back instead. She sighed as the physical memories flooded her, her pulse tripping when her body flared into life at the mere thought of him.

"Snap out of it," she told herself, and reached for the door handle. It was then she noticed the blue lights flashing in her rearview mirror. There was a police car parked up behind hers. "What the hell?"

She grabbed her keys and got out of the car, watching as a tall uniformed police officer walked up her driveway. Stern but attractive, he was built like the side of a house, and he looked vaguely familiar. There was another man in the car, and the way the vehicle was parked, it was completely blocking the driveway, hedging her in like a criminal. What would the neighbors think?

The officer flashed a badge. "Good evening, madam. Are you aware of any traffic violations you might have made in the last ten minutes of your journey home?"

"No!" Chrissie was shocked; she was a very careful driver. She was mortified to think she'd done something wrong. Then she realized she'd snapped at the policeman and tried to soften it with a non-offensive smile. "I'm sorry, officer, I know it's no excuse, but I've had a lot on my mind recently."

She wished he wasn't wearing sunglasses. It unnerved her that she couldn't see his eyes. His jaw looked as if it was made of granite and he had a scar across one cheekbone.

"Turn around and put your hands up against the roof of the car."

A rush of humiliation hit her as she did as instructed, resting her keys on the car roof and then flattening her palms against it.

"Can I get some assistance here?" The officer shouted toward the parked car.

Assistance? Something wasn't right here. Surely you didn't have to be searched for a traffic violation—or even several road traffic violations—and especially not by two of them. She heard a car door slam, then footsteps. The tension at her back intensified, the scrutiny of the two men behind her making the skin on her back prickle. She moved her head, trying to see their reflections in the windows of the car.

"Hold it right there." Strong, male hands moved under her arms and down her sides, patting her down. Blushing furiously, she prayed the neighbors weren't watching. His hands slowed to a stroke at thigh level and he lingered there a moment, before he stood up and drew her hands together behind her back. Whoever it was—and she guessed it was the second bloke—she could feel his breath warm against her neck.

"You've acted inappropriately, but I'm willing to let you off with a verbal reprimand, if you take what I have to say seriously."

Something like déjà vu tickled her mind. Her spine straightened, her faculties gathering. Oh, that voice. Her head jerked as she tried to look back at him. Something cold and metal slid into place around her wrists, and she heard the click as she realized who and what it was—handcuffs.

"Liam," she said in disbelief, staggering on her heels. "You followed me home!"

"Step inside." His voice was gruff. "I need to talk to you." One strong arm around her waist held her steady, the other snatched up her keys from the car roof. "Do you agree to hear me out?"

"You bastard—you can't just come around here and tie me up like you're some egotistical caveman." Jolting forward, she leaned against the car, pulling away from him with all her might.

"If that's what it takes." He grunted, hauling her away from the car, where she had pinned herself. "I'll do it. Chrissie, we have to talk."

She wriggled and twisted in his grasp, but he lifted her off her feet, and despite her kicking back at him with her heels vigorously, he managed to turn her around and wedge her against the car so she couldn't move. Her cuffed hands were slammed hard against the car door and one heel was bending under her as she tried to lever away.

Liam grinned.

"You are getting some sort of sadistic pleasure out of humiliating me like this!"

"It's a means to an end, but you do look extra sexy when you're angry." His eyes burned with lust, and it triggered a response in her that made her press her lips together with annoyance, afraid she might say and do the wrong thing.

"Jesus, Liam," the other man said. "I thought you said she would enjoy this." The police officer standing by had his hands on his hips and looked perturbed.

"She *is* enjoying it, she's just a stubborn, iron-willed little vixen who refuses to admit when she's having a good time." He lifted his eyebrows, letting her know exactly what he was referring to.

Riled, she stuck her tongue out at him.

Liam laughed, and then goaded her under his breath. "What, you can't deny you enjoyed it back there on that desk when you had your legs wrapped around me?"

Her cheeks burned. Her head was reeling, her nerves jangling because he had her locked in his arms. Desperate, she turned her attention to the other man. "Who the hell are you?" She looked from one of them to the other. "He's not a real policeman at all, is he?"

"Actually, yes, he is. Chrissie, meet my older brother, Colin."

The police officer gave her a mini salute and an apologetic glance. "I'm sorry, madam. It was a ruse." He looked rather awkward, as if he'd been forced into this. "Your driving is impeccable," he added in a lower voice.

"Col is the uptight member of our family," Liam added.

"Fuck you," the police officer said, then cleared his throat and adopted a serious expression. "Excuse me, madam, but I have to ask, am I okay to leave you in my brother's capable hands?"

She was about to respond, order him not to leave, when

Liam ducked down and kissed her full on the mouth. His sheer strength demanded she submit, his mouth claiming hers. With his hands holding her so tightly and his body against hers, she could feel the passion in him, the hard pressure of his cock through their clothes letting her know how much he wanted her. She melted, her body betraying her as she wilted against the side of the car, her head dropping back to take his kiss, to return it. One gentle thrust of his tongue into her mouth and her sex clenched, eager for his thrusts there, too. When he pulled back, a soft moan escaped her open mouth.

"There, you got your answer, she's enjoying it," Liam said to his brother.

The policeman nodded, a sardonic smile on his face. "I surely did."

Bewildered, Chrissie stared at Liam. He'd done it again; he distracted her from what she was going to say.

"I owe you," Liam said to his brother. Then he set about moving her in the direction of her own front door, one hand on the bridge of the cuffs pushing her forward, the other examining her keys.

When she saw the determined set to his expression had resumed, her resentment flared and she pulled herself together. What the hell was it with this guy that he could trick her so easily? She ground to a halt and made him pause long enough to kick out in the direction of his shins. "Manhandling women against their will runs in the family, does it?"

He winced when she managed to make contact, but his expression only became more focused. "No, but determination does, and I am determined you will hear me out."

Oh, but that determination ran in his voice and in his actions, too, and it was a huge turn-on. Though she struggled and kicked, a secret part of her blazed in response, the part that wanted to hear what he had to say, the part that battled against her logic and will—the essential woman in her that had reveled in the time they'd spent together the week before.

He jostled her up the path, away from the police officer who stood with his arms folded across his chest, shaking his head, a wry smile playing around his mouth. How dare he? He tipped his hat and headed back to his car.

"I will report you for abusing your position," she shouted out across the lawn.

Liam grabbed her against him, and applied pressure on the bar between the handcuffs, drawing her shoulders back. His breath was warm against her ear as he looked down at where her breasts thrust out through her shirt because of the position he'd got her into.

"He was helping me out, and if you are going to bandy about threats, think about this. I have some nice footage of you on your back, enjoying yourself immensely, on your boss's desk."

He'd been filming it? Of course he had, he'd been on a stakeout, for Christ's sake. She remembered him saying that when Theresa had come into the office. He had footage of the whole thing. Her eyes flashed shut, her entire skin going hot and cold. She was taken right back to that desk, a series of images flashing through her mind, images she'd been thinking about in her silent moments, remembering and reliving. Knowing they were captured on film did bad things to her. The temperature between her thighs built rapidly. "I hate you," she hissed.

"No, you don't." He grinned, sure of himself. "It makes very interesting viewing, believe me. But I'm willing to keep it to a private showing between the two of us." He laughed softly against her ear, one hand against her waist allowing him to caress her beneath her breasts as he spoke. "If you give me something in exchange."

His hands on her felt too good. "What? What do you want?"

"Let's go inside."

When he unlocked the door, he bowed and gestured her inside.

She took her chance and darted down the hall and across the sitting room, so the sofa was between them. He lunged after her, but was thwarted by the unfamiliar territory, tripping on a coffee table. A moment later he was back on course.

Inadvertently, she'd got herself cornered. "Do you always have to handcuff people? Is that the only way they will put up with your cheek?"

He ignored her remark, glancing around. "Nice decor. I like the black-and-white print over the fireplace. So calming…just what you need for that wild temperament of yours."

"You don't know me." She averted her face.

He drew her back by the chin so she had to face him. "I know you better than you give me credit for. Hear me out, I've spent a lot of time thinking about you and I want you to give me a break. Listen a moment, I can prove it." He shook his head. "I know what's going on here—it's not just about us."

"Us? What us?"

Again, he ignored her comment. "You know I couldn't tell you I was an official investigator. I knew you weren't behind it, but you could have inadvertently told someone else I was investigating. Think about it."

She shrugged it off. "So what, what has that got to do with you…handcuffing me?" Even saying it sounded suggestive, and her body liked the suggestion, whatever it was it sounded hot and kinky and parts of her were raring to go.

He stepped back, still blocking her in, but giving her a bit of space as he spoke. "It's the only way I could guarantee you would listen to me. We had a lot of fun that night, and you enjoyed it every bit as much as I did. I want to see you again, but you're angry. I think I figured out why."

"Oh, you do, do you?"

"Yes, you're not really annoyed with me, you're focusing on

me because you are annoyed you didn't figure out who was behind the theft."

She shook her head, tried to find the words, but for some reason they wouldn't come. Part of her was astonished he'd taken the time to think about it.

"So I was right."

"You're unbearably sure of yourself, aren't you? You think you can walk into my life, make love to me on a desk and then come into my house and handcuff me and do whatever the hell you want with me...." She faltered and ground to a halt when she saw the sharp interest in his eyes. Why had that sounded like an invitation when she said it? That's not how she meant to say it. "And get away with it?"

She lifted her eyebrows in what she hoped was a threatening manner. Even so, her heart was racing, her anticipation building. God, she wanted him. She wanted to feel the weight of his body over hers again. She wanted to be possessed by this man who was so full-on and sure.

He laughed softly. He was aroused, his bright blue eyes gleaming as he eyed her up in that incredibly sexy way of his.

Resist or submit? She smiled, suddenly loving the dilemma, and growled at him, making ready to run past him. As she shifted, he dropped into a goalkeeper's stance, arms out to capture her. She ducked this way and that, shot left. His arms went around her. Twisting, she slipped out of his grasp and staggered away, laughing with glee, but was thrown off-kilter because she couldn't move her arms. The sofa was looming into view as she hurtled across the room. There was no other option but to throw herself on it, sprawling uneasily across the cushions.

"Perfect," she heard him declare, as he grabbed her around the hips and lifted her onto her knees. The front of her shoulders were pushed into the back of the sofa. Her hips swayed, her skirt riding up.

"You love this every bit as much as I do," he breathed

against her ear as he climbed over her, arms locked around her. She wriggled in his grasp. To underline his point, he moved one hand to her breast and squeezed her erect nipple through the fabric of her shirt. "You're turned on. You like being handcuffed, don't you?"

Capturing her earlobe between his teeth, he bit.

Pleasure shot through her. She wriggled her bottom against him, the feeling of his hard cock through his jeans too delicious. "Maybe."

"Short skirt again, how convenient."

"I wear a short skirt because it makes my legs look longer, which makes me look taller. Put a long skirt on me and I look like a dwarf."

"Well, now, is that so?"

"I'm sick of the short jokes from the men in the office," she added in explanation.

"I had no idea. All I know is it was driving me mad looking at you in that office, with your short, sexy skirts and your gorgeous legs."

She suppressed a smile.

Pushing the skirt up over her hips, he bunched the fabric at her waist and stroked her bottom through the lacy fabric of her knickers. "And you liked being spanked back there in the office, didn't you?"

Did she? Her mind flitted back. Yes, when he'd been pushing her underneath the desk. It had been practically impossible for her to sit still under that desk, between his legs, and with her buttock stinging in the most arousing way.

He looped one finger over the top of her knickers, and pulled them off. "Beautiful," he whispered.

She squeezed her eyes shut, loving his attention and hating it all at once.

"You look so hot when you're all pensive and thoughtful, it made me want to open your legs and distract you."

"Well, you managed it. You distracted me good and proper." She felt the urge to laugh aloud. It felt good, blaming him for the seduction. It felt good letting it out, too.

He stroked and then spanked her exposed buttocks several times, making her gasp. The sting shot through her entire nether region, a moment later altering to a different kind of sensation in her core. Her sex felt heavy and hot, tingling with arousal, as if the spank had lit a touch paper connected to the very quick of her.

"Do you know how hard it is for a man to deal with computer equipment and think about security while he has a hard-on?"

Laughter bubbled up and escaped at the idea of it.

"So the ice queen does have a sense of humor."

"I'm not an ice queen!"

"Obviously not." His tone was heavy with humor. "My mistake, so sorry." He spanked her again, alternating from one buttock to the other, and she moaned loudly, her shoulders shuddering. She couldn't help herself; it burned in the most arousing way, making her want to wriggle and clench all over. Her upper body jerked up when she felt his fingers exploring her, riding the damp seam of her pussy, chaffing her clit.

"This spanking seems to be making you wet, my dear." He pushed one finger inside her, and her body clenched at it, eager for the hard intrusion. "Oh, yes, you seem very eager. Was it something I said?"

"Everything you said," she admitted, the words coming out on a sigh as he moved his slippery finger, riding it back and forth, stroking the front wall of her sex. Wave after wave of pleasure suffused her groin, building quickly to a peak. Then he stroked her clit again and her hips jerked, the whisper of pressure on her inflamed clit pushing her to the edge. Her body wavered as the orgasm rocketed through her, leaving her weak and dizzy.

For a moment, all was silent but for the sound of her own

labored breathing, and then she heard him sigh loudly. "Guess who's caught in the act this time, Chrissie?"

She glanced back over her shoulder at him. He met her gaze and then looked back down at her exposed pussy. A moment later liquid dribbled down the inside of her thighs. She closed her eyes, tormented, and yet loving it.

"Not even you can deny you're enjoying this."

Jolting, she swore aloud. He'd bent down and licked her; right there on her exposed pussy, and as his tongue ran up and down the damp groove her body went taut as a bow, her mind in turmoil. While he pushed his tongue inside her, he ran his hand down the inside of one thigh, then back up the line of the other. Her pelvis reacted, moving instinctively, she wanted him hard inside her, and soon. She whimpered, her face pressed into the sofa back, one knee bashing into the cushion in frustration. She bit into the sofa, but it didn't help—she still cried aloud with need. "Liam, please…"

Relief hit her when she heard the sound of a condom being opened.

"Here I come," he warned. First he nudged her legs farther apart with his knee. Then, lifting her body around the waist, he hauled her hips back against him. The hard, hot shaft of his erection rested a moment between her folds, maddening her. When he pushed inside her, stretching her to capacity, she collapsed against the sofa. "Liam, I feel as if I'm about to pass out."

He pushed deeper still. With his arms around her waist, he held her locked into place. He moved his face into the curve of her neck, whispering her name over and over as he rode in and out, his cock solid, his thrusts deep and building in speed.

"Oh, God, I'm going to come." She began to shudder.

Incredibly, he stopped moving at that very moment, making her cry out in demand. "You wanted this," he said with no small amount of effort, "didn't you? Admit it." He drew back, making her whimper with need.

She was so close. "Yes, I wanted it, I wanted you."

He rewarded her by thrusting deeply back in, wedging the head of his cock against her cervix. "See, that wasn't so hard. No more denial, Chrissie. Promise?"

She wanted to answer, but it was so hard. She was so close to coming and he was pressing against her sensitive spots in the most maddening way, keeping her on the edge. Her sex clutched at him over and again, trying to push it. He remained still until she spoke. "No more denial," she blurted.

He breathed out, and then began to roll his hips into her. He slammed home, jacking her up against the sofa, pushing them both to the edge.

She cried out in ecstasy. He was there, his cock jerking. He thrust again. Her head rolled back, her body clutching at him. She came in a dizzying rush, her entire groin suffused with heat, her body spasming around the shaft of his cock. A moment later, as he pulled out, he moved one strong arm under her to hold her steady, then kissed the back of her neck and whispered low against her ear.

"I'm going to undo these handcuffs now, and then I want to hold you in my arms and tell you how good it felt being inside you, and you're not going to resist, are you?"

"No, Liam. I'm not going to resist."

He unlocked the cuffs. Then he sat down next to her, and lifted her into his lap. Taking her hands in his, he gently rubbed her wrists. He was being gentle and kind, and when he'd finished fussing over her hands, he drew her chin up and held her steady when she tried to look away. "What is it, sweetheart?" he asked. "I want you to tell me, what is it that bugs you so?"

She was raw, undone, and the words rose of their own accord, her body arching against the shield of his. "It's not you. It's just that it's hard," she blurted, "being an engineer, being a woman in a man's world." She tensed, waited for the laugh, for the inevitable tease.

It didn't come. Instead, he kissed the end of her nose. "It's okay, I understand. But you don't have to be tough all the time. Sometimes you can let me be tough for you now. Yes?" His expression was serious, and his eyes shone with admiration.

She couldn't reply, not with words.

Moving up against him, she closed her eyes and rubbed her face against his stubbled chin, because she liked the way this man took charge of her. She liked how he broke her stubborn will, and she liked how he made her enjoy this thing between them.

She liked it a lot.

Three days later, Liam drove up to Chrissie's office as she emerged from the building. She waved over at him. She was dressed smart; her trademark short skirt part of a fitted suit, her soft blond hair swept up and clipped behind her head. When she climbed into the car, she reached over and kissed him, smiling.

"I take it the meeting wasn't as bad as you thought it would be?" Two of the company directors had traveled to speak with the staff about reorganization in the wake of Theresa's departure.

"No. In fact…" She stared at him, slightly shell-shocked. "I can't quite believe it, but they offered me Theresa's job. I'm going to be in charge of all projects allocated to the design team at this office!"

"Every cloud has a silver lining, huh?" He was glad she'd had this boost.

"Yes. It does." Winking at him, she reached over and stroked his jawline. "And I know exactly how I want to celebrate," she added and unclipped her hair, shaking it free over her shoulders, giving him a smoldering glance.

Why was it that just one sign of interest from her could make him painfully hard? "I'm listening."

"I don't want to go out for dinner after all. I want to get

takeout, go home, strip and drink champagne...from your naked body."

Liam turned the key in the ignition, revving the engine. "Anything you want, Chrissie, anything at all...."

* * * * *

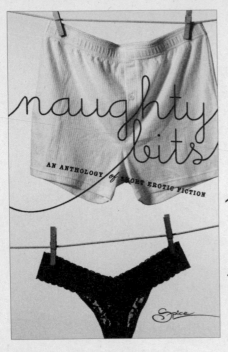

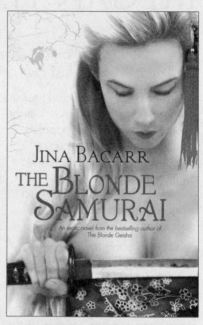

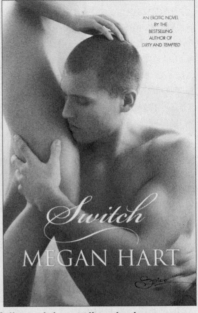

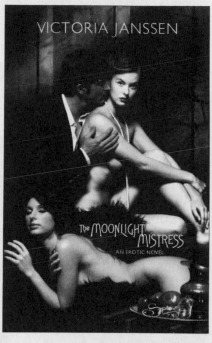